AUTHOR'S NIGHTMARE

BOOK TWO

AUTHOR'S NIGHTMARE

BOOK TWO

Ian B. Urns & A. C. Erinle

Podium

To Deji and Rory, the older brothers.

All rights reserved. No part of this publication may be reproduced, stored in a retrieval system, or transmitted in any form or by any means electronic, mechanical, photocopying, recording, or otherwise without prior written permission from Podium Publishing.

This is a work of fiction. Names, characters, places, and incidents are either products of the author's imagination or used fictitiously. Any resemblance to actual events, locales, or persons, living, dead, or undead, is entirely coincidental.

Copyright © 2025 by Ian B. Urns and A. C. Erinle

Cover design by Mario Teodosio

ISBN: 979-8-89539-353-6

Published in 2025 by Podium Publishing
www.podiumentertainment.com

AUTHOR'S NIGHTMARE

BOOK TWO

CHAPTER ONE

Beam's POV: Day 68
Current Wealth: 118 gold, 31 silver, 14 copper

Several things happened on our seventh day in Elswick, all of them good. The first was that Solitaire's gun was finally finished, and we all hurried in picking it up. I was a bit disappointed to find that it was not, in fact, a giant Browning M2, minigun, or anti-tank rifle. Perhaps it was a bit unfair, but Solitaire's abilities in my head had started to become quite close to Tony Stark's. He did seem a bit put out when I let my disappointment at its rate of fire show.

Which isn't to say it wouldn't change things. For several reasons. It was easy to load, all one needed to do with it was keep one compartment to the left of its barrel stacked with tiny little lead balls—which we'd also commissioned in large quantities—with the other side holding a compartment for the gunpowder to slide down, picked up from its store at the back by an oscillating sort of . . . grip, thing. Being honest, I'm not very good at describing the technicalities of things.

What I can describe is the effectiveness, though. We gave Shango a hundred shots to practice, and by the end of them he was consistently blowing holes in a human-sized target from well over a hundred meters. That was more than the range of basically any bow weapon I could think of, which was good enough for our purposes.

The more immediately exciting bonus, of course, was that we'd also commissioned several sets of plate armor last week, from several different smiths for the purpose of speed, and they were all finally being finished. One each for Helena, Argar, Solitaire, and Shango. None for me—apparently my magic meant I wasn't worth spending the money on. Thrifty pricks.

Well, we'd not had that much to spend, being fair. By the time we'd forked over all the necessary funds, our surplus of more than one hundred gold had quickly shriveled by ninety-seven. Even looking at the results, it was hard to feel like the sum had been worth it.

All the others were testing their movement in the armor, flexing and shifting, feet leaving the floorboards to creak under them as they readjusted to moving bodies now some twenty kilos heavier. Argar's was by far the largest frame, and I wondered how much extra mass his own protection had been packed with. We took the better part of an hour to adjust, grappling and sparring, rolling and falling.

Fortunately, Solitaire had watched everyone being fitted with their plate and assured us all he'd memorized the process of stripping it off. Whether he was lying or not, we had better things to concern ourselves with.

We'd discovered a few convenient facts about our new friends while we were spending the week working and training, most pressingly that Helena, somehow, was actually literate. We still didn't actually know what that woman's past was—I myself hadn't spoken to her much—but I was in no place to complain given how convenient it was having someone to peruse the missives for us.

She did just that, around noon, while we all waited, standing around her and watching, giving feedback on each suggestion.

"Uh, a caravan needs protection moving from here to Dragonsfell and back? It's offering three gold," she noted. We talked, then decided against it.

"Too long." Solitaire sighed. "Not worth it."

"There's a village that's been harassed by a raiding party. They want someone to find their camp and clear it out."

That sparked a bit of thought.

"How big is the village?" Shango asked. Helena frowned.

"Doesn't say here, but the place is Whitan. I've been there once or twice. It's about the size of Rinchester, before the Rotters, I mean."

Our faces soured. We were definitely not clearing out a force big enough to bully hundreds of people single-handedly, armor or not.

"Ah, what about this?" She grinned. "An old Remon fort has been taken and currently occupied by the orcs. The city itself wants someone to take it back. There's a time limit. The guards are being sent in to remove them within a few days, but it's not more than one day's travel away. Thirty gold."

We'd been finding it harder and harder to procure the ingredients for gunpowder, and Solitaire claimed his breath was starting to smell like shit. Thirty gold sounded very, very good, even after the massive profits we'd made over the past week. I knew it'd tempt everyone before I even saw their faces creasing over in thought.

"What sort of fort is it?" Solitaire asked. Helena peered at the paper, frowning.

"Uh, a hillfort. Remon, like I said, built and rebuilt over and over again. Wooden walls, a drawbridge—"

"A motte and bailey," Solitaire cut in, understanding flashing. "Of course."

I should've guessed it myself. The Remons were our version of the Romans. Yes, yes, I know, believe me I know. We did start writing this book when we were fifteen, in our defense. Regardless, if it was something as primitive as that then it probably wouldn't be packed with *hundreds* of the enemy, at least.

"Any idea what the average armament of the orcs is?" Shango asked, clearly giving the idea some considering himself. That almost had me decided on its own. He was by far the most cautious of us. If he thought something was on the table, then it was probably all but a sure thing for the rest of us.

Helena shook her head, though.

"They're not really giving much information in that regard."

"Iron weapons," Argar piped up suddenly. "Mostly, pig iron of the sort you'd see on northerner raiders. Most of them are either wearing furs or some primitive sort of wool armor. The occasional one has nice and big blocks of iron sticking on them, not quite plate, but not quite not plate, either. Those ones usually have actual steel, too, though I don't know where they get it."

We all eyed him, and he grinned smugly.

"There are benefits to frequenting every pub in the city, you know. I hear everything the mercenaries have been saying, and a particularly juicy bit of gossip can actually outpace magical communication on the military grapevine."

I made a note not to underestimate Argar again. The big guy played aloof, but he was about as sharp as the new axe we'd bought him.

"That sounds manageable," Solitaire observed, shooting an approving glance Argar's way. "Very manageable, actually. I'd been assuming our opposition would be as well armed as the local humans."

Even in spite of his good mood, his lip still curled slightly when he said the last word. "Humans," stretching the vowel, wincing as if he'd just tasted something bitter. It was as if the very thought of people disgusted him. That was, of course, because it *did*. I supposed fighting orcs might give me a bit of insight into how my friend felt fighting his own species.

"We'll still be outnumbered," Shango noted. "Right? There's only five of us."

"We're all far more than the average soldier," Solitaire countered. "And there won't be that many of the enemy. At best there'll be a hundred, which will require some farming infrastructure setup to occupy for any length of time. Helena, how long have they been there?"

"Three weeks," the Vit replied, and Solitaire nodded, apparently having anticipated the answer.

"Three weeks," he echoed. "And it's winter, so they can't have been growing anything in any significant amount. Do they have wagons, Argar?"

The giant shook his head.

"Good. That means any resources they brought in would've been basically carried by hand. I think we have good odds of finding no more than a few dozen there."

We all eyed him, far from reassured by the declaration.

"That's still a few dozen." Shango sighed.

"And it's a fraction of a hundred," Solitaire snapped. "I think you're all underestimating how dangerous we are, the Belahonts in particular. Beam alone could probably take ten of the fuckers as he is now, let alone the rest of us combined. For God's sake, Shango, you have a *gun*."

As far as arguments went, it sounded a lot more petulant than usual. I supposed that was just the natural consequence of making it an argument about how we'd totally be able to kick ten guys' asses each. Still, it wasn't exactly . . . flawed.

"We can check it out at least," I noted. "It's just a day's travel. We can easily afford that. The potential rewards are huge."

"Come on, Shango," Solitaire added. "Don't be a bitch."

It probably wasn't the ribbing that decided him in the end, but it certainly looked like it was. Shango's decision to humor us came just moments after Solitaire's poking.

"Fine," he growled through a clenched jaw and closed teeth. "How and when do we set off?"

"Carriage has served us well so far. I see no reason to abandon it now." I shrugged.

"I suppose you're right." He glared.

The preparations didn't take us long. Most of our week had been spent preparing for something on the level of what we were heading for, and we set out with a confidence we'd not felt since arriving here.

After seven days of being cooped up, hurried, and worked to the bone, we were finally having a nice, juicy enemy dropped in front of us. Bodies covered with steel, hands filled with actually high-grade weapons, limbs powered by magic superhumanity accumulated through months of torturous fights and underhanded trickery.

Perhaps it spoke ill of me, but I felt a rush of excitement as I joined my friends in walking. Vampiric rapier at one side of me and skill in conjuring new weapons practiced to the point of taking me less than a second. Here was a chance to finally see whether I stood the test of Redacle's truly hardened killers.

Somehow, I found myself unable to even fathom the idea that we might fall short.

CHAPTER TWO

Solitaire's POV: Day 69
Current Wealth: 21 gold, 31 silver, 14 copper

It *was* a motte-and-bailey-type castle, and we could tell, just peering at it from afar, that it didn't hold that many.

The place was small, for one thing, too little to fit anywhere close to a hundred even at its peak, and there were far too few people shifting around the outside for there to be anywhere near even that amount. I was bad at estimation. Well, no, actually I was excellent at estimation—*humans* were bad at estimation in general. Still, I was confident we'd not be facing any more than forty enemies, and definitely not all at once.

On the other hand, a potential max of forty fucking enemies was a lot for anyone to deal with. Helena seemed more concerned at the prospect than most of us.

"Eight each," she breathed. "We can't manage that, plate or not, magic or not. We'd best turn back now, while we still can."

"Eight each," Beam noted. "I can manage that, plate or not."

The Vittonian glared at him, and I found myself cutting in before either of them could start a doubtlessly irritating argument.

"We don't need to just waltz over and headbutt one of them," I noted. "There's other ways to do this, smarter ways." They all eyed me and started thinking of some.

"Stealth is the obvious trick," Shango noted. "We attack at night?"

"We won't be doing much sneaking wearing sixty pounds of metal," Argar grunted.

That was when Beam piped up.

"I don't have loud armor, though," he noted. "Not loud, not heavy. I could scale that wall easy."

We all turned to it, eyeing the thing. I made about fifteen—no, thirteen—feet. Four meters in noncaveman measurements. Could he?

Yes, easily. And without risk, too. A four-meter fall wouldn't hurt Beam the way he was now, even if he landed face-first. We'd grown more than just strong. Powerful.

But should he? That was the more pressing consideration. There was plenty of death waiting for us on the other side of those walls, we could see as much now, and if Beam got surrounded by it all on his own then even he wouldn't last long.

There was one simple fact that weighed heavier than the others.

"Your armor glows in the dark," Shango hissed. "You'd be spotted in two seconds flat."

Beam hesitated, and I could practically see our brother about to erupt.

"You are not going up there fucking naked!" he snapped. Beam met his fire, for once, with some of his own. That was when I knew the argument would be a painful one. When his heels dug in, they *dug* in.

"We don't have any better ideas," he growled. "I can get in, open the doors, and save us all the trouble of smashing through. We'll all be on them faster than they can believe and probably have one dead each before they're even fighting back."

It was a lot of speculation, confidently stating facts about variables even I'd be hesitant to make into absolutes. Obviously, it didn't convince Shango for an instant.

The back-and-forth proceeded about as expected, with both sides occasionally gaining some opposition or assistance from one of the other three now just watching it all. Finally, when both Beam and Shango were becoming tired enough that their barked arguments started to grow more sparse, I finally cut in.

"We can use Beam," I said at last. "But there's no reason we need him to be the only crux of this."

All eyes turned to me, and I elaborated.

"Firstly, I think we can all agree that, of the five of us, I alone have the advantage of being given a normal, healthy childhood that imbued me with a proper amount of knowledge in stealth and throat cutting."

Argar frowned with the start of a question, and I barged on over it before he could slow the conversation down with any of the usual irrelevancies people liked to bring up when they caught a snippet of how based and awesome my mother was.

"Which tells me that doing much of anything on that wall is going to be easier said than done without a source of light. Targeting the guards, though, who'll be holding some . . . different matter. So I say we send Beam in to try that instead. Meanwhile . . . we don't need to batter the door down."

I nodded to the fort demonstrably.

"We can see from here it's got a door bar. I can judge the height, and Shango can hit a target within six inches at dozens of yards. Give him a few seconds to shoot through the wood and we'll be able to just force them open ourselves. All we need is a loud enough distraction to keep them from gauging where the gunshots are actually coming from, right?"

We all brainstormed, then turned to Shango's spare ammo. He had enough for a good two hundred shots, give or take. Even with his rate of fire that did seem a bit . . . excessive.

It was night soon, and near pitch-black even sooner. All of us squatted outside near the fort. All of us kept quiet and eyed the place, awaiting our signal with bated breath and peeled eyes.

Mind you, that was a bit redundant on our part. As far as signals went, this wasn't one we were particularly at risk of missing. Nor, for that matter, would a mole with tinnitus be.

Something chirped in the night. Something else flapped over our heads. One of the orcs told a joke to his fellow guard, and another laughed at it. Then the explosions went off.

Shango had long since overcome his puerile, childish aversion to something as silly as black powder violently screaming out fire, and he had his gun leveled before we even caught sight of the wispy smoke catching firelight over the fort. His first shot rang out, and I just barely glimpsed splinters flitting away from the wood. Another explosion, barely a second later, this time from an altogether different spot. He fired again, hit a second time. The blasts we were setting off with small things, too small to tear apart thick wood, but those bullets were more than able.

The rest of us were standing now, readying ourselves to hit the door. The third shot came almost in time with the third explosion, so synchronized that it almost looked like the tiny flakes of splintered oak were responsible for the roaring noise as they flew from the door. All of us were charging at once, save Shango. Not roaring, not shouting, not letting out any sound at all except for the scrapes and clatters of steel plate grinding against steel plate. Ten meters separated us from the door. We cleared them in seconds.

Argar was ahead of us, partially by design. His shoulder hit the surface like a battering ram, two hundred kilos of man, forty kilos of steel, all driven by musculature so strong it would've beaten any Olympian in Earth's history without the slightest competition. Both doors shuddered, widening a few inches. The rest of us added our momentum onto his and turned those inches into feet.

Inside the courtyard, orcs were running about, arms flailing, eyes wide with confusion. Up close, I could make out a few details on them. All were tall, for Redacle, maybe the height of modern humans. They were broad, grey skinned rather than green, thick fleshed and tusked. True to Argar's word, most wore leathers and wools, clothing more than armor. There were maybe a dozen with us in the courtyard.

A dozen dead men, then.

Beam dropped down onto them from the wall, his armor on, his weapon conjured. He was like a ghost, glowing and pale, missing only a color coded horse. He rode in without it, though, and it wasn't needed for death to come with him.

One orc turned, too late to keep from losing a leg to one heavy chop. I crashed into its friend before they could encircle me, bowling the bastard off his feet—we probably weighed about as much, but my magical strength and armor mass gave me more stability by far. From the corner of my eye, I saw Argar's axe flying, taking an arm off at the shoulder, and then two of the fuckers were closing in on me too fast to swing. I tossed my weapon at one—a short sword, or long knife depending on who you asked—and kicked the other in the chest. He went down just as his friend recovered, and I tackled the unlucky orc.

First I tried to bite him. I couldn't; my visor was down. Being the clever lad that I am, I improvised. Smashing the metal into his face, once, twice, three times. Each headbutt came down like a guillotine blade, and by the time I was finished his head resembled . . .

Well, certainly not a head, that much was sure. I rolled off the corpse, climbing up just in time to catch a hammer across my head.

It was an unlucky blow, breaking one of the latches on my helmet, tearing it free. Unlucky for the orc, that is, because now my head was uncovered, and he was unbalanced from his swing. My gauntleted fist pulverized a big, grey nose and flattened the bastard, then I was on him. My teeth found what was left of his face, taking off lips, cheeks, brows, and finally the nose. Truth be told I don't really remember much of it, only that he stopped struggling about a minute in, and that my face was wet when I next stood up.

Around me, I saw that everyone else had just about finished their killing, too. Argar was pulling his axe out of a split skull, Shango busy fixing a new box magazine onto the side of his gun. Beam was nowhere to be seen, and Helena answered my confusion as she rested momentarily against her spear.

"One of them ran inside." She breathed. "Your brother went after—"

I was running before she finished speaking.

CHAPTER THREE

Beam's POV: Day 69
Current Wealth: 21 gold, 31 silver, 14 copper

Thinking about it, with hindsight being twenty-twenty and all, I think there's a good chance that making the decision to spring into the heart of our enemy's base had been poor judgment on my part. Even I wasn't sure why I'd done it. At first. But then I felt that familiar, grating presence inside myself, rooted right down in my core, driving me to act, to fight, to kill. I'd thought I was getting used to it, managing a handle on it, keeping it nice and separate from myself.

Obviously, I'd thought wrong. One does not get thrown face-first into enemy territory by something one had a handle on, no matter what Solitaire insisted.

Inside the fort felt a lot bigger. I'd not thought it would have room for corridors, let alone several, but I'd found myself within one, and I could hear enemies on both ends of it. The rational, clever part of me was tempted to wait for them and ensure that I fought them in a cramped and tight environment where their numbers couldn't be brought to bear. Partially, it was the knowledge that they had bows that kept me from doing that, and partially it was simply raw, primal fear. I continued onward in any case, not stopping until I found myself stepping out into a wider chamber.

There were orcs in it, of course, close to a dozen. And one of them was taller, wider, and dressed from head to toe in thick, jagged plates of pig iron. Just perfect.

Behind me I could still hear more coming, and the place wasn't big enough that it'd take them more than a few seconds to be right at my back. That made my options fairly limited. Option, singular, really. I attacked.

Fortunately, my sole advantage seemed to be that the orcs hadn't expected me to be mad enough to try to hack all of them apart by myself. I closed in on one before he could even react, crossing a half dozen strides in no time at all, swinging wide and hard. My ethereal blade found that magic spot in his neck, fountaining blood in all directions as it scythed open an artery and continued to take the head almost fully off. Before he'd even fallen, I was onto the next, swinging again, finding my blow blocked but still sending the orc stumbling with the force of it. One tried to circle me, so I twisted around and threw a back kick into its body, catching a hip and breaking bone on impact. Out-racing gravity again, I was back at the blocker, this time taking a foot off and moving on.

There were a lot of them, but as long as I kept moving, kept killing, I'd be changing the fight's dynamics before they could properly organize themselves. Just needed to leverage my momentum and keep blocking theirs. Easier said than done, though.

Easier said than done when the big one suddenly reared up in front of me. He swung a hammer so big that I doubted I could've even lifted it over my head before coming to Redacle, and I barely evaded the bludgeon. I felt it pass me by, air displaced by the sheer strength involved, and stumbled back to retake my balance before another blow followed it up. I struck first, this time, stabbing hard into the orc's shoulder. Somehow the iron deflected my blade, leaving nothing but a deep furrow in the shoddy metal as I went off-kilter. The next swing caught me full in the chest, actually lifting me off my feet with the impact.

My armor was tough. We'd not exactly had the equipment for modern-day stress tests, but over the past few weeks Solitaire had taken the time to confirm that it was at least in the same ballpark as steel, albeit more rigid. That stiffness probably saved my life. The hammerblow cracked my breastplate with a terrify-ingly loud noise, cutting through my ears as I flew back entire feet before finally landing. My shoulders hit first, and I used them to roll back, managing to turn my momentum around and bring myself up into a crouch just in time to dart back from another swing.

The orc kept coming, like a tornado with steel jutting out, and I just carried on scrambling away from the hammer, still feeling a sharp throb in my ribs where the first swing had almost split my torso open. It was a delaying response, and something that would only last so long. Even moments after starting, I could see the enemy drawing in close, death coming toward me inch by inch.

Well, that wasn't ideal, so I took a leaf from Solitaire's book. See, he'd learned to fight, not win contests, and in a fight you had to do more than just touch your opponent to gain an advantage. Which meant when I lurched forward and let the hammer's handle clatter off my shoulder, my enemy was no closer to killing me than if he'd thrown some mean words my way.

I was closer, though. Close enough to press my sword into a gap posed by his bending knee, then twist it inward. It tunneled through the skin and flesh below easily enough, leaving thick, sludgy blood to free itself from the wound. The orc snarled, swinging for me with a fist this time.

Again, Solitaire's bag of tricks worked wonders. I lowered my skull and headbutted the creature's knuckles, letting the ethereal plate guarding my brow take the brunt. My head snapped back, wits shaken for a second, but I wasn't too stunned to feel the sensation of bone crunching against me, nor hear the cry of agony from its unfortunate owner.

Things took a sour turn there because, as the leader seemed to lose his advantage, more orcs closed in to snatch it back. I wasn't that fast, and I couldn't dodge everything if ten attacks came from ten directions. I didn't get the chance to find out how many I *could* manage, though, because that was around the time the cavalry showed up.

Solitaire came in first, helmet gone for some reason, but axe still tight in his grip. He buried it in one orc's head, splitting the skull open like a watermelon and battering the corpse to one side. A gunshot rang out, blowing a nice chunk out of another, and then Argar charged in. He went straight for the leader, of course. Argar was prone to Argaring, after all.

It was just when Helena had joined the fight herself that I snapped myself out of the stunned stupor I was in, pouncing on the nearest enemies to help my side out. I have to say, as far as melees went, it was a brutal one.

The main orc was probably the one making most of the difference because even nursing a broken hand, he was good enough to tie up Argar. One or two others were tougher, bigger, and quicker than the ones outside, however, and I started to consider that our enemies had some sort of hierarchy based on fighting power. The weakest got stuck with the shit work guarding the frigid air outside, while the strong got to snuggle up nice and warm behind walls and ceiling.

Mind you, it wasn't my most thoughtful reflection because every time I started to so much as polish a coherent idea in my head, someone interrupted me by trying to chop it off. I fought more defensively now that I wasn't racing to thin the herd, forced to take fewer risks, and obligated to guard my allies' backs as I darted around between swings. Now, with some breathing room, I could take in the sensations of the battle, and more particularly of the enemies. It was remarkable.

The vampire had been faster than me—it was a vampire, after all—and I'd be lying to claim the world was exactly slowing down now, but the physical swiftness of my body meant that it might as well have. Compared to that, every swing my way was sluggish, every dodge clumsy. Compared to me, my enemies were drunks or toddlers.

I almost felt bad killing them. Almost.

A club caught me in the head, bouncing off my helmet, and I flailed back with a retaliatory strike that drove the offending orc away but left me open for two more with spears. One I sidestepped, the other I stepped *into*, forced to trust my armor again and feeling my heart skip a beat as the metal tip slid dangerously close to a joint before passing me by. Another of my swings struck home, this one successful in taking most of a jaw off, then I was barging an orc off its feet with a body check.

Turning, I looked for the one who'd swung the club, only to find Solitaire already had it pinned against the wall, snarling with his teeth bared like some vicious animal, thumbs pressing down on its eyes. He didn't stop, even when the creature's struggles weakened and blood started to fountain down both cheeks, didn't stop even when its screams turned to whimpers. Only when Shango asked him to step aside did Solitaire acquiesce, and even then he seemed reluctant.

My guts were hollow as I watched my friend blow the thing's head off, my eyes not even on the execution, falling instead onto Solitaire. He seemed impassive as ever, or as impassive as one could seem with a flood of adrenaline coursing through his veins. Eyes clear, face relaxed, hands opening and closing casually to work the excess energy out of him as he looked around the room.

"So," my friend asked. "Anyone hurt?"

I looked around, too, seeing the carnage we'd made of everything. I had a few cuts, some bruising for sure, but nothing that was more serious than aches and pains. Nothing that would persist for more than a few days or eat into our precious profit margins by demanding a magical healer's touch.

"None," I replied, cold. It'd been my mistake, thinking like that. A sword didn't think, question, or feel for the throats it cut.

A sword didn't worry about what its wielder might do next.

CHAPTER FOUR

Shango's POV: Day 69
Current Wealth: 21 gold, 31 silver, 14 copper

Solitaire stood before me, just a few meters away, and smiled. He smiled cockily, grin lopsided, confident, charming. It was a grin that promised trouble, mischief, a grin worn by a man who knew perfectly well how clever he was and didn't see a damned problem with showing the world. It was a grin that said, "Quick, look over here, before you miss how great I am!"

And yet it was a grin that promised no great cruelty or harm, no real damage done, and no line crossed. It was the grin of a troublesome little boy because it *was* the grin he'd worn back when he'd been just that. Impish, not demonic. Dastardly, not evil. The grin of a man who'd never even humored a dark intention.

Blood dripped down from his fingers, pooling by his feet. A meter beside it there was another pool, made from the twin rivers of ichor drizzled out of an orc's eyes, then bolstered by the flood released when I'd put it out of its misery with a head shot. Whenever I blinked, that momentary darkness was filled by the sight of a screaming enemy and the sound of its agony. By the twisted, snarling face my friend had worn while he made himself the cause of both. While everyone held their silence, I heard the sounds of crimson droplets hitting the floor, of limbs jerking with the last spasmodic impulses of dying nerves.

Solitaire looked at me. He grinned. It was the grin of a man who'd never even humored a dark intention.

"So, looks like there were few enough for us to take, after all," he noted proudly, turning and eyeing the room as a whole. "Actually, I reckon we could've taken a few more, too. Worth noting, that."

I wanted to scream at him, to storm across the room and punch that lying grin off his vicious face, but Helena and Argar were here. Our friends? No, not yet. Our companions, maybe, but our subordinates before anything. People who believed in us, who followed us, and whose help would be compromised if they thought we were fracturing. If they saw us doing so before their very eyes.

So I bit my tongue, mastered myself as quickly as I could, and forced out the most convincingly neutral answer I was able to.

There'd be time to confront my friend later, but that time was not now.

"Yes, well, it could've easily been more," I replied curtly. "A lot more, not just a few. Let's not make a habit of this if possible. I'd prefer we deal in sure things."

Solitaire shrugged, and even I couldn't tell whether he was aware of the struggle I'd just gone through in giving him a response other than fury.

"Hopefully we'll have a few more men next time, too. They are cheaper than plate armor, aren't they?"

He'd done it on purpose, must have, but that didn't change that the candid intellectualization gave me something starkly practical to think about, and my mind rushed toward it eagerly.

"Less reliable than plate," I noted, and we all started our search of the place, looking for potentially valuable loot. Orc teeth were, sadly, too mismatched in human mouths to be of much use to this world's dentists. We'd found that much out from one of the more experienced mercenaries in Elswick. On the bright side, knowing early had saved us the cost of some pliers.

As might have been expected, there wasn't a whole lot of value to be scavenged from the hideout. That didn't stop us from drawing every possible droplet of wealth that there was, however. The orcs hadn't been raiding as much as many of their kind, which meant we didn't find much in the way of precious metals. They still had a few stolen human weapons, which would sell for a nice bit for their steel make, and plenty of various knickknacks that if nothing else could be melted down for the metal fittings worked into them. All told, we ended up with about a sack and a half of various items we'd all gauged would be relatively expensive compared to how much they weighed.

One gave me pause, though. A little doll, made of clay and straw, lying beside the tools I could see had been used for chiseling and etching it. Lying next to one of the orc's beds. It was a child's doll, surely, and my stomach dropped out of me at the sight.

In Redacle, orcs were violent, and they weren't as smart as humans. But that didn't make them animals. They could still feel emotion—fear, love, empathy. They could learn to be good—much like almost any sapient thing could. They still took care of their children.

Feeling suddenly sick, I considered leaving the doll just on instinct, but an impulse had me take it with me. It'd be destroyed, surely, whenever the fort's new human garrison reclaimed it. Something about the thought bothered me. The work was ugly, but it'd clearly taken time and effort. Time and effort the workman would never see bear fruit now because of us. Had he been the one Solitaire had—

No, I stopped that thought before it could exit its infancy. Pocketing the item, I turned back to the group and forced a strength that was entirely absent from me to show on my face.

"Alright, let's head out now. The carriage should still be waiting, but I'd rather not risk giving that moneygrubbing prick the time to ditch us."

A few grumbles of agreement rang out, and we started trudging for the exit.

Neither me nor Solitaire nor Beam had asked about stats. That was because we'd already talked about the notion before departing, in private and away from Argar and Helena. It wasn't that we didn't trust our new companions with the knowledge of how exactly we grew so strong so quickly, of course. It was that Solitaire, specifically, did not trust them. He'd come around—I knew he would—it'd just take him a while. He'd required a full year to stop wiring trip mines into my walls just in case my father's company tried to have him assassinated back on Earth, after all.

Odd, that. I could so confidently convince myself he was still the person I knew. No, so confidently *know* it, without any convincing required. I'd seen him torture a man for seemingly no reason at all, and somehow that wasn't even slightly at odds with knowing he was the same person I'd met as a kid. What did that say about me?

Well, obviously that I had a twisted fucking taste in friends. I kept on trudging out through the fort, loot bag slung over one shoulder.

[Appraisal]
Class: Emperor
Level: 13
Condition: Fine
Modifiers: +5 Toughness, +3 Strength, +3 Speed, +1 Alertness
Statistics: Strength 9, Speed 9, Dexterity 6, Stamina 5, Toughness 10, Alertness 9, Charisma 9, Intelligence 9
Inventory: Local wear, plate armor, repeater, shortspear
Class Abilities: Appraisal II
Current Experience Points: 13/460
Unspent Skillpoints: 2

It was interesting to see the name of my new local clothing. Then again, we'd known already that the menu seemed to give things names based on what their owner thought of them. More interesting to see we'd gained a level, however. Only one, though. I suppose that made sense. Orcs were big and strong, but a few dozen of them weren't exactly on the same level of danger as the giga-troll, or that vampire. One level was plenty for our means, anyway. Every little bit of power we got was one step closer to . . .

Well, to whatever we were going to do with it, I supposed. Rule the world? It sounded so silly, put like that. But it was a matter for later. I focused on spending my points.

It was tempting to just go with Alertness and Speed, but Solitaire had assured me that his little repeater didn't hit that hard compared to Redacle's real monsters. One day I might regret not having the extra Strength, and there were plenty of situations where brawling would still be needed. I decided, in the end, to put my points into Speed *and* Strength, a happy compromise. No need to keep away from mobility entirely just because I'd still need to crack heads open in the future.

[Appraisal]
Class: Emperor
Level: 13
Condition: Fine
Modifiers: +5 Toughness, +4 Strength, +4 Speed, +1 Alertness
Statistics: Strength 10, Speed 10, Dexterity 6, Stamina 5, Toughness 10, Alertness 9, Charisma 9, Intelligence 9
Inventory: Local wear, plate armor, repeater, shortspear
Class Abilities: Appraisal II
Current Experience Points: 13/460
Unspent Skillpoints: 0

I must've been getting used to the feeling of power infusing my body, but it still sent a flutter of excitement running along every nerve I had. Giving yourself superpowers would do that, I supposed, and it certainly helped that the sack on my back suddenly felt that little bit lighter. As did the plate armor, for that matter. I frowned at that, considering the implications.

Could we have our armor thickened as we got stronger? Yes, of course we could. I actually remembered Solitaire mentioning something about centimeter-thick sheet metal plates being used by certain factions, back when Redacle had just been a project we were working on together for fun. I'd have to ask about it later.

I trudged back to the carriage with the others, finding the walk made a lot more tedious from the weight of my thoughts than the weight of my luggage. Of course, I took in the sight of my friends' new statlines as I did.

[Appraisal]
Class: Revolutionary
Level: 13
Condition: Fine
Modifiers: +4 Speed, +5 Toughness, +3 Alertness, +4 Strength
Statistics: Strength 11, Speed 11, Dexterity 8, Stamina 6, Toughness 10, Alertness 11, Charisma 3, Intelligence 10
Inventory: Local wear, plate armor, shortsword, shortspear, knives (x3)
Class abilities: Detect Element II
Current Experience Points: 8/460
Unspent Skillpoints: 0

[Appraisal]
Class: Dragonknight
Level: 13
Condition: Fine
Modifiers: +3 Strength, +4 Speed, +3 Toughness, +4 Alertness
Statistics: Strength 12, Speed 12, Dexterity 8, Stamina 9, Toughness 11, Alertness 12, Charisma 6, Intelligence 5
Inventory: Local wear
Class Abilities: Beloved II
Current Experience Points: 86/460
Unspent Skillpoints: 0

CHAPTER FIVE

S hango was giving me one of his angry stares again, and I'd figured I was in for it. Probably it'd been the orc whose eyes I'd gouged out.

Certainly, that had been impulsive. But the bastard had deserved it—almost skewered me with his spear while my helmet was off, and I've had a long-standing policy to do mean things to anybody that tries sticking a bit of metal in me. Still, Shango almost definitely wouldn't see things that way. He was one of those reformist types, not really a fan of revenge or payback.

It didn't exactly surprise me when the talk came, despite it happening the literal first instant we were both relatively alone and secluded. I was working on more black powder, and he was jotting down notes for our inventories in preparation to sell them. Early morning, a bit too early to be making our profits just yet, sadly.

"Why did you torture that orc?"

He asked it straight, and that was a relief because I was far too tired to deal with some runaround answer. Ever since getting my armor, I'd felt incomplete without it, unsafe. Like I was leaving myself open, sleeping without a nice knife under my pillow or minefield around my home. That destroyed helmet strap meant that I essentially always had an exposed head, at least until we had it fixed. And my head was where I kept all my brains.

"It pissed me off." I shrugged.

Shango glared.

"He," he corrected, and I only shrugged again.

"Right, anyway, given that he had a spear about three inches from my eye socket just seconds before, I think it's more than fair that I returned the favor with interest. Any more questions?"

"Why did you enjoy it?"

Interesting question, that. I'm sure the answer would vary depending on which psychologist you decided to ask, and I for one had never really taken much interest in that particular dumbass field of study to begin with. I shrugged again.

"Because a million years ago, the monkeys that smashed things to bits with rocks in revenge had better survival rates than the monkeys who curled up into balls and started crying when they were hurt?"

He glared at me again.

"Do you really think this is the time to be joking?"

God, it was exhausting to talk about this. I just sighed.

"No, obviously, but I don't know what you expect. A promise that I won't thumb any more eyes out in the future, no matter how pissed off I get?"

He blinked, staring at me for a moment. I suspected that the expression was covered fast enough for most people to miss it. Oh me and my big brain.

"Yes." Shango glared. "If I can't get you to *apologize* or understand why fucking recreational torture is wrong, then at the very least I want you to assure me it won't happen again."

I eyed him and considered my cards. Without me, Shango would be losing all the black powder he'd gotten so used to selling, as well as any of the other things I had planned. If I mentioned that then I'd be adding pressure to him, and surprise, too. He wasn't nearly nervous or hesitant enough to have realized that I might threaten him over our technology already. Maybe I could unbalance him enough that he would move past this conversation and never quite realize that he'd been played.

But . . . No. Shango was my friend. He was a good person. Even if he hadn't been, he was clever enough that social bludgeons like that would only keep him wrong-footed for so long. Best to just appease him.

"Fine," I told him, suddenly feeling a lot less . . . glib. "I promise."

He held his stare for a long moment, then nodded shortly. His face wasn't much less tight as it turned away from me. I figured that probably made sense. Shango was just another person, at the end of the day. People tended to . . . freak out.

Shango headed off soon after that, and I had the rest of the morning to myself. Feeling the rush of adrenaline, a certain animalistic . . . something overcame me, and I headed right for Helena.

Remarkably, she proved immune to my roguish charms, actually shuddering when I asked her if she was up for a tumble. Never one to have my ego so easily bruised, I killed the remaining hour or so with some quality me time, imagining all the ways I'd kill her if it ever came to it.

I wasn't particularly bothered, mind, because we all had a nice treat awaiting us the moment the shops opened. Shango practically dragged Beam with him, while Helena reluctantly trudged after to make sure nobody tried to murder us while we were out. I skipped along with him, though, almost drooling in anticipation of our profit.

As it happened, we made almost one gold—forty-three silver and three copper, to be precise. Not bad just for salvaged loot. The real payout was our actual reward, though, which we followed our Vittonian soldier in search of. Turns out it had been the actual city who made us the offer, which was good. At first. Cities tended to be more consistent than nobles or oligarchs, in my experience, and it left me a lot more confident that we'd be actually getting paid.

Unfortunately, that confidence didn't last. Because we soon found out that we'd be heading to the Main Hall of Elswick to receive that reward. I swear I've been told more gut-wrenching things, but not often enough to recall off the top of my head.

Well, obviously that started a nice, big discussion. Not about whether we ought to go, of course. Self-preservation was good and all, but thirty gold was thirty gold. We'd kill for that much money, as evidenced by us killing about forty fucking people for it not half a day prior, so we'd sure as shit risk putting ourselves in the eye of this world's real bigwigs over it, too.

The only question was *who*. And the answer, obviously, was Shango.

It was the only choice that made sense. Neither Helena or Argar were our leaders, Beam wasn't nearly as good with people, and I'd sadly not been able to guarantee that my body wouldn't react to the presence of an aristocrat by pinning them down and eating their neck veins.

We got him as ready as we could, then sent him along on his way.

"I think I might be about to cry," I breathed, watching him make his way to the big palace thing that the city's councilors had declared their main base of operations. "It feels like just yesterday when he was a freshly hatched trust fund kid, getting wailed on and mugged for his money, relying on his friends to protect him."

"Friend," Beam corrected, turning back to me with an arched eyebrow. "I was the only one who protected him early on. *You*, as I recall, were the one mugging him."

Ah, yes, that. Well, what was I to do? The only ethical consumption under capitalism was consuming the rich, and I'd yet to learn what a stand-up guy he was.

"Details." I shrugged. "Regardless, we have more shopping to do. And not just armor repairs. I have something really clever planned."

That interested him, and I filled him in while we headed to the blacksmith. It was nice, just talking about a topic we were both interested in. Beam and I hadn't done that together since . . . well, since we'd created the hellscape we were currently stuck in. It helped that Beam actually had a knack for metallurgy.

"Tool steel," he echoed, thoughtful. "That's modern, though, isn't it?"

I actually wasn't sure.

I knew the classification didn't exactly show up before relatively recent history, but not how recent, or whether we'd already *had* what we ended up calling tool steels before finalizing their name. What I did know, though, was that the name was descriptive. Tool steels were named for being well suited to making into any kind of tools, including those that cut. Wouldn't hurt to see what kind of weapons metal like that turned into.

Another thing I was fairly confident in was that certain kinds were apparently shit hot for sword making. And I knew their formulas. Well, sort of knew them. I had to do a bit of rummaging around in my head to finally find them, but that kind of thing was just a natural hazard of having such an enormous depth of memory.

"I'd like to learn blacksmithing," Beam said abruptly, and I glanced his way, dragged out of my cognitive cocoon by his voice.

"Good idea," I noted. "Your physical strength and coordination would help, and I'm sure your *other* ability could be modified in some way to make it even easier."

Bellows, protective gloves, compressive grips, or blast chambers. Off the top of my head I could think of half a dozen ways he might use his weapon conjuring to enhance the otherwise mundane art of working metal. He'd need skill to start, though.

We continued on our way to the smithy.

CHAPTER SIX

Shango's POV: Day 69
Current Wealth: 25 gold, 24 silver, 14 copper

I'd walked into bigger buildings than Elswick's Main Hall, much bigger. Any given skyscraper, for one, had it beat in sheer volume by more than just a few times. My father's house—or the main one, rather—would've been a runner-up for sheer width, and not too far behind in height and depth. Really, it wasn't that special by Earth standards.

By Redacle standards, though, it was a giant. And so help me, I actually felt some whisper of the primitive awe that might have struck the world's locals upon seeing it. I must've been acclimating to the general lowered state of things here, which was a scary thought in and of itself.

Within the building, I was walked through long hallways packed full of obnoxious decorations. Suits of armor on display, big heavy swords and shields mounted on walls, stuffed animals . . . a stuffed troll. It all demonstrated an excess of wealth that I might've expected from the ruling body of an entire city.

And it irritated me, too. Those suits of plate armor could've kept fighting men alive, just as ours had kept Solitaire alive when that orc took a swing for his head. The money gone into stuffing and hanging those animals might've bought medicine, or food. Any of the things we'd spent so long doing without. It seemed my flirtation with poverty had changed the sight of wealth, maybe forever. I wasn't entirely sure how I felt about that.

It was a bunch of servants who led me through all the pomp and privilege, and not one of them actually spoke to me as we marched deeper into the building. All looked slightly nervous, though I wasn't arrogant enough to assume it was on my behalf. Probably they just had mean bosses. You learned to recognize that sort of thing through the state of a person's subordinates. Actually, the way people's workers acted could tell you all sorts. I noted no lack of refinement in these ones, backs all straight, body language all prim and carefully trimmed away into an almost mechanical finish.

So the city's councilmen, one or more of them at least, had a thing for propriety and formality. That was useful to know ahead of time. I didn't have the chance to figure out much more, though, because we were soon at our destination.

In my head, I'd been marching toward some big chamber full of imperious glares from wizened old politicians. Instead I found myself dumped into a warm office, fire burning hot beneath a mantelpiece on one side, and papers stacked high along a ridiculously sized desk on the other. My host was seated behind that desk, and he, at the very least, did meet my expectations in being an elderly man. Spectacled, face lined, eyes hawkish. Other than that, though, I found the affair far more like being taken to some CEO's presence than a nobleman from any fantasy novel, my own included.

I tightened my eyes, surveying him the moment my gaze caught sight.

[Appraisal]
Class: Heir
Level: 1
Condition: Fine
Modifiers: None
Statistics: Strength 3, Speed 3, Dexterity 4, Stamina 4, Toughness 3, Alertness 3, Charisma 5, Intelligence 4

Average stats across the board, when scaled to the standards of a sixty-year-old fat man. I should've expected no less.

"Belahont," the man said without looking up at me. "Shango Belahont, correct?"

He mispronounced my name, vocalizing the vowels in accordance with British phonetics. Which told me that he'd probably seen it written without hearing it spoken. That was interesting in and of itself. In a world as illiterate as this one, it was no small thing to have people write about you without even hearing your name aloud.

I tucked the information away for later and nodded.

"That's right, my lord," I replied, keeping my tone respectful and voice formally still and cold. He paused, glancing up at me, thoughtful.

"I'd heard you were a foreigner," he noted. "You certainly sound like one, but . . . not off continent?"

Solitaire often said my accent sounded a bit American. Beam often said it sounded a bit English. It seemed Westerners heard it as whatever Western countries they were most familiar with save their own.

"I've moved around a lot," I deflected. "I'm afraid my accent is probably quite strange to your ears, my lord."

The man grunted, peering at a sheet of paper. I habitually glanced at it, trying to glean whatever info I could, before remembering that I was, in fact, illiterate. That would be a side objective once I got back—learning to read this world's language. And perhaps discovering why only spoken words were apparently translated for me.

"What you did at the fort, whatever it was called, has made the routes around town. Five soldiers against four times as many isn't unheard of, but still . . . It's impressive enough that it doesn't happen so often. Particularly with a chieftain among the orcs."

Chieftain? Right, that was the rank name for the bigger, better-armored ones.

"I thank you, my lord," I replied, bowing respectfully. I'd learned plenty about scraping around arrogant old men, fortunately, and this one seemed no harder to please than most I'd met. He eyed me.

"You're here for the reward, I take it?"

"That's right, my lord."

He sighed, then gestured to a servant just beyond my field of view, who quickly stepped into it with a fairly heavy bag in one hand. It jingled encouragingly as they handed it over, and I resisted the urge to count the coins. It'd probably just end up offending the noble, or, at worst, I'd actually have been shortchanged and forced to choose between accepting that and confronting him about it. No way of knowing if he was the sort to take things like that as blows to his ego, so I just tucked the money away.

"Thank you, my lord."

He grunted again.

"Not much for conversation, you commoners, are you? Very well then. That was all. Be off with you."

I hesitated and finally risked speaking again.

"Forgive me, my lord, but I had assumed there would be . . . perhaps more work that you could use—"

The man cut me off, sneering.

"Use someone of your group's resources? Please, we have more blade-wielding idiots than we know what to do with. Don't tell me you thought killing a few orcs had earned you some kind of esteem."

It fucking had, and he knew it. He was just being a dick. But when someone in his position decided to be a dick to someone in mine, there wasn't a lot that could be done to prevent it. I nodded apologetically and bid my leave before heading out through the door.

Right outside, in the hall, I ran into a new face. A woman this time, with hair colored a lighter blonde than I'd even known hair came in, and eyes of emerald green. She was pale, with blemishless skin and full cheeks that told me she'd grown up enjoying quite a lot more food and health care than was normal in Redacle. When she spoke, her voice sounded like something straight out of Buckingham Palace.

"You're Belahont, the mercenary, yes?"

Instinctually, I readopted the same deferential politeness I'd worn when speaking with the nobleman, nodding respectfully even while I studied her.

[Appraisal]
Class: Schemer
Level: 9
Condition: Fine
Modifiers: None
Statistics: Strength 2, Speed 3, Dexterity 6, Stamina 3, Toughness 3, Alertness 3, Charisma 7, Intelligence 8
Class Abilities: Finesse 3

Holy shit, *eight* Intelligence. That was high, higher than anyone we'd seen so far, outside of ourselves. I tried to remember some of the figures Solitaire had estimated for rarities. Seven, I know, was extremely uncommon in any stat. On Earth most people would only ever meet a single individual with anything that high. Eight was definitely one in several million, and possibly more.

I swallowed, hardening my thoughts and forcing myself to focus. Staring me down now was a goddamn genius. It was almost enough for me to overlook that she had magic to boot.

"Yes, my lady, how may I—"

"Tell me, when did you start learning magic?"

I paused, thought, weighed things. If she knew already then denying it might draw her ire, and I'd not done anything public to demonstrate that I'd made any sort of progress to mark myself as worth noting. That was important.

Some magi didn't like being supplanted by those younger than them, and they had a tendency to take matters into their own hands when it came to ensuring that didn't happen.

"A few weeks, my lady," I replied. It wasn't that many, really, but it had been long enough that rounding up a bit wasn't such a stretch. She weighed me.

"And you were able to afford these lessons almost as soon as you came to Elswick how, exactly? From my understanding, your family was haggling over a few silvers."

Fuck, shit, shitty fuck, and fucky shit. She'd done her research. That was bad, very bad. I couldn't know what she knew—couldn't hold probable informational paths in my head and follow them all to guess what everybody was learning the way Solitaire might. Which meant that I couldn't be sure whether she'd *know* any given lie was a lie or not simply by being familiar with the events.

"My brother made the arrangements," I replied. "He's very persuasive."

"Ah, yes, another new student of magic. It's quite rare to find two in one family, you know," she noted. "Do you want to hear what I think, Belahont?"

I nodded because of course I did. She continued.

"I think your family has a knack for magic, and the intelligence to know better than flaunting it until you're better established. Am I wrong?"

Several thoughts occurred to me, all leading to the inevitable conclusion of just nodding. There was no getting my way around this. The woman hummed thoughtfully.

"Interesting. You may go now. Good day." She turned, taking her leave without another word, and I watched her go. Memorizing her face and appearance.

We'd been operating, so far, on the assumption that Redaclans would continue being their idiotic selves. That had been a mistake. Every generation had its geniuses, and that was true of Redacle's people, as well. I wasn't sure whether I'd been lucky in the results of running into this one or not.

In either scenario, she was a threat.

CHAPTER SEVEN

Beam's POV: Day 69
Current Wealth: 25 gold, 24 silver, 14 copper

Solitaire had more magic lessons, so he'd headed off and left me with only a hastily scribbled shopping list on a piece of parchment. The sheer luxury of having readily accessible writing tools again, after so long, was almost enough to make me overlook how god-awful his handwriting was.

Seriously, it was almost supernatural how bad it was. Like reading something a five-year-old had scraped out. A five-year-old who was busy being tased as he wrote it. Maybe people only had so much brain, and geniuses like him just put it all in a handful of places rather than spreading it out more easily.

Thankfully I could still just about make it all out, and the amount of it, at least, was extensive enough. It was a nice change of pace after seeing the illegible script of Redacle everywhere.

He'd separated the list into two main sections. The first was elements; the second was various materials that those elements were found in. I assumed all would be easy enough to get in Elswick. Solitaire tended to avoid making the sort of mistake it'd be to accidentally suggest I somehow find gasoline or something—but either way it was hard to imagine that I'd actually need to worry about such things.

Probably, my friend was vastly overestimating how quickly I'd pick up blacksmithing. I'd done some back home, of course; it hadn't just been a passing fancy on my part that I mentioned it. But it'd never been more than a hobby for me. I knew the simple techniques of the trade, and I'd take a while longer than most to get blisters, but if I tried to make money from my meager skills, I'd starve to death.

The blacksmith was right where he'd been when we'd first entered, hunched over his anvil, face down and eyes tight with concentration. I knew better than to interrupt a look that compressed, so I just waited patiently while he tortured the hot metal in his hand. He was nice and quick about it this time, and it occurred to me that he probably found himself hurried by the knowledge that he was keeping the people that had dumped one hundred gold on armor and given him a design from the future waiting.

"Morning," he grunted, eyeing me, and I smiled.

"Morning," I replied. My glance flickered to his forge, already hot despite only having been ignited a few minutes ago. Amazing how quickly things could get started. "I'm here for a few repairs."

He snorted at that, actual amusement, unhidden and unabashed. The blacksmith's look wasn't derisive, though. "I'll bet."

I frowned, uncertain suddenly. "I'm sorry?"

"No, I'm sorry," the man answered quickly. "I assumed you knew. News of your group's attack on that fort has already made it across Elswick. I'm not surprised you took a few lumps in it. What needs fixing?"

I held up Solitaire's helmet. "My brother's piece. One of the fittings was damaged, and a bit of the metal got buckled, as well."

He took it between his hands, eyeing it studiously, humming to himself. "Could've been worse," he noted. "Orcs are bloody strong things. Their muscles are double the power of our own even disregarding size, maybe more. Judging by the angle, I'd say it was probably the armor that kept this from being a death blow."

I was glad Solitaire wasn't actually here because he'd definitely have been an asshole about hearing someone note that their armor stopped an attack. I had more tact, just nodding and going along with it. Hiding my eagerness to sidestep the beginnings of our conversation.

"So can you fix it?"

The man glanced at me sidelong, baffled.

"Of course I can. It's just a broken fitting. I can have it done by the evening if you're really in need of it. Won't cost you more than five silver, either."

That was a relief. I'd not liked the thought of possibly waiting with a big, vulnerable opening for Solitaire's head. It was hard enough keeping him alive already. That man collected ass kickings like Pokémon cards.

"We can pay that," I replied quickly. "But . . . would you mind if I watched you work on it? Or . . . helped?"

His expression shifted quickly, eyes hardening.

"I'd rather just get the full price."

"No," I answered. "No, no, I'm not asking for a discount. I'm asking to . . . I suppose, apprentice under you?"

Fuck, I was awkward with things like this, and I just knew the guy could tell. He weighed me in that way people often did when they were trying to figure out whether they were talking to an idiot or being one. He seemed to be zeroing in on the former conclusion, and fast.

"Do you have any experience?" the smith asked me after a few moments. The question was a pleasant surprise.

"Some." I told him about my past steps into the career, and he looked pleasantly surprised himself.

"It's not usual to find a man with so much time spent in a trade he doesn't practice," the smith observed. "You and your brothers, you . . . nobles? Something like that?"

I'd probably have made the same guess in his position, and I racked my brain trying to think of which way would be best to handle it. Shango and Solitaire had both seemed settled that nobility would be a good way of gaining the kind of influence we wanted, but Redaclans weren't lax about plebs just lying about their station of birth like that. It could be more than just risky if we tried to. It could be dangerous.

Better to play it safe, at least for now. Maybe one day we'd have nice, big steam-powered tanks with giant rotary cannons sticking out in every direction, and I could be rest assured in my level-fifty self protecting us all. Maybe. That sure as shit wasn't today, though, and you had to take certain precautions when you were on the lowest rung. I decided to just avoid the question.

"Oh, that depends on which land's rules you decide to play by. Anyway, what do you say? Up for a new apprentice, or at least assistant?"

The smith eyed me, thought about it, then shrugged.

"Let's give you an hour and see how much or little you slow me down."

I grinned. That was good enough for me.

Ardin, as I soon learned the blacksmith was called, was, in fact, a shit teacher. Or maybe I was just a shit student. Either way, it was difficult to follow his instructions. Largely because every other one was just a monosyllabic grunt. I watched for a lot of the process, stepping in only when he decided an extra pair of hands would speed him up. Though rusty, I felt a lot of the old skills resurfacing for me, muscle memory reigniting and sending fingers to twitch away.

My greatest use, apparently, was in actually beating the metal. Ardin appreciated my strength more than a little, and compared to the difficulty of cleaving through solid armor, working the heat-softened materials was ridiculously easy. My nostrils were filled with the fumes of screaming metallurgy, my skin prickling with the irritation of ambient heat, and my eyes watered as hot air blasted my face every time we squeezed down the bellows. But I persevered, and the metal started shaping itself bit by bit.

He kept me there for much more than the hour, which I realized was probably evidence that I'd at least earned his approval. By the time the work was all done, a few more had passed, and Solitaire's helmet looked good as new. I grinned, feeling a flood of satisfaction as I eyed it.

The metal was smooth and flawless, glinting the way good steel did in this world, without any blemishes or seams that betrayed the fact of it ever having been reworked at all. I could see Ardin was pleased, too.

"How did I do?" I asked him eagerly. The man shrugged.

"You're a good apprentice," he noted. "Not sure about taking you on, though."

An idea came to me. A really, really clever one. The sort that Solitaire and Shango would have, share, and then move on without ever even taking the time to dwell on the impressiveness of it.

"What if you work for me and my brothers?" I suggested. "You're a good smith—a brilliant smith—and we could use brilliance. There's all sorts you could test your skills on with us."

He didn't look convinced, and I felt the pressure of a conversation slipping out of my grip.

"Think about the things you've made already. We could show you more. You . . . Have you heard about Shango's new weapon?"

"The black powder?"

"No, the thing that spits fire and punches through plate. You built it, but I guess you haven't seen it in action."

Ardin's skepticism was thick enough that a bullet would've bounced off it, but I could see I'd gotten him thinking, at least.

"Show me what you're talking about," he grunted, and I paused, then sighed.

"I can't yet, but I'll be gathering some materials for my brother soon. If you want you can help us mix them into the final product."

His face was like an iron mask, and Ardin just nodded. "Tell me when, then, and I'll be there to see it."

I nodded back. "Will do. Now if you'll excuse me, I have some shopping to do . . ." I took my leave quickly, helmet carried with me, and moved out into the streets. Starting the long process of pondering just where the fuck I'd be finding a sample of molybdenum. And, indeed, what the shit molybdenum even was.

CHAPTER EIGHT

Shango's POV: Day 69
Current Wealth: 24 gold, 48 silver, 14 copper

After my shock at the council's building, I was more than a little eager to just hurry my way back to the others and take it easy. Life was never so nice as to make things like that possible, though. I returned to a fair amount of chaos.

Solitaire had been busy with his magical training, and Beam had been busy with a lot more. The two of them were hastily explaining why, exactly, they'd dropped dozens of silver on random piles of metal scrap and bizarre clumps of material. That was when Argar barged in.

The giant was in an unusually good mood even for him, grinning broadly and eyeing the entire room, twitching with anticipation as he prepared to speak.

"Elswick," he declared. "I was an idiot to forget it, Elswick. The Elswick that hosts a melee every year, eh? That giant tourney with all the best fighters in the surrounding nations gathering around for it—it's starting in a few weeks."

I was interrupted in soaking the words up by Solitaire cackling and patting Beam on the shoulder.

"Excellent, I have about a million things I can show him to sway him over to our side. Having a smith like him will be *very* helpful. Good work!"

It took me a moment to realize he was ignoring Argar, talking instead about his and Beam's outings over the day. Argar looked a shade irritated at being so handily dismissed.

"Are you listening to me?" he growled. Solitaire glanced at him, irritated himself now.

"Of course I am. I'm listening to everything, all the time, whether I want to or not. You're suggesting we put ourselves up to enter this big bout, right? Well forget it. The competition in something like that will crush us. We'd be better served directing our energies to other things."

Argar opened his mouth to speak, and Solitaire interrupted.

"No, you can't take them. You're in the top percentile of Redaclans, in terms of sheer statistical prowess, but a tournament drawing in people from as big an area as you just described will be looking at a sample size orders of magnitude larger than that. Thousands, tens of thousands, maybe as many as millions. Which means that the best among them will be in the top percentile of the top percentile. Get it?"

Argar was a clever enough guy, but Solitaire had used a few too many modern words, and it showed. He sighed as the giant eyed him, clearly *not* getting it.

"If you're one in a hundred, we don't have a chance because this tournament is attracting a big enough number of competitors that anyone who gets close to its end is likely to be one in thousands or more."

The giant snorted.

"Bah, there isn't a man alive who can take me. Just throw me in and see what happens."

While he was blustering his way into having Solitaire start reenacting another feral-animal attack, I was considering the idea. My thoughts toward it were a shade less egoistic than Argar's, and rather more practical.

"Aren't you working on some godly metal, though?" I asked Solitaire and saw his face spasm that way it always did when someone made a good point at him. As if the very muscle fibers beneath his skin had been wounded upon hearing it.

"I'm working on modern-day tool steels," he replied. "Good metal, very good metal, but if you're asking whether it'll let Argar beat some of the sorts I'm expecting to show up, no. Fuck, you've already met at least one person in this city alone who'd wash him, right?"

That much was true, and I sighed. Beam cut in then, though.

"What about me?"

We all turned to him, and I found my friend seemed somewhat eager. No, not somewhat, entirely and unabashedly eager. He was barely grinning less than Argar.

"No offense," Beam said to the giant. "But I'm the best fighter of us all. Where do you reckon I'd rank in the grand scheme of things, Solitaire?"

Solitaire eyed him, clearly not impressed.

"Not high enough. I'm telling you, this isn't a winning proposition for us."

It looked like I was in for another long bickering session then, but Helena rescued me from its clutches. She cut into the conversation, speaking with that icy, scythe-like way she always did, calm and candid as she nudged every other voice aside.

"I happen to know a thing or two about the tournament that you might all find interesting to hear," she volunteered. Obviously that had all our attentions captured near instantly, and she didn't hide the smug grin that sprouted along her face at the knowledge. "It is famous, like Argar said, but it's famous for more than one reason. For commoners, it's a source of free entertainment, but the wealthier attendees have been betting on the outcome of its matches for years."

We all considered that, Solitaire quickest of all.

"Alright," he said. "We'll enter it, then. When exactly will it take place?"

It never took him long to make a decision, and it never took him long to move past one, either. I suppose I'd seen that demonstrated well enough recently. A shiver ran along my spine as I piped up.

"What sort of money tends to get exchanged?"

Helena shrugged.

"A fair amount. It depends on the circles you bet in, but we'd certainly be able to make a nice profit depending on how much we put in and at what odds."

"I said we'll do it already." Solitaire sighed. "This just became a math problem, essentially. If we can risk our money at the benefit of multiplying it, then we should. As things are now, we have the means to make extra income by selling gunpowder. The losses won't hurt much, but a victory will put us weeks, maybe even months ahead of schedule depending on the payout we manage to take home."

It would also mean putting Beam out into the public eye and risking that the world realized our growth rate. Solitaire eyed me before I could say it, a fractional nod conveying instantly that he'd already considered the idea.

But Helena and Argar were present; we wouldn't be discussing it in front of them. I bit my tongue.

"When will the metalworking be done, anyway?" Argar grunted. "I quite like the idea of some miracle plate." He eyed Solitaire, lip curling suddenly. "It won't explode, will it?"

Solitaire grinned and didn't answer.

"We're better off getting the smith, right?" I asked. "When will you do that?"

He shrugged. "Could try now, really. All I'm doing is flashing some designs in front of him. Just letting him know there's more where the other stuff came from should bring him over, right? Everybody wants things from the future." His lip curled. "Except Twitter."

"Work on that quickly then," Beam cut in. "I want him with us sooner rather than later."

Solitaire sighed.

"Always something more for me to do, isn't there? Every—"

I saw where he was going and decided to cut in and save us all a very long and tedious rant.

"Yes, Solitaire, we all know what a poor, tortured genius you are. You can complain about how tragic it is for you to be capable of doing transatmospheric-propulsion calculations in your head once you've gotten us our blacksmith. Just hurry up and do that first."

He glared at me. "Fucker."

I glared back. "Prick."

Beam eyed both of us, shrugged, and turned to Argar.

"Well, we don't have as much to do. Fancy a quick spar outside?"

The giant grinned again, and the two of them headed out. I glanced at Helena.

"Watch them, will you?" I asked her, and she rolled her eyes.

"They'll probably be through to ask that I give Argar a hand soon, anyway." The woman grunted, following them out.

The moment they were gone, I turned to Solitaire.

"You're really sure about just gambling to make money?" I asked, not hiding my uncertainty. He didn't hide his bulletproof confidence, either, grinning widely as ever.

"Not really, no, but I'm sure about it being *probable* to give us our best odds in the long haul. Everything I said still stands, right?"

I sighed, sitting, nodding.

"You just want to build your fortress," I noted, eying him. Solitaire shrugged.

"We all have our little weaknesses. What can I say? I'm a creator at heart."

Right. A creator, provided one defined creation as the art of turning floorboards into death traps capable of ripping someone in half. I didn't meet his eyes as I pondered things.

Solitaire, being Solitaire, knew what I was thinking, and knew, more, what I was feeling. His voice rang out with the perfect tone to project the perfect words.

"It's a while away, anyway," he noted. "We can have a think on this, see if any other options come up. It doesn't all need deciding right this instant, eh?"

Raising my head, I looked at him and found myself . . . confused.

"How can you be this?" I asked him. "How can you . . . Fucking, how can you know exactly what you need to say to help me, and always do it right when I need it saying? How can you be so . . . good? And still . . ."

A screaming orc, thumbs compressing eyes, the smell of optic fluid and sludgy blood staining the air. A friend's face twisted unrecognizably with glee. Words failed me.

They didn't fail Solitaire.

"It's simple," he replied. "You're a good person; the people here aren't."

CHAPTER NINE

Solitaire's POV: Day 69
Current Wealth: 24 gold, 48 silver, 14 copper

Once Shango was finished flaunting his virginity at me, I was free to turn my attention to matters slightly more important than the ethics of thumbing out a Cro-Magnon creature's eyes. More specifically, what the hell could I do with elements, and where were the limiting lines drawn?

There'd not been much point in experimenting before, outside of the very broad tests needed to confirm that I did, in fact, need to boil and heat the ingredients for black powder regardless of how hard I wished them into rearranging on their own. Now, though, there'd be a much wider variance in the methods and techniques done to all the metals Beam had bought on his little shopping trip.

Ores and minerals, some in crystal form, others powders or stony blocks. All of them had things I wanted, tucked away inside, keeping the good stuff from me like meat inside oysters. Well, that was fine. I wasn't exactly the classiest of fellows, but I knew how to eat an oyster at least.

I picked up a rock and started smashing the materials apart.

This wasn't just a discharge of masculine energy. Breaking things to bits was a vital first step in a strange amount of chemistry. Square-cube law and all that. The smaller something is, the higher its surface area—the thing that correlates to reactivity—is in relation to its volume—the thing that correlates to time taken to react. Which is to say, breaking one volume into a thousand smaller ones will make them react a lot quicker and easier. Ten times so, actually. Worth remembering.

We'd started a fire up because that was all I'd need for the purposes of this little experiment. If it failed then we could always just use a proper smithy, but if it worked then that knowledge alone would be worth more than the actual products of my labor today. The molybdenite was first.

Different ores melted at different temperatures, and this was one of the various principles I planned on using to separate the useful agents Beam had gotten from the worthless sludge their atoms were bound in and around. By my estimates, we'd be looking at maybe eight hundred degrees Celsius for the fire, well below the point at which stone would liquefy. Which was the first test. Could I make things more vulnerable to heat?

I waited, eagerly watching the churning flames. Twenty minutes passed without so much as a stone going runny before I was forced to conclude that, apparently, just sapping the thermal resilience of a material was beyond me. Irritating. I considered the matter further, at that, and turned my attention to the fire itself.

Fire isn't really anything special; it's just chemical energy becoming heat. Fuel turning to energy and gas. The temperature was . . . what? I didn't know exactly how it was determined, but I didn't take long to figure it out. Materials didn't have arbitrarily determined burning heats; they were variable. Variable along with the amount and size of the fire, so . . . the faster fuel burned, the hotter it would become. Made sense, of course. For more heat to be transferred across the same medium, the temperature differential had to grow.

So what would happen if the *coal* started reacting faster? I decided to try and find out.

I'd had my suspicions, of course, and they proved well-founded. More and more coal needed dumping on the flames as heat and entropy ate it, CO_2 filling the air with dangerous density. Within minutes, even my superhumanly toughened flesh was starting to throb at the feeling of heat pressing against it, lungs feeling coarse at the scraping inhalations I took. My eyes didn't hurt—they were too resilient for that—but I knew instinctively that looking at the light of the blaze would've been dangerous for a normal person's. It was almost like burning magnesium rather than a standard fire.

And it got hot, very quickly. Worked perfectly for separating my ores and causing all those nice, convenient chemical reactions, but unfortunately I had to dial the temperature down a shade. On account of the stone floor starting to melt.

That was inconvenient, but I somehow didn't mind. I'd confirmed my little theory, knew, now, that I could at least *influence* reactions on a chemical scale. So I got to work testing it out a bit more.

Now originally I'd only actually planned to find my limits, gauge precisely where the lines were so I could work around them. What I *hadn't* intended was to actually stretch those limits, and it came as a brilliant surprise when I started accidentally doing just that. Well, it didn't stay accidental for long.

I worked, and worked, hours soon flitting by as I concentrated on hastening reactions, then triggering them, then amplifying them. I could hear the laws of chemistry screaming at me while I did it, soyjaking as they watched me violate conservation of matter and energy both, leaving products that outweighed the reactants and thermal releases that left equations seesawing rapidly. The more I did, the more I felt spurred on to do.

Shango came in as the sun was setting, the world suddenly darker, and I glanced up at him with a grin. Had all that time really passed? I flitted my focus back, sifting through memories to verify. Yes, sixteen thousand seconds, in fact. And worth every moment.

"Watch this," I instructed him, holding my hands out, closing my eyes, and concentrating for a second. I felt hydrogen in the air, and I took that. Nitrogen and oxygen, too. There wasn't as much carbon as I'd have liked, but I fixed that by just exhaling. It wasn't hard to separate the oxygen out of my breath and add what was left to the mix, balancing and weighing, calculating it all at once. Becoming the catalyst myself.

A few droplets condensed in the space between my fingers, smaller than raindrops. I jumped back as they fell toward the ground, bracing myself for—

They landed and exploded apart, sending a crack of noise and a rush of air to run through the room. Shango practically jumped out of his skin, and I laughed at the sight as he leaped back. The ground was slightly scuffed where they'd fallen. Not a lot, just a few ruffled feathers on the surface of the stone. But not bad for a subgram mass.

"What the fuck was that?!" my friend demanded, glaring at me. I grinned back.

"Nitroglycerin," I told him. "The sports car to our black powder's space hopper. Pretty cool, eh?"

His excitement was strongly felt, and long-lived. Shango quickly called Beam in to witness the effects himself, and they both waxed lyrical about the implications of them. Just seeing them react to it had me bubbling over with anticipation all over again.

"What else can you do?" Beam asked. "Make a nuclear explosion?"

I opened my mouth to answer, but was cut off by Shango.

"Solitaire, do not try to make a fucking nuclear explosion."

I closed my mouth, then glared at him. Fun-ruining asshole.

". . . Could you, though?" he pressed. I sighed and shook my head.

"No, probably not. I can de- and recombine molecules, but I can't change the actual elements themselves. New quantities of some seem to appear— otherwise I wouldn't be able to create a bit more mass than would otherwise be possible with whatever reactants I'm using in their quantity—but that seems to be limited to just a pure chemical reaction, nothing nuclear. Though . . ." A grin flitted along my mouth. "Level me up a bit more and I might be nuking people regardless, right?"

For some strange reason that I couldn't even begin to comprehend, neither of my friends looked particularly pleased with the idea. Still, their dissatisfaction didn't last long.

"So how much nitro can you make at once?" Beam asked.

I considered that. There was always the option of just checking, of course, but if that amount happened to be much more than a few ounces, it'd mean we'd need a new warehouse . . . and possibly a new genius. I calculated it instead.

Previously, I'd managed to make around fifty percent more of whatever product I was aiming for than the reactant masses would have otherwise allowed. What would the limiting factor be here, then? My breath, definitely. I could draw in oxygen, nitrogen, and hydrogen from far around myself—a few meters at least—but if I wanted a decent amount of CO_2 I'd need to bring it out of my lungs. I did some quick calculations based on caloric intake and respiratory efficiency, arriving at . . . 0.04 grams, turning to about 0.01 grams of pure carbon. Not a lot, hardly anything in fact.

To calculate how much of one chemical you can make from others, you just need their molar masses. The total atomic mass of what you're making, compared to the fraction of that mass made up by any particular reactant. Nitro had a molar mass of 227, with three carbon atoms being part of that. Carbon's molar mass was twelve, multiplied by three that became thirty-six, making it about 16 percent of the total mass. So I could make just under ten percent of a gram of nitroglycerin if I used all the carbon in one breath.

"Uh, Solitaire—" Beam began. I shot a glare at him.

"No talking, brain thinking," I snapped, and continued to do just that.

Breath wasn't going to help much. How much CO_2 could I get from the surrounding atmosphere?

Three grams, as it happened. Enough for about thirty grams of nitro. That wasn't very much, not at all, but it was a start. And it'd also shown me there was a limit to how far I could manipulate chemicals from—about two meters or so. Would that increase as I became more powerful?

It annoyed me that I couldn't know yet, but I moved past it and shared the information.

"So how much is that?" Shango asked eagerly. I considered it, then shrugged.

"I have no idea. Wanna go and see?"

He did, and so did Beam. Almost as much as me, in fact. The three of us headed outside, and I worked my magic, congealing atoms together into that special fluid that had made us so good at killing in the twentieth century. I was careful to get it moving as I made it, sending my arms out in an arc to ensure that the fingertip-sized blob of nitro was already flying away as it congealed into existence. It struck the stone floor about a dozen meters ahead of me.

The difference in explosive power between it and the black powder is hard to describe.

Our ears didn't ring, but I saw stone break and dirt jet upward like a puddle being stamped on. It rained down while we laughed.

"What can you make with this?" Shango asked, grinning. I sighed.

Nothing, obviously; it was fucking nitroglycerin. But I wouldn't mind giving a go at stabilizing it into something that didn't explode when you looked at it too hard. Dynamite would be a solid bet if I ever found a reason to put the extra work in.

And if nothing else, the ability to make a hand grenade out of literal air was nice to have. I could think of a certain fucker I'd quite like to test it out on.

First things first, though. I had to fix the ventilation in that damned warehouse.

CHAPTER TEN

Beam's POV: Day 72
Current Wealth: 74 gold, 17 silver, 22 copper

Time passed, and several things started to happen. I began my new career in smithing, as the blacksmith—Ardin—was suitably awed by some of our designs to join up. Unfortunately, it involved working myself close to ten hours a day in the process of learning. Fortunately, I was well used to that sort of exertion, and I quickly discovered all the right ways of moving to ensure that I was working as many of my muscles as possible in the process. It didn't take me long to fall into a rhythm with it all.

My friends kept themselves busy, too. Both of them continued learning their magic, though Solitaire cut his practice down in favor of concentrating on his chemical fuckery, and of course we sold plenty more gunpowder to keep our coffers topped up. Our accommodations soon grew with our funds, and all of us got accustomed to hot meals, baths, all the little luxuries we'd spent our earliest days missing. It was good, peaceful, and relaxed. Except for Solitaire's ever-growing paranoia.

Now, Solitaire was a great guy. Well, okay, fine. A good guy then. Or, not actively bad. Certainly there were worse people one could meet . . . if you searched enough. He wasn't actively dangerous, at the very least. Under most circumstances, and as long as you didn't make any sudden movements in his peripheral vision. The point being, I liked Solitaire, really, he was one of my best friends. But he had a tendency to . . . freak out when he thought trouble was approaching.

And in this case, he was absolutely fucking right; trouble *was* approaching. Corvan must have heard of us by now, and we were rapidly closing in on his expected arrival time. Solitaire dealt with that kind of pressure—or any other pressure, for that matter—about as well as a land mine. A nuclear land mine that knew how to make other nuclear devices.

Suffice to say, I was a bit worried for him. Every day he was developing a new conspiracy theory, moving around, muttering to himself all twitchy and dark. He spasmed whenever something even slightly unexpected happened, went for a knife whenever someone startled him, and otherwise made himself resemble a rabid wolverine occupying the body of a human.

"We need a fort," he snapped for the fiftieth time. "A bunker, a . . . a defensible position, choke points all around it, with overlapping fields of fire and barbed wire and minefields and—"

"We need to relax," I tried, and he glared at me in that magical way he had. The one that left me convinced, even after all our years of friendship, that he was about to come flying at me and start chewing bits off.

"You need to fuck yourself," he snarled. "Fucking morons, all of you, idiots, cattle. Happy to just waddle around chewing grass with your mouths open, waiting to get killed. Well fuck that. I'm too clever to die. I'm too clever for anything to even hurt me. I'm—"

"Being a cunt to your friends," Shango cut in, eyeing him coldly. Solitaire snapped around, glaring his way. Shango kept talking before he could reply. "Or am I stupid, mindless cattle for pointing that out?"

Solitaire hesitated, tightened his jaw, swallowed as if something bitter were in his mouth. Then looked away.

"Sorry," he managed. A few moments passed, and I saw his frenzied rage replaced by something else. Shame.

It always came to him after an outburst like that, and like always he pretended it didn't, and we pretended not to have seen it.

"We do need to protect ourselves," Solitaire grunted after a moment. "Corvan will be here tomorrow, at the earliest, and not much later at best. This isn't an ignorable problem anymore. We need to be ready for whatever he tries to do."

"Alright," Shango answered, warmer now. "How do you suggest we go about that?"

Solitaire hissed, thinking.

"I want to know when he's coming and from where, so . . . I've sent along a few bribes to the gate guards. Figured if it worked for him, it'd work for us. Our reputations probably helped with that, too."

Shango didn't look surprised, just nodded.

"Okay, what else? How do we take him?"

"I can have one of his hands off before he's even cast," I volunteered, and Solitaire eyed me.

"He shielded himself from an explosion within seconds of waking up. I don't think I'd like to bet on you managing that."

Truth be told, I would have, but he wasn't exactly wrong that it'd be risky at least. Certainly, there were easier ways.

"Shango has a gun," I noted. "That'll be helpful. How do we make sure he gets the chance to use it?"

His accuracy was improving, though not as quickly as it had a few days ago. Little, fractional changes we noticed by the day. He had about one and a third times the hit ratio now than when we'd headed out to take back the fort.

"Unless Corvan blocks it with magic," Shango answered back. Solitaire sighed.

"We should have Ardin cast us some iron balls to shoot. They won't weigh as much, but they'll hold together a lot better than lead. Might keep their energy concentrated enough to punch through, maybe."

It depended, of course, on how strong Corvan actually was, which was a bit inconvenient given that the fucker happened to be stronger than any other magus we'd met. Hell of a person to piss off.

Then again, he'd started it.

"This'll all be useless if we don't have a decent place to catch him," Solitaire noted. "This warehouse won't do. He could probably bring it down in a minute or two."

We were talking about it now, I realized, properly talking about it. Corvan's attack wasn't some future event anymore. It had drawn close enough that we had no choice but to actually engage with the threat. A chilling thought.

Our back-and-forth didn't last us as long as it might have. Mostly because it was helped by a man who'd spent more of his life thinking about the best ways of defending himself from the kinds of power we'd be assailed by than any modern citizen ought to have.

It wasn't long before our plan was finished, and we went about enacting it. Argar was sent grumbling from the place with a big burlap sack, Helena was marched away to gather more, and Shango went out looking for a new hire.

Days passed, we worked, we grew more and more scared. And then we grew less scared.

Argar and I were in charge of gathering little stones and pulverizing them with hammers, on Solitaire's insistence. He wanted sandbags, the weirdo. Well, maybe it was fair enough. If they stopped machine gun fire then it was worth trying them out against a wizard, at least, and it gave us something to do. He was keeping himself busy, as well. Making more gunpowder, filling our pockets by the day.

Shango kept himself busy, too.

He'd told us about the blonde noble lady who'd approached him, of course, and we'd all kept her in the backs of our minds, worrying as she was. Well, she made herself known again, soon. Calling on Shango for a meeting about . . .

something, something we weren't allowed to be told beforehand, apparently. That sparked a new discussion among us, which ended in the only way it could have.

Ideally, we'd have all gone. But we were busy, preparing, and ill-suited respectively. Solitaire in particular could activate a woman's fight-or-flight response just by coming within a fifty-foot radius of her, which made him a poor choice as company for such a meeting.

So Shango readied himself to head out alone. I was still stacking sandbags when he was finally prepared, and Solitaire was busy mixing, so neither of us really gave him much of a look as he headed out of what was rapidly transforming from warehouse to bunker.

We turned around soon, though. Because he wasn't so much as five feet out the door when all of us felt magic in the air, and then a wave of fire rolled down toward him.

CHAPTER ELEVEN

I had about a second before watching my friend become the world's nobbiest barbecue, and I was acting on it before most of my brain even knew what was happening. Thinking, reaching my focus out into the air around me, grabbing all the components I could find, drawing them in, and throwing them.

Even after training for weeks, I'd never have been quick enough to do something with magus magic that fast, but my new powers were different. More innate, instinctual, limited only by the speed of my mind. And those were no limits at all.

By the time I saw the light, I'd already filled the surrounding atmosphere with my will. By the time I felt the heat, I'd already started reaching into it for water. By the time I saw the fire, I'd already thrown it out in a great torrent to wash around Shango. Sixteen cubic meters of air, with at least a few percentage points of it made up of moisture. Then the ground, then my clothes, then my breath. And then all the loose hydrogen and oxygen I could manage to boot. Probably, I hit my friend with close to a ton of water, likely bowled him off his feet, likely saved him, maybe killed him.

Unfortunately, I was denied the chance to know because I discovered something new about my power, too. It wasn't exempt from Newton's third law.

My feet left the ground instantly, body tossed back like a rag doll, forced to take more than its fair share of momentum as I propelled the torrent outward. It more likely than not weighed ten times as much as me, and was moving easily dozens of miles per hour. I had just enough time to realize that I might die before the wall caught me.

The heavily sandbag-coated wall. It was that that saved me, slight deformations to the covering burlap sacks decelerating me more gradually, reducing the force and keeping my skeleton from crumpling apart. It didn't stop me from seeing stars, however.

I bounced off it, fell down, groaned, and coughed. Blood was in my mouth, salty and iron tasting, flavoring the death I was choking back and leaving me spasming for precious moments while I waited for my organs to settle. By the time I came to, the room was empty except for me, and Shango was just barely visible outside, flitting by the door. I got to my feet, coughing, but no more blood came up. That was a good sign, and I lurched my way to the door with a grunt.

Outside, everything was mad. The air smelled of smog and smoke—it was all hot enough to sting even my supernaturally toughened flesh—and Shango didn't so much as glance at me. I felt the magic instantly, but it took me a second to realize that some of it was coming from him, and all of it directed in the same vector as his eyes.

Fire, more fire, more fire than I'd ever seen before. Slashing through the air in great waves, heating the stone ground to a cherry-red glow, and Beam was right in the center of it all. Dodging, diving, jumping, and flipping.

He was moving fast, almost faster than I could keep track of, like he was passing through air while the rest of the world swam its way through water. The glowing armor clung to him, as always, trailing light, but I could see that he was moving to the limits of his abilities.

Corvan was hovering high above, eyes alight with hate, power extending down in great sheets of flame. My friend didn't have long, so I got to work.

The air was drier around me now, but not so much so that I didn't find plenty of moisture to separate and throw out. I kept the speed down this time, just enough to reach a few meters overhead and intercept one of Corvan's attacks, hissing on impact as the heat was absorbed and diffused as pattering rain. I didn't look at Shango while speaking, but I didn't need to to know he'd be listening.

"We need your gun," I told him. "I'll focus on buying us some time."

Even as I said it, I called on more water, moving to ensure that I could keep scraping fresh patches of air after depleting others. I sent my next blast out as an elongated lance, aimed for the magus himself, and watched as Corvan shifted his flames into an opaque wall of air. The liquid scattered on impact, of course, but by then I was already preparing a follow up.

Fire rolled down for me, and I threw up more water—felt it boil away, but near enough that the wave of heat made my eyes water and skin itch. So I fixed it, drawing on more moisture, wringing the heat out of my flesh by boiling the liquid myself. An endothermic reaction that gave me the perfect chance to cool myself a bit, and gave me an idea.

More fire, more water, this time farther from my body, leaving me safer and unhurt. I took the extra time and used it to gather more water, drawing the heat from it as I did. I needed somewhere to put it, so I separated my mass of moisture into two blocks, one vaporizing while another, much larger, froze solid. I shaped the liquid even as it hardened and crystallized into ice, making it a great, long lance with a jagged tip. Then I lashed it out at the magus.

Corvan blocked it again of course, his shield shattering the material with ease. Something strong enough to turn away an explosion as big as we'd thrown his way last time would've never failed at something so trivial.

I'd been counting on the fact.

As the ice broke apart, its hollow interior was exposed, venting out the pressurized steam I'd left trapped inside—all the waste heat I'd needed to move away to solidify the water now free to shoot out and bathe the magus. He was fifty feet away, at least, but I still heard him scream, and nobody could've failed to see him fall.

He could still breathe while using his shield, after all; most magi could. I knew enough about our magic system to be aware of that much. If air could get through, why not gas? God, I wish I could marry myself.

Corvan slowed himself before he landed, climbing, waveringly, to his feet. And then the bricks were on him; Argar, Helena, Beam, all moving like a pack of hunting dogs, encircling him within an instant, attacking in unison. His shield was fast in raising, and great in warding them off. I called out a warning right before the shock wave he conjured rang out to send them all flying back. Beam, though, didn't need it.

He'd already leaped away from the concussion, twisting to land feetfirst in a crouch, then lunging again. His conjured sword was barely deflected, and the sheer force of it sent the magus skidding back, fighting for balance. Argar rose behind him just as he did, letting Corvan's momentum carry him toward his axe swing, sending him spinning and rolling away with the strength of it.

Fire, then water. My and Corvan's magic met in the air, sizzling each other to death, and Argar charged through the conflagration. The magus sent another jet of flame out, smaller, but enough to heat his plate to glowing and launch him back—I screamed at the sight, the magus turned to me and raised his shield.

My ice shattered again, but this time Corvan's barrier was far enough in front of him that the steam dispersed before it could scald his body. I could see the effects of my last attack still, red, cracked patches along his skin, but it was all superficial, too little to truly hurt him. I should've used more steam, and trapped it in a smaller space, increased the pressure and mass so that it would hold heat longer and shoot out faster. Might've melted the bastard's face off with my last hit, might've hurt him again with this one. Too late now.

The gunshot snapped me out of my self-pity.

Shango had taken his sweet fucking time in fishing out his rifle, but it was free now, and I heard it announce itself with a sharp crack of supersonic flight and the sizzle of burning powder. Corvan's barrier flashed, then buckled, and I saw a spray of crimson in the air all within a time frame so small even my enhanced eyes couldn't pick out any individual moment from coming before or after another. The magus stumbled, cursing.

Yeah, that was right, old fucker. A bullet wasn't quite the same thing as a wall of air, however pressurized it was. I wasn't surprised to see the victory of technology over magic.

Beam chose then to slam his newest weapon into the man from the side, a giant halberd that might've been too big for even his own superhuman musculature were it made of metal instead of light, and hit with about as much force as the entire River Mersey. The poor old man went flying so hard he looked to be challenging *Apollo 11*'s record.

Corvan hit the ground, bounced about a meter back up into the air, then hit it again. He slid this time, rolling and grinding along the floor before finally stopping as his face hit a wall and his body flipped one last time. I saw him twitching. Still alive, then, odd.

Clearly he'd shielded himself from the subsequent impacts, as well as just the initial strike, because the streak of blood he'd left along behind him wasn't nearly a dead amount of leakage. That was fine, though; it meant more fun for me. I stalked after him, a sudden energy vitalizing my movements as I thought of getting my hands on the fucker and twisting bits off. Where would I start? Perhaps a rib. That'd be ironic; we'd needed him to fix Beam's ribs first, after all. Then again, one couldn't beat the old classics. I reckoned I'd take off his cock.

I reached him, and he turned to look up at me with focus in his eyes and magic in his hands. It didn't last long. My fist cracked across his jaw and launched the coherence right out of him, leaving his head to loll back slack and boneless as his eyes fogged over with concussion. My fingers were just tightening about his chin, my other hand just reaching for the nearest cluster of pain receptors, when something important occurred to me.

Glancing over my shoulder, I looked back to check on Argar. The man was still lying still, a smoldering wreck covered with smoke and steam. My anger flared, but I stabbed it in the kidney and put it to one side, glaring back at the magus.

"Alright, cunt, listen up," I hissed, bringing his face to within an inch of mine, resisting the urge to start chewing through his cheek and bite out his tongue. "You just hurt a mate of mine. You're going to unfuck him, and if you don't manage that I'll be teaching you things about human anatomy that your moron civilization won't discover for another five years."

Corvan did not appear to be any less grumpy than usual.

CHAPTER TWELVE

Shango's POV: Day 76
Current Wealth: 168 gold, 47 silver, 29 copper

I hurried to Solitaire and Corvan, all too aware that every moment passing by was another opportunity for my brother to do something horrific, irreversible, and, in this case, disastrous. He wouldn't, though, would he?

A stupid question. Of fucking course he would.

To my surprise, though, he hadn't. When I came to the pair they were talking—or, rather, Solitaire was snarling, and Corvan was cowering. I supposed that much made sense. Magus or not, he was still just an aging man physically. Within the reach of Solitaire's arm, there would be no real contest between the two of them. Which made it even more remarkable that Corvan's physiology hadn't been rearranged yet.

"You're going to heal the big one," Solitaire growled just as I came to within earshot. "You're going to do a really, really nice job of it. He's going to live a long and healthy life, and he'll even have that knee problem gone once you're done. If you don't, I'll kill you. If you fail, I'll kill you. If he turns out to be too hurt for any magus in the world to fix, I'll fucking kill you so slowly you'll end up wondering whether it was old age that got you in the end. Understand?"

Corvan nodded, his face sheet pale. I could see blood dripping from one side of him, just under the ribs. It formed a patchy trail behind him, too, little droplets and flecks on the ground. Not a deadly amount to lose, I thought, but running out fast enough that it would be soon. Solitaire hauled him to his feet with one arm.

"Then let's get healing," he spat.

Argar was in bad shape. Somewhere between "hospital visit" and "something I just hauled out of a blast furnace" levels of hurt, barely moving, not making a sound, covered with burns and covered even more entirely by mangled, glowing armor that kept us from seeing the extent of it. We'd needed Beam's help to even examine him, twisting and tearing the ruined plate's remnants free of his body.

Fortunately, the heat left his steel coating just about weak enough that it surrendered to my friend's physical power. Unfortunately, what it revealed was more harrowing than I'd dared fear.

There were men out there who'd have sent a steak back to the kitchens if it had been as cooked as Argar was. His iron-tough skin was peeling back, blackened and charred, cracked apart to reveal bloody meat below. That meat wasn't anywhere near as glistening or moist as it ought to have been, its residual water currently permeating the air around him as a thin, steady trail of steam. The giant twitched, groaning with pain, and every motion sent fresh rivulets of blood to ooze up from his ruined body where the tissues were fused unnaturally together, then forcibly torn apart by the shifting movements.

Without magic, he'd have been dead. Even in a modern emergency room I wasn't sure what his chances would've been, but we had something better. I turned a glare to Corvan, tried to think of something to say, then gave up. Looking, instead, at Solitaire.

"If he doesn't save him," I said quietly, finding the words coming out of me as if someone else were speaking with my mouth, "I want you to kill him as slowly as you're capable of." Maybe it was a betrayal of my ethics, but I didn't care in the moment. Would I have gone through with it? Who knew.

Solitaire nodded and, for once, didn't smile.

The magus got to work.

I watched him like a hawk, Beam watched him like an eagle, and Solitaire watched him like the most paranoid man Liverpool had ever produced. All three of us kept our eyes on him with laser intensity, and Helena was crouched right behind, her spear ready to drive through the magus' spine if things looked like such an action would be necessary. The worst part was how difficult it would be to tell. We could all feel magic hemorrhaging off of him, but none of us were yet skilled enough in magery to tell one kind from another by sensation alone. He might've stopped healing and started readying another fireball, for all we knew, and the only warning we'd get was the light and heat.

Corvan's face didn't twist into a treacherous sneer, though, and his magic didn't convulse into a deadly ambush. He just looked exhausted.

When creating Redacle, we'd made any kind of magic exhausting, difficult, and time-consuming for a reason. It was to avoid compromising our dark-fantasy atmosphere by making it easily commonplace for people to have limbs grown back, or fevers purged from them. Well, that was biting us in the ass now because Argar's tortured body was being repaired far, far too slowly for my taste.

It certainly didn't help that we'd forced the magus to use so much of his power in the fight just minutes prior.

The blackened, carbonized flesh that was beyond saving fell off, detaching from its healthier dependencies and falling away like leaves in autumn. Below, the ugly red flesh slowly lightened, turning from crimson to scarlet, then pink as new skin grew over it. I saw the heat die down, the mangled connections rethreaded as soft tissue reformed and reattached. The more was done, however, the slower things became. Corvan was panting and sweating long before Argar was past the point of danger.

"I can't keep this up much longer," the magus breathed, his words strained. I eyed him, deciding that if he was that good at lying he'd probably have seen our little betrayal coming a mile away in the first place.

"What can you do?" I asked, and he scowled.

"Nothing, I just—"

Solitaire hit him, hard, in the spine, and the magus coughed out his agony for a moment before continuing in a slightly milder tone.

". . . Not much. My power is failing me."

"What can we do about that?" I snapped, sending a furtive glance at Argar. He didn't seem to have improved much, if at all. For all the damage that was *physically* gone, his strength was just as diminished and his agony just as apparent. Maybe people only had so much life in them, and an injury like this left it all squeezed out even when most of it was fixed. Maybe there was just more damaged tissue deeper below the exterior.

I was spiraling, focusing on minutiae, giving myself something trivial to consider so I didn't worry myself with what actually mattered. Stupid. I stopped.

"We can't do anything," Corvan replied, a touch of panic to his voice. He'd answered fast, fast enough that I might've been the delaying factor in our conversation had I not snapped myself out of the panic when I did. But his answer was useless all the same.

"That's not good enough," Solitaire growled. "If you can't do anything then you're a scrotum-themed rug in my warehouse."

He wasn't even kidding. I knew Solitaire kidding, and this was certainly not it. He looked far too sincere in his smile, far too subtly eager, for it to be anything but a promise of what was to come.

If he decapitated our subordinate's healer, then it would probably get in the way of his healing Argar. I decided to intervene before that could happen.

"What about a power pool?" I asked. "Can you draw on my strength?"

It was a concept in our lore, but not a commonly used one. I only even suggested it out of desperation, and before Corvan could answer, Solitaire was leaning in.

"Everyone shut up," he instructed. "I'm being clever."

I struggled to acquiesce. Every instinct in my body wanted me doing, not watching, but I was fresh out of useful ideas, and by the look on Corvan's face, a power tap wouldn't have changed anything at all.

"What do you think you're—"

"Shut," Solitaire snapped, interrupting the magus before his question could continue. It occurred to me that Corvan suddenly seemed a lot less cowed, his posture a lot less fearful. Was that intentional?

Yes, it must have been. Somewhere along the way he'd managed to slip himself out of the subordinate position in our conversation. Probably around the time we let him see he was fucking invaluable for healing Argar.

Whatever the implications of his newly perceived status were, Corvan had asked a valid question.

"What *are* you doing?" I frowned, figuring Solitaire had at least a bit of wiggle room in answering. He was quite the multitasker when he wanted to be. Most of the time he just asked for silence because he was a cock.

Sure enough, I got my answer.

"Cooling his body down," he replied. "Specifically, all the bits that are still hot enough to keep cooking. If nothing else, I'll keep his burns from worsening on their own."

Corvan barked out a new answer before I could.

"I was doing that," the magus exclaimed. "If you can do it yourself instead, then I'll have more power to spare on other things." Wordlessly, Solitaire made room by his side for the man to kneel down and continue his work in healing Argar, and I just stood back and watched them both go at it.

Minutes passed before they were finally finished, Solitaire leaning back with a snarl, Corvan with a sigh. Both of them were exhausted, but Argar looked . . . better.

He was breathing consistently, at least, not interrupting every other inhalation with a sharp gasp, not twitching or spasming anymore. There still wasn't a lot of color to the man's face, but there was at least a life to him. He looked less categorically dead than asleep, and I'd call that progress. All eyes turned to Corvan, who glanced up at us and scowled.

"I really am done now," the magus growled. "Nothing left in my reserves. If you want him healed more, it'll take you a few hours of waiting."

I resisted the urge to swear. Magi were powerful, but not for very long at a time. Depending on how they paced themselves, they could output maybe a few minutes of magic each day at full strength, with long stretches of recharge time in between. If he'd been healing at close to full capacity then he probably did have truly nothing left in the tank.

If he was lying to keep our guard down, though, then there'd not be any real way of knowing. I knew a lot about our world's magic, but not what different levels of it *felt* like, or how to compare them. I had no way of matching up the power we'd seen from Corvan to the exhaustion he claimed he felt, nor even how strong he was to begin with.

Solitaire must have gone through all the calculations already because he spoke before I could.

"You're going to make your offer soon," he noted. "To keep healing him, now that you've seen how we can kick the shit out of you."

The magus glared at him the way people tended to glare at Solitaire when he opened his mouth.

CHAPTER THIRTEEN

Beam's POV: Day 76
Current Wealth: 168 gold, 47 silver, 29 copper

Negotiating with a half-mad wizard had not been on my bucket list, but I surprised myself with how quickly I adjusted to the task. I figured everyone only had so much awe and shock in them, some finite amount assigned at birth, and that I'd already emptied mine long ago by spending those frantic first few weeks in Redacle. Maybe I was just resilient.

Certainly, the fact that we'd just beaten up the wizard in question had helped to mitigate the intimidation factor somewhat. Either way, he looked a lot more nervous than Solitaire and Shango. A good sign.

"How do I know you won't just kill me anyway?" Corvan asked us all, eyes flitting between us as he did. "The moment your friend's healed, you don't need me anymore."

Shango's eyes practically rolled out of his head at that.

"We won't kill you because we don't want to kill you, you fucking moron," he snapped. "We never wanted to kill you. We just wanted to live our lives and not lose a friend because some bear came flying at us one day. You're the one who tried to fuck us all over, and you're the one who chased us halfway across the country because we escaped."

Corvan's eyes narrowed.

"After trying to kill me with your magic powder," he growled. Solitaire hit him again, and the magus glared up at him.

"I'll try a bit fucking harder if you want," the Scouser snapped. "We did that because you threatened to kill us with magic if we didn't give you all the money that was keeping us alive, you shit-heel."

For a second, the magus looked like he might argue, then, instead, he bit back whatever words had been foaming at the back of his mouth and just sighed.

"Well, anyway, what can you do that'll make me certain I'll still be alive after whatever deal you make me think we've cut?"

Shango answered that, shooting back as quick as ever with a response so carefully worded it left me wondering, as always, whether he'd had it prepared an hour in advance. Given we'd been fighting for our lives not fifteen minutes ago against the recipient, there was perhaps cause to doubt it just this once.

"We're going to be employing you from now on," he said confidently.

Corvan blinked at him, taken aback. Being honest I probably looked about the same.

Instantly the magus' eyes moved to Solitaire, who was currently foaming at the fucking mouth glaring at him, eyes bulging and veins jumping out against his skin. Evidently, he wasn't too fond of the idea that we might be *working* with this one, let alone leaving him alive. Fortunately, despite his currently ongoing impression of a feral wolverine, he didn't seem like he'd be jumping the gun and lynching him.

For now, at least.

"Why would you work with someone you hate?" Corvan asked wearily. Shango sighed.

"Because we want to actually achieve something of worth, and you're powerful enough to help us do it. And, believe it or not, none of us actually enjoy viciously killing people, even ones we don't like."

Solitaire growled like a pit bull caught in a trash compactor, and I saw Shango checking with a quick glance to ensure our friend hadn't started closing in on the magus.

"*Most* of us don't enjoy viciously killing people," he amended.

"You want my magic," Corvan sneered, and Shango rolled his eyes as if he were talking to some screaming toddler.

"Yes, genius, of course we want your magic; it's fucking magic. If that surprises you, you're an idiot. If it's not a deal you want, then you're a dead man, and I'm afraid my brother won't make it fast."

Solitaire took a step forward, maybe for emphasis—the bad cop to Shango's good cop—and maybe because he really did just want to dismember the old man that much. Corvan barely glanced his way, though, seeming more thoughtful than concerned.

"Brothers?" he echoed. "You were friends when we first met."

Shango kept whatever surprise he felt hidden well, but mine must've shown because the magus grinned.

"Interesting lie to tell," he noted.

"Interesting time to get distracted," Shango shot back. Solitaire took another step forward, and I swore he was actually drooling now. "Work with us, yes or no?"

Corvan's eyes flickered between us as he thought about it, and it looked like he'd be taking his time in answering right up until Helena's spear tip prodded him in the back again. His face wrinkled in a wince. He swore, then glared back at her.

"What sort of conditions?" he asked.

Shango groaned.

"Fucking seriously?"

"I want a gold coin every week, whether I do anything or not," the wizard pressed. "No less."

"You get forty silver," Shango replied, "And you get to keep your nuts."

Solitaire didn't say anything at all, just stared at the magus, who seemed to consider the lunatic about as carefully as was appropriate before answering.

"What exactly are your plans that you still stand to benefit from having a magus join you in them, even now?" the man asked carefully. Shango met his question with the most severe, earnest stare I'd seen him give anyone yet.

"This world is wrong," he said simply. "It's twisted, diseased, evil. People starve in the streets, die of easily treatable wounds, work themselves half to death just to keep a grip on the shitty slivers of land their feudal lords have decided are theirs to work and die on. It's a disgusting, immoral ruin. We're going to fix it."

Corvan stared, then sneered, then in a few moments he was laughing out-right, cackles echoing out in every direction, chest heaving and shoulders lurch-ing. Such was his amusement that I actually saw tears threatening to form in his eyes and wet his cheeks, which was doubly impressive with the severe scald marks littering so much of his flesh. Apparently Solitaire's little steam missile hadn't quite seared the tear ducts closed.

Finally Corvan seemed finished with his convulsive chuckling, and his face grew serious, even as sporadic laughs still moved it a shade.

"I'd taken the three of you for fools." He snorted. "Now I see I was wrong. You're madmen. Fine, I'll help with your fool's errand, but don't expect me to die for it alongside you."

It was, I decided, about as good an offer as we could reasonably expect to have gotten from him. Shango just nodded dutifully, as if he were simply recording Corvan's help down as some relevant factor, without any particular emotion attached to it one way or the other. Solitaire, on the other hand, looked as if he might go into convulsions at not being allowed to tear him apart. I still wasn't sure whether he was just acting for the sake of leveraging a better deal, and probably never would be.

It was Helena who broke the silence, punctuating her words with another spear prod to Corvan's back.

"We've been talking for a few minutes. Shouldn't be too much longer until you have the power to make another crack at healing, should it?"

The magus craned his neck back uncomfortably to glare at her.

"Who let the woman talk? Oh, God, and she's a savage, too. I really—"

Solitaire interrupted him by dropping down to one knee, blood flecking his mouth and chin as a sudden cough seized him. We were all by his side in an instant, concern creasing our features.

"What's wrong?!" Shango demanded. Solitaire only shook his head.

"Threw myself into a wall using my powers," he whispered, volume forced low and feeble by the strain of his injury. "Think I broke a few ribs. Funny thing is I don't think the adrenaline's worn off. Can't feel any—Oh, no, there it is. Fuck."

"Get back, idiots," Corvan instructed. "Let me handle this." The man's hands lit up, and I saw them move to Solitaire's side. Every instinct in my body told me to take the magus' fingers off at the knuckles, but I curtailed them. He'd healed Argar, and he didn't have the remaining power to fight the rest of us again no matter what. With luck he'd heal Solitaire.

We all watched as our friend's agony slowly abated, and the strength slowly trickled back into him, but in less than a minute the regeneration stopped. Solitaire blinked, testing his ribs as Corvan spoke.

"Didn't have the power to fully remove the wounds," the magus explained, panting with exertion. "But you can treat this as about a week's head start on healing them. He's not in any danger now at least."

"And neither are you," Solitaire noted, eyeing him. "You're oddly relaxed for a man standing around enemies with none of his magic available."

Corvan's face stiffened, but only a shade. The magus shrugged.

"As of just now, I think we've established my usefulness," he retorted. "As I said, you're all madmen. But you're not fools."

CHAPTER FOURTEEN

Solitaire's POV: Day 76
Current Wealth: 168 gold, 47 silver, 29 copper

It'd been a pretty shit day so far, all things considered. I'd gotten the hell kicked out of me in a fight with an old man, spent several minutes watching a friend of mine convulse, and at the end of it all I'd gotten blue balled on playing reverse-Operation with Corvan and the nearby pile of metal scraps.

Oh, and my rib cage currently resembled a jigsaw puzzle. All in all, not exactly a win in my books. Still, it could've been worse. Things could always be worse when one fought a wizard.

Shango had made himself scarce about half an hour earlier, right after he was finally, properly sure that neither Argar nor I would spontaneously drop dead. Which had left the rest of us alone with Corvan. I'd surely lived through more awkward silences, but for the life of me, I couldn't actually think of any examples.

"What's your brother doing?" Corvan asked abruptly. It was just the two of us alone, for the moment. He'd decided he could trust us, going by the lack of our beheading him as soon as we knew he wasn't immediately needed anymore, and I'd decided I could trust him on account of the magus seeming to understand what would happen if he killed any of us and left the others alive. He'd seen our growth in power and was quick enough to realize we'd not hit the end of it.

Not quick enough to realize we could've just been holding off on killing him for fear that he'd done something to sabotage the healing process, though. Moron.

"He's busy doing important things," I replied, not even bothering to hide how dismissive I was, and barely resisting the urge to deliberately emphasize it. Fortunately Corvan was, apparently, just about sapient enough to notice anyway.

"You're not very good at answering questions, are you, boy?"

"You're not very good at understanding answers, are you, prick?" I shot back, only to find the magus grinning. Clearly he was well aware how much he got under my skin, which meant the only way to equalize our conversation would be getting under his even deeper.

"How did it feel getting the fuck knocked out of you by a bunch of people less than half your age?"

As far as gibes went, I had to say I'd come up with subtler. But sometimes a sledgehammer was more useful than a scalpel, and with an ego as big as Corvan's I had a feeling this was one of them. It seemed I was right because his face soured like milk in a desert, and his response was launched back as quickly as Uzi fire from an amateur.

"How did the three of you grow so much stronger so quickly?" he asked, the creases of age deepening across his features.

"We're really, really hard workers," I replied, and he scowled at me.

"Don't play me for a fool, boy. I know magus magic when I see it. What you did wasn't that, nor was whatever let you survive that impact against the wall. Your *brother* in particular was using something else, too. So what is it, and how?"

I considered his words, thought about all the cards I had available to play. Truth might give him the tools to shine some light on our abilities—as a practitioner of magic he might well know a few things the world's authors didn't, considering how much was "filled in" without our input. But it would also give him more confidence, and that tended to move people against you. Keeping him in the dark altogether would only sow his distrust. How could I deny him an answer without making him think he'd never get one from me?

Simple.

My foot lashed out, and it connected hard with his face, knocking him flat on his back and sprawling all four limbs outward. I'd held back, not wanting to actually kill or seriously injure the old fuck, and all too aware that my growing strength left me closer in raw power to that bear we'd met upon arrival than my former self. By the pained groans coming from Corvan, I deduced my kick had been successful in not snapping his spine and instead only just giving him a mild headache.

"Don't call me boy," I said coldly. "And don't forget to apologize the next time you set one of my friends on fire." I stood up, taking my leave before the wrinkly fuck could right himself and start asking more inconvenient questions. With any luck he'd have run out by the next time we spoke.

Beam interrupted me before I could even begin to consider what I'd be doing next, wandering over with that twisted, concerned look he always had when something was seizing his head into thoughts he'd rather it avoid.

"You alright?" I asked him, knowing full well what the answer would be already. As I am simply a giant bleeding heart with a skeleton and nervous system, however, I asked regardless, intending to coax my friend into speaking and venting out whatever had him so worried.

It worked; his words came fast.

"We've been having trouble with some of the new metals. Specifically the, uh, molybdenum. Ardin says his forge can't get hot enough to properly work it, let alone melt it and mix it into the rest of the alloy."

That wasn't what had been troubling him—I knew that much without even *needing* to think about it—but likewise I knew that Beam had been deliberate in sharing the practical issue rather than whatever emotional one was clearly gnawing away at him. I'd offered my hand, and he'd chosen not to take it. That was fine, ideal actually. I was much better at dealing with practical matters than humans, anyway.

"I'm not surprised," I confided, starting on my way to the forge. "Molybdenum melts at . . ." I paused, sifting through my memory for the relevant data. It came quickly. "Two thousand six hundred degrees Celsius."

Fuck, that hot? Military ceramics melted at a lower temperature than that. You'd have a hard time generating that sort of heat with thermite, let alone some caveman's furnace. Apparently Beam had some understanding of the implications, too, because his face fell.

"I don't think we can get anything that hot, Solitaire," he noted, crestfallen. He wasn't exactly wrong.

"Well our idiot gene mates can alloy it with things somehow," I thought aloud. "There must be a trick." It was irritating that I hadn't already learned it, but then I'd had a fairly narrow education. Already I'd stepped off the rails of my lunatic mother's teachings just by recalling the properties of various modern alloys, having learned that much from my sporadic interests and rapid-googling habits rather than any proper teachings.

Fuck, what I wouldn't have done for some internet access. Even just an hour, I'd have the city wrapped around my pinkie by the fiftieth minute.

Beam, however, seemed to have other, pettier concerns.

"Did you just call the human race your gene mates?" He frowned. I ignored the irrelevant question, focusing instead on the more pressing concern.

"Beam, concentrate. How do we make this work if we can't generate the heat needed to melt our products?"

"We don't." He frowned again. "Right?"

Was he right? No, I decided.

"Have you ever heard that modern furnaces are all made of tungsten?" I asked him. He shook his head, as well he should. "Me, neither," I concurred. "I've not heard that they're made of anything particularly special at all. Which tells me that the trick here isn't just finding a more heat-resistant material."

If it was, we were fucked. I didn't know how much tungsten was in the air, but I knew that I'd probably have visibly aged before gathering enough to assemble something as big as even a grain of sand, let alone proper industrial equipment.

But it couldn't be that, could it? I was getting distracted, focusing on irrelevant details. What mattered here was whether I could coin a way of heating something up regardless of container material. How might that be done?

Well, obviously my one major advantage was that the air inside my furnace wouldn't all be a uniform temperature. Particularly, the space near its center could be a lot hotter than at its edges, which in turn would likely be cooler than the metal walls. As heat differential increased, convection and conduction both shot up, as well. This was essentially why holding your hand against a five-hundred-kelvin piece of metal for one second was a lot less painful than holding it against a five-thousand-kelvin piece for one-tenth of a second. It also meant that cooling down the furnace itself would cause heat to be sapped away from the air within ever faster.

But how fast? Was there a point at which we'd have the coals burning so fast, the fire flooded with so much oxygen, that there'd be no time for all the excess energy to get dragged away into the metal?

I couldn't know. That was annoying, and unexpected. Usually I just intuited things about the world without even meaning to, but not, it seemed, today. And I didn't have the knowledge required to sidestep the failure of nature's gifts.

I did have the means to find out, though. The slow way. The practical way. I smiled, thinking of how I'd almost melted a crater into my warehouse floor experimenting with those coals the other day, and began to explain to Beam what exactly we'd need to do things the fun way.

CHAPTER FIFTEEN

Shango's POV: Day 76
Current Wealth: 168 gold, 47 silver, 29 copper

It didn't say anything about me that I was more afraid of being late for my meeting than any other consequence of Corvan's attack. It said something about the horrible, nasty, no-good world I'd made with my evil friends. There were consequences to pissing off a noble, and they very much depended on what sort of noble it was you'd annoyed. A nice one might have you flogged, but something about the blonde woman I'd been summoned by had struck me as . . . mean. Hard, like she was the sort to pull out fingernails as an appetizer. Perhaps it was just my Nigerian DNA reacting to the presence of a white aristocrat.

My walk to the council's building was, as a result, about as tense as any walk I'd ever had in my entire life. And made all the worse knowing my friends weren't there with me. I'd have basked in the relief brought by Beam, fighting wrecking ball that he was. Or Solitaire—there was something oddly reassuring about having him there to all but guarantee that the first blow thrown would come from our side. I'd left them both behind, regardless. If this went bad, I wanted them to have a head start in running once they heard that a bunch of big, horrible soldiers were looking for them.

Besides, everything we'd discussed before still applied. I didn't want them shitting up my negotiation.

I found guards awaiting me as I approached the entrance, and wasn't even able to get a single word out before they spoke.

"Dark skin," one noted to his friend rather than me. "Six feet. The foreigner."

Both sets of eyes rested on me at that.

"You're here for Lady Velaharo?"

Discounting the small possibility that they were mistaking me for another African giant who'd been summoned by an entirely unrelated noblewoman, I nodded. Both men turned.

"Follow us," the first of them grunted, and they led me inside without much further ado.

The place was very much as I remembered, though a little bit more claustrophobic for my fear of being put in a penis guillotine. Fortunately the walk didn't last long enough for me to actually wet myself, and I was soon ushered not-so-politely into an office.

It was different from the other one I'd seen, smaller, tighter, less indulgently decorated and more . . . economic. I could see far more work left done and undone on the desk, and behind it the lady Velaharo eyed me. My guess, it seemed, had been right. She was the blonde who'd approached me the other day.

And she didn't look up at me, not even a glance. She just kept on writing like the other noble had. Rude? No, surely she was too clever for that. She needed me to see her contempt. To keep up appearances. Which meant she wasn't the sort to get genuinely offended when someone saved time by stepping on past them.

"You wanted to see me?" I noted, not *quite* going so far as to sit down opposite her, but letting my voice ring out with a confidence that wasn't anywhere to be found inside me. This wasn't entirely new ground for me. Nigerian elders, particularly those who simultaneously had age and authority in abundance, tended to behave this way. It was all about respect. As I had come to understand it, I was to respect them by treating them like gods, and they were to respect me by not treating me like filth.

At last she glanced up, green eyes running over me with a scrutinous glare.

"Word has been spreading about your activities," she replied coolly. "I take it they are the reason for your tardiness?"

I didn't wince, nor did I violently shit myself. That was about as much as I could say in defense of my reaction to her words. I was quick in playing damage control.

"My apologies, my lady. I was delayed by—"

"By an attack by one Corvan the Coal Hearted," she interrupted, eyes twinkling at my surprise. "Yes, I looked into your previous whereabouts. Apparently you made quite a fight of it when he came for you. Tell me, how did you manage to kill him?"

Was she bluffing, lying? Trying to test me, pretending not to know he was alive when she did? Or had the word just not gotten around yet that we'd spared the magus who attacked us? It all depended on how she knew it was Corvan specifically. An eyewitness who gave his physical description, if she'd used that to piece his identity together, would've likely let her know he was still breathing, too.

It would be a risk to do anything but answer honestly, and so I told the truth. Just not all of it.

"Dumb luck," I replied. "And a badly hurt friend."

She seemed amused rather than disappointed.

"Luck does not kill a magus, not of that caliber."

"How do you know of him?" I asked abruptly. "Seems odd to me that you'd have heard the name of some village mystic."

By the look on her face, my attempt to blindside her with a question and wring out an answer before she'd considered denying me one hadn't worked. But she replied anyway. Odd, that. I tucked the fact away for future examination.

"I know many names, particularly those belonging to men I'm considering bringing into my employ."

That was interesting, but she didn't let me dwell on it.

"Now, how did you kill a magus? A more specific answer this time, if you don't mind."

I hid my irritation. Evidently this line of questioning would not be moved past. Which was inconvenient because it moved very, very closely to Beam's and Solitaire's magic. I wasn't certain whether they'd be burned for using unnatural forms of it like they were, but it was a risk I'd rather avoid.

"We had the numbers," I explained. "And each one of us was armored in steel plates. I know a bit of magery myself, as does my brother Solitaire, and our third brother Beam is a fighter like you wouldn't believe. That, and we got lucky."

She hummed at that, thoughtful but not amused.

"I heard talk of great flames engulfed in water," the woman noted. I hid my surprise and shrugged.

"I'm sure I'll hear it soon, but honestly I can barely even control air myself."

It was true. Magery started with subtle influence over the simple things around you. Air being the most common. I'd used that much to push Corvan's attacks aside, but I'd never really overpowered them. If I'd been defending someone less durable than Beam or Argar, the heat of his magic coming even as close as it had might've been deadly regardless.

Being true didn't make something believed, though. Fortunately for me the lady Velaharo didn't seem particularly distrusting today.

"I had heard reports that your brother Beam fought the magus with . . . interesting equipment. Armor and a sword glowing like firelight, pale white and near transparent, yet harder than steel and seemingly without any weight at all."

I ran cold, recognizing, instantly the dangerous proximity of her questioning. It was a tempting instinct to swallow before replying, but that would be giving away one emotion too many on such treacherous ground as this.

"An interestingly specific rumor," I replied slowly. "I've heard people say things about us, but never quite that . . . particular."

But this woman was clever, really clever, and my misdirection didn't throw her off-kilter by even an inch.

"Odd, I've heard people talk about your innovations quite a lot. Magic powder capable of erupting into great releases of heat, light, and force; some curious staff that can cleave through plate and kill a man from double the range of any bow; and a warehouse filled with alchemist's things. Even Rinchester, oddly enough, seems convinced your family saved them with . . . What was it? Ah, yes, some arcane weapon crafted from the town bell, that spat fire like a dragon's breath and tore apart dozens of enemies at once. All coincidence I presume?"

She didn't seem annoyed to have been lied to, which was by far the smaller source of relief for me. If she thought Beam's magic weapons were just an invention on our end, it would keep him that much further away from being lynched.

Better to lean into her misconception, but reluctantly. As if I'd been caught by a shot in the dark rather than watched it whip by a mile from my heart.

"My brother Solitaire understands the world in ways that the rest of us . . . just don't," I replied, telling the truth, at least in isolation. It was the best way to be believed, the best way to keep your stories consistent. The more you lied, the more lies you had to remember not to contradict later, the more cracks you were laying in your own mask. I didn't have Solitaire's memory; I couldn't hold a photograph of the whole world in my head at once to be studied at my leisure. We mere mortals had to simplify things to account for our own limitations. Above all, we had to make sure he didn't know that was what we were doing, the smug prick.

Velaharo was listening eagerly. With luck that meant that I could distract her from my lies with the sheer unbelievability of my truths.

"We come from a foreign land," I told her. "And our people know things about this world that yours do not." True. "They are better educated, better nourished, and even our children are freely handed secrets that a lot of magi would kill to keep hidden." True. "Those people are gone now, and we're the last of them." False, but close enough to the truth. "Of us all, my brother has a unique knack for intuiting more with our knowledge, filling in the blanks. Not the most educated of us, but possibly the most brilliant." True, if flattering.

I didn't believe Solitaire was the most intelligent man alive, back on Earth, but that was pure guesswork on my part. I'd certainly never seen anyone near his level of cleverness, though I'd certainly read of a few historical figures who might have been. Velaharo was believing me, so far at least, and that was good. I continued.

"Solitaire has been using this talent to re-create some of the technologies and magics we had back in our country, and . . . Well, Eregar seems to be appreciating them so far."

She eyed me, with her crushed-emerald stare, and nodded lightly at my words. Thinking for a few moments before replying.

"Interesting," said Velaharo. "Then I have an offer for you."

CHAPTER SIXTEEN

Shango's POV: Day 76
Current Wealth: 168 gold, 47 silver, 29 copper

A deal?" I frowned, stupidly, but recovered from my surprise quickly enough. Truth be told it'd been an oversight on my part to be surprised at all. *Of course* she'd wanted a deal. She was smart, staggeringly smart, and she knew enough about me and my friends that it'd take a drooling idiot not to want in on what we were doing. Gunpowder was a big deal in a world that'd never known it, and if she thought Beam was running around in magic metal, as well . . .

"A deal," Velaharo repeated, interrupting my thoughts with the words. "Do I need to explain what exactly I wish to gain from it?"

In fact, she did not.

"You want the fruits of our knowledge," I guessed. Her lips thinned.

"I want your knowledge," Velaharo corrected. "But, as I am not unreasonable and know that you are no fool, I will settle for simply what you can create with it."

An obvious lie. Whatever we gave her, she'd have it studied, taken apart, and put back together until whatever alchemists and blacksmiths and scholars she'd summoned up had figured out a way to replicate it for her. That's what I'd do; that's what anyone with eyes that reached the horizon would do. More money later, not a little money now.

But surely she realized I'd know that. So was she hiding her plans? One good way to find out.

"You want to study it," I noted. "To figure out how to replicate it."

She arched an eyebrow.

"Obviously. Are you only just realizing that now?"

So, not trying to hide it then. Unless she was a better liar than Solitaire, which was unlikely.

"Not really." I shrugged dismissively. "Just making sure we're on the same page. What sort of offers can you make that'll be worth more to us than any of the others we'll get?"

"For one," she replied, quick as lightning. "I can assure you that I won't hire some big, horrible men to club you over the head until you either tell me everything for free or end up an idiot."

I eyed her, considered what I knew of Redaclan nobility, and decided that she was neither joking, nor making an inconsequential point.

"Go on," I urged her, and she did.

"For another, I don't think you're likely to find very many other nobles willing to protect you as I have already."

It was a deliberate tidbit thrown out, casual as anything, but done knowing that it'd hook my attention. Well, it fucking did, and I didn't have the patience or temperament to make a show of not caring about something as immediately important. Not when Velaharo would just see through the performance, anyway.

"How exactly have you done that?" I challenged her. "I was attacked by a magus capable of leveling houses a few hours ago, and I did not feel very protected while suffering through it."

I'd spoken without remembering who she was, without thinking about what her sort's temperaments tended to be, and I almost winced anticipating some vicious aristocratic retribution for my disrespect. But it never came. I saw anger, fury even, but it didn't blossom into retaliation. And there was something else with it, too. Shame?

Whatever the emotion had been, she didn't let it sit for long. Lunging past so quickly I barely even caught it.

"I am talking about the actions of my fellow nobles, and the numerous thugs in this city. Mercenaries, *criminals*. Gods know what other sorts. You continue to draw breath only because I have kept the growing tides of confrontation from reaching you, even as the pressure they bring forth has intensified."

Her answer brought a wave of skepticism to me, and I decided to wear it openly. Sometimes the truth could do a lot of heavy lifting for you, even when you were searching for lies rather than hiding them.

"That's a very convenient accomplishment," I noted. "You protected me and my family, so hard, in fact, as to leave no evidence at all that we'd even been in need of protection in the first place. Remarkable. Tell me, do you have a stone to sell that turns lead into gold?"

She eyed me for a single moment, then rose from her seat and slapped me across the face. Her strike was not powerful; I barely even felt it. She was a woman, an untrained, noncombatant woman, and with all my level-ups and points thrown into Toughness I wasn't even sure if most grown men could hurt me anymore. In fact I was more concerned for *her*, and sure enough I caught the fingers of her hand flexing with pain, as if she'd just struck a tree trunk rather than a face.

That didn't make the fury in her eyes any weaker, though. Pain didn't tend to.

"You will not speak to me like that," Velaharo told me, her voice icy, sharp, and . . . hollow.

Strange, but true. There was no passion to her words, no weight, none of the emotions I'd expect from a woman so shocked and repulsed by a thing that she'd felt no recourse at all except to lash out physically in some knee-jerk fury. But my cheek still tingled with the sensation of impact, all the same.

I'd been hit by a woman who was completely calm and lucid, who hadn't even felt particularly enraged by the thing I'd been hit for. Why did that happen? To send a message, obviously, but the message being sent here clearly wasn't just not to disrespect her. She didn't care about that—I could see that clear as day.

The message, then, was that I *couldn't*. That I needed to show her the respect due, that . . . that she was someone I couldn't sass the way I had been.

And if she was sending a message like that, even when she didn't give a shit in the slightest about that disrespect, it was because she had something to hide. Because she knew that her message was a lie, that I *could* disrespect her, that she *was* someone I could sass.

She hadn't cared about my contempt or snark because she was fucking used to it. All the pieces fell together at once, and I felt a powerful, idiotic surge of confidence as I knew for certain that I was right.

Slowly, I massaged my cheek, smiling as sweetly as I could muster.

"I'd advise against that," I said idly. "My family happens to be quite strong, as far as mercenaries go. Unless you'd like to take a moment and don some nice steel gauntlet, slapping me just won't have the usual bite. Though I can pretend it hurts if you'd like."

She stared, taken aback, and there was no feigning the flash of uncertainty and worry in her eyes. Not a scrap of anger, just the fear of a woman whose facade of strength was being broken. I decided to break it harder, taking a seat now, putting my legs up on her desk as I leaned back in the chair.

"If I accepted your terms, what sort of protection could I expect to get exactly?" I asked, moving on to business quickly, while her shock and concern were still strong, wanting to ensure she was as unbalanced as possible.

It didn't work, not really. This one recovered as fast as she thought.

"It depends on what kinds of secrets you would be willing to part with," she replied. "What kinds of equipment or material I would receive."

I thought about that, considered the black powder I couldn't calculate, the alloys I knew nothing about the parameters of, and decided to just offer her an answer in broader terms.

"Steels that are far, far stronger than any you'll have seen before. Able to hold an edge for numerous battles without sharpening, or be tempered into holding one for a single battle that might cut a person right down to their bones with the strength of a normal man. Just for a start."

Velaharo thought, nodded, considered. Then sighed.

"Very well then," she breathed, tense suddenly. So tense in fact that I half expected her to order some guards in and have me beheaded. What she did instead was even more shocking. "My offer is for a marriage between us."

CHAPTER SEVENTEEN

Beam's POV: Day 76
Current Wealth: 168 gold, 47 silver, 29 copper

Solitaire was concerned—I could tell that much from the fine, subtle behavioral patterns I'd learned to read in him over our long years of friendship. The slight arching of an eyebrow, the twisting of a lip, the tightness in his jaw. And, if one were particularly observant, the fact that he was pacing around swearing at everything that moved.

"Shitting metallurgy," he snarled to no one in particular. "Thousands of years we've been using it. About time to swap it out for something else. It's fucking pitiful! Iron! *Iron!* What's so special about fucking *iron* that all we can make after thousands of years is steel?! I should skip the bastard entirely and just figure out how to scale up nanoparticles. That'll show them."

I did my best to tune the rambling out, deciding to just let him tire himself with it rather than try to engage. Ardin, perhaps understandably, was less at ease with it.

"And yet here you are, relying on primitive metallurgy to do yer amazin' ends," he growled, shooting a glance back at Solitaire, then quickly refocusing upon his work. Upon my work.

We were grinding metal ores to bits, ready to blast them in our new furnace. It hadn't taken Ardin long to create the thing, a nice, big iron chamber with an additional compartment around the outside to pump and circulate water. Cooling the container while hell itself coiled around inside. We weren't entirely sure what level of heat it could survive, though, and until we were, we'd be taking no chances. Thus the grinding. Make things powder and they reacted faster, demanded lower temperatures. With luck, saved us all one giant furnace.

It was that need for luck, more than the need for work, that seemed to be needling Solitaire so much.

"Here I am," he agreed with Ardin, practically spitting the words. "Taking things one step at a time, I suppose. Not like we ever moved past metal at all, to begin with. It'll keep being useful for centuries more. Sorry, Ardin."

He flashed a glance at the blacksmith, who caught it and nodded in silence, seeming mollified at least as he continued grinding. Conversation was fleeting past that point, interrupted by sporadic blasts of focus on our end as we all hurried to finish our menial work and test out the furnace. Ardin, above all of us, seemed eager for that.

Finally the time came to test our creations, and we all watched eagerly as Solitaire concentrated on the coals and fires, soon conjuring a roaring, snarling mound of flame within our furnace.

One of the largest issues, of course, had been in storing the molten material within something that melted at a higher temperature than it did. We couldn't. So instead we'd all built the furnace to tilt and rested our metals in a trench at its bottom.

The hope was that we could pour whatever mixtures we ended up with out of it. If not, we were all in for an annoying, painful, and quite possibly dangerous time scraping the stuff free.

"How long will it take?" I asked Solitaire. He paused, then shrugged.

"No idea. I don't know the specific heat capacity of molybdenum. Give it a few minutes?"

As reassuring as that was, it actually wasn't reassuring in the slightest, and I found myself chewing a lip in thought as we all stood around the furnace and watched. By the time it was finally ready for us to open it up, I felt the tension reaching a crescendo. Half expecting some big explosion to erupt from the interior as we tilted it over and unlatched the door.

Even kept surrounded by circulating water to drag away the excess heat, it was hot to the touch. Hot enough to feel through the pair of specially thick leather-and-wool gloves I'd worn for just such an issue. I tilted, the contents poured, and all of us watched.

It wasn't liquid, and we practically deflated at the knowledge. Solitaire was the first to notice why that deflation was mistaken, and Ardin was just a moment behind him.

"The powder," I gasped as it finally dawned on me. I saw it all only as the stuff cooled enough that it was no longer glowing, homogeneous, luminescent white fading to orange, then red, then nothing at all. The steaming metal was different, its shades changed, its substance transformed.

Notably, it was an it. Singular, one powder now, where we'd added in a mixture. Solitaire laughed.

"Powder metallurgy," he noted. "I've heard the term. Never actually bothered to google what it was. I'd guess this is it, though. It looks . . . compressed somehow?"

He sounded uncharacteristically confused, and I resisted the urge to spoil his good mood by teasing him for it. He'd been on edge since Corvan had started working for us, very on edge. This little triumph might've been the first relief he'd gotten from the fact.

Solitaire did strange things while under pressure, typically resulting in a lot of breaking and not very much mending afterward.

"Powder metallurgy," Ardin mirrored, thoughtful as Solitaire reached for the metal. Solitaire looked thoughtful, too, but in that special Solitaire sort of way that usually led to him doing something that would've been stupid even for a nongenius. I'd long since learned to keep him from such tactical blunders and slapped his hand aside.

"Is it cool?" I snapped, glaring at him. He met my eye, glaring back harder.

"Should be," he replied. "It took twenty-eight seconds to lose enough heat to go from orange to dull red in its blackbody emissions, and that was fifty-three seconds ago. Would you like to see my math?"

It stung a bit, having him jab that at me. He knew full well I couldn't make sense of it, but before I could say anything Ardin piped up.

"Still hot, idiot," he grunted, eyeing Solitaire sidelong. "Too hot for most people at least."

Solitaire scooped a pinch of the metal powder up, sneering.

"I'm not most people, am I? I'll have you know these fingers were tough enough to go through an orc's e—Ah, piss and shit." He dropped the powder, then shook remnants from his fingers where it still clung, cursing more.

"*Ah* shit, wank, wanky shitty shit wank, fuck." He breathed, waving his hand to and fro, as if he hoped to make the pain lose its grip and fall off. He didn't succeed, but where he failed in relieving his own agony, he put on quite the show for Ardin and me. We watched, grinning to each other as he did his little dance.

"Stop smiling," he snapped, glaring almost as hotly as the metal now. "It's not funny."

"Can I see your math *now*?" I asked him, trying not to laugh as I did. "I just suddenly got the strangest feeling that, somehow, it might possibly be slightly flawed."

Solitaire might have cut through glass with the look he gave me after that, but it only bounced off my smile like so many other things before it. Ardin looked even less daunted, and actually took things a step further by scooping up more of the powder himself.

"Hmm," the smith noted. "Looks like my fingers will go through an orc's eye, too."

"Bite a cock," Solitaire snapped, kneeling down and taking some of the metal himself to examine it. "Now shut up and let me study this. I'd like to learn as much as is possible about the shit we're about to be wrapping around our friends, particularly how heat resistant it is."

A silence fell over us at that, Solitaire's from concentration, mine from the memory of a fallen giant and nostrils filled by the scent of seared flesh. Ardin, clearly, was quick enough to read a room when it was as obviously flavored by emotion as this one. He kept quiet, too, and we all just sat in waiting.

Fortunately, Solitaire was a fast bastard. He didn't take long to be nodding to himself in satisfaction.

"Right, that's all I'll learn from it as powder. Now we need to make it a single solid to do some proper stress tests."

Another silence, this time broken by Ardin.

"How do we smith it?" he asked. "We couldn't melt it, and this powder metallurgy doesn't seem to fuse things, eh?"

Solitaire paused, glowering suddenly, but before he could reply a new voice cut in.

We all turned to see Corvan eying us.

"Well." The old man leered. "I happen to know quite an effective way of generating heat, if you're willing to negotiate for it."

Kenny hadn't wanted to be paired with some crazy white kid, and certainly not on his first day. Taiwo would have been his choice, always. But Taiwo wasn't with him; he wasn't even in the same school. Kenny was alone, surrounded by white faces and Western faces and mean faces, sticking out like a sore thumb with nobody to speak to and the all-too-confident knowledge that, even if he did, his accent alone would be yet another difference. It was like being crushed from all sides, so much so that he almost jumped at every noise, almost ran at every glance.

And to top it all off, he'd been paired with the class psycho. The mutterer, eyes flitting around, hands slowly curling and uncurling. There weren't many twelve-year-olds who looked like they'd be more at home behind an acrylic sheet and fifty security guards, but this new boy—Bernard, his name was—did a splendid job at conveying just that. He glanced up at Kenny as he approached, looking like he was considering then and there whether to kill or eat him. Perhaps both, hopefully both, if it was to be the latter at all. Kenny would rather be dead when that happened.

But he was spiraling, distracting himself, wasting valuable mental energy. Kenny steeled himself, forced a veneer of friendliness he didn't feel, and smiled at the kid.

"Hi, my name's—"

"Lying cunt," Bernard snarled, glaring at him. "You're a lying cunt. You're not pleased to see me, so why are you smiling? What are you hiding?"

Well, he'd certainly had introductions that went less smoothly, but for the life of him Kenny couldn't think of any then and there. He hesitated, and in that moment he noticed a few things about the boy. The first was that he was shorter than Kenny, but not by much. The second was his accent—Western for sure, but clearly different from the people around them. The third was the bizarre rictus seizing his face as he spoke, as if the muscles beneath were trying to escape from under their fleshy covering.

"I'm not hiding anything," Kenny said slowly, eager not to startle the lunatic standing before him. "I'm just being polite. We're on the same team, right? We need to work together for this project, so let's work together. I'd rather we not be at each other's throats while we do so."

His eyes flitted across Kenny's face, body, hands. As if he were looking for concealed weapons. Concealed somethings, in any case, and apparently he found none. Bernard grunted with something almost mistakable for satisfaction.

"You're not as much of a cock as everyone else," he noted. Kenny couldn't help but let a smile crack his mouth at that.

"You barely know me." He grinned. "Give it some time."

Whatever budding common humor was about to grow between them, it got interrupted by the arrival of their group's third member. Cádo, his name was, from what Kenny recalled. The only boy in the class as tall as him, and the one, so he'd heard, who had yet failed to give up even a single school sport for another to claim first place in. He smiled as he approached, and oddly enough the expression seemed sincere.

Fortunately, Bernard seemed to agree because he didn't give nearly as hostile a greeting to the newcomer as he had Kenny.

"We're only in threes, right?" he asked. "Nobody else is joining us?"

Cádo hesitated, then answered with a nod. Kenny saw Bernard deflate. Evidently he wasn't a particularly big fan of people. Kenny supposed he could relate.

"Good, what are we doing then?" the smallest of them—the maddest—continued. "I want to hurry up with getting this over and done."

Their assignment had been a fairly broad one, creating a diorama somehow. All arts and crafts, handiwork and glue, it wasn't something Kenny had really bothered to think about. He'd never been particularly bad with his hands, but nor did he enjoy using them. It would just be work, and he'd sooner get it finished fast, as well.

Fortunately, despite the obvious differences in personality and the frictive interactions they caused, it wasn't much effort to coordinate on a design. A simple concept, the interior of a cell, and an easy way of organizing it. Bernard, Kenny found, was near-preternaturally good at keeping track of the steps and dimensions involved, to the point where he suspected within the hour that the boy had already mapped the entire project out in his head. Cádo listened intently, and seemed excellent at lowering the otherwise neurotic boy's guard, while Kenny himself did his usual thing and kept both of them on task and well structured. Things were moving far, far smoother than anticipated.

But then the hitch came, as hitches were wont to do.

The three of them had taken to continuing their project after class, for no reason that any one of them, save Cádo, would have admitted. They were beginning to enjoy it, and enjoy one another's company. Kenny appreciated the quickness of Bernard, the ease of communicating with him, how deftly he grabbed the finer nuances of a point and reconstructed their conclusion without being prompted. He liked Cádo, too, for the boy was simply pleasant, and all of them were starting to get along. Enough so that their pretense of finishing the project out of class to earn themselves a free period during the continuation the next day was growing thinner as feigned disinterest crumbled and plans started forming of how to spend their free time together.

It was in this crucial stage that the interruption came. Kevin was responsible, the largest boy in the school, and over two years their senior.

Though not academically lacking, Kevin had been regarded by all as dull, and his cruelty was prodigious. Almost as much so as his size and strength. The boy towered over even Kenny by more than a head, and was actually larger than most of the adults in their school at only fourteen. Much of this weight was muscle, too, for he'd done well for himself on the school's wrestling team. His reputation was more for brutality than skill, however, for though there were none better at hauling other boys off the ground as they scrambled on the mat, the difference in fouls and visits to the nurse's office was far more skewed around him than any records of winning or losing.

"Not surprised you weirdos are hanging out." He grinned, marching over with his broad face twisted by a vacant, animal smile. Cruelty glinted in his eyes, as if often did, and even Kenny, the newest of the three, felt a stab of anticipation. He knew something was coming.

"I know Bernard," the older boy grunted. "And I know Caydough, but you're new." His eyes were on Kenny now with an eerie focus. "Name."

The question was phrased like a demand, and Kenny found himself swallowing before answering it. Kevin really was very big. He'd only seen him from a distance before that moment, only heard about him from others. It was quite another thing to find the two-hundred-pound sack of muscle rearing up before him face-to-face.

"Kenny," Kenny answered, knowing full well the sort of response he might enjoy from sharing his Nigerian name. "I—"

Kevin cut him off.

"What's wrong with your accent?" he grunted. "You can't even talk right? That's why you're so desperate to spend the extra time on your project?"

He closed in, fingers closing about Kenny's lapel. Everything Kenny knew about people, about talking to them, started to crumble at that. Words failing him, the situation falling into violence and madness. He forced himself calm, wove together a suitable answer, and opened his mouth to give it voice.

But the words never left him. Bernard's forehead was faster than his tongue.

Kenny heard the crunching, and when Kevin's eyes rose again, having fallen with his wince of pain, it was clear that the cartilage centering his face had been mangled beyond recognition. His nose was smashed to pieces, lumps jutting out in every direction, broken down to its very base as blood streamed out of its bulging nostrils. Hate burned in the boy's gaze as it fell on Bernard, who sneered back.

"Fuck off," the smaller boy growled, speaking like a feral thing. Kevin was undaunted.

"I'm gonna kill you," he snarled, closing in on big, loping strides. Bernard moved forward, not back, eyes wide with madness.

"Kill me? You couldn't kill me with a nuke, you fucking moron. Come near me and I'll *actually* kill you. I'll smear a bit of rat shit on my fingernails and scratch ya, let you catch something and die pissing out so much blood that ye bedsheets are red."

It gave Kevin pause, even gave Kenny pause, and in the resulting silence, Cádo moved. He threw a kick, more dexterous than any Kenny had seen before, and his heel found Kevin right beneath his ribs, sinking in deep as the soft tissue before it deformed.

The boy dropped down to his knees, vomited an amount that was, if anything, disproportionately large for his frame, and crumpled face down. The boys eyed one another, silence broken by Cádo himself.

"We should do this again sometime."

CHAPTER EIGHTEEN

Marriage. It was such a strange thing to hear mentioned, such a bizarre thing to be brought up during hardball negotiations. You didn't *marry* the people you were making deals with. It just wasn't done. Not unless you lived in Westeros and had blond hair and DNA written in Comic Sans.

Except Redacle had been based on A Song of Ice and Fire, as well as a dozen other dark-fantasy worlds. And in our world, political marriages were about as common as politics. I shouldn't have been shocked, shouldn't have even been surprised. I was, though, and Lady Velaharo was quick in noticing.

"You're concerned with our difference in station?" she guessed, misreading the situation completely and giving me a very convenient out.

"More surprised that you aren't," I answered, recovering as quickly as I perhaps ever had. "I . . . would be rising in social rank and taking your family name?"

She eyed me, unimpressed.

"Do you need to ask? Yes, obviously, you will be taking the name Velaharo and joining my family. I will not be making myself a commoner."

I didn't miss the faint twist of disgust in her curled lip as she said that, and I breathed another silent thanks to my past self for knowing better than to have Solitaire negotiate with this woman. He might well have buried her head in the wall for that.

"And I'd be in charge?" I pressed, needing assurance. She scoffed.

"In charge. Is that how your people phrase it? You will be the head of our family, yes. As the husband, it is only proper."

Well, there was one convenience about medieval culture. As a man, it did tend to help you get your way in the world. I buried the flicker of distaste even as I leaped on the chance.

"Alright," I breathed, nodding. "Then all that's left is for you to tell me what's fucked your family badly enough for you to make this offer."

I could see the surprise on her face at being seen through, fleeting though it was; however, it'd be a lie on my part to claim I'd simply outthought her. Velaharo's performance had been excellent, and I'd not found any fault in it, but she'd been undone by the simple fact of my knowledge regarding her world and culture.

Redaclan nobles did not offer to let commoners into their ranks lightly, certainly not as an opening arrangement. Something more was going on here, and Velaharo swallowed before addressing it.

"I'm sure I don't know what you're talking about," she lied, unbalanced enough for me to see the cracks in it now. I sighed.

"Don't treat me like an idiot, please," I replied coolly. "I'm afraid my brother got his brains from the same place I did. You're being pressured into this offer, I'm guessing by circumstance, so tell me what problems your family is facing. Financial?"

She hesitated, which all but confirmed my guess even before she replied with words.

"Yes," Velaharo answered reluctantly. "Financial issues, debt, the usual. You noticed that my guards have been the same pair between this meeting and the last?"

I hadn't actually, but hearing her mention the fact made it seem obvious. I kept my lapse to myself, in any case. Never a bad thing to be thought cleverer than you were, particularly in a negotiation.

"That, and I'm afraid your opening up with it as an offer tipped your hand a bit. What sort of debt?"

"Fifteen thousand gold coins."

She might've stood up and punched me in the gut and still left more air in my lungs than that bombshell did. Fifteen thousand gold. It was a ridiculous sum, almost one hundred times our current stockpiles, enough to buy and equip a small army.

"When does it need to be paid off by?" I tried, finding myself less confident at the prospect of this deal with every passing moment. Velaharo, clearly, could see my growing hesitance because I saw a desperation blooming to match it.

"A year, thereabouts," she answered hastily. "Quite far, quite distant now, and with your sums growing so quickly—"

I'd just about finished the math by that point, and cut in once it was done.

"More than one hundred times our current stores, with only thirty times longer to make it."

She met my gaze with a sudden intensity.

"Can you not make such a sum over that time?" Velaharo snapped. "Do you intend to be counting gold by the dozen forever? If so, with your technology, you must be a fool. And I will not curse my family with ties to a fool."

It was such an abrupt, savage assault on my ego, so clinically aimed and forcefully delivered, that for a moment it actually succeeded in distracting me enough to almost fall into her trap and let her seize the conversation.

"You're deflecting," I observed, having learned long ago that stating the bare facts of a failed manipulation was among the best ways to unbalance the one attempting it. "You know this is a risk. There could be factors at play that only become relevant once I reach the levels of production needed to meet your debt's deadline."

Could I have fallen for her attempt at throwing me off-balance? Yes, definitely. On an off day she might've gotten me. Could Solitaire?

I almost laughed aloud. Solitaire would've fallen for it hook, line, and sinker. However brilliant he was, leveraging that bastard's ego against him had always left him as helpless as a kitten. It was almost tempting to do it myself sometimes.

Velaharo was shaken to have been seen through. Clearly she was as impressed by her trick as I, but as always she overcame the shock quickly.

"A risk, then." She shrugged. "Every decision is a risk. The question is what do you stand to lose, and what do you stand to gain? I'm offering you a noble title, aristocracy. I'm offering you *rulership*. Do you think you'll ever find that elsewhere, in your station, for a price as low as fifteen thousand gold coins?"

Oh, she was good. She was very, very fucking good. As good as me? I didn't know, and that was the first time in my entire life I'd ever *not* known. Even on Earth, I'd never met a person with this woman's knack for persuasion, manipulation, and deception. I felt something stir below the belt and quickly tucked the sensation aside.

It'd been a while, what could I say? Still, I wasn't Solitaire. I *could* restrain myself.

Several questions had come from the woman's reply, all of them good. How useful would her position be, how likely was I to find it elsewhere later on, how large really was the risk at play?

Risk first, and it couldn't be dismissed easily. If all went well I was fairly sure we could meet the quota, but that wouldn't allow for potential setbacks, expenses, other unforeseen problems. It would be something breathing down our necks right up until we finished paying it off. Not to be scoffed at.

So how useful would the position be? Well, fucking very. It would be nobility, in feudalism. Not easy to overstate what an advantage we'd find there, very much a promotion comparable to going from rake to farmer. On top of that, there was her apparent position as councillor for Elswick, which at worst would be some honorary position we might leverage even further politically.

Which brought me to the final point, perhaps the most important. What were the odds of me ever finding a deal like this again?

No, that wasn't the important point. I could overcome the good or bad of this deal with whatever wealth we might get later on. What mattered, what would really decide things, was how much would be gained from making this deal, right now, and how likely a similarly useful deal was to come around later on. The correspondence of timing and scale, the combination of social power and the particular point at which we got it.

How likely was I to, at any point, do something that would make all the long-term benefits I stood to get from nobility this instant? It was a question that barely needed answering.

"Alright," I said at last, almost catching my words as I said them. Uncertain, worried, resisting the urge to tremble. But speaking anyway. "Let's get a marriage contract written up."

CHAPTER NINETEEN

Solitaire's POV: Day 76
Current Wealth: 168 gold, 47 silver, 29 copper

Being honest, it was quite useful to have a magus on staff. A proper magus, I mean, not a half-trained one. Corvan really did simplify a lot of matters in a lot of ways.

Take the prospect of heat, for example. Ordinarily I'd have spent an hour thinking of how to make the coal burn even faster, considering cooking it to get it even hotter, pulling out half a hundred little chemical and physical tricks to wrangle extra temperature out by the degrees. Not with Corvan present. With Corvan, I just stood back and watched the old bastard magic all the heat up for us.

It was simple geometry, what his powers did. From meters away, in an instant, he'd blasted Argar with enough heat to leave his plate armor glowing red and his flesh blistering and mangled. Hundreds of degrees, at least, diffused across multiple cubic meters of volume. We didn't need multiple cubic meters heated up now, though, and so Corvan concentrated all that temperature into the space of liters instead.

The metals didn't stand a chance, liquefying near instantly into a boiling, bubbling elemental broth. He didn't bother hiding his smugness as he saw all of us staring at the mixture, sweat beading on our foreheads, legs trembling.

Oh, sure, he was on our side. Sure, he realized what would happen if he gave Shango cause for revenge. But I couldn't shake the feeling that the bastard had more planned, had some move up his sleeve, and I wouldn't let him pull it off unmonitored. I had every intention of sticking to that bastard like stink on a shit.

Not openly, though. First rule of stopping people from trying to murder you: Don't let them know that you know. Dear old Mum had been very clear on that fact. The best way to start a fight with someone is cutting their throat while they're asleep.

"So this mixes into a stronger kind of steel?" the magus asked, voice barely audible over the magic. It wasn't that the flames were loud, rather that the air around them was. Displaced by the kinetic waste of too much thermal energy concentrated into too little a space. He'd conjured a wind inside without even meaning to, just another little reminder of why I'd be best killing him in his sleep when it came down to it.

"It does," I replied calmly. "The actual mixture is a secret, though, and frankly I don't think your tiny, shriveled brain could even store all the information anyway."

Corvan glared at me sidelong, but said nothing more. He finished up the heat after a moment, and Beam and Ardin quickly doused the furnace's outside in water to cool it enough for touching. They tipped the liquid out.

"You can work this as it cools?" I asked Ardin. He glanced up irritably.

"Probably not now," he grunted. "But I can learn it at least. Just give me more metal, more time. I'll experiment with techniques."

I nodded, and he and Beam disappeared from the room. Leaving Corvan and me alone. For one wonderful moment I thought the magus would fuck off by himself and leave me to my business. Instead he spoke.

"You're going to be attracting attention with your technology, you realize," he noted. "The bad kind. People are already eyeing you. I heard that the Dead Edge have been looking into your business, or at least I did before heading over here myself."

To his credit, he talked about his journey to come over and murder us quite openly, quite calmly. The prick. I resisted the urge to hit him again.

"Who are the Dead Edge?"

He glanced, smug now.

"Ah, not so streetwise, then?"

"Answer me, prick."

The magus clearly relished doing so.

"A gang, an old one. They've been operating in Elswick for about half a century. I actually had a run-in with their founder when I was just a boy. Big, powerful, and clever. They don't cross people they know they can't, but they're quick to spot and lunge for opportunities."

"Opportunities like a group of half a dozen mercenaries who are making magic powder capable of blowing up buildings," I finished for him. Corvan shrugged.

"There were advantages to selling it openly, money wise, but you must've known it'd get you looked at by particular types."

We had, of course; we weren't idiots. The simple fact was there'd been too much to gain for any real thought of keeping the stuff to ourselves. If we hadn't been shoveling off black powder, we'd still be diving into forts and battlefields, still trying to fund our little operation by the skin of our teeth. Now, though, we were just about ready to start acting as proper agents.

Still, that didn't mean we weren't in a fuck pile of trouble now.

"How strong exactly is this Dead Edge?" I asked wearily. Corvan shrugged.

"A few hundred men, at least, and I hear they have a magus or two among them. As I said, they're a powerful gang, not the sort you want interested in you."

Well, that little tidbit could've come earlier. I was about to say as much when Shango walked in. He looked nervous, his features twisted with the kind of thoughts that always bubbled under his face before a serious conversation started between us. I braced myself for what he was inevitably about to tell me.

Then frowned, as he turned to Corvan instead.

"What do you know of the Velaharo family?" he asked abruptly. Corvan seemed surprised—I certainly was—but the magus overcame his stunned silence quickly enough to give an answer.

"Old," he replied. "One of the oldest in Elswick, even in Eregar itself as I recall, but they've fallen on bad times. Dirt-poor, lambasted in reputation. As I hear it they haven't been a real political factor in years."

Shango winced but didn't look surprised. It was a combination that immediately set off alarm bells for me.

"What did you do?" I asked him.

He took a second, weighing each word before he spoke.

"I should've asked Corvan before going to meet with Velaharo." He sighed. "But, being fair, it wouldn't have actually made any difference. Just as a precaution, I should have."

"What did you do?" I pressed, fighting for calm as I found myself growing more anxious and antsy by the moment.

Shango paused, considered, then sighed reluctantly and lurched into his explanation.

"I married her," he replied, practically trembling at the words even as they left his lips. I just stared at him.

He. Married. Her.

Certainly, there were stranger sentences in the English language, even stranger combinations. "Will will smith smith" came to mind, quite quickly, and that was only scratching the surface.

Still, even knowing that, somehow the revelation that my friend was marrying a fucking aristocrat struck me differently.

My first, reflexive response was, of course, to immediately behead the offending noble. That was after all what good Liverpudlians did in front of an aristocrat, but my righteous answer was paused as I mulled the situation over some more, glaring at him.

Finally, the meat of it hit me.

"You didn't consult us first," I noted, glare deepening. And to think, after all that whining I'd had to endure about not killing people without permission, the bloody hypocrite had gone and gotten himself hitched!

Shango even had the nerve to be defensive rather than immediately apologizing and telling me I could decapitate as many bandits as I wanted, as any good and reasonable person would have.

"It was a heat-of-the-moment decision," he snapped. "There wasn't exactly an opportunity to say no."

"Why wasn't there?" I pressed, and he glowered.

"Because, as I was about to tell you, Phelia has enemies, and she reckoned one of them—"

"Phelia," I cut in. "Your wife. First-name basis already? I thought that was a sixth-date sort of intimacy with your lot."

"Oh shut up," Shango snapped, and I bowed.

"Of course, your divine holiness, please continue telling me why you married a woman you've spoken to for less than half an hour."

His irritation brought a smile to my face, but Shango was quick in wiping it away.

"Because she has enemies," he continued. "A Lord Byror, for one, who from what I've heard has been working with quite a powerful gang, and has a habit of using them to do *extrajudicial politicking.*"

I almost groaned. It was just a classic, too perfectly fucking horrible. Perhaps God really was a woman. It was the only way I had of explaining how vindictive she was.

"The Dead Edge," I guessed, and didn't even manage to relish the look of surprise on Shango's face.

"That's right," he breathed. "How did you know?"

It was a good question. How did I know?

Well, obviously, I knew because we were living in our own little fucking nightmare.

CHAPTER TWENTY

Solitaire had been right about one thing: The new steel was exceptionally good. Once Ardin had finally figured out the process of working it, that was. He took his sweet time in doing it, apparently far less economical with the samples he was being handed once he found out we could keep making more with Corvan. What we heard from Shango, about the new attentions of one Lord Byror and his gang of bastards, was seemingly too insignificant to meaningfully hurry the smith. It would've been admirable, if it weren't *my* neck he was gambling with alongside his own.

A few new factors came into play now that we knew we were dealing with potential adversity and making things that any idiot could possibly mimic here. The first was the need for a more secure workstation. Solitaire, unsurprisingly, was the one who gathered all of us up to discuss that.

"We need a defensible location," he explained. "Somewhere safe, easily warded. Does your new girlfriend have any ideas?" He directed the question at Shango, who did not seem particularly bothered to have Phelia's relation to him misstated. Perhaps he was just used to Solitaire's Solitairisms.

"She doesn't own any property," he replied coolly. "Except for her family estate, which I'm not sure she'd be okay with us using."

"It's not up to her though, right?" Solitaire pointed out. "You're in charge of the family now."

Shango blinked, thoughtful.

"I'd rather not just boss a woman around, all domineering like that," he noted. "I mean, you know, I was born in the twenty-first century. However things are here, I still have certain . . . values."

Solitaire placed his hand down on Shango's shoulder, nodding in empathetic consideration, then met his eye.

"Stop being a bitch and tell the cunt we're moving in," he said simply. Shango glared at him.

"Don't call her a cunt," he replied calmly. Solitaire stared at him.

"Pardon?"

I took a step back, sensing what was coming. Shango took a step forward.

"She's my wife now, my family. Please don't call her a cunt."

Solitaire eyed Shango in a way I'd not quite seen him do in a long time. I was speaking up before he could.

"I think we're all getting distracted here," I noted. "We're talking about moving our stuff. How do we do that exactly? Carriage?"

Both of them glanced at me distractedly and nodded.

"Yes," they said in unison, and Shango sighed before continuing.

"I'll tell Phelia we're using one of the spare rooms. You all get ready to move."

He was off soon after, so quickly that it only dawned on me once he'd already left that we'd all been left with the job of hauling the heavy equipment onto a carriage.

"Typical." Solitaire sighed, preparing to do just that. I bent down to offer him a hand, as the two of us hauled our new furnace up while Argar and Helena headed outside for the carriage. It was easier than it would have been a few months ago, which was to say, it was possible. The furnace must've weighed over half a ton, at least, but we hauled it up to waist level and carried it over next to the door to wait for their arrival.

We weren't waiting long, but it was still enough time to get plenty of other lugging done. The distilling gear from Solitaire's gunpowder manufactory, our remaining supplies of coal, even a few work desks and tables—why not, after all. They might even have helped to disguise the actually unique equipment.

Through it all, we eyed Corvan as he waited in one corner of the room.

"Oh don't rush to help," Solitaire snapped after one particularly heavy desk refused to budge under his own strength. "I'm sure your fucking magic powers wouldn't be of much help anyway, really. Just stay as you are and relax."

Corvan eyed him through his bushy brows and beard, a pipe pinched between his teeth, wisping smoke out into the room.

"Magic is good for many things," the magus replied. "The greatest force in Redacle, perhaps the universe, but it is not to be used for trivialities such as lifting desks and hauling luggage."

Solitaire shot back instantly, as I might have expected. The sentiment was a common one shared by magi in our book, and almost always with the intent of giving some veiled, esoteric reason for why it would be vaguely untenable for them to help with more mundane matters like manual labor.

Obviously, it wasn't the sort of excuse that would work with a person who'd helped to fucking invent their culture in the first place.

"That's a pile of wank, and we both know it. You're just lazy."

Corvan opened his mouth to argue, then Solitaire cut in.

"Your people are taught early in training to use that excuse because it's part of a carefully woven layer of cultural mystique that keeps you seeming unreachable and superior, one of the many things that have kings taking your advice and commoners trembling in fear of you."

The magus eyed him, wary now, and Solitaire continued.

"Sadly, your moron fearmongering has the same weakness that every other example of its use was prone to throughout history. Knowledge. You'll have to find more ignorant targets to try it on than us, I'm afraid."

"Where are you from?" Corvan asked, thoughtful now rather than bitter or smug. "You know things you shouldn't know, far too many things. I've heard you discuss Earth, your homeland. Where is it?"

Solitaire shrugged, dismissing the barbed question as if it were no more than some idle observation.

"I don't see why I need to tell you that. Ask Shango if you're so curious. Then again, you tried to burn him to death, too."

Corvan held Solitaire's stare.

"You know why I joined up with you, I assume?"

"Because you know we're going to be powerful one day, and you want to get all the goodwill you can while we're still weak enough for it to come easily."

The magus nodded, unfazed.

"One day," he echoed. "And if it looks like that day won't come because you pissed off the wrong person or picked the wrong fight, I'm gone."

Solitaire met his gaze, nodding. He didn't look the least bit surprised. Solitaire never did when people spoke to him of betrayal.

"Then I guess we'll be careful not to fuck up," he answered, then grunted as I added my muscles to his, and we worked to haul the last of our stuff over to the door. It was just in time, too, because outside a carriage waited. Not the shoddy, small kind we'd sent Argar and Helena for, though. This one was tall, pulled by proud horses, made of polished wood, and so evidently expensive I half expected it to glow.

A woman was standing beside it, with hair as gold as the trim of her possessions and eyes as green as grass. She smiled the way an angel might, though her lip curled slightly as she moved across the grimy road to speak with us.

"Solitaire and Beam, yes?" she asked. "Belahonts. Shango, my husband, sent me. It's a pleasure to meet you, brothers-in-law."

I extended a hand, then quickly lowered it as I remembered this region's customs on women shaking the hands of men. Simply smiling instead.

"It's lovely to meet you, too." I beamed. "You're here to help us transfer our, uh, equipment?"

"I am," she replied, eyes twinkling in a way that told me she wasn't at all as reluctant as Shango had predicted. "Shall we get a move on? I'm rather eager to see what you can all do with it."

CHAPTER TWENTY-ONE

Solitaire's POV: Day 78
Current Wealth: 229 gold, 37 silver, 6 copper

I'd gotten used to carriage rides since coming to Redacle. In fact I'd actually come to regard them as something of a luxury. That was what hours of constant walking would do to a person, I supposed. Still, it came as quite a surprise how comfortable Velaharo's vehicle actually was. Apparently the working class' tears made for quite effective wheel lubricant because the journey was smooth sailing from start to finish and found only one hitch.

We were about halfway to the manor, or so I was told, when I heard something outside. Turning to look at it, I found a woman sprinting down the street, something clutched tightly to her chest and a frantic look on her face. She was short, brown-haired, and slender as a whip, but the wind under her legs was a thing and a half.

The pair of guards chasing after her, red-faced and empty lunged, barely managed to snatch my focus away from her. Neither one was close to catching the woman, and the distance between them and her was only growing. It wasn't that that caught my focus, though. Instead I found myself noting the way she wove between obstacles, always choosing the ones perfectly sized, shaped, and placed to impede her as little as possible, while doing the opposite with her pursuers.

As I turned to Beam, I found he was already eyeing the scene, as well, a thoughtful look on his face.

"You want to recruit her?" I guessed.

He glanced at me, as if surprised I was even there, then nodded.

"She's fast," he noted.

"And smart," I concurred, looking back to see her rapidly disappearing from sight. No time for a prolonged think, then.

She could be trouble, with what looked like a stolen object, but given the sheer fear of the men chasing her I could only guess that it was a *valuable* stolen object, too. Possibly that meant we could profit by seizing it ourselves, but at worst it was very strong cause to believe that this one had permeated quite a strong security setup to snatch it.

In the end, there wasn't really much doubting where my decision would land.

"Go after her," I sighed to Beam. "Helena, Argar, and I can take the stuff from the carriage, though . . . do keep a low profile."

I didn't like the idea of him getting murdered by the Dead Edge just because I'd sent him off alone, but Beam only grinned and dove out of the window. He took off faster than either of our fighters could have managed, armor or no, and . . . yes, I saw, almost as fast as the sprinter.

With luck, he'd be fast enough to escape a killing.

The carriage carried on, rolling away and soon pulling in to stop before a sprawling mansion. Velaharo stepped daintily out from her door, and I trudged down from mine. Argar and Helena, stored on the back, were already beginning the tedious process of hauling their gear toward the house.

"Where's Shango?" I asked Velaharo. She eyed me impassively.

"He should be inside somewhere, looking through the place. Said he had a study to make, or something to that effect."

If it were me, I'd be making sure the mansion was a nice, defensible position. Located on the city's edge, it was unpleasantly vulnerable to assault from anything that bypassed the outer wall, and painfully exposed. Remote. A lot could happen in this part of the city with nobody noticing elsewhere. A lot could be gotten away with.

Knowing Shango, though, he was doing something stupid, like appraising its worth or calculating storage capacity. Some people just had no appreciation for basic safety.

The long, tedious process of hauling gear had only just begun, Velaharo eyeing it as it panned out with a thoughtful look, when the sound of hard footfalls caught my ear and turned me.

I wasn't sure what I'd expected to see. A messenger perhaps. Maybe my very own noble to offer a proposal of marriage—that would've been brilliant. I'd have loved to see the look on her cunt face when I turned her down. But instead it was a man, then another, then another. All big, all hardened by and for violence, spears in some hands, axes and clubs in others. Weapons, proper weapons, made for war and killing, not just improvised in some alley.

At their head was a tall fellow clutching a cocked crossbow, handling it with the gesticulations of a man who knew what he was doing. Everything seemed to slow at the sight of him, and I noticed a few things all at once.

These people were staring right at me, obviously here for me and with no pleasant purpose. They were also attacking now. Not when some of us were already inside unloading, or when we were on the road. Now. After we'd disembarked, after we'd traveled the farthest possible distance. There weren't enough of them that our remote location would provide any cover a suitably dark alley wouldn't, which meant . . .

Velaharo, they were worried about her. About hurting her with an attack on the carriage, or trespassing on her property by heading into her grounds. That made sense. Noble blood was sacrosanct after all. In fact, Shango managing to gain his own nobility was probably why these animals were here. They'd heard the Belahonts were becoming aristocrats and realized that taking us out and wringing us for knowledge was now or never.

Which made my next action very, very clear. I turned, hurrying at a sprint to Velaharo's side while the enemy was still fifty feet away. Close enough for a crossbow to hit, I thought, but with any luck my sprint would be surprising and fast enough that I'd cross my five paces before catching a bolt.

I wasn't wearing my armor, which meant that it really was fortunate when I reached Velaharo in time, shocking the woman by grabbing her and violently dragging her body in front of mine, keeping it between me and the now-stunned men still approaching. I'd drawn my knife somewhere along the motion, and now held it pressed against Velaharo's throat.

"Try to shoot me and you'll hit her!" I roared, keeping my gaze flitting from one man to another. "Shoot my subordinates and I'll cut her throat. Good luck explaining the dead noble to your bosses!"

Silence followed, and I used it promptly.

"Argar, Helena, take the carriage inside."

I heard a fortunately hasty scraping of boots on ground behind me, knowing my bodyguards were scrambling to do just that. Good. My charade here wouldn't keep the bastards delayed for very long.

Velaharo twitched in my arms, body moving against mine, a wrathful gasp escaping her.

"Let go of me, you pig!" she snarled, speaking with that vehemence that women always seemed to have. "How dare you? How dare you use me as some fucking shield!"

I tightened my grip on her and said nothing as I glanced up at the men. Surprisingly, Mr. Crossbow was already leveling his weapon my way.

Human shields were a fairly bad idea back on Earth. Plenty of guns could pierce right through a Homo sapien's torso and still have a fair amount of wounding—if not killing—power when they hit something behind them. In fact, humans made for such shit shields that we were forced quite early in our history to invent actual shields.

But there were no guns here, just a crossbow, and by the looks of it, it wasn't one of those fancy arbalest types with a five-hundred-kilo draw weight and the power to punch clean through steel. Which meant if it hit Velaharo, it probably wouldn't be blasting out her back to injure me.

That, I realized, might well have been the only reason I was still free of a fight. Because the crossbowman clearly wasn't held back by the thought of killing a noble anymore, subtly trying to move around Velaharo for a clearer shot, subtly growing more annoyed as I maneuvered her to deny it to him.

Seconds passed, then more, and things were closing in on a minute before the situation finally boiled over.

"Just get him," the crossbowman—the lead man, I now confirmed—said with a snarl. His fellows started moving in, five of them, marching swift and determined. The decision was forced on me. If I let go of Velaharo, I'd be shot and die. If I kept hold of her, I'd have my arms busy when the others fell on us and die. If I tried to back away with her, she'd slow me, we'd be caught, and I'd die.

My options were slim, and the only one remaining was fairly obvious. I waited until the men were close, then violently shoved Velaharo into the nearest of them.

Reflexively, he caught her, seeming just as surprised as she was as the screaming, thrashing, swearing woman almost bowled him over.

I was already moving by then.

CHAPTER TWENTY-TWO

Beam's POV: Day 78
Current Wealth: 229 gold, 37 silver, 6 copper

We really did have fucking awful luck of the draw, thinking about it. How often did we, all three of us earthlings, split up? Not that frequently, not back then at least. And yet, just as both Shango and I were elsewhere, Solitaire got attacked. Well, I didn't know anything about what was going on at Velaharo Manor until later on. I was still preoccupied with my own little escapade. Chasing a woman.

Saying it like that, one does wonder whether Solitaire might have been better suited to it.

Maybe not. This one was quick, disappearing around corners, hopping stalls, tearing down the streets with a frightful speed. More speed than me, easily. I could feel the distance between us growing with every stride, see her disappearing farther and farther ahead into the distance.

Early on I'd assumed there'd been no high-profile guards in pursuit of her. It had seemed like a reasonable deduction, but seeing the way she moved, I could easily believe that there had been, and she'd just torn on ahead of them. No human had ever moved like this in the Olympics, that was for sure, and the longer I chased her, the more convinced I became that there weren't all too many animals who'd have given her a decent chase, either.

But I still had to catch her—there was really no two ways about it—and so I did what we earthlings—Belahonts—had started to develop a bit of a reputation for doing. I cheated.

Not in a particularly sophisticated way, mind. If I were Shango I might've shouted something really clever and evil to trick her into turning around, or slowing, or falling over. If I were Solitaire I'd probably have stopped for a few seconds to assemble a jet pack out of the fruit I was running past, then swooped down on her from above.

Instead I just climbed a building, putting my supernatural strength to good use as I hauled myself over it, and cut along the side.

The woman was heading through a part of the city I recognized, and her path would doubtless take her through the street I was dropping down into. All I'd have to do to get her was wait, so I did. And did. But she didn't come.

It took a good few minutes before I finally caved, stepped out of my hiding place, and started perusing the path I'd expected to find her shooting down, scrutinizing every wall and gutter for any trace of her. Perhaps expectedly, she was in neither the brickwork nor the gathering street sludge washed to either of the road's sides.

My heart started to spasm. I couldn't have *lost* her. It just wasn't possible. She was right there, I'd had her, and I'd had one fucking job. I—

I checked myself, forced as much calm as I could manage, and made myself go through the bare facts of things. Obviously, she hadn't just evaporated into nowhere. So how could she have slipped away?

Over the walls was the obvious solution, but eyeing them I found it hard to be convinced. They were steep, close to ten feet high, and without much in the way of grips or handholds. I'd only managed to hoist myself up by pinching down so hard that I almost dented the crumbling mortar, and while the woman was definitely not as heavy as me—perhaps even beneath half my weight now that blacksmithing had started packing on my muscle—I doubted she had the physical power needed to fight gravity under those circumstances. Climbing was a much harder exercise than most people gave it credit for, even under ideal conditions.

Had she backtracked? That one sent a shiver down my spine. If she had then there'd be no finding her. With her speed, with my delay, she could have turned down half a dozen different streets, made her way a literal mile from me. A few minutes wasn't very much time at all, except for her.

I took an embarrassing pause deciding what to do next before logic won out over panic. I was certain she'd not gone over the wall, and knew I was fucked if she'd doubled back on herself, so there was only one thing left. Check more potential hiding places. If she was tucked away in the alley somewhere, or anywhere else along the path she'd cleared while I was climb-ing, then I might just find her. And if she wasn't, then I'd lose nothing by searching because she was already easily too far away to catch again with how much time I'd spent.

Even as I began my search, the tension bled away to smugness. I couldn't twist mere mortals to my will or remake everything mentioned in the Geneva conventions, but I could get plenty of thought done myself when the situation called for it. I almost wished we hadn't left Ardin back at our original ware-house to go and get his stuff from the shop. It would've been nice to have someone with me to appreciate it.

The search was long and tedious because it was quite the shortcut I'd taken. Easily thirty meters of alley to sift through, and one particularly fast person to sift it for. I was well aware that even a second's delay in reacting to her might let the woman get irreconcilably far ahead, so I kept my diligence as I worked. It soon proved worth it.

She saw me before I saw her, a little glinting eye piled away in some shadows beneath a few scraps of rotting wood. There was lots of debris in the place, plenty of patches she *could* have been in, especially with a body as small as hers. But I didn't let my guard down, and my reactions were fast as ever. I was mov-ing just an instant after she was.

An instant was a long time for that one, and she almost slipped out of my reach in the time I took to fully turn and snap out an arm to grab her. My fingertips just barely grazed her clothes, a painful tug dragging on their liga-ments as tearing cloth snagged and halted her momentum, then she was stum-bling away, half stopped and trying to restart her sprint as I began mine.

My shoulder caught her in the stomach, bowling her over flat against the ground, and I was atop her instantly. She struggled, writhing beneath me with the sort of strength I'd half expected but still found instinctually hard to believe. It was like the feral power of a cat, all weight-efficient force generation and explosive energy. But pound-for-pound strength only did so much when one had as few pounds as her, and up close I could tell she was just as small as I thought. Fifty kilos, probably less, short and wiry for this world, let alone mine.

Which was to say nothing of my own magical strength. I didn't even budge as she thrashed beneath me, just remained still and kept her arms pinned, wait-ing for her to run out of steam.

But she surprised me before that could happen.

"Saw you chasing me. Pretty determined for a rapist, aren't you?" she spat, glaring up at me with eyes that betrayed so much blind, searing disgust that it actually gave me pause.

Too late, I realized the trick for what it was. She snatched her hand out of my grip and half leaned upward for an elbow to my jaw before I could even think to grab her again. My head snapped back, vision dancing for a moment, then refocusing. She'd freed one of her legs by then, but I pressed down instan-taneously and tightly, compressing her against the ground.

With her arm still free, she hit me again, then again. But I ignored the blows. She had no leverage, and no surprise this time, her fist just bounced off my face and neck like it belonged to an infant. I glared at her, meeting the woman's eyes and finding my temper suddenly short.

"Very clever," I snapped. "Now will you stop struggling? I want to fucking talk to you."

She froze, and for a second I dared to hope I'd gotten through to her. Then she went still, and I realized what was happening. A giant fucking six-one man, pinning down a four-eleven woman, snarling orders at her. I almost puked.

Carefully, I moved back, standing slow, making sure not to let any sudden moves escape me.

"I'm sorry," I pressed. "Really, I am, but I do want to talk with you, I have an offer I'd like you to hear, and . . . that's all. You can leave if you want to. You don't even have to say anything." To illustrate the point, I took a few steps back, giving her enough room to doubtless escape if I started for her again. Even as each one stabbed me with reluctance. "There, your choice."

She stood, eyed me, eyed the alley behind her. Made to move, body tensing the way a cheetah's might. Then paused. With a sigh, the woman met my gaze once more and spoke.

"Go on then," she said, speaking with an admirable level of steel in her spine. "I'm listening."

CHAPTER TWENTY-THREE

Shango's POV: Day 78
Current Wealth: 229 gold, 37 silver, 6 copper

I'd been having a nice day, a relaxed day. A good day. My big, stressful decision was made and behind me, my schedule was freed up, and I'd just found myself with access to a sprawling mansion. Exploring the Velaharo Manor was an exercise in . . . frankly, therapy. It was an aged place, but not simply withered. More . . . dignified. Though also withered.

Clearly the Velaharo fortune had not been at its peak for quite some time, as I found a lot of maintenance in need of doing around the mansion. Undusted surfaces, uncleared cobwebs. They became more common the farther I moved from its more human-touched areas, which told me that there was at least *some* effort to clean the place ongoing. Clearly, it was just of limited scale and effectiveness. Which was understandable. There was a lot of it to clean.

Ordinarily I'd have loved to ponder the logistics of such a job, busying myself with the hows and whys, the mundane considerations of scheduling and workload, informational diffusion and organization. It was probably diagnostic of something, but I'd always found myself relaxing through mental work like that.

Solitaire ruined it, though, as he often ruined my downtime. In his defense, he had a bit more of a reasonable cause to do so this time compared to his usual antics. It was hardly his fault we were attacked.

Helena barged into me from behind, shaking my focus onto her and meeting my eyes with a tight, fearful stare.

"Men, gang members, well armed and attacking," she gasped desperately. "Outside. Solitaire and your . . . wife."

I barely even noticed that she'd called Phelia my wife, barely even noticed anything at all as my mind blanked with adrenaline and my body moved with purpose. I was tearing down the hallway not even a second later, torturing the aged floorboards with the force of my strides.

Helena was fast behind me, and the two of us burst out of the mansion in unison. The scene awaiting us made my stomach churn.

Argar, apparently, had headed back for Solitaire quickly, and he was already tied up fighting alongside him. Giant axe swinging one way and the other, he seemed unable to connect with the man facing him. Though smaller, his opponent was quick as any I'd ever seen—including the vampire—and fought with a pair of stiletto knives that glinted with thirst. Once, twice, three, then four times he evaded the heavy-handed swings of my bodyguard, before calmly stepping into his guard and thrusting one weapon in between a pair of plates.

The giant folded, groaning with pain as the knife dug in, then withdrew an instant later. Its wielder backflipped to land some three meters free of him, glancing at the blade. He didn't seem pleased to see the meager amount of it tipped with blood, and Argar bulled on after him without another word.

I was an instant away from rushing in to help when something flew past my vision, a woman. She hit the ground hard enough to bounce, rolling and sliding another five meters, and a glance showed me what had launched her. Solitaire.

My friend was covered in blood, and I wasn't certain how much belonged to his enemies. He fought two at once as I watched, throwing himself back and away from a pair of chasing weapons, one a long, heavy machete, the other some sort of spear. Both looked like their wielders knew what they were doing with them, and a more scrutinous inspection revealed plenty of smaller gashes across Solitaire's body.

He was moving well enough that I knew none were too deep, though, and just as I was starting to decide whether he needed my help as much as Argar, Helena made the decision easy. She rushed over to the giant's side.

Solitaire didn't say anything as I hurried to him, but he acknowledged me with a single glance that told everything. There was fear in his eyes, actual fear, and seeing that in Solitaire was enough to chill me to my core. The machete came for my face. I sidestepped. My armor was lying strewn out in my room somewhere, and I'd not taken the time to grab my sword while I was gone, but I still had two good weapons. The first was born from a simple habit I'd picked up, the knife I'd learned always to carry with me. The second, though, was something far more inherent, and far, far more powerful. My magic. I took a step back from the swing, extending my hands and feeling the air, caressing it to test out those magic points where the currents interlocked. Then I let the words echo through my mind and pushed against them.

Air shifted, shooting out like a thrown brick and crunching into the attacking man's ribs. His feet left the ground as he tumbled back, flipping head over heels like a rag doll struck by a bat. I didn't look long enough to see him land, focusing instead on the remaining enemy.

Solitaire was on him already, in past the spear tip, hands gripped tight across the shaft. Without looking, he called out to me.

"The bowman, get him!"

I took an instant to see what and whom he meant before the last enemy struck me, a tall Redaclan with a large crossbow aimed dangerously our way. My hands moved fast, my mind faster, my magic fastest of all. The bolt left his bow and flitted through the air so quickly I could barely react in the time it took to cross ten meters. Then it hit my hastily constructed wall of air.

The bolt slowed but didn't stop. Moving past the air with a mass and velocity that Corvan's flames had never possessed, however hot they'd been. It clipped my shoulder but registered more like a beesting than a stab wound, barely breaking the skin as it bounced off and skidded away. Apparently my little barrier was enough to exhaust most of its momentum.

Clearly, the shooter realized that, too, because I saw him stash his weapon away and replace it with a large metal bar. He closed in, moving with a disconcerting confidence.

My attention snapped back to Solitaire just as he broke the spear over his knee and jabbed the steel tip through his enemy's face, running it into one cheek and out through the other, then tearing it fully free in a spray of blood. I actually felt queasy watching it, but he only snarled, then whirled with alarm.

I turned to see the woman from before closing in, readying myself for her. I didn't like the idea of hitting a woman, modern instincts threatening to bubble up at the worst possible time. Fortunately, I was partnered with a man who not only didn't share such compunctions, but had actually given me considerable reason to suspect that he hit women *even harder* than men. Solitaire tossed his opponent into the attacker to knock both her and him down into a heap, then shoved after me.

"You take the bowman," he instructed. "Just buy me a bit to wrap these two up, then I'll be with you."

I moved to obey instantly, knowing that however mutually Solitaire and I respected one another, there were situations when one of our minds was more than equal to the other's. Under the cover of death's robe, he was master, and I knew better than to argue with whatever logic had decided his priority. Only one thing gave me pause.

Going by the glint in his eye, our bowman enemy had decided that fighting me first was in his best interests, too.

CHAPTER TWENTY-FOUR

Solitaire's POV: Day 78
Current Wealth: 229 gold, 37 silver, 6 copper

The cunt lunged for me, and I sidestepped. My fist came down for the base of her skull, but she was faster than me, rolling out of the way, springing back up to her feet. I could've tried to grapple her, would have done so a few weeks ago, but now I had better options. I extended my thoughts to the air, started feeling for bound molecules and particular elements, drawing them together.

Her attack came fast, but I'd gotten a lot of practice at my power since first discovering it. The globule of nitroglycerine was already clinging to my fingertip by the time she came in. I flicked it off with one move, dove back with another, and there was no dodging the droplet at such close range. It caught her stomach and detonated loud and hard enough to cut timber in half, sending her stumbling, then falling as her balance gave. I didn't check on the body, just tried to make more of the stuff.

By the time she was up, I'd wetted my hands with tiny little patches of explosive condensation. Gathered them together again, making a larger drop this time, and flicked it just as the last. This one caught her between the eyes, and by the time the explosion cleared there was little left of her face.

I turned, grinning, to see how Shango's fight was doing. But life was a cruel bitch, and plans were made to be fucked up. I could see at a glance that we'd made a mistake. My friend was on the ground, scrambling back from our enemy, hands wide and jaw tight with pain as blood ran down his side. The bowman—now without a bow—held some big length of metal in his hands, something I might've called rebar if we'd been back on Earth.

The tedious matter of categorization would have to wait because it was about two seconds away from opening up my friend's skull and spraying the surrounding area with the world's second most remarkable brain matter. I closed in to keep that from happening, conjuring again.

Nitro was a no-go, not with Shango so close to the enemy, but I racked my memory for a potentially suitable replacement. It didn't take long for my horrible, awful, nasty, sexual hunting hound of a brain to think something up.

$H_2SO_4 + H_2O_2$, all things I had in abundance around me, save the sulfur. I fortunately had a bit of that on my person—some residue from working on the explosives, clinging to my clothes and patches of my skin. I'd meant to wash, hadn't gotten around to it with everything happening with Velaharo. Now it looked like that slipup might save us.

I mixed my chemicals as I rushed the guy, conjuring and almost-telekinetically holding them in the air ahead of me, then splashing the resultant concoction across our enemy's head. I missed his eyes, sadly enough, but his hair and scalp got doused. For a moment only confusion colored his face, then I saw the pain start.

Piranha solution. It's a particularly strong kind of acid, the one responsible for how most kids think all acids behave, stripping meat from bone in under a minute, melting things into nothing. It didn't seem to be working as quickly as I'd have thought, and its effects stopped after only a few layers of skin were removed. Did magical resilience help ward off the corrosion of acid? It made sense if so.

Either way, the man didn't exactly look much better off.

His head was a gory, bloody, soggy mess, hair clinging tight against a ruined scalp and slick with foamy blood, left bubbling by the gaseous products of the particular reaction that had stripped him of his flesh. With an expression of pain clinging to his face as tightly as steel clamps, his entire body spasmed with the agony of it.

I would've killed to hit him with another splash, killed even more to get the next one in his face, but I'd more or less exhausted my sulfuric reserves, and he was recovering dangerously quick. I had to be realistic, compromise with the simple pragmatics of my situation. Besides, there was more than one way to skin a human.

As I moved, I rushed past one of the fallen fuckers I'd fought already, the idiot with the spear. I snatched the splintered tip of his weapon up off the ground next to him while he was busy bleeding everywhere, twisting it in my grip and holding it like a dagger. The bowman had recovered already by then, but it didn't faze me. I'd hurt him. Now I just needed to kill him. I started work on another batch of nitro, exhaling the necessary ingredients out into my palm as I conjured it.

He recovered before I could finish, lunging with his bar and thrusting it at my face like a rapier. I darted to one side, but the metal twisted after me, clipping my head and bouncing off with a dull clang. I felt the sound more than heard it, noise echoing around in my skull as I stumbled back.

My arms rose with the nitro ready, then went wide as my legs gave out. A sudden dizziness took me, one I recognized instantly for the nausea of serious concussion, and I dropped to my knees as the explosive went wide.

The bowman was on me instantly, bar raised high and ready to bring down. It was only the shimmering air between my head and the cold metal that spared me, the atmospheric barrier deflecting the impact and forcing a wince on the man's face as his joints rebelled. He took a step back, thrown off-balance by the unexpected impediment, and I knew there'd not be another chance than that.

Shango had saved me once, but I saw his shield fray and come apart before the next swing fell. It was all me now.

My shoulder caught the bowman hard, but my tackle was ill-judged. Balance still escaped me, slipping through my fingers like something slick with oil, and he was clearly practiced in holding himself up. We shifted for a few moments and filled the air with scraping leather as our boots scuffed and dragged against the stone, then my momentum ran out, and we both stopped.

I was practiced in holding myself up, too, and I was practiced in what came after you managed to do it. We'd stopped. He was free to shift his center of gravity, and I was still hunched over leaning against his gut. That meant I had about a second before an elbow came down into the back of my neck. If he was as strong as me, that would be dangerous. If he was stronger, it would be death.

Well, I had about a second, and I've never been the sort to take injury well. I used my precious moments to lift the man's shirt and sink my teeth deep into the flesh of his stomach.

His body was lean and toned, barely an ounce of fat on it. That was good; it meant there was less in the way of me reaching all the delicate muscle beneath. My teeth ground together, and my head thrashed side to side like a pit bull in an orphanage, vision turning red with adrenaline, hearing becoming so distant that the man's horrified screams seemed like a shouted message from far below.

The bastard couldn't move. His body was being held tight and still by its own pained convulsions, and he didn't have the strength required to dislodge me with whatever simple motions he could've made. Moment by moment, I tunneled deeper through his belly, drawing close to the more vital meat below.

It was Shango's voice that told me something was wrong, just an instant before it killed me.

"Get back!" he cried, and I did, lunging away from the man on instinct—trusting my friend's warning more than whatever sensory input my body had taken. The iron bar caught my right shoulder and broke it, turning me in the air, flipping me one way and the other. I rolled, jarring the limb and finding the world disappeared beneath a curtain of searing, hallucinatory pain.

CHAPTER TWENTY-FIVE

Beam's POV: Day 78
Current Wealth: 229 gold, 37 silver, 6 copper

Elizabeth, as I had learned the woman was called, was still more than a little bit guarded around me. I wasn't too surprised, nor was I unfamiliar with the behavior. It reminded me a lot of Solitaire, back when we'd first met, all caution and suspicion, self-preservation and inquisitive defense.

Just like back then, it was a hard barrier to get through. Every inquiry I made was interpreted as some sort of attack. Every innocent observation had, apparently, at least two double meanings that had escaped even my notice, and God help me if I made a sudden movement.

The two of us were walking, at least. That gave me the *illusion* of progress even if none was actually coming.

"You're fast," I noted, making yet another attempt to break the ice. She glared at me.

"Obviously I'm fast. How'd you catch me?"

It was, at least, a change of pace from the usual retorts I'd been getting, so I decided to answer her. If nothing else to keep the woman from getting suspicious again if I didn't.

"I climbed a wall. Already saw you heading down this way so I figured I could jump down beside you when you came past. I hadn't expected you to hide, but you didn't see me anyway, so."

She bristled.

"The guards were only chasing me from one direction," she snapped. "I hadn't expected to get caught from the other."

"Right," I replied, eager to soothe her before she could go off on another tirade. "And, if you don't mind me asking, why exactly *were* they chasing you?"

Elizabeth glared at me.

"Because they're bastards, all of them. Every single guard is a bastard. It's just what they're like."

All guards are bastards. I almost laughed. This one *had* to meet Solitaire, but later. For now she still had answers being kept to herself that I needed to get in on hearing.

"They had something specific to be going for you about rather than anyone else, though. Right?"

The woman grew testy, not meeting my eye.

"So did you want to meet me just to pry into whatever I had?"

"No," I replied honestly. "But I think it's only fair that I be told, considering I'll be putting my skin on the line by moving around with you while you carry it."

I could tell she didn't want to tell me, but not why. Was it fear? Embarrassment? Basic caution? Whatever emotions flared up in her features, they died down quickly, and she didn't meet my eye as she replied.

"Just this," she breathed, fishing around inside her clothes for a moment, then producing a . . . cup. An old-fashioned goblet to be precise, bronze, battered, and . . . remarkably shitty. It was old, though, so I figured there was a story tied to it.

"Some sort of . . . family heirloom?" I guessed. She looked at me like I'd just drooled on myself.

"This is the chalice of Mozen Drayri, one of the relics left behind by God during his last visit." She smirked. "Not much to look at, but it'll sell for a fuck ton if you find the right buyer. One hundred gold at least."

Our new uptick of wealth wasn't old enough for that sum not to hit me like a sledgehammer, and I found myself eyeing the goblet with a new respect.

"Hands to yourself," Elizabeth growled, stuffing it back inside her clothes quickly and glaring at me with unguarded suspicion. I almost sighed out loud.

"I'm not going to steal it," I snapped. "My family is already making plenty of money anyway. Relax."

That gave her pause.

"You . . . don't seem like a rich person," she noted, looking pointedly at my clothes. "I figured you were a foreign worker, a mercenary or something. Nobody who isn't a fighter moves as fast as you did, at least."

She was strangely close to the mark, reminding me yet again of Solitaire. But there were more important things than how impressive she was.

"You're probably going to need to lie low for a while, right?" I guessed. "Why don't you do it with my family? We can shelter you better than alleyway debris, at least."

Elizabeth hadn't been on edge before. I found that out quickly enough by seeing what she looked like when her guard was *actually* up. Apparently, it was knife wielding.

"And no witnesses, right?" she glared, hostile instantly.

I took my time thinking up a response, all too aware that I could blow everything by giving the wrong one. Finally I landed on something that sounded good enough, if a bit more edged than I'd have liked. I'd tried doing things gently, kindly, but we really could use someone like this woman, and she'd made it abundantly clear that the soft approach wasn't one she'd allow to work. I steeled myself.

"I didn't have any witnesses back beside your hiding place," I noted slowly. Even saying that much brought back the memory of her fear, but I kept myself steady against it.

Elizabeth seemed more affected by the reminder than me, which was fucking fair enough, but that also meant that it sank in deep and did a good job of knocking her second-guessing and worries aside. I watched as the thoughts dawned on her and waited for her to consider my offer with a lens that was less . . . paranoid.

"Why would you offer me this?" she asked finally. It was a definite improvement to get questions like that. At least those I could do something with. Those I could answer honestly.

"Because me and my brothers know what it's like to have nothing," I said frankly. "And we know how cold it is out here. Do you want to sleep somewhere warm for a while?"

Her face sort of spasmed for a moment, the way Solitaire's did whenever he was failing to hide a strong emotion, and then Elizabeth turned away from me, nodding.

"Yes," she said quietly. "I'd . . . like that. Thank you."

I didn't say anything, just started walking and let her follow after. Some people weren't comfortable with owing someone, and some people weren't comfortable with expressing their thanks. Elizabeth, I could tell, was both.

God, I needed her to meet Solitaire.

We'd covered a good portion of our journey before I hopped off the carriage, which was lucky for us. Elizabeth's adrenaline rush was starting to run out, and the woman seemed to shiver more intensely with every stride we took toward our destination.

"Where exactly is this mansion of yours?" she asked. We were a few minutes into our walk by then, and if anything I was surprised she'd waited that long. More surprised by our pace. My legs were well over a foot longer than hers, and I had more strength than a powerlifter twice my size, but she was keeping up easily. Even forcing me to push myself in haste. That speed was something we'd have to examine further.

"It's near the city's outskirts," I answered. "Velaharo Manor, I think it's called—"

Her head whipped around so sharply I thought I was about to be stabbed, but the only edge that sank into me was Elizabeth's glare.

"You could've mentioned that sooner," she snapped. "Bloody noble's house. How'd you even manage that? Last I heard, your family was bulk buying horse shit and brawling with magi."

I'd told her who I was, of course, and she'd taken it in stride.

"Truth be told, I barely know myself. My brother just announced . . . it. My other brother will probably be drilling him for more details as we speak. It's not like him to do things unilaterally like that, so he must've had a reason not to consult us."

She frowned.

"So none of you are in charge of the others?"

It took me a moment to realize why she'd even ask that. Redacle's families tended to have a more traditional structure. Primogeniture and all that. Whichever of us was oldest would be expected by most to be the head or something similar.

"No."

Elizabeth considered that, and if I wasn't wrong it seemed to impress the woman. But I didn't get to study her for much longer, as the few miles remaining between us and our destination were eaten up. The two of us were practically jogging before long, and doing so almost as fast as a normal human might sprint. It took about ten minutes to finally reach our destination with all the shortcuts and hasty climbs we threw in.

It took me less than a second to recognize the sights around the gate. Solitaire lying down, shoulder mangled and bleeding, Shango barely standing and staring blearily at some unknown enemy. Argar and Helena were the only ones in armor, moving to encircle the foe, and Corvan was nowhere to be seen.

"Stay here," I breathed, stepping away from Elizabeth and focusing for a moment, feeling the hum of magic as armor encased itself around me once more.

This one's strong, a familiar voice told me. *Stronger than you. Kill it this time. Don't spare it like you did the magus.*

My eyes flickered once more to Solitaire where he lay bleeding, and my heart hardened.

I didn't need telling not to pull any punches.

CHAPTER TWENTY-SIX

Shango's POV: Day 78
Current Wealth: 229 gold, 37 silver, 6 copper

I should've brought my gun. I knew it. It had been the big trade-off. My weapon was stored in my room, on the opposite wing of the mansion to where I'd been when I'd heard of the attack. Making my way to it would've cost extra minutes. Solitaire might've died during those minutes, but I'd have come here with a gun.

No, not might have. Solitaire would've been a corpse had I shown up even thirty seconds late. I'd made the only choice I could in the moment. The one cause for irritation was that I'd let myself get so separated from the weapon in the first place.

The bowman's stance had changed, and I could see why. The iron bar he'd been using before now hovered around him, spinning and flying, looking almost like some boomerang capable of powered flight. It was what had smashed into Solitaire while the two were grappling, and going by what it'd done to his arm, I wouldn't particularly enjoy the sensation of being on the receiving end of it myself.

Just our luck, I supposed, to find a magus on the enemy's side right when ours was fucking nowhere to be seen. My thoughts were interrupted as the bar came shooting for me.

My hands splayed, and the air hardened, thickening into a barrier that sent the iron ricocheting off to one side. Right behind it, though, was the bowman himself, sprinting toward me and shouldering past the remnants of my barricade. I tried to step out of his reach, but his hand snapped out and caught my lapels, halting me just in time for a punch to find my ribs.

I felt something crack, folding over as tears flooded my eyes, and through the pain I barely thought to keep mental track of the iron bar. My barrier came just in time to stop its second impact, but the bowman's knee caught my face while I was busy blocking it.

There was nothing under my feet, and then there was everything under my head. The impact raised me high, turned me halfway around, and left my face to strike the ground on its own. I rolled a few more feet, vision spinning, and barely raised my head in time to see the bowman leaping back from some giant, jagged streak of ice.

Solitaire was up, and active. Hurling projectiles just as he had against Corvan. I could see he was choosing smaller ones, though, perhaps limited by the speed he could make them, and our enemy—the ever-considerate person that he was—didn't take more than a second to adjust.

Iron broke ice, as iron tended to do, then came right for him. Solitaire stayed put, though, holding his focus on it for a second, conjuring a particularly thick wall of ice just an instant before impact. The bar struck it lengthwise, its tip piercing the ice like a chisel, digging in deep and sending a thick crack to almost bisect its structure. I saw the weapon remaining where it was, quivering and vibrating as its wielder fought against the grip imposed around his tool.

Solitaire had conjured more ice around the embedded metal almost as soon as it stuck, holding it still, and his face was pinched now with focus. I wasn't sure why.

Seconds passed, then the bar was free. I saw something flake off it as it erupted out, its shape suddenly less uniform, thinned at parts. It still did a fine job of smashing through Solitaire's new barrier and knocking him flat.

Argar and Helena were beside the bowman instantly, a spear and axe flying in unison, both moved with the strength to kill a troll. He danced back from them, focus shifting to the pair as his bar hurtled over. I rose to my feet, trying to move, cursing as I realized how dizzy and fatigued I still was. I needed moments to recover.

I needed to recover, and I needed to know the plan, too. Solitaire wouldn't have taken a hit if he hadn't had one, so I made myself over to his side.

He'd certainly seen better days, and today I doubted he could see at all, eyes bleary and unfocused, blood running down his side. I tried to make sure he was coherent, and Solitaire's first words rang out.

"The bourgeoisie," he breathed. "They're using foreskins. Circumcised-baby foreskins. They grind them into paste and eat them, keeps them young. They use them in skin cream. That's why it gets rid of wrinkles. Youthful flesh."

It did not necessarily mean he was less coherent than usual, so I tried a more pointed question.

"What are we doing?" I asked. "How do we stop this guy?"

Solitaire focused at that, meeting my eyes with an intensity.

"Rust," he croaked breathlessly. "On his weapon. I rusted it, oxidized. It's . . . weaker."

I could see by the fog in his eyes that I wouldn't get much more from my friend, so instead I stood back up and forced myself to breathe deep. Nothing felt too broken; nothing felt unworkable. I was more winded than wounded. As far as I could tell, at least. As far as I could hope. I raised my hands and forced myself to focus, even as I watched the two bodyguards readying themselves to attack the bowman.

Evidently, he'd backed off because there were now a good dozen paces separating them. His eyes were affixed on the pair with icy coherence, his bar orbiting him as fast as ever. I took my time readying an attack, then sent it out.

Air was good for speed, for precision, and for motion. It wasn't good for offense, not on its own.

Fortunately, I didn't need it to be. I turned my concentration to the carriage nearby—still just a few meters from me—and felt the atmosphere snag around some of its contents. Wide, semispherical, iron. The cauldron, perfect.

It was a heavy thing, a really fucking heavy thing, and I felt the veins stand up in my body as I hoisted it through the air. My power wasn't much. It could throw a man only slightly better than Argar might have, but it could apply its force for dozens of meters. That meant a lot more room to build up energy. I kept the cauldron flying straight as an arrow, angling it just right to intersect with the bowman's body as he strode toward my bodyguards. Fifty pounds of cast iron flew and flew, accelerating until it was moving fast as a running man, then a galloping horse, and then a baseball pitch.

Ridiculously, I was almost tempted to look away before impact, but I made myself keep watching as the bowman's head whipped around at the last second and his bar shot into the cauldron. The collision sent sparks flying out into the air, and I learned two things very quickly.

The first was that cast iron, apparently, was brittle. The second was that whatever material our enemy's bar was made from, it was far stronger than normal metal ought to have been. The cauldron erupted into multiple fragments, passing harmlessly around the bowman as its energy dissipated uselessly.

But my work was done. He'd been distracted, and Argar and Helena moved in well to take advantage of the fact.

The former was faster, or perhaps more eager, clearing more ground with his loping strides and swinging as if his enemy were some giant tree in need of felling. Helena moved with more reserve, waiting until Argar attacked to circle around and stab from the side, aiming low, going for the bowman's knees and shins, then cursing as he leaped back.

I watched as a punch caught Argar clean across his visored head, sending the big man a step to the side, then saw Helena's spear flash again. The steel parted fabric, and I saw blood flecking its tip as she drew it back. The bowman backed off farther, eyes narrowed, testing.

Our fight wasn't going well. Argar and Helena were beyond the capabilities of any normal humans, and well equipped, but I saw the man's bar rising back up behind them. The barrier I conjured at their backs wouldn't hold long, and once it fell they'd be outmatched. I was already planning a retreat when the light caught my eye.

Beam knew how to make an entrance; nobody could ever take that much from him. He came in like a rocket, tearing across the pavement and just flying straight for the bowman.

Instantly, the iron bar had its new priority, and I watched as it shot straight for my friend. Anyone else might've been in a bind, but Beam only jumped, letting the metal crunch hard against his breastplate, splitting the ethereal material making it up and still jutting out even as he soared close to ten meters and landed within arm's reach of our enemy. Beam swung his conjured weapon, a dagger—odd choice—and I watched as the bowman leaned back.

Only then did I realize what my friend had done because the blade lengthened as fast as a blink, becoming a cleaving saber and biting deep into the enemy's side. He stumbled away, ichor drizzling from his flank as his face twisted with pain, and I acted fast.

The fragments of cauldron were too far for me to grab with my air, but the iron bar wasn't. I ripped it out of Beam's armor and launched it across the space between him and our foe, watching as the rusted metal crunched hard into his nose. More blood spurted free, but he was quick in grabbing it, then twisting his weapon around at Beam. My friend blocked, sliding back entire feet as his balance struggled against the combination of our enemy's strength and magic.

My air was too slow to do anything more as the bowman stepped forward again, bar dropping down for Beam's head. And snapping as his ethereal weapon rose to meet it again.

For a moment, nothing happened. Everyone was too stunned, too surprised. Then everything exploded with motion at once. Argar's axe carved, Helena's spear skewered, and Beam's sword sliced. A triangle of crimson appeared on our enemy even as he turned to flee, ruined weapon spinning around behind him like a shuriken, keeping us at bay for precious moments.

I watched him disappear into the streets, dropping down to my knees and panting.

CHAPTER TWENTY-SEVEN

Shango's POV: Day 78
Current Wealth: 229 gold, 37 silver, 6 copper

Corvan did return, eventually, and when he did the old bastard looked quite surprised by what had happened. That was more or less what decided me on not waterboarding him for answers. It was hard to fake a reaction as sincere and authentic as his had seemed to be.

We were all huddled inside the mansion, having retreated to one of its numerous living rooms with Solitaire. All his gear was stored there, as was his body. He'd lost consciousness as soon as the fight was over, apparently having held himself awake purely to ensure the enemy was seen away, and Corvan got to work on him quickly. All of us stood back and watched the magus do his thing, nerves frayed at the sight.

Despite bearing witness to the exact process more than once, I still managed to hold a grain of fear for it. Certain something would go wrong, cripplingly wrong, that Solitaire would be hurt beyond repair, or that we'd have spent too much time waiting before he was healed. There was a snag, as it happened. Corvan winced.

"Magic," he grunted. "This was done with magic, someone else's."

I went cold. It was harder to heal an injury left with magic in Redacle, one of the ways we balanced healers, but Corvan persevered. He was finished soon enough, and Solitaire's breathing became heavier and more consistent.

"When will he wake up?" I asked, surprising myself with how dry my throat was. The nerves. I kept expecting to be over them, somehow, kept hoping I'd one day have moved past fear, worry, panic. Kept proving myself wrong. It seemed I'd never be too powerful for fear. Not while I was weak enough to be threatened.

"I should've been there," Beam breathed, and I glanced over to see his knuckles squeezed white against the seat of a chair. His face was tighter still.

"I should've been holding a gun," I replied. "Solitaire should've been in armor. Corvan should've been fucking with us"—I glared at the magus as I said that, then continued—"and in all, we should be stronger than we are already."

I took a moment, eyed Beam.

[Appraisal]
Class: Dragonknight
Level: 13
Condition: Fine
Modifiers: +3 Strength, +4 Speed, +3 Toughness, +4 Alertness
Statistics: Strength 12, Speed 12, Dexterity 8, Stamina 9, Toughness 11, Alertness 12, Charisma 6, Intelligence 5
Inventory: Local wear
Class Abilities: Beloved II
Current Experience Points: 86/460
Unspent Skillpoints: 0

Beam's powers were just as they'd been for days now. We hadn't grown stronger at all since our attack on the orc fortress. We'd gotten lazy, let ourselves stagnate, focused on money instead of the ultimate currency. The ability to kill a fucker before he killed us.

"We were sloppy," I finished, realizing even as I said it how similar I sounded to Solitaire.

A chair creaked, Argar's chair. They often did that when he sat in them. Most furniture was simply not built with two hundred kilograms of ginger in mind. I turned my gaze to him to find the man looking, surprisingly, rather put out himself.

It was then that the idea struck me.

"That tournament—it hasn't happened yet, right?"

Argar's eyes lit up quickly, and he shook his head. I nodded, beginning to pace as I thought.

Winning that, progressing through it, would mean contests and fights. Difficult ones, against powerful enemies. The exact sort of thing that we tended to gain experience from, if our observations were correct. It seemed our most promising prospect.

"I say we enter," I said at last. "For a few reasons, the major one being it's a good way to make money fast, which we'll need to do to make a dent in the debts."

Beam frowned.

"Debts?"

I resisted the urge to swear as I looked back at him.

"Yes, debts. We . . . uh, inherited a few with the marriage."

It had been my big conundrum, whether to consult Solitaire and Beam before signing Phelia's contract or not. Ultimately I'd decided against it purely because I was aware a certain fucking noble and the Dead Edge had us in their sights. Evidently, given how quick the attack came, I'd been right to. We'd probably all be dead before a second meeting if I hadn't agreed to Phelia's terms in the first.

I was fully prepared to tell Beam as much, but he didn't seem in the mood to even discuss it. That, I supposed, I couldn't really blame him for. I took my leave from the room soon after that, finding myself suddenly cramped inside it. Being close to Solitaire's slumbering form made it hard to think, and I had something else to attend to, as well.

We'd found Phelia inside her mansion, after the altercation. Sitting in a living room, drinking. Drinking a lot. She'd already emptied half a bottle of wine by the time I stumbled into her room, and as I headed back for it I expected to see a lot more lying empty around her. But I didn't. As I stepped inside for the second time, I found her reading, sitting upright and forcing some veneer of calm.

She still trembled, fidgeted, moved in all the ways I'd learned people did when adrenaline was filling them with lightning. But her composure had hardened rather than softened in the hour since I'd seen her, and it didn't look like she'd touched another drop of booze. Once more, I let myself appreciate the woman for a moment.

Then she noticed me, looking up questioningly.

"Husband?"

It felt strange to be called that, so strange that I took a moment mulling the word over before I let it properly register. Fuck.

Then I stepped over it and answered her.

"How are you doing, after the incident?"

I'd expected some uncertainty, residual fear, trauma. What I hadn't been anticipating, though, was the immediate incendiary anger.

"The incident," she spat. "That's what we're calling it, I suppose, when your brother uses his family members as shields?"

Her words gave me a moment's pause, and I used it to chew on them. Solitaire, obviously. I hadn't heard about that particular misdeed of his, though.

"He . . . Why did he do that?"

"Because he's mad?" she snapped. "I really couldn't say. He's *your* brother."

I considered my next words very carefully and decided that this was not the subject I wanted to have a screaming match about. Not at a time like this, in any case.

"We can discuss this once I've heard more specifics about the attack," I replied coolly. "Until then . . . How are you feeling?"

Phelia was far from happy, but no secondary rage came. I considered that a victory.

"Scared, obviously," she replied stiffly, and I saw a sudden flutter of shame in her eyes. "I almost died. I was helpless to save myself. I . . . I found that the limits of cleverness are exposed against the power of violence."

It was so poetic, I almost didn't catch her trembling as she said it.

"You've never been in a . . . situation like that before," I noted. There was no guesswork involved, no speculation. I simply saw and knew, with no more conscious deliberation than was used to see two fingers held up and label them a pair. She nodded, her usual bullwhip humor absent. Devoid of her sarcasm, I found her somehow smaller in my sights.

"I hadn't, either, until recently," I told her, and found myself almost surprised to realize it was the truth. "You're probably trying to process things, to make sense of it all. You're probably not certain whether all the things you've spent a lifetime learning still apply. You've seen a new set of rules, and you're trying to figure out how to unsee them."

She met my eyes, held my gaze. Then nodded. I sighed.

"Well, I don't think there's an easy way to help you do all of that. All I can say is that you'll figure it out eventually. I did."

"And what did you figure out?" she asked me suddenly. The intensity in her stare told me that this was more than just some petty challenge. She *needed* to know. Desperately. More than that, even, she was terrified of not knowing. It made me feel all the guiltier.

"I figured out that everything I'd learned still applied, most of the time. But your life will be as violent as the most violent people in it, and gathering attention will guarantee that that'll be a very violent kind." I paused, surprised by my own words even as they left my lips. Somehow, though, it all made sense. It all felt right. "I learned that peace isn't something you choose for yourself. It's something you force onto others."

Phelia didn't say anything. She just stared at me. The silence between us only lasted a few moments before interruption. The door flung open, and I turned to see Helena standing and panting in its frame.

"Solitaire," she breathed. "He's awake!"

CHAPTER TWENTY-EIGHT

I had to apologize to Argar shortly after waking up, even though his being thumbed in the eye was mostly his own fault. I mean, I'd been asleep, unconscious, even! Not an hour removed from a death match! Holding his face that close to me had just been asking for trouble. It hadn't even been on purpose, either. My arm had just done that.

Still, I said I was sorry, on account of what a kind, generous soul I was. And the fact that I didn't want to be used as a drumstick by the biggest ginger I'd ever met.

"It's fine," he grunted, still blinking and rubbing his watering eye as he said it. Evidently I'd closed the physical gap a bit since our last fight. It was almost satisfying to see confirmation, though I was a bit preoccupied to dwell on it.

"Did we win?" I asked, memories of the fight swimming back before my eyes. Argar nodded.

"You're still alive, aren't you? Course we won."

"I mean, did they manage to destroy any of our equipment?"

He hesitated at that.

"A few bits and pieces, but not much. We fought them off well enough."

A few bits and pieces. My blood boiled even at that much. *Those stupid fucking rats.*

"Thanks for your help," I told him, realizing that it needed saying. One did not live long with bodyguards whom one failed to make friends with. History had taught me that. Argar, though, didn't look particularly happy.

"Should've done more," he said, face dark. "We were next to useless."

I considered replying, but hesitated. Argar didn't look it, didn't seem it most times, but he *was* smart. Always thinking behind those beady eyes, slow, steady, but deliberate. He wasn't the sort to eat up my typical bullshit.

"You did as much as you were capable of," I replied, watching his face as I said it. "Kept enemies tied up, fought well enough. I don't think anyone can blame you for not winning the entire fight for us."

"I wasn't the one who ended up almost dying," he scowled.

"Yeah, well, you were last time." I sat up with a grunt and climbed off my . . . couch. I was lying on a couch, apparently, and that realization led to more. I studied the room around me, the size, the pomp, and realized it was probably what the Velaharo Manor looked like on the inside. Ugh, I could *smell* the aristocracy. It had the scent of stolen relics, dead poor people, and uncommonly numerous chromosomes.

Argar looked for a moment like he'd say something more, but the opening door distracted both of us. I turned just as Shango stepped through it, his face plastered with worry, eyes wide.

"You're okay?" he asked instantly. I forced a grin, knowing how much it would soothe him.

"Of course. They build us Liverpool boys different from the rest of you. How do you think we survived the seventies?"

Shango didn't answer at all. He just hugged me. Well, he tried to, I assumed. It was more of a deduction really, given that he didn't manage to complete the motion. I saw him quickly stepping in with arms raised, and all the old reflexes just took over. It was all I could do to shove his face back and send him stumbling rather than thumbing an eye out.

He glared at me, and I felt that old feeling. The stab of guilt, going in deep and twisting wide. I didn't meet his eyes.

"Sorry," I said pathetically. Shango remained silent, and after a few moments I was forced to look up by the sheer weight of awkwardness closing in around us.

There was a new look to him then, and I took a second to digest it. Shango smelled of fury, all of it directed my way . . . but too strong to just stem from my shoving him.

"You used my wife as a human shield," he growled, answering the newfound mystery in one quick breath. I took a second to let his words sink in.

Really? *That?* He was annoyed by *that?* It was too ridiculous for words, but pointing that out would hardly mollify him.

"It was a heat-of-the-moment thing," I said coolly. "I realized why the bastards were there, what they intended to do, and I figured they'd be hesitant to kill her compared to me. I was right. If I hadn't kept myself hidden behind her I'd have gotten a crossbow bolt put through me long before you showed up. I'd probably be dead now."

"And so you decided to risk her to save your own skin?"

Yes, I had. Obviously.

I was the cleverest human who'd ever lived, carrying the knowledge and ethics required to save this entire steaming shit pile of a world. She was one of the tapeworms living in her society's gut. The choice between which of us needed to die, if it came to that, was clear.

Shango wasn't behaving like a man who'd accept that sort of retort, though, so I tailored my words a bit more strategically.

"We were both already in danger," I replied calmly. "As far as I could tell, she was in much less than me, which meant that the only way it could have been right to *not* shield myself with her is if you somehow think my life is simply worth less."

He was not, in fact, mollified. Rather, Shango got that look in his eye that only ever came when he thought I was being stupid.

"This isn't just a numbers game, you fucking reptile. You don't just shield yourself with someone on our side. In our family, even. You should've tried to get *both* of you to safety."

I considered explaining the particulars of how difficult it would have been to get myself, let alone myself and Velaharo, behind cover in the time we'd had. I considered, further, testing Shango to see just how much he valued this woman he'd known for less than a week. But I stopped myself.

"I'm not going to pretend to care about some fucking aristocrat," I told Shango, meeting his eye. "Not in the slightest. I hate her. I hate everything she stands for, even more than I hate the other monkeys inhabiting this world."

I gave him a moment, letting it sink in. Only a moment though. Shango was brilliantly quick. Less than a decisecond passed before understanding exploded across his face. I spoke up again just before he could let it give voice to an argument.

"But I realize that you, clearly, feel differently," I finished. "And I didn't before. I'm sorry for that."

Clearly the apology took him by surprise, which probably should've made me introspect about what sort of person I was, but instead just made me pleased to know that the sheer novelty of it would add weight to my feigned concession.

It did.

"That's . . . big of you to say," he noted with the tone of a man being forced to say something he didn't want to. Well, that was Shango all over. Always forcing himself, instincts nice and chained up like a loyal hound. God, I was jealous of that sometimes. The sheer mastery he had over himself. If I had his mental stability—or if he had my raw mental prowess—the result would be . . . terrifying.

"I should hope so," I replied. "I think one of my nuts just ruptured in the process."

I didn't smile, despite the joke, and I could see the balance of levity was well picked. Shango relaxed a hair, then spoke again.

"Solitaire, I don't like that you're only apologizing because *I* care about her."

I met his eyes.

"And I don't like that I'm apologizing at all."

Shango held my gaze for a second, a dozen separate thoughts being born, reared, then put down behind those brown irises within the span of his consideration. Then he sighed.

"Just don't try to fucking kill my wife again."

It was then, finally, that I flashed him a grin.

"Of course I won't. What do you take me for?" Shango didn't grin back, so I moved on quickly. "Now then, who the fuck tried to kill me, and how stretchable is their urethra?"

CHAPTER TWENTY-NINE

Beam's POV: Day 80
Current Wealth: 279 gold, 31 silver, 16 copper

We found out quite soon after the attack that it wasn't just the outside of Velaharo Manor our enemies had struck. Ardin's shop had been hit, too.

Fortunately the blacksmith was alive, not being present during the time of the vandalism, but when he made his way to the mansion and told us, I could see the guy was shaken. A stab of guilt hit me as I saw his trembling features and heard him go over the state of his place, a livelihood smashed to bits all in one go.

"I don't know what I can do," he croaked. "I'm . . . I was that shop. That was my life, my work. Without it I . . ."

I cut in while he was still mid-panic, desperate to make things right.

"You can work here," I told him, drawing an astonished look from the man. "Velaharo Manor has a smithy of their own. Not quite as big as yours, but we can expand it as we go, and it's a hell of a lot safer behind the walls of a noble's courtyard. Work from here."

Ardin looked relieved, but only a bit.

"What will the rent be?" he asked tentatively. I waved a hand.

"No, forget about that. You don't pay any rent. It's all on the house. Just keep doing your thing, alright?"

There was some admiring, borderline venerating look in his eyes as he heard that that I turned away from, never quite enjoying such things as much as either of my friends. Once that conversation was done, though, things began moving on. We had a lot to do.

Solitaire and Shango had become obsessed with the tournament, and I couldn't exactly blame them. I'd heard the reasoning, and agreed wholeheartedly that we needed more power, and soon. Even if it came at the cost of tipping our hand on how quickly we could grow stronger through leveling up.

Their disagreement came from a different matter, that of our attackers.

"Dead Edge," Solitaire repeated soon after waking. "And Lord Byror. Those are the cunts after us?"

Shango nodded cautiously.

"They are," he confirmed. "And you can't go running around for revenge just yet."

Solitaire paused, eying him as if he'd just drooled on himself. "They tried to kill me."

"They did," Shango agreed. "And they will try again, even harder, if you run over picking a fight with them."

"I don't want to pick a fight with them." Solitaire sighed. "I want to find out who their leaders are, find out where they live, crawl in through their windows, and do them while they're asleep. Nice and easy."

"Which the rest of them will, of course, interpret as a completely reasonable and nonaggressive deed that certainly won't escalate things and will *definitely* not bring any heightened level of retaliatory violence our way." Shango sighed, looking suddenly exhausted. Solitaire hardly looked better. I could still remember my own magical treatment, the sensation of being hollowed out it left me with. Clearly that mental fatigue was lasting a while longer for him than me. Perhaps my years of exhaustive training had left me used to such things. Perhaps Solitaire was just a bitch.

"The tournament then," Solitaire sighed, at last, clearly reluctant to make his concession, but making it anyway. Shango seemed relieved as he nodded.

"The tournament. It starts in a few days, which gives us plenty of time to prepare, if we work hard enough that is."

We *did* work hard enough, or at least I had to hope we did, seeing it was Ardin and me who did almost everything. The two of us hadn't taken long to get set up in the Velaharos' smithy, and barely longer to adjust to the downgrade in workstation from the smith's own shop. If nothing else it was a good excuse to practice some new techniques and give Corvan a hard time as he was forced to help us out with his magic.

It wasn't that we *blamed him* for being absent during the attack, more that we felt it was unfair he alone hadn't lost anything in it. Ardin's shop had been destroyed, Solitaire had gotten the crap kicked out of him, Argar and Helena fought for their lives, and Shango was stuck sharing a bed with the angriest woman currently alive.

Anyway, Corvan proved as helpful this time as he'd been before, and we made quick progress in mixing the metals and elements. Before long we had a few sheets readied, thick plates of our experimental steel cooled and worked, prepped for use. Solitaire had them propped up alongside normal steel, and called on Argar for help in testing them.

"You want me to hit it," he echoed, trying, and failing, not to seem pleased. Helena watched it all from one corner, trying, and failing, not to seem curious.

"As hard as you can," I told Argar. "The plate on the left first, then the one on the right. And use that." I nodded to the huge work hammer we'd leaned against the far wall, its iron head bigger than even Argar's gargantuan fists. The thing weighed twenty pounds, apparently, which made it heavy enough that most Redaclans were too small and weak to even wield it.

I had a feeling that Argar wouldn't find himself so limited, though.

"Must be my birthday." He grinned, striding across the room and snatching the tool up into one giant hand with a single motion. It barely seemed to weigh anything in his hands, and Argar showed no real strain in raising it up to rest across one shoulder.

"Better stand back," the giant grunted. We did.

His first swing was like a hybrid between a landslide and an anti-tank weapon, his mountainous muscles driving the metal head so violently against its target that I saw sparks explode out upon impact and drift down to the ground below. The point of contact wore a clear mark of his strength.

"Not bad!" I grinned, studying it. The steel was blemished with a big, broad dent. Easily a few inches at its widest, and buckled inward deep enough that I thought it might well have driven ribs organ deep, had it been equipped over a human torso as armor. Argar hefted the hammer in satisfaction, shrugging.

"Would've done less if it'd been on a person, moving back on impact," he said, as if that made smashing steel almost in half any less impressive.

"Not bad," Ardin echoed, looking far from pleased. It was, after all, his own steel we'd just watched a crater get planted in, and like so many good craftsmen he had more than a touch of his own ego wrapped into the fruits of his labors. "Now what can you do to the new metal?"

Argar grinned again, and the hammer was moving in an instant.

There were no sparks the second time. And that was the first thing I noticed. The second was how the sound didn't contain any screech or grind of metal, only a sharp rattle. Argar cursed, taking a step back, reeling with the hammer as it bounced from his target. I studied the point of impact with a grin quickly spreading across my features.

It had dented, just like the first sheet of metal, and it had dented noticeably. But there wasn't anything that could be called a crater. The metal had deformed perhaps one or two inches across, and was shallow enough at its deepest that I suspected my fingertip was thicker.

"Stronger," Ardin noted, gifting the room with a rare smile as he said it. "Much, much stronger."

I just kept staring at the spot where the impact had occurred, grinning. It hadn't been an anti-armor weapon, of course, and I had no doubt that Argar would've done a hell of a lot more if he'd hit the stuff with a proper polearm, anything with a nice big spike to concentrate all the force behind really, but even so the difference in effect was proof of . . . something.

"We need to make more then," I breathed, looking around the room. I got nothing but nods.

"We need to make more," Ardin concurred.

CHAPTER THIRTY

Shango's POV: Day 80
Current Wealth: 279 gold, 31 silver, 16 copper

W hat in the world is a protofascist?"

It was the first sentence I heard entering the library, and I heard it in Phelia's voice. Her aristocratic accent practically colonized every syllable as it left her lips, marching them toward Solitaire's ears like poor people into German machine guns. Solitaire looked about as pleased as I might have expected.

"Sorry," he replied, sounding about as sorry as he ever did. "I forgot you were a mud person. A protofascist is what we civilized humans call you aristocrats, nobles, authoritarians. The people who, in a few centuries, will lay out the framework necessary for a generation of mindless egotists to become rich by torturing children and polluting the air."

Her eyes narrowed, but Solitaire was far from finished.

"You know, the funny thing is, you and I are actually quite alike. Or your ancestors and I, at least."

Phelia scoffed.

"I highly doubt that."

"No, no." Solitaire grinned. "It's true, really. I'm a violent, selfish megalomaniac, just like all the idiot warlords who made themselves the first aristocrats by killing everyone that argued. If I'd arrived here a few centuries ago, it'd probably be my descendant sitting on the throne right now."

"What's this about?" I asked before Phelia could say something Pheliaish and run the risk of causing my brother to *do* something Solitairish. "The two of you are arguing. What about?"

"Your brother wants to turn my house into a death trap," my wife—fuck, I had a wife—replied instantly, glaring at Solitaire as she said it. Solitaire for his part just shrugged, seeming entirely unbothered.

"A death trap for anyone who tries to sneak in and kill us, yeah. There's a lot of ground to cover, but I reckon we can set up plenty of traps."

I took a second to process that, and then I replied. Very, very delicately. Solitaire was not exactly a patient man, but somehow, remarkably, when the topic moved on to curtailing his paranoia . . . he became even less so. It had taken me almost a week of reasoning, screaming, begging, and threatening to finally make him agree not to booby-trap our shared house back on Earth. Now that people who existed outside of his neurotic fucking head were trying to kill us, I wasn't sure even I'd be capable of persuading him otherwise.

"Solitaire, I understand—" I began.

"Don't tell me you understand what it's like to constantly think everyone wants to murder you," he cut in sharply, glaring. "Don't."

I paused, swallowed my irritation, nodded. He had a point.

"I can *appreciate* what you're thinking, and that our current situation is somewhat different from the ones we've had these conversations in before—"

"He's tried to do this before knowing a huge gang was after him?" Phelia asked aghast. I sensed there would be no positive outcome of discussing that with her, so I tactically ignored it.

"But you really need to try to rein in your . . . instincts."

Solitaire took an uncharacteristic moment before replying to me, then did so. In the same way artillery batteries tended to reply to things.

"It is not fucking instinct, Shango, to take precautions for when people attempt to kill you. Pre. Cautions. Acting to stop something before it begins, utilizing knowledge and intellectual reasoning. That's about as instinctive as physics."

A migraine was starting to prick at my brain. It really was fascinating, sometimes, how Solitaire's mind worked. Or, in this case, how it didn't work. If he'd been anyone else, not racked by his ridiculous suspicion and borderline schizophrenic delusion, he might've changed the world.

He would change this world, regardless. In this world, an average earthling was an adult among children. A genius? That was something else entirely. Something barely even human. And now I was watching one's own mind threaten to tear him apart. I steeled myself and thought back to all those times I'd been panicking here and had Solitaire there to help talk me through my worries. He was a rational man, a brilliant man. He understood, eventually, when his mind was mangling his thoughts. I just needed to make him understand sooner rather than later.

"What could you be doing instead of this to keep us safe?" I asked. "How could you be advancing our influence, our technology, if you dedicated your time to that rather than bombing the house?"

Solitaire shot back instantly. Most times I found his cognitive nimbleness refreshing. Today it was just exhausting. Arguments were far easier when I had an ice age between each of my opponent's thoughts.

"Not a lot," he replied confidently. "This is something I can do in my spare time. We've not been selling as much black powder recently, either, so I'd just be using spare materials for a lot of the traps. It'd also give me the chance to map the house out and get a good list of rooms and their potential uses, as well as study it for anything else we might turn to our advantage."

Phelia piped up before I could. Rare, that. Finding a person who could beat me to a sentence. Rare, and a bit exciting.

"You are not salvaging my fucking house," she growled. Solitaire looked like he was on the verge of growling back, so I cut in.

"Alright," I said. "Tell you what, Solitaire, you head to the stadium and begin the tournament preparations. Sign us up, as many as you can manage. I'll discuss this with Phelia and see if we can . . . come to an arrangement."

Both of them glared at me, clearly not happy, and Solitaire stormed out angrily enough to make me wonder why I even bothered with the fucking compromise in the first place. Phelia spoke when he was gone.

"A lot of families have people like your brother," she noted, eyeing me sidelong. "Mad dogs. Best to get rid of them early, before—"

"Talk to me about getting rid of my brother again and you'll fucking regret it," I said coldly. So coldly I almost surprised myself. She froze at the response, paused, then nodded slowly. Deferentially.

"Of course, husband, I apologize," Phelia said. Her voice was a little quieter, but her words were sincere, as far as I could tell. There wasn't a hint of resentment, and that made me feel worse.

"I shouldn't speak to you like that. I'm sorry." I sighed, turning around so I didn't have to see the expression she was wearing. Phelia's voice made it vivid enough in my head, regardless.

"I am your wife. I shouldn't have spoken to you so . . . defiantly. I apologize."

It was surreal to hear. Most modern women would be dripping with sarcasm as they said such a thing, but Phelia wasn't modern. Her tone was entirely sincere, and it actually sent a chill down my spine to realize it. I cleared my throat, suddenly awkward and . . . sobered.

"Was there anything else?" I asked, more to move the conversation along than anything, but as I turned, I saw Phelia with a considering look across her features.

"There is one thing," she replied delicately. "I . . . haven't brought it up yet, as I assumed you would be the first to, but . . . there is the matter of children."

I forced my mix of surprise, horror, and reluctance not to show all at once. Keeping myself calm, leaving my face paralyzed into stoicism through a carefully measured application of will. It helped that Phelia's request wasn't exactly unexpected. I'd gone into our marriage fully aware what Redaclan women were like, and more particularly what society expected of them. Particularly the nobles. Raised to essentially be a breeding machine, it was no surprise she was asking what she was.

"I'd rather not have any just yet," I said, deciding to buy time rather than deny her outright. Now of all points, it wouldn't be ideal to give her any cause to turn against us. But Phelia was, of course, fucking smart, and I didn't see her buying the deflection.

"I've waited days," she replied. "I've been patient, but we've yet to even consummate our marriage, and we have duties, you understand. I'm not certain what you know of the proper way of things given your station, but we've already delayed more than is normal, and far more than is necessary. It's a compromise on my part already that we're only talking about this now."

Fuck, I needed more time. I needed time to think, to misdirect, to reroute her. Was it a coincidence she'd broached the topic while I was so distracted? I found it hard to believe so. But that could work against her, too.

"There's so much going on at the moment," I replied. "Can we not talk about this sometime more convenient? After we've dealt with the Dead Edge?"

"That could be weeks," she replied testily. "Months."

I eyed her, and Phelia sighed.

"I'll wait another week. After that we're discussing this."

Just fucking perfect.

CHAPTER THIRTY-ONE

Solitaire's POV: Day 80
Current Wealth: 279 gold, 31 silver, 16 copper

I was exposed, out in the open, vulnerable and unguarded. They were all looking at me, staring, plotting. I knew it. I could smell it. Bastards, all of them. Rats and killers, little rotting pieces of shit with brains and teeth and knives and hatred. I wanted to kill all of them. I wanted to build some nice, big fucking bomb, set it off, and finally get myself some peace. Watch the skin boil off them, the bones smash into dust, the air finally fall still and *quiet*. Just me, on my own, nothing to worry about, nobody to watch my back around. An endless party where the only one invited is the only person I knew wouldn't try to do me.

Except I wasn't the only person I knew that about. There was also Shango and Beam. I sighed. One day I'd be able to go through with killing everybody. One day.

Seen without the veil of neurosis I'd been wrapped in since setting foot outside the Velaharo Manor, the outside wasn't all *that* scary. Within reason. It helped of course that I had two notable figures with me, one towering, plate-clad Helena, of course, but more importantly Corvan. The magus had been rather grumpy to get dragged out and forced to bodyguard me while I moved toward the arena, but I considered that more of a bonus than anything.

"You're being paranoid," he whined nasally. "They won't send another attack so quickly. They'll still be reeling from the first failure."

"I'm being cautious," I replied, deciding to keep it to myself, for now, that attempting to convince a person they were paranoid is just how a double agent would go about orchestrating their death. It seemed awfully convenient to me that Corvan had been absent during the attack. Literally awfully. It was fucking awful how convenient it was. Practically left me gibbering with worry and expecting the bastard to jump out from behind every corner trying to fireball me.

The timing, though, just didn't line up. Corvan hadn't been out of our sight in any real capacity since we beat the shit out of and recruited him like a Pokémon. He'd have had no chance to organize any sort of betrayal after that. If he was working with the Dead Edge and that Lord Byror, he'd have been working with them already when he came for us himself. And if that had been the case, he'd have come with help. Corvan and the crossbowman alone, I thought, would've had better than even odds of killing all of us the other day. Not a chance they'd failed to cooperate given how much of a reputation for killing ability we'd built.

"You alright, sir?" Helena asked, snapping me out of my thoughts and whipping my head around to her with the question.

"Of course," I replied. "Why?"

Behind her metal visor, I couldn't see any trace of facial expression, and the reverberations of words through steel distorted her tone a shade. Even so, I could sense the sardonicism in her answer.

"Because you had that look on again. The one you had when you set off that trap in Rinchester, and we all had to pretend not to notice your cock pressing against your clothes."

Silly me. I must've forgotten to keep my face guarded. That'd teach me for not being properly diligent when thinking about *them*.

Our walk was long, which served well to prolong my itching anticipation of violence and raise Corvan's whining to a new height as the magus began to complain about aching knees and a poor back. I ignored both as best I could, just concentrating on the act of putting one foot ahead of the other, right up until I came to the arena.

It was a big thing, as one might have expected. But only relative to the other structures of this world. Ten of it might've fit inside an Olympic stadium back at home, and though the architecture was made of far more stone and metal than was normal, it didn't reach all that high into the air. Ten stories, maybe as few as eight.

"Huge," Helena noted, as if we might've missed the fact. Corvan seemed less impressed, but not by as much as I would've hoped.

"Magic," he grunted, nodding toward it. "Built with magic, I'd bet. Probably tempered the supports with it."

It was a funny thing to be so sure of. Back home, we wouldn't have blinked twice at a building that size, even one three or four times it. But back home we'd had innovations like . . .

Rebar. Just bits of steel, run through stone. Instant multiplier of its strength and supportive power, and about as simple as anything. That'd be worth mentioning later.

"Come on," I grunted. "I'd rather leave the window for murdering us as small as can be managed, eh?"

Corvan and Helena didn't say a word, which was annoying. I was suddenly nervous, suddenly feeling exposed and open all over again, as if a great big eye were perched atop the stadium and glaring down at me. I could've used something to distract me from the sensation of my neurons eating one another.

We got inside fast, recognized before we were even at the door and ushered past it by some poor sod who looked worried I'd gut him for taking too long. Made me wonder about the sort of people who typically signed up for this event, until I remembered it was people who'd gained a lot of experience hitting one another with bits of sharp metal.

Inside the place was musky, dank. It smelled of sweat not yet broken and blood still waiting to be spilled, almost exciting. We made our way through to the main desk, where a tiny bespectacled man sat. I'd not have made anything of his glasses, usually, but they were a rare thing in this world. Not many could afford them in Redacle, even with magic to help the shaping of glass into focal lenses. Which meant he was probably high in the event's pecking order.

"Names of applicants," he said lazily. "Heights, weights, chosen events."

I told him, signing up myself, Beam, Argar, Helena, and Shango to fight in the melees. There was another event, too, some sort of magic-dueling-type deal, but Corvan vehemently refused to be added into it.

"Only a fool lets the world see what he can do in a fight," he spat. "If you'd known what I was capable of, that weapon of yours would've killed me in my sleep."

He had a point there, I had to admit. Information was a weapon like no other. Reluctantly, I opted not to record his name. We continued the business until a new detail came up, one that gave me pause.

"You are aware, sir, that you bear sole responsibility over the injuries gained during this contest, and must have them healed out of your own pocket?"

I had not been, and it fucking changed things. If I wanted to attack someone under the protection of a noble, what would I do? Well, that depended very much on the circumstances. If one of those circumstances was an event where crippling them was as easy as signing up to swing a sword at them.

It was live combat, real weapons, and automatic loss by forfeiture. If ever there was a time . . .

But we needed the experience, we needed the power. I had to pick between vulnerability now and vulnerability later.

No, I decided, I didn't. If I didn't sign up now, Shango or someone else would anyway. Reluctantly, I steeled myself.

"We understand," I replied.

CHAPTER THIRTY-TWO

Solitaire came home when it was still light, and his and Phelia's bickering followed me through the house. I felt it grinding against my every nerve, posing the question of how, exactly, they could manage to leave such an absurdly huge mansion feeling so laughably cramped.

The answer was obvious of course; we weren't actually *living* in most of it. At Solitaire's insistence, the upper floors had been all but abandoned, and we'd started to concentrate ourselves in the bedrooms over the ground floor. He'd actually rekindled the screaming match with Phelia by letting her catch him bolting big sheets of metal over the windows.

"Where did you even get the iron?" had been among the barrage of questions first thrown at him, which had been Phelia's first mistake. In assuming it was iron, she'd opened the door for Solitaire to fixate on the fact that it was, in fact, bronze he'd made from tin and copper in the garden soils. All Phelia's futile attempts to discuss anything other than the particular kind of metal being used to reinforce her house had, sadly, failed.

They just kept going at it, for an hour, for two, for almost three. I needed a break, somewhere I knew their bitching couldn't reach me, so I hurried through the house until I came to the forging room.

The one place that had required utmost silence on pain of disturbing men while they handled thousand-degree steel and rooms full of toxic fumes. My sanctuary. Ardin was working away as I entered, Beam helping him, Corvan nowhere to be seen. The magus must've been fresh out, though, because the actual forge itself was hot, special-made furnace glowing cherry red on the exterior as it worked on mixing a new batch of Solitaire's tool steel.

"Alright." I nodded to them. "Mind if I sit in here for a bit?"

Beam looked up from his work of shaping some weird, ethereal tool around Ardin's hammer, grinning.

"They're still ballistic?" he asked. I didn't share in his amusement, a consequence of having been tortured by their going at it for about fifty times longer than was reasonable, and ten times longer than was humane.

"Please don't talk about them." I groaned. "Talk about anything except them. Talk about us almost getting eaten by a bear, just not that bullshit, not now."

Beam grinned his beaming Beam grin, and I knew in an instant that he had no intent of stopping.

"Marriage troubles?" he asked astutely. My glare bounced off him as they usually did.

"I'm married to the most British aristocrat ever born outside of Britain," I told him, resisting the urge to throw a bit of swearing in for good measure. "Yes, Beam, I'm having marriage troubles."

He looked sympathetic at that, humor evaporating, eyes growing serious.

"Would you like to talk about it?" he asked. I considered for a moment, remembered what exactly it was that Phelia had asked me last time we'd been alone together, then found my answer.

"Definitely fucking not."

Beam looked just a shade relieved at that, and to fulfill my end of the social contract I pretended not to notice.

"How's the armor going, then?" I asked, and that brought a spark of excitement across his face.

"Good," Ardin grunted. He didn't look up, just continued to work in that strange, split-focus way he had. He was almost like Solitaire sometimes. "We've been concentrating on getting the measure of the metal before anything, but I reckon I have that down now. Just need to produce and work enough to actually make the stuff."

A flutter of anticipation went off in my gut as I eyed him.

"And how long will that be?" I asked, daring to hope. He glanced at me, after that, with a face that dashed my stupid optimism.

"A week, probably, maybe one or two days less if we really hurry. Sorry, boss."

The tournament started in about half a week, and from what Solitaire had told me the earlier matches—the ones with the most fights, before as many people had been eliminated—would last at most a day going by historical precedent.

I felt my temper fray, but forced the burning coals of my anger to die out before they could even start burning. There were a lot of reasons for why our metalworking wouldn't be done before the start. The Dead Edge's attack had cost us probably a day, just off the top of my head, but it wasn't something I could fully blame on anything except simple circumstance. The question now was how to work around it.

"Concentrate on a suit for Helena first," I instructed, earning a few surprised stares from the pair. "She's smaller than Argar, and her name comes up after his and Beam's. She'll be the quickest to finish a set of armor for and has the best odds of it being ready for her first fight."

If any of us were injured in the tournament, it would be horribly costly to restore our wounds. Corvan couldn't keep pushing himself to heal everything after all, and if those wounds were extensive enough, they might exceed the limit of our wealth. Best to ensure we were going in with maximized protection from the start.

Beam and Ardin continued working away while I watched, and I found myself eyeing the whole process. It was oddly satisfying to see. The hot metal deforming, bits of glowing shrapnel breaking off and hissing away, great big cracks dispersing across its face before it all flaked off like some snake shedding its skin. I could tell in an instant that they'd practiced long and hard, and after a few minutes they invited me to ask. Clearly, they were proud of the techniques, Beam especially, and I was curious. Might as well give all of us what we wanted.

Apparently, the biggest obstacle in actually working the metal had been the same thing we'd been looking for in doing so. Its strength. Even heated, even to the point of almost melting, it retained enough physical resilience that all Ardin's and Beam's not-inconsiderable physical prowess was needed just to meaningfully shift it. This led to a process of turn taking, painstaking repetition and patience, constantly cooling and reheating it over and over again until their tiny little deformations and changes in working it had added up.

It was, I gathered, easier with Corvan there, as his magic could add some additional pressure, but they could still manage between the two of them. Once finished, the metal had a strange luster to it that normal steel didn't, almost whitish in its finish, and they gave me a nice long demonstration of the more practical differences.

"We finished this yesterday, as the final stage of our weapon-testing process," Beam explained, holding a blade out to me. There was no handle, no guard, but he'd wrapped its base in enough leather that I didn't worry about hurting myself as I seized it. Surprisingly light. Heavy, of course. All swords were—I'd learned that quite fucking quickly—but given its size . . . light. More in line with what you might expect watching movies than the two-pound pieces of iron we'd grown accustomed to seeing swung around.

I swung it, and watched as it came down hard into a wooden post I could only *hope* had been prepared for such a test. The edge bit in, easily, and soon enough I was struggling to pull the thing out from where it'd gotten more than a few inches stuck in. Beam laughed.

"And that's just for a start," he declared. "You're going to go nuts when you see the armor—"

"Metal!" Ardin snapped, dragging Beam's focus back to what was, apparently, a particularly tricky bit. He winced, glanced at me with a hurried good-bye, and got back to work. I knew when I was being bothersome, so I took my leave and headed back out into the mansion. Quiet. It'd quieted down. Good, I was feeling tired. Wearily, I trudged my way back to my quarters, rather looking forward to dumping myself into bed and letting sleep take me.

But there wasn't a peaceful, empty room awaiting me when I walked in. Only an occupied one, with a devastatingly beautiful blonde seated on the bed. Phelia was in what I first took to be some sort of nightwear, but realized after a moment was a bit more . . . exposing. Her face was tranquil, eyes intense, posture upright, and body language open.

"Uh," I said, about as intelligently as I could have managed. She blinked, seemingly in slow motion, and I was suddenly aware of how long her eyelashes were before she spoke.

"Husband," Phelia began. "I think we have some overdue business."

CHAPTER THIRTY-THREE

Shango's POV: Day 80
Current Wealth: 279 gold, 31 silver, 16 copper

Phelia," I said at last, looking her in the eye and not the tits. "What a . . ."

I was going to say "surprise," the fucking moron that I was. I was in my bedroom, which was also her bedroom. Seeing her there was many things, but it was not surprising.

"What a lovely dress you have on," I finished, wincing almost as I said it. Great, genius, mention the lingerie. That'll surely not give her an opening to do whatever the fuck she wore it to help do.

She smiled at the praise, flushing that way white people did when they felt the slightest emotion at all, like cartoons.

"You like it?" she asked. "It was my, uh, mother's."

Her face turned even redder, and I resisted the urge to wince again. So I was being seduced with generational lingerie. Spectacular.

"What are you doing, Phelia?" I asked at last, realizing that turning this into a discussion, a thing of pure questions and answers, was about my best chance of coming out on top. I was a smart guy, but a giant brain only helped you if it had enough blood to work with, and all mine was dangerously close to pumping down the wrong end.

Phelia's head seemed perfectly fucking clear because of course it did, and her eyes narrowed at my question. This, I could tell, was very thin ice I was treading on.

"Excuse me?" she asked, suddenly sounding at least four times as upper-class, five times as British, and six times as angry. A combination to send a chill running down every Nigerian vertebra I had. I pushed through it, though. Unbalancing people was one of the major uses of one's emotions—Solitaire had taught me that much when we were kids—and I'd always been quite inured against such techniques.

"I mean what are you trying to do here, or do you expect me to believe that you were just suddenly overcome with womanly passion and *had* to have ravenous intercourse this very night?"

By the look on her face, she *had* expected me to believe that. It was another reminder that Redacle was a different world than mine, and the men inhabiting it were made from levels of misogyny and horniness that Earth had left behind centuries in its past. *For the most part.*

Phelia looked at me, then she stared, then she glowered. Finally she folded her arms, irritated, but not enraged.

I'd learned in our brief time together that she was a woman who tended to understand when she'd been beat, and I let myself draw some satisfaction at having managed such a feat. The quick glance I took at how her gesture left her frankly magnificent breasts bulging almost out of her clothes was purely for celebratory purposes.

"What's wrong with you?" she asked after her silence had lived long enough to start thinking about retirement. "We've been married almost a week, sleeping in the same bed for barely less time, and you haven't so much as touched me. Are you . . . ?"

Redaclans had a concept of homosexuality, and some of them even accepted it as normal. I didn't think we were in one of those progressive regions, though, and Phelia's line of questioning wasn't something I'd expect from someone that was. I shook my head.

"Then why?" she pressed, back to angry now. "Why are you so disinterested in sleeping with me and properly consummating this?"

I surprised myself by not actually knowing. Was it because she was a bitch? No, not really. She barely was. Was it some distaste for her customs and values? Again, no. Certainly, I found her attractive enough. It was all I could do not to leer at her like some piece of meat. So why?

"Because this world is a disgusting, evil hellscape that grinds human lives into nothing for no reason at all, and I don't want to bring another person into it, let alone my own child, until I've done something to make a dent in that."

It was the truth, but that didn't mean she'd accept it. If anything it meant the opposite—were humans inclined to value honesty and reality for their own sake, then we'd have had no cause to invent lies.

Seconds passed, and I braced myself. Waiting for some snarl of anger, some cultural knee jerk, some snapping, ranting retort to remind me that I lived in a world of fucking animals. Nothing came. I frowned, seeing Phelia's face shift, but only fractionally. Her features creasing to some dull, cold acceptance. Wordlessly, she nodded, and I surprised myself by being the next to speak.

"Are you . . . alright?" I asked because I really was on a roll today when it came to saying the fucking stupidest thing I possibly could. Phelia only sighed.

"I understand," she answered me, not meeting my eye, and drew herself down under the covers.

"Phelia, what's wrong?" I tried again, but this time no answer came at all. She just remained where she was, still, silent. My first thought was that it was some kind of manipulation, a careful act made to pluck at my heartstrings, but I'd seen this woman lie and danced with her at politics. Something like this didn't feel like her style at all.

My second consideration was that I'd stumbled onto something more raw in her memory than I'd guessed, but all the moves that seemed to prompt were either bad, worse, or unthinkable.

In the end, I couldn't bring myself to even lie down beside her. Just made for the door and let myself out in silence.

We'd slept in snow on our first night in Redacle. And the second, and the next few after. Slept in shitty leaking inns after that. Slept in carriages, hotels, spare rooms. We'd lived off stale bread, jerky, or nothing at all. Every single fucking moment I'd lived in this world had been a struggle, and it had all been because of people like Phelia Velaharo and her fucking family.

So why, I found myself wondering, had I seen her eyes twist into the very same expression Solitaire's and Beam's had during the hardest of those times? What in the world had her so desperate at a time like that?

The thoughts followed me as I made my way through the frigid halls, soft carpets feeling hard, exorbitant decoration casting jagged, ominous shadows across the walls to chase me. I'd roped a woman under my power through some contract, turned an unjust system to my advantage just because it was the fastest path to power. How the hell was I any different than the oligarchs we were aiming to depose?

I kept walking, and the answer wrapped itself around my heart like a constricting snake made of ice.

We were different, I knew, because we weren't just doing it for ourselves. We were actively hurting ourselves, forgoing a good, easy life to try to grasp at long-term power and influence, build ourselves up outside the establishment. We were self-sacrificing, not-serving.

I paused, my heels ground the carpet, and my throat tightened like a vise. I turned around, heading back for Phelia's room.

Self-sacrificing. But we were pragmatic, too. If you refused to choose between the lesser and greater evil, then you were committing an act of evil. And my choice was clear. One person meant nothing compared to a world of millions.

Even a person who called me father.

CHAPTER THIRTY-FOUR

Beam's POV: Day 84
Current Wealth: 299 gold, 30 silver, 41 copper

I'd fought in front of crowds before. In fact I'd probably still had more fights before an audience than without one, even after my months in Redacle. That was the natural state for a career Olympian. I'd spent the entire day of the tournament's beginning wondering what feeling it would evoke in me to see the assembled masses staring and calling out as announcers dropped names and fighters readied themselves out of sight.

As it happened, the feeling was absolutely nothing at all. I might've known. I was a fish in water here, a bird in the air, a writer in the middle of an overextended metaphor. I was in my element.

But I wasn't fighting. Life just wasn't fair sometimes. We'd been given word that Argar was to go up first out of us all, which told me that Shango had probably been right on the money about the organizers choosing based on alphabetic order. It was lucky he had been, too, because we'd not even come close to finishing a suit for Helena yet. A lot of the hardest parts, the most time-consuming, we'd already started practicing and preparing, but even so it'd be a close thing to have her armor ready by the next day.

Argar, despite finding out he'd be thrown into the ringer with nothing but a few piddly millimeters of normal steel, didn't seem particularly worried. Then again, I'd yet to see any real evidence that he was capable of being particularly worried.

"Never been a man who can beat me," he said confidently. "'Cept you, on account of you cheating."

I sighed. Apparently my leveling up and weapon conjuration violated some previously unobserved rule of engagement, and as a result discounted all of my wins over Argar ever. Somehow that didn't seem fair, *or* make me feel his confidence.

"You ever heard the saying, 'Pride comes before the fall,' Argar?" I asked, not really expecting him to have. He just shrugged.

"Hear it all the time," he grunted. "About half the fights I've won ended with someone tossing it at me. Never fallen, though."

I had half a mind to bring up the vampire, but that was a bit of a touchy spot for him. And mentioning his relative effectiveness against the Dead Edge would just have been cruel.

"Alright, let's see a few swings," I said instead, watching as Argar hefted his axe and started hacking away as if the air had insulted him. It was impressive, watching him move, almost surreal. Seven feet tall, four hundred pounds heavy, every inch of him muscled like a bull. Magic had given me strength beyond the limits of mere flesh and blood, but there was something about the raw physicality Argar brought to a fight that was just terrifying to see.

Advantage us, a terrified enemy was half beaten. Solitaire liked saying that. I could only assume he'd gotten it from some book about historical warfare or integrated circuits.

"Good luck then," I said to Argar at last, slapping him on the shoulder and slightly hurting my hand against his plate. I must've been more nervous than I thought to use such an excess of strength, but Argar only grinned more broadly before tipping his visor down.

"Luck is for people under seven feet tall." He laughed, tone only slightly marred by its passage between the metal grate.

I didn't watch Argar step out from the contestant's area, as much as I wanted to, but instead headed back up to where Solitaire and Shango had stashed themselves. The noble's box.

A long walk rested between me and it, punctuated by many stairs, and I'd donned a set of chain mail under my clothing just in case the Dead Edge got ballsy. Even still, I practically sprinted my way to my brothers and barely even felt out of breath in doing so. My body weight felt increasingly slight these days, preternatural strength making a mere two hundred or so pounds less significant than it had once been. It felt wrong. I'd still not retained all the athleticism and bodily efficiency I had on Earth, and yet I was stronger than ever. Much stronger. Moving so easily it was like living under low gravity, like my flesh and blood were being slowly replaced by something lighter. And the *speed* . . . That was something else, too. Something almost unnerving.

Once I reached the place, I was struck by an inexplicable wrongness. I stepped into the noble's box and found myself surrounded on all sides by enclosed seating areas. One section seemed to be a kind of common room, where a dozen or two people stood around and chatted. Many more were split off into separated miniature lounges. Sofas strewn out, foodstuffs laid about for pickings, wine and other such drinks displayed invitingly. It reminded me most of those Roman living rooms I'd seen art of, with the people lying side-long as they chatted, eating grapes and whatnot.

Still, that inexorable disquiet remained. Gnawing at me, grating on my nerves, scratching my spine. It was everywhere and nowhere, imperceptible but unmissable. And after a few moments spent standing around gawking like a moron, it hit me.

The place was *clean*.

Now, I had been in Redacle for a while, but three months isn't enough time to go native. The very concept of cleanliness had not yet become alien to me. A public place as well maintained as that, though? Well, I'd be lying if I said it didn't have me stunned like a gut punch.

"Oi!"

Even in a generic medieval-Euro fantasy world, I knew of only one man British enough to use that greeting. I followed Solitaire's voice, finding him staring at me from one seating area, gesturing for me to move over. I acqui-esced, hurrying and soon finding the others in my sight. Shango and, of course, Phelia, the reason we were even allowed in an area like this.

"What's up?" I asked eagerly. I hadn't been gone long, maybe a few min-utes, but give my brothers a few minutes to work and they'd turn tables like spin tops.

Solitaire answered me first, his grin nearly splitting his head.

"We've figured out the betting," he said quickly. "Turns out it's not actually that difficult. They came over and invited us. I suppose things needed to be kept simple for—"

Shango coughed, Solitaire paused and then continued more slowly.

"For those few people among this particular class of guest who might, by some perspectives, appear less intelligent than those of a more challenged and tested lifestyle."

He glared at Shango, taking a moment before continuing.

"Anyway, that's not the cool part. The cool part is I know who Argar will be fighting next. Someone called the Soldier. Nicknamed at least, not sure what their actual name is."

I eyed him, finding a genuine surprise at the revelation, but not a particu-larly strong one. I'd known, after all, what happened when one gave my broth-ers a few minutes to work.

"How did you learn this exactly?" I asked. Solitaire shrugged in an Ozymandaian display of modesty.

"I used my giant brain to ask a few questions, make a few logical leaps, and follow it all to a guy who knows a guy who's in touch with a few of the organizers. Apparently they have loose tongues, but then again you know how their kind like to—"

Shango cleared his throat pointedly once more. This time I was glancing at Phelia when he did and saw the glare that shot toward Solitaire from her.

"Their kind being overpaid executives of course," Solitaire amended, about as enthusiastically as Henry VIII's ass wiper. "And the long and short of it is I know whom our friend will fight."

"Do you just have the inherent ability for criminal activity?" Phelia asked politely. Solitaire turned to her, just as sweet.

"Did you manage to fit all of Shango at once last night, or are you still working up to that?"

She went red as a sunburned tomato, and Shango himself just about convulsed. It took me a second to realize what was being referenced. My first thought was congratulations for my friend.

My second, of course, was amazement that it'd taken him so bloody long.

"So who is this Soldier?" Phelia asked, not meeting any of our eyes.

Solitaire grinned wider than he'd grinned yet, sitting back and savoring the moment of expectant silence before he replied.

"I have no fucking idea."

CHAPTER THIRTY-FIVE

Beam's POV: Day 84
Current Wealth: 299 gold, 30 silver, 41 copper

Argar strode out like he owned the place, armor glinting in the high sun, giant body almost silencing the crowd with its sheer scale. I wasn't entirely surprised. God only knew what kind of awe a man his size would evoke in people who fell short of even average Americans by a good few inches.

His opponent, by contrast, was . . . less impressive. Not a short man, by Redaclan standards, but far from tall. He strolled out in a heavy gambeson with a shield on one arm and a shortspear in the other. Even beneath the thick armor I could tell he was built, broad, almost box shaped. Whatever musculature was going on under those clothes, it probably left him even heavier than I was.

Which wasn't to say he had as much mass as Argar was bringing to the table, maybe not even half as much. The giant would've outweighed his armored body even while facing it naked, and I wasn't certain the axe he had resting across one shoulder could even have been swung with the smaller man's strength. But builds could be deceptive. I had to remember that.

Redaclan rules were in play here. For all I knew the Soldier was—

"Level eleven," Shango said from behind me, sounding almost bored. "Strength eleven, Speed nine, Dexterity seven, Stamina twelve, Toughness eleven, Alertness nine, Charisma five, Intelligence five."

He was bored, eyeing the Soldier, because of course he was. The ability to look at a person and boil their abilities down into a list of numbers did have a way of killing the fucking suspense in a situation.

"Is that the farthest you've ever used it from?" Solitaire cut in. Shango blinked.

"Oh, shit, yeah." He grinned. "Guess my range is over . . . uh . . ."

"Ninety-two meters," Solitaire replied, wiping Shango's grin away.

"Let's watch the match," he grumbled.

It was a good thing he grumbled it when he did, too, because if he hadn't, we might've missed the fucking thing. Argar moved in quick and heavy as a stampeding ox, axe coming down with so much force that I actually worried for a moment that he'd fucking kill the poor enemy in that single swing. He didn't, though, shield rising up just in time to meet the edge.

Wood splintered and cracked, steel biting through a centimeter, then an inch. A jagged split ran up and down from the point of contact, almost reaching the iron rim, and I watched as the smaller man stumbled back.

He might've tried to stop a speeding motorcycle and kept his balance better. Argar roared, grabbing his weapon with both hands, tightening his fists, and pulling.

For one moment I thought the Soldier might manage to hold himself in place. Then Argar's motion was completed, and the man simply came uprooted in an instant. Feet plucked off the floor, body lurching forward into a stumble as his shield dragged him after it. He was smart, though, and turned that momentum into a stab that left the tip of his shortspear sliding off the metal plate of Argar's chest, an ugly scratch marking the point of contact and a shower of sparks marking its violence.

Argar took a step back, maybe from shock, maybe from fear. The Soldier was quick in exploiting it. He thrust again, going high this time, then whipping his spear back down to lurch for Argar's knee. I realized it was heading for an opened joint, widened and exposed by the giant's move to block the stab at his face, and the metal tip passed between plates with drill-book precision.

Then Argar's fist hit the man like a thrown anvil.

The Soldier was staggering, almost falling over as his torso was forced so far off-kilter. He rebalanced, readied his spear, then froze as Argar's hands closed around it. One swift motion and the shaft broke apart, splinters flying in all directions, plate-clad giant bashing them aside and bowling the man off his feet. They went down together, Argar on top, hammer fists raining.

In the end, it was a referee who called it, and I was left to worry that Argar might've just smashed a man to death for the second time that day. He exited the arena without much hesitation, though.

And the crowd didn't like him. Oh, fuck, they *hated* him. Argar the brute, Argar the savage, Argar the half troll. The names were as numerous as they were uninspired, thrown out like volleys of arrows into the center of the stadium. He didn't seem to mind.

Solitaire definitely didn't, and Shango seemed downright pleased. That was when I remembered the betting.

"We . . . won something?" I asked, hopeful. They both grinned.

"I put a gold on Argar." Solitaire shrugged. "Five-to-one odds in his favor, so we're about ten silver richer. There are disadvantages to being as big as a grizzly bear, apparently."

Yeah, that I could see. I'd have bet on the big guy, too. But it didn't explain their grins, which Solitaire quickly rectified.

"Argar gets a lot of good bets from sheer size, right?" he noted. "And the more he wins, particularly like that, the better his odds will grow."

I stared at him, understanding dawning.

"You want to rig a match?" I asked. He shrugged.

"It's an option. I doubt Argar'll throw one, but I can make something that'll give him a bad enough case of the shits he won't have much choice. Oh, look, next fight's starting."

And so we all turned to the arena as a new pair walked out, and we kept turned to it. Hours passed with fights dotted between them, some immediately following another, but most delayed by half an hour or more. I guessed the event wanted to keep people seated and buying food for as long as it could, which wasn't exactly dumb. We were actually starting to get a bit bored, seeing the competition, before a particular figure made themselves known.

Bachton Anophes, one of the city's more prominent nobles. And, as even I noticed from the name, a relative of the fucker Phelia had gotten us tangled up dealing with. He was a big man even by modern standards, close to six feet in height, and covered in plate armor. He clinked his way into the center of the arena to an absolute avalanche of applause, so much so that I turned a questioning look to my brothers.

"The Challenger," Solitaire said as if quoting something. Because he was. "That's what they call him," he explained. "On account of him almost beating the King of Blades, apparently."

That did not leave me with a net decrease in questions.

"The King of Blades," he explained, "is the reigning champion. Never failed to show, never lost, never even visibly hurt. Apparently the Challenger got closer to winning than anyone else."

"So he's tough." I nodded.

"Twelve-to-one odds here," he replied.

"And level thirty-two," Shango added. "Strength twenty, Speed twenty, Dexterity eight, Stamina six, Toughness twenty, Alertness twenty, Charisma five, Intelligence three."

My mouth went dry. With the stat differences Shango had described, the scarily numerous points separating him from us would've made a lot of difference. I kept my eyes peeled for the guy's movement.

From the other side of the arena, his enemy emerged. Bigger, broader, also in plate. Shango read his level off at thirteen, and he didn't need to tell me his Strength. I could guess by the sheer fucking size of the hammer he was one-handing that there wasn't a man on Earth who could've made him break a sweat in that department.

The fight began, then it ended. One moment, the big man moved. Another moment, he raised his weapon. A third moment, the Challenger shifted where he stood, lurching to one side with blinding speed and sending his sword right into the enemy's exposed joint. Chain mail ruptured, blood spurted, and the man's arm fell limp at his side, refusing to obey the instructions he was doubt-less sending its way.

"Yield!" the Challenger ordered. Big Man didn't, moving in again, perhaps hoping to surprise him. He did not. A boot caught his chest, lifting him from his feet and sending him to slide almost a meter backward along the ground. This time the ref called it for him.

The entire thing hadn't even taken three seconds, and by the looks of the Challenger, he hadn't even taken a bet.

"Well fuck," Solitaire remarked. "I bet our ten-silver winnings on the big guy."

CHAPTER THIRTY-SIX

So we were fucked if we wanted to actually win the tournament, no surprise there. One did not world build while one had a compulsive personality unless one compiled a list of what different kinds of characters could do at different points of the series' power scale. I knew there were people out there who could pick up that bear we fought on day one, lift it fully over their head with a single arm, then forcibly insert it into the giant troll's asshole while it tried, and failed, to stop them. Tearing the troll in half after the fact was doable, but entirely optional.

The real question was how far we might get, and what we might manage to gain before inevitably dropping out. Argar wasn't the best of us anymore, after all, and I'd be willing to put fifty gold on Beam over him in a heartbeat. With luck, we'd make a pretty penny off the bookies here.

"We'll get hurt," Shango observed once we got home. Argar's chain mail had stopped the Soldier's attacks, and his impossibly hard body had weathered the blunt force of them, but it still looked like he'd be coming away with bruises. "A stronger thrust and that would've gone through."

My friend held the coat of mail up for me to see, and I didn't miss the section of links that had been mangled by the fight.

Redaclan armor tended to be built thicker and heavier than real-world historical counterparts, but there was only so much you could do against a stab made by someone who'd have been in the running for Earth's powerlifting champion. I took Shango's point. Making a habit of letting weapons get past his plate wouldn't do Argar many favors.

"We can make chain mail out of that new steel, right?" he asked abruptly. I grinned. It'd been about half a day's work for Ardin and me to figure that particular challenge out, but we'd managed it, and the look on Shango's face when I told him as much was well worth the delayed sleep.

"It was luck," I chimed in. "That none of us fought except Argar for the first day, but we'll almost definitely be seeing action tomorrow."

That put a bit of a downer on things, but then psychotically depressed paranoids had a tendency to do that.

"We'll have Helena's armor ready by tomorrow," I said hopefully. "Which is a huge advantage to her. Not to mention the spear." I'd watched the edge Beam and Ardin put on that do its work already, and it was nothing short of terrifying. The normal issue with making the sharpest weapons you could was that they wouldn't *stay* sharp. Sharpness was, after all, just how thin the edge was, and a thinner edge would be easier to break and damage for all the reasons that it had an easier time breaking and damaging other things.

And that was the convenient thing about a metal with quite possibly several times the strength of what most other weapons were made from here. It could survive several times the pressure, and thus be made several times as sharp. I had no doubt that if someone had skewered Argar with a tool steel spear using the Soldier's strength, it would've carved through that mail like it wasn't even there.

"We'll have Helena's by tomorrow," Shango noted slowly. "But what about Beam?"

There was the question, the concern. Beam would be the one actually fighting if any of us did the next day, and we *had* made a start on his armor, indirectly. It'd be a lot easier to work the second set than the first. With Helena's fit to be done within the hour, we might well have a full twelve-hour crunch to prepare for his bout. Twelve hours wasn't a great stretch by the standards of armor smithing, though. If I recalled my research properly, it usually took around ten times longer than that for a single worker to manage a suit.

Ardin was fast, superhumanly so. His levels had all gone into Dexterity, smithing skills. Probably, he could work at double or triple the usual speed, and he had Beam actually helping, too. Not to mention Corvan providing heat and pressure with his sorcery. But twelve hours still seemed like a stretch too far to hope.

I recalled the sight of the Challenger's strength and worked through the calculations in my head. If my friend went up against an enemy like that, he wouldn't be getting very far.

Night came shortly after, and I slept about as well as any other man worrying he might watch one of his best friends get cut in half. The fights weren't to the death, I knew, but they weren't exactly safe affairs, either. Real steel was being used with real edges, and the digging I'd done had established that there were at least a few deaths every year. Short of skewering the other guy while he was down, people could get away with all sorts in the tourney.

It wouldn't take much for Beam to get killed. Bad luck, a superior enemy, his own moronic stubbornness, even. I made a mental note to hurl a rock at his head if he wasn't quitting when I thought he should. Getting disqualified for a foul was better than getting dead.

Eventually sheer tiredness won, and I drifted off.

I didn't dream like other people. I'd figured that much out when I was about two—oh, I can remember being two by the way—and mentioned to my mother how I'd replayed a particularly cool cartoon the previous night about ten times. She'd been confused, surprised. I'd been a toddler, so it was only looking back on it when my brain was finished hacking apart synapses and growing itself that I realized she'd not been capable of that herself. I asked around, subtly, and eventually figured out it was just me.

When I'd dream, I was still there. My senses were apart, and it was hard to establish any real causal consistency between one event and the next, but my consciousness remained active. Anything I looked at, focused on, solidified. My dreams were an empty vacuum for me to build whatever I wanted in.

Yeah, it was really fucking annoying watching *Inception* and knowing that I'd never be able to tell people this without getting accused of copying it.

Anyway, that night I built a pyramid. There wasn't any particular reason. I just felt like it. Pyramids were cool. Some of the most iconic ancient structures mankind ever made, with a simplicity that had survived well into the age of modern geometry. They were the ultimate evidence that we'd not really changed in thousands of years, just updated our software on the same old caveman hardware. Humans loved our pyramids, hierarchies, orders. And we loved making sure all the wrong people ended up at the top even more.

I made mine from skulls, eyeless, tongueless. Unable to watch, to whisper, empty and vacant. Perfect structures, inert and ready to be positioned by my will. As I built, I climbed, and as I climbed, I looked out. I saw the landscape around me and quickly plucked a suitable image from my memory.

Redacle, odd. I saw it all, the hills, the landscapes. Copied directly from my cerebral cortex with a perfect accuracy just barely short of silicon. It was beautiful in a way, seen from such heights. But then I saw the maggots. The rot that fed them. Running across the land, putrefying and poisoning everything it touched, spreading. Spreading, always spreading. Multiplying. They just couldn't help themselves. No matter what they were, no matter where they were from or what fucking genes they carried, they were all the same. All had to make more of themselves. Had to narcissistically put themselves in the next generation.

I watched the rot build their castles and cities, their laws and nations, their delusions and evils. I watched it all, and my dream was making me sick. I blinked, screamed, then the fire came, taking it all, purifying everything in that way only total obliteration could. Soon I was choking, lungs tortured by the carbonized gases and broiling atmosphere as smoke wafted around on thermally displaced gusts.

My dream didn't last long after that, ending briefly, time distorted as it so often was during unconsciousness. I woke up smiling.

CHAPTER THIRTY-SEVEN

Beam's POV: Day 86
Current Wealth: 306 gold, 0 silver, 17 copper

My match was earlier in the morning, which was about typical of our luck, and we only found out a few hours in advance. We'd all known and agreed beforehand that my using my magic to conjure armor and weapons would be too risky. Redaclans didn't tend to react well around foreign magics, so I was sticking with a slightly refitted set of plate made for a particularly big mercenary who'd never paid up to Ardin a year ago. My weapon, of course, was the vampire's rapier, still as light and balanced as ever.

"Remember your training," Shango said wearily. I frowned at him.

"What training?"

He shrugged.

"I don't know. It just seemed like something useful to say. Go out and kick the shit out of the other guy with your Olympic-athlete training I know nothing about and can't comment on. Better?"

We shared a grin. The brittle kind that shattered like glass under the weight of the moment.

In this case, it had help shattering. Solitaire spoke up.

"No idea about the guy you'll be going up against," he cut in. "Except that his name's Baldrick, like the *Blackadder* character."

We looked at him blankly, and Solitaire sighed.

"Fucking hell, the good shit never makes the transatlantic trip," he muttered, then spoke up again. "Point is he's an unknown factor. Baldrick the Stonearm. Whatever he can do, best to figure it out before deciding on anything."

It was better than Shango's advice, but still not great. Solitaire was a good fighter, and an absolutely *terrifying* brawler, but . . . He just wasn't a contest competitor. Oh I'd want him at my back in a street fight any day, but I'd spent my whole life sparring against people who'd knock him around in a one on one, and I wasn't about to start taking his advice now.

Still, I knew how easily his ego bruised. I politely didn't say anything.

The crowds were louder when I stepped into the arena. They were always louder from the inside, their cheers closing in on me like a vise, sending electricity to run along my nerves. I felt my stomach convulse, squeezing itself so tight that I knew I'd have puked if it'd been holding anything, and the alien strength surging into me as adrenaline widened up blood vessels had me wishing my enemy would hurry up and show himself already. He must've been almost as eager because he did.

Average height for Redacle, well-built. He had plate on, too, which had me worried given the difficulty we'd found in getting ours. The man carried some giant glaive, another issue in and of itself. I was used to fighting against other swordsmen and could only imagine different techniques would be involved with defending against a weapon like that.

"Strength and Toughness ten," Shango said. "Dexterity seven, Speed and Alertness eight."

So he was slow but powerful, then. And not even that powerful. By stats alone I was fairly confident in winning, but that glaive worried me. It was a big thing, big enough that he probably needed all even his near-superhuman Strength just to use it in combat. The reach difference between us was going to be a problem.

"Good luck," Shango breathed.

"Go for the cock," Solitaire added. I nodded absently, heading forward just as the announcement came that our bout was starting.

I came in fast, then slowed. Hesitant, circling the guy, stepping in and out as I tried to gauge the distance between us. Hard to read movements beneath plate, I realized. All those little muscular twitches and tensing joints that came before a strike were obscured by the stiff metal encasing them.

When he moved, I found the motion so poorly telegraphed that it was raw reaction time that saved me from the kilograms of steel lunging at my head. I stepped back, smacking it aside with my rapier at the same time. The enemy's weapon was heavier. Mine swung with more effort, and I felt the impact shake my arm up to the elbow as I knocked the attack away. I closed, aiming to take the chance to get behind the tip, but obviously the bastard fighting me now was used to tactics like that. In one twisting motion, his glaive was arcing back for me, this time in a swing aimed low for my knees.

He should've aimed for the thighs instead. As things were, I just about managed to jump over the weapon, feeling the wind of it run beneath my feet, and land before a new thrust came at my belly.

Just barely, I was back in time to see it sweep in front of me, and I kept backing off with my eyes held tight on the enemy. He was closing in, confidence apparently bolstered by the exchange. His glaive came high, on the verge of lowering, then he did something with the shaft and his shoulder to rotate it into a sidelong swing. This time I dropped myself, angling my rapier and letting it slide up and over me, straightened just in time for his boot to catch my chest. It bought him a moment, which he used to crack the shaft against my helmet, and then that fucking glaive's blade was back at me.

Our fight wasn't a fight for long, soon devolving into a simple chase. Me backing away, eyes always on that blade, feet always on the next step behind me. My enemy closing in, like a homing missile, entire world apparently lost to him. He swung, and stabbed, and cleaved, and swept.

And all the while I studied him.

I'm not a genius. People say I am because they've never met a true, honest-to-God genius. Solitaire, he's a genius. Shango is a genius, and my fucking brother was a bigger genius than either within his field. I'm gifted in some way. I doubt anyone could learn as fast as me, but mostly? I just practice.

My enemy's moves were something new, but that was fine. I'd practiced new things already. I kept my focus on him and started to realize that the exposed chain links beneath his plates were jostled with motion, and the sounds of creaking steel were ever so slightly different based on position. I realized he favored thrusts to answer some things, slashes for others. That the weight of his weapon, and its sheer length, would force him to attack with the shaft or butt if I slipped by once. That he couldn't manage its balance while his feet weren't planted in a certain way.

He'd never been closer to winning, I saw now, than during his first attack because each failed attempt just gave me more information to work with. I didn't remember things like Solitaire, or needle out secrets like Shango, but somewhere in my brain a deep, speechless part of me was compiling the methods and motions of this new threat. Before long, the ape part took over. I started predicting.

A thrust missed me, and before he could follow it up with a backstep and swing, I closed in. The man twisted his weapon to drive me back with the butt, and I timed my stab just perfectly. Overextended, and with such timing, I couldn't have made a scratch on his armor, but my rapier made its way right through the joint of his inner elbow just as it was most exposed. It found the chain mail beneath spread out in the motion and unable to disperse force as it normally might. And it was driven with more strength than two of me could ever have mustered before coming to Redacle.

I saw blood leaking from it as my enemy staggered away, and I followed up. He'd not brought his weapon around in the shock. I punished him for that by flicking mine for his visor. People protected their eyes on instinct of course, and when he did I thrust down again for his knee. This one backstepped whenever an attack came, and did so in a very particular way so as to ensure he could pivot just right to bring his glaive around quickly. It meant that the joint—my second target—was open and placed just perfectly to replicate my first swing. This time, though, I was a lot closer.

More blood, a clear, visible flow now running down his calf and touching the ground in a moment. Not arterial, not quite, but it was enough that I knew I'd not just imagined my enemy slowing. He swung. I ducked, stepped close, and darted back at the last second to bait out an overhead cleave. My feet took me sidelong, and I nicked his wrist, then kicked the weapon aside as one of his arms was taken off it in shock. It went wide, too wide to be brought around in time, and I lunged.

I didn't put my sword through his eye. Instead I used the cage-like guard as a makeshift bludgeon and punched the metal into his armored face. The difference in our strength was immediately apparent, unbalancing him, then letting me kick a leg out from under the bastard as he stumbled. A bit of martial arts, I'd learned, did tend to help in a sword fight. He landed hard, and my boot was on his chest before he could rise, sword right at the joint of his helmet and gorget.

Unsurprisingly, my victory was called soon enough.

CHAPTER THIRTY-EIGHT

Solitaire's POV: Day 86
Current Wealth: 307 gold, 2 silver, 33 copper

I loved gambling. It was one of those wonderful pleasures in life, like blowing up a building or taking a limb off with a machete. Had all the right synapses screaming at one another for more, electrical ecstasy running through the brain in a nice clean circuit. Particularly, I liked doing it early.

My mother took me betting a few times as a kid, and eventually the fun always evaporated. Spend enough time seeing horses race, and I'd learn what the actual odds were for each one winning, more or less. There were always unseen factors of course. I wasn't capable of observing every particle in the universe—yet—but it meant that I could place a bet and be reasonably sure I'd win. The major limit, naturally, was not wanting to get my head cut off by a bunch of gangsters.

Thing was, we *already* had a bunch of gangsters trying to cut our heads off, so I had no incentive not to bet away to my heart's content. Life was good.

Elizabeth, the new join Beam had found the other day, was helpful for a lot of it. She'd learned all the right people to go to for information on things like this a long time ago, flitting from place to place, needling out the relevant information.

Of course we didn't have nice, big seasonal display boards to compile and record people's previous win-loss ratios, and there were a lot fewer repeat fighters from what we'd gathered. What I was doing was basically no more than guessing, but I was a pretty good guesser, and the money started flowing in.

A few silver here, a few gold there, and patterns started to emerge. Big guys had less of an advantage in weapon fights than brawls, but reach was far more of a factor. Stamina became the decider between people who were both well armored, and polearms reigned supreme. By the time Beam's fight came, I'd started to get some hint of what was happening, and I only grew more confident as we watched more. Helena surprised me by fighting on the same day as him.

However much I enjoyed betting around in the smaller pools, Helena's fight was one I had to see with my friends. Particularly when her reputation, as a member of the Belahont Company, was big enough that a few *nobles* might've actually been putting some cash on the outcome.

Shango was already seated among them when I returned, Elizabeth in tow, and the two of them couldn't have had different reactions. Shango was evidently pleased to see me, and I was pleased to see him. Since his marriage with Phelia had been finalized, the Dead Edge had seemed to quiet down a bit, perhaps worried about making themselves a pressing issue for the people who owned a magic boom stick. Even so, it was always a relief when nothing came of us venturing out for things, in spite of our ongoing rule not to do so alone anymore.

Elizabeth, on the other hand, looked as if I'd dragged her into a shit-filled lower intestine, only for her to find it crawling with tapeworms. Which was to say, she was a working-class girl dumped in the middle of a noble's gathering. I sympathized.

It's not that I don't like people, of course. I just understand them. Which means I fucking loathe the cunts. Their stupidity, their casual vicious cruelty, their animalistic selfishness. Most of all, their possessing the precise amount of intelligence needed to impede any effort to better them.

Give me a dog and I'll have it obedient and trained within a week. Give me a human and there's not a force on Earth that could guaranteeably move them out of whatever arbitrary evils they felt like, not even the force of my towering intellect.

"You alright?" Shango asked her, making mistake number one. Phelia wasn't with him, which was something, but I'd learned enough about our new friend to predict her response even before it came.

"Shut it, bauble," she grunted. Shango looked utterly baffled, and just a little bit wounded. Eyes suddenly creased with a frown, face wavering as if he were about to cry. It might've been cute, had it been a little boy's expression rather than a grown man's. As things were, it just irked me.

"Don't be so surprised." I sighed. "Beam told us she was based. Now move along. I want to sit down."

Truth be told, there was easily enough space on the couch, but asking for more gave me an excuse to bring up something that wasn't Elizabeth's entirely justified classism. It seemed to work. Shango shifted his position rather than ask any questions or hurl any retorts.

"Lovely." I grinned, looking out into the arena. "Elizabeth, tell him what we found out."

She did, quickly, without needing any clarification on the topic. Elizabeth, I'd learned, was a very clever person, and Shango had taken a peek at her stats when she'd first been introduced. Intelligence seven, one of the only ones we'd seen of such a level. She certainly spoke like she had a mind found only in one among every few thousand.

"The War Hound," she said, throat tight. "Also known as the Pit Hound, also known just by his name, Aja. Presumably signed up under another name beginning with *H*. He's a Vittonian, like Helena, and used to be a slave in one of their city-states. Fought as a gladiator. Won. A lot. Ended up here eventually, where he serves the Anophes family—the city governors—and continues to win. Also a lot. Only one who's ever beaten him was the King of Blades. That's the most I know."

I did like that about her, the way she'd proclaim her information dump as all she knew, but throw in that little twisty smile. Letting a perceptive eye see that she knew full well how impressive she was, and agreed with whatever praise might be about to get shoved her way.

Well, Shango certainly agreed with it, too, and he grinned.

"Bloody brilliant addition to the team you are," he noted, which seemed to stun Elizabeth. I supposed she'd had even less experience around *nice* rich people than me. Come to think of it, it was bloody weird how both of my best friends were in the top percent.

Shango's approval didn't last long, though. Soon eaten by the dawning facts of what Elizabeth had told him.

"Helena's fighting a guy like that," he breathed, frowning. Drawing the same conclusion I had.

"I don't see why she would be," I noted. "If the only name that'd put them together alphabetically was one Elizabeth didn't even hear."

Shango eyed me.

"You think it's a setup?" he asked. I nodded without hesitation.

My friend was about to say something, I thought, but a new voice rang out before he got the chance. Prim, glass sharp, and silk soft, all sleek and slippery like oil on waves, reaching my ears with about as much aristocracy as a genocide. I shuddered, head turning around to gaze upon a short, plump man with a pencil mustache, bright eyes, and a smile so false it made me want to claw his tongue out.

"Remarkable." He grinned jaggedly. "I'd heard the tales, of course, of the famous Solitaire Belahont, but to see you in action is . . . Why, I'm humbled, truly." He took a seat on the end of our couch without asking permission and turned to look at Shango that way people often did after finding out he was the one with the connections and money. Peering through me like I was transparent.

Perhaps he'd feel inclined to pay me more attention if I started twisting his nuts off.

"Do I know you?" Shango asked with the tone he used when he thought he *did* know someone and hoped he was wrong. The man only smiled wider. I had my suspicions already, of course, my brain tended to generate such things before even I knew it'd done so. But it still made my heart sink to hear them confirmed.

"Lord Joshuit Val Byror," he proclaimed, dripping with false pomp. "At your service. Might I be the first among my most esteemed class to congratulate you both on your unprecedented ascension. Crawling one's way up from street rats to nobility in only a few weeks? Remarkable."

Everything he said, I thought, was some sneering little mockery, but there was no use in bringing it up. Shango evidently thought the same because he was all business with his answer.

"What do you want?" he asked coolly. "Run out of gangsters to throw at us?"

Byror smiled.

"Oh, believe me, I haven't. But I shan't be *throwing* anything at you again, not unless my hand is forced. I'm afraid I was . . . hasty in doing so as quickly as I did. I am merely here to watch your subordinate's match."

I went cold, as he turned to the arena, and Helena strode out in her plate.

"After all," Byror continued. "I've sunk rather a lot into it."

CHAPTER THIRTY-NINE

Shango's POV: Day 86
Current Wealth: 307 gold, 2 silver, 33 copper

Aja the Pit Hound was a big guy. Not Argar big, but he was upsettingly close to it. Six foot three, maybe six four. Rippling with musculature that I hadn't even known people in Redacle had the nutritional and training quality to build. His hair was black, greasy, and frizzy like mine, eyes dark, face darker. All twisty skin and scar tissue, pulled at in a dozen different directions by the puckered knots of mangled flesh and seemingly trapped into a permanent snarling grin.

He walked like a panther, as if his own weight was nothing at all, and I couldn't help but take a look at his stats. Couldn't hide my horror as I did.

Nineteen for Strength and Toughness, seventeens in Speed and Alertness. High Intelligence, massive Stamina. I could see now why he moved as if his body weighed nothing at all because from his perspective it probably did. Even with all the glinting plates of . . . metal?

"Draconian bronze," Solitaire breathed, staring at the coppery-colored strips of lamellar and mail as if they were some giant pack of animals barreling for him. Byror only smiled wider.

"Correct!" he proclaimed, as if speaking to some little kid who'd done something clever. "Impressive eyes you have there, my friend, and admirable knowledge for a mercenary."

By the look on Solitaire's face, he was trying to figure out if Byror really meant to say "mercenary." I decided to speak up before he decided the noble hadn't and did something Solitairish in response.

"Expensive for a pit fighter," I noted.

"Oh, the Anophes insist on keeping their little monsters draped in only the finest." Byror laughed. "And believe me, the result is rather impressive."

I jumped to my feet, intending on storming down to warn Helena of what we all knew was coming. Just as I turned to the door, though, I found more than a few men barring it.

"Terribly sorry." Byror sighed. "But you won't be getting to her. Just sit back and enjoy the show."

The Pit Hound strode toward Helena just as the match was called, and he lashed out with some giant curved weapon. A khopesh, I think it was called. Didn't seem like the kind of thing that'd get through armor, but his strength was mountainous, and its edge seemed to . . . glow. Incandescent in my sight, like someone had taken a blowtorch to it and left it bright with heat.

Helena caught it, her shield twisting up high. She was equipped with something similar to a hoplite's aspis, though we'd reworked it from tool steel, made it thinner and lighter while still adding a bit of strength to a typical example. It did stop the Pit Hound's swing, but barely. The metal trembled at the impact, sparks flying out, and as Helena stumbled back I glimpsed the sight of a deep gouge in her shield's face. She regained her footing just in time for him to lash out again.

Helena had the range, with her shortspear, but her enemy had been so quick in his first strike that he'd gotten past its length before she could thrust. Now he just lashed his weapon against the wall of steel between them.

It didn't look like a fight, more like a giant psychopath trying to sledgehammer his way through a concrete wall. And the wall was cracking, every impact sending Helena stumbling a half step farther, each space between the next swing and her shield adjusting its position was by a narrower breadth. Every dent that rested in the tool steel of her aspis was deeper. Whether she broke first or the shield did, it looked like a breaking would be on its way no matter what, and not one that helped us.

But this wasn't just some meathead; it was Helena. She was one of ours, smart, tough as boot leather. She lasted a good while before her body started to slow and weaken with the strain of keeping her enemy back, and while she lasted, she thought. Between each impact, the straps on her shield grew a shade looser, until finally she cast the thing off and sent it whipping for her enemy's face as a thrown projectile.

As far as hurled metal went, it wasn't the most effective attack. But it kept the man's reflexes focused on the one big, glinting object coming for his face, so much so that he didn't quite step back in time to keep Helena's spear from finding the joint of his hip.

Tool steel, that was what Solitaire said the alloy had been called. I saw why. In an age of piston-driven mechanisms capable of grinding stone to powder, the requirements of metal tools had become extreme. Pressure resistance, impact resistance, an unyielding, unbreaking strength that was to the primitive metals of this world as they were to raw iron. Helena's weapon bit in, carving through mail and sending her enemy back a step, beads of crimson running down the armor just beneath where she'd skewered.

But only beads, not a river. My own blood went cold as ice at that, and I heard Byror exhale.

"She had me worried for a moment there." The man grinned, leaning back, folding his hands behind his head. "But the Anophes seem to have put some thick mail beneath the plates."

Helena didn't get even an instant to breathe before her enemy was coming at her again, his fury redoubled, as if the injury had somehow offended him. This time, though, she was ready for him.

Even without her shield, Helena kept her distance and lashed out at the man's face and neck, forcing him to abandon the all-out assault he'd used before.

Her own body was struck plenty, metal screeching as that bronze khopesh carved rents out of the steel. I felt Solitaire wincing at the sight. Helena kept fighting, though, kept circling. And for just a moment, she even gave me hope that there was a chance.

Then the War Hound's khopesh found her elbow, cracking the carefully articulated joints and cutting deep. Blood fell in a sheet, but it had barely even hit the ground before Aja's second stroke caught Helena's knee, leaving her to collapse as the leg gave out under her. He kept swinging, blood kept flying, her body kept changing.

It should've taken the announcers maybe a few seconds to get over their shock and call the match off, but instead they waited for minutes. Minutes of Helena writhing around, slowly ruined more and more as one piece after another was stripped off of her.

When the match was finally brought to an end, she barely even looked human. Just a pile of mangled meat lying in armor. Still alive, I saw, still fucking alive. Moving around like a maggot on the ground.

Slowly, I turned to Byror and found him grinning. Fucking grinning. His eyes were as pointed as ever, teeth on full display as he smiled.

"Consider this a learning experience, my boy." He beamed. "The Velaharos were old enemies of my family once. No longer. For the same reason that the rats in my privy are not counted among my foes. You've risen fast and well, and so I imagine you actually let yourself feel some measure of hope that you might overturn me, perhaps even goaded on by that pretty little whore you married for a title. Now you know better."

My heartbeat was in my ears, and so loud that I could barely even hear the crowd as they screamed away in the distance. The world was a dark, tight tunnel, and Byror sat alone at one end of it.

"Oh, you don't need to say anything," he pressed, still smiling. "I just wanted to make sure we understood each other. That the rules of noble engagement, as they were, do not make you untouchable. Good day, my boy."

Byror got to his feet, slithering away and leaving me and Solitaire alone. Instantly I turned my eyes to my friend, opened my mouth to speak. And froze.

Solitaire looked through me as if I was made of glass, and I knew, instantly, there would be no reaching him. No dissuading him.

He wore the same face he'd had on after staving that bandit's skull in with the hammer, after gouging that orc's eyes out, after every casual cruelty I'd ever seen him do. But more so. It sent a shiver down my spine and left me feeling an unmistakable sense of vertigo.

"Let's go and find Corvan," he said slowly. "And see how much he can do for Helena."

Mouth dry as a desert, I just nodded.

CHAPTER FORTY

I felt it all. That's what people never got. That's what Shango never got. I wasn't just observant and clever. I wasn't just good at guessing. I felt everything. Every feeling and thought running through other people would run through me, as well. My brain was a crowded highway; other people's emotions were the cars. And all the drivers were drunk.

Shango didn't say anything as we hurried down to Helena's side, finding her dumped just beside the entrance to the arena. The fucking animals had just left her lying there, and she seemed even closer to death by the time we were kneeling down. One of her arms still worked, so I wrapped my fingers around hers and held the hand while I waited for Corvan to come, heart pounding so fast she could probably have felt it through the skin contact. If her own agony hadn't blotted out everything else.

Corvan took his sweet fucking time to show up. He'd been nearby of course, but I guess the old wanker had struggled with the stairs. Even he looked disturbed to lay eyes on Helena, his face paling, eyes twisting with horror. But he was made of hard enough steel to get working quickly, kneeling down beside her and doing what he could as soon as he could do it.

Magic healing worked best the more recently after injury it was applied, and became exponentially less effective the more healing the body itself had been allowed to do naturally. It was why it couldn't really do much for old age, a form of damage that was entirely caused by the body itself, and had its treatment of cancers limited to simply vaporizing the tumors out. It made the sight a tense thing because I'd already seen Corvan's magic had its limits with Argar. How much had we exhausted the magus before he treated the giant?

Only one way to find out, and I felt my guts sloshing around like meat in a blender while I did.

Flesh went wet and runny like water, melting back together, severed ligaments re-fusing, smashed bone re-forming. Corvan was exhausted quickly but kept working. Skin knitted itself back, soft tissues regrowing where they'd been hacked away entirely, new blood letting itself bubble into the emptied husk of her body. Just when she'd started to resemble a human rather than some raw steak, the magus leaned back panting.

"I can't." He shook his head, exhaustion palpable. "My magic, it has its limits." I felt my hands curl into fists.

"So we take her to another healer."

"There's maybe one or two in this entire city," he snapped. "And neither are as powerful as me, or as cheap."

"They'll be something," Shango pressed, just as forceful, and I saw a flicker of emotion twist along Corvan. The sort of strained sympathy one feels for an idiot when they drool on themselves.

"Do it," I replied, standing. "I'm heading home." Shango looked at me as I left, and I could feel the blend of worry, disgust, and anger even without looking at him, but it only made me leave faster. I needed to be gone, needed to be free of other people's misery as soon as I could. To clear my head enough for some actual thought, or at the very least my own emotions.

It wasn't so much to ask, I thought, that I be allowed to feel my own feelings. And it wasn't fair that I have it demanded otherwise by people who didn't even realize what they were asking.

Elizabeth accompanied me to the mansion, for all the good she'd be in a fight. I saw terror in her eyes, tasted it on my tongue, felt it coursing through my veins like poison, urging me to act. I knew what she'd say long before she said it.

"I didn't know you were feuding with a noble," Elizabeth began, firm, combative. Ready to be challenged. I didn't challenge her, just told her how things would be.

"I'm going to kill him, every other member of his shit-eating class, then use their heads as bowling balls while I civilize the moron species they emerged from. If you're not in the mood to help that then you can flee whenever you want, but a bit of danger is going to be found anywhere, and if you leave our service then I can't guarantee you won't be captured and interrogated for whatever you know about us."

She glared at me, but it wasn't a glare made for me. Elizabeth was just in a glaring sort of mood, her face simply doing that to let some of the thoughts swirling around behind it leak out. Our journey didn't have much more talking involved before we were back at the mansion.

I didn't waste my time marching farther inside, not even when Beam came over with a frown across his face and worry deep in his eyes.

"What happened?" he asked. I didn't say anything, just let Elizabeth explain as I knew she would. I had other things to concern myself with.

Phelia was in her study—Shango's study now, I supposed—and looked up at me in confusion as I entered. Her confusion turned to worry as I closed the door, picked up one of the thick oaken chairs opposite her desk, and propped it up under the handle. Beam's hammering came an instant later, handle turning, frame rattling, but he couldn't force it open with how well I'd lodged the chair legs into the fixtures between wooden floor panels.

Me and my sister-in-law had a bit of privacy.

"Solitaire," she said, eyes widening as I stalked around the desk. Phelia was on her feet instantly, backing away, sensing what was coming. She wasn't as fast as me. I was on her in an instant, hand closed about her jaw, grip squeezing just to the line where I was certain I wouldn't crush bone and cause any permanent damage. I lifted her off the ground, brought her around, and pinned her down against the desk, leaning in to stare into her eyes as I took her hand with my other.

"Fingers," I said slowly, holding one of her digits up while she struggled against me. "You have ten. I'm going to ask a few questions. Some I already know the answers to, others I don't. I won't tell you which is which. Every lie I hear is another snapped bone."

Her fear was slick and painful, like boiling oil running over my tongue. I resisted the urge to spit and clear my mouth of the phantom sensation, forcing my glare to sustain itself on her eyes.

Phelia nodded, shortly, sharply. Terrified. Good, terror would lubricate this conversation.

Beam wasn't an idiot, and he'd known me for close to ten years. His banging intensified, bodyweight hitting the door, then bouncing off. It was a sturdy thing, inches thick, hardwood all the way through. Shango had confirmed that our friend hadn't gained any XP from winning his bout, and even with a superhuman's strength an object as tough as that wouldn't yield. If he was as clever as me, or as cool as Shango, he'd already have left to go and find a hammer or axe, but he wasn't, and so the pointless impacts continued.

"Why does Byror consider you an enemy?" I asked Phelia.

She was clever, I knew that, and I could see the gears turning behind her eyes. Doubtless she knew that something had happened to make this question pressing, so she'd be trying to calculate what, worrying that I might just kill her if I found out she'd had reason to suspect anything of what had been done to Helena.

Which wasn't wrong.

"His family and mine have been rivals for generations," she croaked. I couldn't falsify that, and it actually did get corroborated by what Byror had said himself, so I moved on, looking for more specificity.

"What does he think of you as an individual?"

She hesitated, taking another moment to think. I gave her finger a twist, just enough to hurt, to hurry her.

"Quickly now," I snarled. She obeyed.

"He tried to marry me ten years ago, wanted my . . . mind. He considers me intelligent."

Dangerously intelligent? I almost asked, but there were better ways.

"Why?"

Another hesitation, quicker this time.

"I once saw through one of his plans, warned my mother of it, but she told him of my suspicions, thinking of him as a friend. His plan came to fruition, and he wanted to marry the girl who'd seen through it at just fourteen. My mother refused."

I considered that and snarled.

"So one of the most prominent nobles in the city considers you actively dangerous, and you didn't fucking tell us before marrying my brother."

Her eyes widened with raw, undiluted panic. The sort a bunny might have in a bear trap.

"I had to hide it," Phelia croaked, speech constricted by the tightening of her own vocal cords. "I . . . My family, we're on our knees. My sisters can't even stay in Elswick anymore because of—"

My hand came down on her mouth, smothering her words into silence.

"You have one chance, right now," I said, "to tell me anything else that might be relevant. After that I'll fucking kill you if I find out you didn't. Understand?"

Her face paled. I elaborated.

"I'll wring your pretty little neck like a chicken, I'll cut you into tiny little pieces, and I'll burn you in a fire so hot you'll be cremated into ash within minutes. Nobody will ever know what happened to you, who did it, or why. You'll just stop existing."

Phelia nodded, eyes wet with tears, heart thundering like a drum. I released her and smiled.

"Wonderful. Now I suggest we keep this conversation between us."

I waited for her to nod again, then turned for the door, opening it and letting my face fall blank. Beam was on the other side, staring confusedly between me and Phelia.

"Sorry." I winced. "Decided to get a bit of privacy breaking the news to our sister. She's quite distraught, as you can see."

He turned to Phelia, who remained quiet, and nodded in understanding. Buying it without a thought.

CHAPTER FORTY-ONE

Shango's POV: Day 86
Current Wealth: 214 gold, 1 silver, 39 copper

It had cost us close to a hundred gold to heal Helena, and the worst part was how unsurprising it was. Magic was costly to use, insofar as exhausting its wielder. There were limits to how much could be done at once.

Which didn't mean it wasn't *exploitative*, the amount we were charged. The moment our first magus healer smelled my desperation, I could see their prices increase. And I'd paid them. There'd been no fucking choice in the matter. That was what the weak and desperate did to the strong and secure.

I stood by Helena and watched as her body slowly mended. Far, far too slowly, as it happened. Corvan had done just barely enough to keep her from dying on the way to her new healer, and they were able to advance her condition even less. By the time it was done she was . . . able to heal the rest on her own. Eventually. That's the promise I received, and Corvan backed it up with a careful study of his own. We took our leave before I could lose my temper and smash the damned magus' fucking teeth in.

"Lucky," Corvan grumbled as we carried Helena out. She felt lighter, largely because a considerable fraction of her new armor had been left in the arena as shredded scrap metal. "Just help me take her to the others. They can bring her back to the mansion."

I did, and they did. Leaving me in the arena to fight after only a few short hours. The fights were moving quicker.

The biggest worry with my own match was no longer losing, but rather losing in the same way that Helena had. Finding myself attacked with paid violence, overwhelmed and taken apart piece by piece. As I stepped out into the arena, I found myself thinking back to Byror and what he'd said, thinking back to the Pit Hound and what he'd done. There was just no contending with either of them, I knew. And if we weren't in the clear from their continued focus, then we might as well just give in.

My mouth was dry, body trembling, and hands equipped with a tool steel sword. A sword, a fucking sword. We'd been contacted before my match, told by the referee that my gun had been discounted for being "unsportsmanlike." I saw an enemy behind that almost as surely as Solitaire had, and it ended up being Beam who'd gently reminded us that sports events of any kind had generally disallowed shooting holes in each other, even back on Earth.

God, everything could've been a trap, and every trap could've been the end of me. But we needed money. I stepped out to get it, heart beating like a drum.

A big bastard came up out of the other end of the arena, and my blood was basically molten by the time I saw him. Easily Beam's height, and built like a linebacker. Shoulders like a draft horse, eyes all tiny and mean, hands like dinner plates. He held a giant fucking hammer in one of them, with a round shield in the other. The most *vikingy* man I'd ever personally seen, or even heard about.

Magnus was his name, of course, and he had a reputation for doing well in these things, having competed twice before and gotten past round one both times. If there was a person to be bribed into crippling someone, it might be him.

"I've heard about you," the man grunted, coming in just as the start of the match was announced. "Belahont, yes, rising stars."

He spoke with such a European accent I was almost surprised not to see him magnetically dragged toward Africa at supersonic speeds. Politeness compelled me to answer, regardless of our circumstances.

"Heard about you," I answered. "Magnus the Dozen, named after the number of men you killed at once in a battle."

I had done my research, and I did a little more as I spoke, peering at the man.

[Appraisal]
Statistics: Strength 11, Toughness 11, Speed 8, Alertness 9

Those were his big stats, the threatening ones, and they were big and threatening enough already. But I knew that this one probably had ten, even twenty times my actual experience fighting with swords. This did not seem to be a fight that would end well for me.

He came like a viper, whipping in for my face, forcing me to jerk back, then letting his shield crunch down at my dragging knee. Slower than me, but just as skilled as I'd feared. I felt a jolt of pain, snarled, and limped away from him. The joint wasn't broken, I thought, but it fucking hurt.

"Not as fast as I thought you'd be," the man grunted, and despite everything the words filled me with relief. People didn't usually talk to those they intended on ruining, not of their own volition at least.

"Maybe I'm just trying to lower your guard," I suggested, figuring that if he was a talker, I might as well get him talking. If nothing else it might distract him into letting me score a hit. He was covered with ringmail, but not plate. A solid strike would badly wound him, especially with my strength.

"Fought lots of talkers," the man grunted, slapping my blade aside, then swinging back for my head. I ducked, feeling my armor creak around me. His hammer clipped my helmet, sent me stumbling, but didn't break anything. He certainly tried to fix that mistake with his next swing.

My sword came up, which was a fucking bad move. The heavy end of my enemy's weapon knocked it almost out of my grip, then a second one whipped back before I could react, sending the blade skidding off along the stone floor, leaving my hand empty.

"Are you looking for a job?"

I just barely got the words out in time. They were clever, I thought, a nice distraction. Gave the man pause, but that hesitation only lasted long enough for me to move an inch with my sword. Then his hammer caught me again, and I went down. My back slid along the stone, world tilting, stars dancing before my vision before something caught my shoulder, and I turned.

Without thinking, I moved with the roll, trying to end up with my legs and arms beneath me, knowing that if they weren't I'd probably be knocked out of the fight before I could get up.

The hammer caught the sun, and I rolled again just as I did, hearing it hit stone behind me, then I was up, running, looking around desperately before I saw my sword. Then a shoulder caught me, and my feet left the ground again. This time I stayed face up as I went sliding back along the stone, and Magnus was standing over me before I could move, hammer high.

"I wasn't joking about the job!" I managed, voice sounding strangled even to me. He didn't hesitate this time, just swung down. I thought quickly, remembered how easily I'd slid along the stone, how little friction seemed to have grabbed me. I raised my forearm, angled it just right so that his hammer met it with a fleeting contact, then watched as metal glided across metal and his swing went wide.

Magnus wasn't as used to fighting men in full plate, it seemed. The man's balance was broken, temporarily, as he overswung, and I lashed a kick out to his knee to help him lose it entirely. Solitaire had done the move a lot, always vicious, snarling, always precise. I didn't have nearly his experience, but it seemed physics was on my side because Magnus went down.

I was on him almost before I knew what I was doing.

Weight was weight, right? Wrong. My weight was less than Solitaire's and Beam's—not by as much as it once had been, but even the extra muscle I'd gained in Redacle didn't leave me as tall or broad as them. The armor helped, an extra twenty-five kilos of force pressing Magnus down, but the man I was trying to pin beneath it could've sprinted with a sumo wrestler on his shoulders.

He shifted, turned, moved like a coiling snake. Staying on top was a losing proposition unless I did something to offset his ability to turn me off, so I slammed a gauntleted fist down for his face. His head jerked aside fast enough to avoid one hit but not the second, and the third hit him as cleanly as I'd ever hit anyone at all.

Magnus must've been made out of pop-culture Viking because he barely even flinched, but his struggling got a shade weaker, bought me another chance, gave me a few more precious moments to think of something new. I didn't, though, just kept trying the same old plan. Sometimes I wished I could scheme like Solitaire, then I remembered that I didn't think the president had been replaced by a clone and decided to settle for the level of intelligence I had.

"I'm serious," I repeated, still hammering down. "Don't you want armor made of metal that can stop draconian bronze, a staff that spits fire and punches through plate?" He hesitated, just for a moment, then grabbed me, leaning up and dragging my head down, twisting me into some lock before I had the chance to resist. Our heads were close by, his strength too much to overcome with the leverage I had.

It surprised me, then, that he chose to speak instead of starting to twist.

"What sort of pay?" he asked. "Answer quickly. This won't stay convincing for long."

Sometimes you didn't need to think of a million plans at once or calculate the length of a man's cock from ten meters away to have a functional strategy. Sometimes you just needed a single good idea and enough versatility and focus to push it through to the end.

And sometimes you needed to keep from getting distracted by your own cleverness.

"Five silver a day," I said instantly. "Plus free housing, food. We're holed up in a mansion right now—Velaharo Manor—with room to spare."

Obviously he'd heard of the place because he went a bit still before his voice rang back out.

"And that's a guarantee?" he asked after a second. "How do I know?"

My heart raced. It cost a bit of money to get into this tournament, and someone who'd entered twice already probably wouldn't throw away his chance to win for another year. I'd have to pick my words carefully.

Then a thought struck me, a really, really clever one.

"You were paid to hurt me, right?" I guessed. "So I couldn't continue through this tournament even if I managed to beat you? You know we have enemies, and I know you're trustworthy because you haven't been fighting to wound. We need the help, and we need good men we can rely on to give it."

Another pause, this one fleeting.

"Hit me," Magnus whispered. "Make a show of breaking free and slam your fist down."

I did so, moving almost without thought. It was satisfying, how he flattened out across the ground, wind seemingly knocked from him. The match was called soon after.

CHAPTER FORTY-TWO

Beam's POV: Day 87
Current Wealth: 224 gold, 18 silver, 2 copper

Solitaire's fight was over quickly, and nastily. I won't describe it because I can't. Not without feeling a bit queasy, even after all these years. To give the broad strokes: His enemy had been paid to hurt him so he'd have a harder time fighting through the rest of the tourney. Solitaire noticed, and was stronger than them.

It took three men to carry the poor sod out of the arena. He wasn't that heavy; it's just that after he regained consciousness, he kept flinching and clawing at any hands that came near him, screaming so loud nobody even understood what he was saying. Solitaire's mood seemed improved as he returned to the box.

Slightly.

"Got it all out of your system?" I asked, throat tight as I awaited his answer. It was good that I was here instead of Shango. However awful it had been seeing Phelia break down at what had happened with Helena, my brother's need to head back to the mansion and comfort her meant he hadn't watched what I had. My guts still squirmed at the very memory.

"To some extent." Solitaire shrugged. "You know how it is, eh?"

I didn't, and I didn't want to, but I also didn't want to make any further mention of the fact. The day had been long enough already. "When's the last match?"

"Soon. Possibly right now."

That perked me up a bit. I glanced at Solitaire, whose eyes were affixed almost unblinkingly on the arena.

"We're already pretty far back in the alphabet, and things are moving along faster as they progress. I don't think we have much of a wait before round one is over."

As usual, Solitaire was right. The two of us were seated there for much of the day, watching fights, betting, winning. Time dragged on around us, and eventually we came to the crescendo of it all. Dozens of bouts fought and won, with only a single one remaining. Solitaire was leaning forward in his seat as it got called.

"Do you know who they always send out first for these?" he asked. I glanced his way.

"No?"

"Anyone but the King of Blades. He comes last, every time. He's the climax."

Before I could even answer that, Shango's voice made me jump from the side.

"What have I missed?" he asked, barging into the room. He looked about as good as I felt, which was a grim thing to witness. My confusion was quick in bubbling up after the observation.

"What are you doing here?" I frowned.

"Solitaire." Shango shrugged. "Sent word to me about twenty minutes ago. Apparently the King of Blades is fighting?"

It really was annoying, the way he just made things correspond to his timing, but it was a lot more useful. Solitaire grinned, clearly aware of both facts.

Shango took his seat, twitching, shifting. I thought for a moment he was eager, then I saw the curled fists at his sides. Idiot. He was still worried about Helena, still dealing with Phelia. None of us had expected his wife to take things as hard as she had, and it was only more salt on the wound of what had happened.

I turned to the arena, silently urging the King of Blades to hurry up. We could all use something new to look at.

Fortunately, we weren't kept waiting for long. The crowd probably saw to that, their impatience growing at an exponential climb as the seconds sluggishly trickled by.

The King of Blades was not the first to emerge; that honor belonged to one Xerght, a man with no last name and a height that rearranged Argar's position on our hierarchy of stature. He was big. So big, really, that to even frame him in relevance to other humans was redundant. It was like looking at a great marble statue come to life and striding around, so toweringly huge that he barely even fit in through the mouth of the arena's entrance.

Next to him, the King of Blades looked absolutely diminutive. Which was not to say the near-seven-foot giant entering second and covered from head to toe in golden plate armor wasn't an impressive figure in and of themselves.

"What are their stats?" I asked Shango, who looked suddenly rather disturbed.

"I . . . don't know," he breathed. "I mean, I can see Xerght's, but the King of Blades . . . Nothing. It's like I don't have the ability at all."

"The armor?" Solitaire asked, sounding more concerned, even, than Shango. "Might be enchanted. If it resists magic then it'd probably resist your Appraisal, right? We do, fundamentally, use magic abilities here."

"Right." Shango nodded. "Yes, that makes sense. Fuck, so we're going in blind."

"Not blind," he assured him. "Xerght's stats, what are they?"

"Uh, Strength seventeen, Toughness eighteen, Speed ten, Alertness six."

Not a bad set, I had to admit. Could I beat him? I watched as the giant moved forward, crossing as much distance in one step as a short man would have in two. He had to be nine feet, or even more.

No, maybe I couldn't. Scary.

"So we can learn about the King by looking at his performance here," Solitaire finished. "Just keep your eyes peeled. We'll be gleaning information from this, as long as we focus. There's always information to be gleaned."

For once, his rampant intellectualization was actually reassuring. At the very least it gave us all something to do, and my expertise was rather uniquely suited to this task. I kept my damned eyes peeled.

The match began quickly, and it began with Xerght stepping forward and swinging. He wielded an axe, a giant, heavy thing that looked like it'd been made to hack boulders rather than wood. It came down like a battering ram, and I waited for the King to sidestep.

He didn't, simply raising his sword one-handed and catching the axe-head against its blade. The sound was so loud, I actually heard it over the crowds, and the King's armored body slid back a good few inches along the stone. His opponent was reeling, unbalanced by the shock of his swing being stopped, fighting to right himself.

I never saw the King's move; it was just too fast. All I knew about it was more deductive than perceived.

His sword stopped a few feet beside the giant, and the blood came out after. Xerght shuddered, took one stunned step backward, then toppled over and fell. Like watching a house fall down. I almost expected the ground to shake as he hit it.

The crowd was silent for a long moment, then the cheers came. By then the King had already turned and started back for the entrance, making his way out without so much as glancing at the roaring audience, as if he'd been alone with his enemy. It was so cool, I actually felt a little bit angry just watching it.

"So . . . Uh, we probably shouldn't try to fight him," I noted.

Solitaire and Shango did not bother responding. They both just sort of went quiet. I couldn't blame them. Hell of a thing to see, what we'd just watched. Hell of a thing, to find out in one moment that our chances of actually winning the tournament were literally zero.

We watched as the tournament's announcers strolled out, pretty women dressed nicely to catch the eyes of the audience and quiet everyone down while the information was conveyed.

"Ladies and gentlemen, you have just witnessed the first round of Elswick's Tourney of Wolves. We've had quite an exciting show of it so far already, with a potent turnout if I've ever seen one, but believe me, things will only get better and more hot-blooded from here! Please give a hand to this year's first-round victors . . ."

Names started being rattled out, ours, thankfully, among them. I started to zone out after that. It was Shango who snapped me back to focus, and he did it with an excited gasp. I turned to him, eyes wide, half expecting some disaster to be awaiting me. Instead, I saw a wide grin splitting his face.

"Experience points!" He laughed. "Finally, we've got experience points. Fucking hundreds."

As far as revelations went, there were certainly less pleasant surprises to be faced with.

CHAPTER FORTY-THREE

Shango's POV: Day 87
Current Wealth: 224 gold, 18 silver, 2 copper

[Appraisal]
Class: Emperor
Level: 14
Condition: Fine
Modifiers: +6 Toughness, +4 Strength, +4 Speed, +2 Alertness
Statistics: Strength 10, Speed 10, Dexterity 6, Stamina 5, Toughness 10, Alertness 10, Charisma 9, Intelligence 9
Inventory: Local wear, plate armor, repeater, shortspear
Class Abilities: Appraisal II
Current Experience Points: 153/480
Unspent Skillpoints: 0

I'd put my points into Alertness and Toughness, but not just to round everything out at ten. I reckoned they were the most useful at the moment. Alertness was almost a limiting factor on my fighting speed, and Toughness was all the more influential for a person in full plate armor. Everything I took would be an impact now, and that was just the thing that Toughness helped most with.

It would've been nice to get more than just the one level, but I barely concerned myself with what could have been. A huge experience dump was still a huge experience dump, and it seemed our decision to join the tourney had paid off.

The knowledge that we were now more or less stuck in it, as the path of least resistance for strengthening ourselves, did take a notch out of my good mood in any case.

Solitaire was next in my sights, and he'd chosen predictably.

[Appraisal]
Class: Revolutionary
Level: 14
Condition: Fine
Modifiers: +4 Speed, +6 Toughness, +3 Alertness, +5 Strength
Statistics: Strength 12, Speed 11, Dexterity 8, Stamina 6, Toughness 11, Alertness 11, Charisma 3, Intelligence 10
Inventory: Local wear, plate armor, shortsword, shortspear, knives (x3)
Class Abilities: Detect Element II
Current Experience Points: 148/480
Unspent Skillpoints: 0

Toughness really was in our best interests right now, and Strength was always good. I took a moment to appreciate how much even I dwarfed Beam as of our arrival, then moved on to Beam himself.

[Appraisal]
Class: Dragonknight
Level: 14
Condition: Fine
Modifiers: +3 Strength, +4 Speed, +4 Toughness, +5 Alertness
Statistics: Strength 12, Speed 12, Dexterity 8, Stamina 9, Toughness 12, Alertness 13, Charisma 6, Intelligence 5
Inventory: Local wear
Class Abilities: Beloved II
Current Experience Points: 226/480
Unspent Skillpoints: 0

Alertness, interesting that. I supposed he hadn't seen the King of Blades' swing, either. Made sense that he'd be trying to stop a miss like that from happening again. Though I wasn't sure how much difference one point would make, our Speed points seemed to make less of a difference than our Strength or Toughness. Otherwise a real-world human sitting at ten would be outrunning horses.

Which wasn't to say it was useless; that just meant it wasn't by default the only thing worth getting. We'd already been doing this long enough to know the benefits of iterative, long-term improvements. One step was better than no steps, and turned directly into two.

More to the point, there was no guarantee this was as good as our tourney rewards were going to get.

"This wasn't that hard, right?" I asked, suddenly feeling . . . suspicious. Things weren't this easy in Redacle, never. If something looked too good to be true, it probably was. I'd learned that better than anything since coming here.

"Mixed bag," Solitaire agreed. "But we got lucky."

Beam piped up, seeming more confident on this than either of us. Which was fair enough.

"We did." He nodded. "Sixty or so fighters who weren't with us, and a good few are dangerous enough that none of us would even have a chance against them. Even putting aside the King of Blades, Aja the Pit Hound, the Challenger . . . Fuck, that giant the King actually beat would've had better than even odds against me as I was in round one. And I'm not that much more confident I'd win now. The risk was high, and we got fortunate. We can't bank on that happening again."

"Particularly because we're now fighting the top half of the last round," Solitaire concluded, looking suddenly less pleased with his new statline.

I couldn't blame him. My own optimism was starting to dwindle. I wasn't half the fighter Solitaire was, or one-tenth the fighter Beam was, but I knew enough to know there was some fierce competition. Even ignoring the top five of the tournament, more than one of the other competitors were good enough to give Helena, even Argar a run for their money.

"Which means more experience if we manage to reach round three," I breathed. Even to me, it was a pretty fragile reassurance, but Solitaire looked happy enough. I supposed that was the major benefit to being an insane megalomaniac. Optimism. Shame his paranoia usually canceled it out.

"Either way we have some preparation to do," Beam noted, and we all agreed once more.

"Let's head back," Solitaire breathed. "I want to keep working on our . . . defenses."

Neither Beam nor I contradicted him. It would just have been cruel, for one thing, to deny him so vital a mental lifeline at a time like this.

And for another, I rather liked the idea of leaving ourselves better protected myself.

We arrived back at the mansion with no great incidents, apart from an incredibly embarrassing moment where Solitaire almost killed a man who he thought was walking up behind him, but had actually just been moving past us to get in front. It was a refreshing, almost surprising thing to see that our new home was not under attack. It was no less glorious than ever, from the outside at least. Expansive lawns, proud towers, sprawling wings.

You only saw the desiccation if you paid attention to subtle things, like how the gardens were strategically trimmed only around the outer perimeter, hiding the decay nearer the center.

"God, it's so . . . *insecure*," Solitaire spat, lip curling, eye twitching. I did my best to ignore him as we strode in.

Beam disappeared soon after our return, heading off to find Argar and the others. Solitaire and I were quick to leap back into discussion, however. We had a lot to touch on.

"Do you have anything you can make that might let us stave off a bigger attack?" I asked him, not really all that hopeful. He was either quicker than usual or had already been considering just this question because he got back with an answer so fast I didn't even notice a pause.

"I can make more guns. Well, Ardin can make them, but it'd take time out of armor we might use in the tournament. Mines, those I can do myself."

I decided not to directly contest him on literally mining my home, and instead moved the topic on to less *volatile* means of defense.

"I was thinking more along the lines of barricades and such."

Solitaire sighed.

"Yeah, I can set those up, but it won't be much good until we have more men. And recruiting en masse now just opens the door for whichever bastards are after us to sneak spies in by paying them more."

I hadn't thought of that, and found myself suddenly less confident about having hired Magnus. All the more reason to mention it fast.

"I did pick someone up in the tournament," I told Solitaire, spitting the details out quickly. I half expected him to go insane on the spot. Instead he looked pleased.

"Perfect. Beam didn't think he was trying to kill you, and Byror almost definitely isn't smart enough to pull off an infiltration this complex, not with the sort of double bluff it'd need. Or stupid enough to think that sending some-one from within the tournament to join us wouldn't be the most suspicious method possible after what happened to Helena. Nice one, mate!"

He hit my shoulder, and I smiled. Forgetting, for a second, all the things he'd made me remember since we came here.

Then it was back to business.

"Well, try to get him here sneakily. Send Elizabeth on it actually. It'll be good to see who else we can draw in from the tournament. And . . . Hmm, rival gangs might be another source of recruits, trustworthy ones at least. Trustworthy enough to give guns as long as we're ready to put them down if they act up."

It was dizzying, watching his paranoid considerations, and more dizzying knowing that Solitaire could only physically speak fast enough to voice one for every ten that flitted through his mind. I did my best to stay focused despite the radioactive psychoses playing out before my eyes.

"Assembly lines," Solitaire said at last. "We can get extra smiths for our guns, several. Making different components, which will then be modified in different ways, and assembled as a group. The factorization approach but used for disguise rather than just for speed. If nobody knows more than a single component of what we're making, and nobody knows how to make the ammo, then none of them will have the ability to replicate what the final product is. We can easily outfit our recruits with repeaters like yours and not need to worry about the secret getting out, or drawing Ardin away from armor smithing."

Thinking about it for a moment, I decided the plan sounded solid enough. It left only one question.

"What's Beam up to during all of this?"

CHAPTER FORTY-FOUR

Beam's POV: Day 87
Current Wealth: 224 gold, 18 silver, 2 copper

I sought out Argar first because frankly I considered him my highest priority. Helena could wait, as awful as that sounded. She was stable, I knew, and that meant I had no limit on the time I could take to speak with her and offer whatever comfort I could.

Argar, though, had to make the most of every hour we had. Every minute. There were only so many days before the second round finally started, and I didn't want to see a repeat of our other bodyguard's performance when it did. I found him in one of the central lounges.

God, he was still ridiculously big. Like someone had stretched out a normal man in every direction. I supposed a single freakish giant sighting wouldn't take the edge off seeing a seven-foot man just a few yards from me, particularly when that man was lounging and moving. I almost felt sorry for the chair he was strewn across. His weight was torturing it almost to the limits of breaking.

"Alright, boss," Argar grunted without his usual grin. I couldn't blame him for that in the slightest. Grins of any kind, usual or otherwise, were in rare supply around our company these days.

"Alright, Argar," I echoed, not entirely sure how else to respond. Then I paused, and realized I couldn't actually have cared less about beginning the conversation *properly*. "We need to talk."

Argar turned to me, confusion and suspicion written clear across his features.

"Nobody ever starts a nice conversation like that," he correctly pointed out. I just moved past it. Didn't matter how right he was; it was still coming.

"I'll be blunt then. We're into the next stage of the tourney, and the competition is fierce. We can't be sure you'll remain a cut above the enemy."

Argar scoffed.

"Please, I'm twice the fighter—"

"No you're not, Argar," I snapped. "I'm sorry, but you're not. You need to train. You're a mountain of muscle already, and your natural talent is absurd, but you still just lounge around most times and treat fighting like a game. It's not a damned game anymore, and we can't afford to have you charging in like it is. I need you to start properly training with me, not just enjoying practice bouts, actually training. Concentrating on learning, pushing yourself physically, burning fat and building muscle."

And building whatever magic infused those muscles to strengthen them. He couldn't level up, but the people of this world still grew more powerful, and generally through training. With luck Argar could at least follow us up as we strengthened.

But I saw defiance in his eyes, as I might have expected. His stubborn streak seemed to be holding strong regardless of my appeal.

"What do you know about what I need?" he growled. "I've got northern blood. We never needed to train. My people's heroes did their deeds while sleeping rough and struggling between meals. They didn't have time for some fancy instructor or tutelage. They never set foot in some nobby training halls, and they definitely didn't swing weighted swords or any crap like that. They were strong because the world had built them like that from birth. That's what strength is, natural and inevitable."

I almost didn't know what to do about the tirade it was so out of left field. I supposed different sorts had different views on things, but still. Something as alien as being opposed to *training* . . . How did I even go about contradicting that?

Slowly, I guessed.

Northmen, of which Argar was apparently descended, were our . . . Well, they were generic pop-culture Vikings basically. And Celts, sometimes. Your typical hard men doing hard things while hard. And a lot of what Argar had said was true: They tended to produce freakish mutants capable of wrestling trolls before they'd even finished puberty.

What he was overlooking, though, was that they weren't morons. With luck that'd be a worthwhile angle to pursue.

"And do you think any of your heroes would've done without proper training if they'd had the chance? Hell, do you think they even did without it in the first place? That they just knew how to use shields and axes, how to form walls, all that? Come on, Argar, you're taking this to a ridiculous extreme."

"Because I'm already living better," he snapped, angry now. "How do I make a name for myself, how do I even follow them at all, if my entire life has just been luxury and comfort? I'm in the bloody south, and I can't afford to go to where the really hard living is. I'm soft. So I won't train, no matter what. I'll get where I get with my own talent and nothing else."

I sighed and thought about it for a while. Argar was speaking again before I could finish.

"And I don't know what you think you're saying about me keeping up with you, but I've been holding back every time we had a practice bout. Don't get so cocky over nothing, you tiny little bastard."

Idea time.

"Why don't you prove it, then?" I challenged him, taking a step back.

I had my rapier on me still. It had rarely left my side ever since I nicked it from that vampire, but I didn't reach for it. Conjuring one of my magic weapons instead, making it a challenge.

"I'll make this fair and not use my armor," I promised him. "Seeing as you're naked, too."

Argar's eyes narrowed.

"You're going easy on me?"

I thought a moment before answering.

"Yes."

With a roar and an explosion of motion so instantaneous it even surprised me, Argar was flying at me like a thrown brick. I stepped back, raised my weapon, and caught the axe-head just as it came at my chest. I realized two things in an instant.

One was that Argar must have been as jumpy as the rest of us to be keeping his weapon so close by. The other was that he was fucking *strong*. My grip almost surrendered at the impact as I stumbled back, weapon too light and muscles too weak to fully meet his strength. Argar's own came flying back with ridiculous speed, coming for my head this time.

I ducked it, by inches, and felt a boot thud into my chest for good measure. My preternatural reflexes let me roll with the blow and mitigate some of it, which is probably all that spared me a broken rib. Still, it hurt.

My back hit the ground, and I rolled another few feet before finally stopping in a crouch. Argar just kept coming, though, like a damned flood. I scrambled into a roll and came up swinging for his face.

It had been a reflex, really. And it was damned lucky my sword missed a solid connection. Argar moved a single inch a single instant before impact, and the edge of my weapon opened up the skin from just atop one ear to just behind an eyebrow. Blood fountained down, but he didn't even shift his face in response.

Just kept on fucking swinging.

One missed, another missed by less, and I was backing up again, swearing as Argar kept on tirelessly as a damned machine. Something caught the back of my leg, a fallen chair, and I threw myself over it in a sightless dive, rushing back to my feet, melting away from Argar's swings.

I bought myself a moment, at least. And as he closed again I had my balance set, my stance ready, my mind keen. His next swing didn't get close, and I saw the one after it coming before it had even started. I took a half step with each parry, calmly controlling the space between us, smacking Argar's weapon away once, twice, a dozen times. Soon enough beads of sweat were starting to make themselves known across his face. With a growl, he closed faster to try to body check me.

That, of course, had been well within expectations. I punched him the moment he came within range, an ungauntleted fist that nonetheless carried enough speed and force to crack open a normal man's skull. It thudded squarely into Argar's chin and stunned him.

Stunned only, though. It was a testament to his ludicrous durability that he remained standing, so I helped him down by taking a backstep, shifting my sword into a blunter shape and swinging *that* for good measure. Argar's Toughness did not prove the equal of that.

He fell hard, actually landing on the chair I'd caught my leg on and crushing it flat. The floorboards creaked, and the room shook slightly as four hundred pounds of dumbass smashed into the ground. I watched, waited for Argar to regain his wits, and stared as he struggled to stand a few moments later. Glaring up at me.

"You held back," he growled. "When we sparred."

"I'm stronger now," I told him. "Because I focus on improving myself. And yes, I held back. So did you."

Argar spat. "Doesn't change anything."

"Yes it fucking does," I growled. "You stubborn asshole, who's legacy do you think you're upholding by losing to a weaker talent because you sat around drinking beer all day instead of training?"

Argar had no answer for that.

For the last few days, life had been pain. Helena accepted it readily. The pain was nothing, an irritation, a prick, a bother. It was no fact at all measured against the knowledge that she'd not live as a cripple.

She made her way around the house, feeling her body slowly mend, silently wishing it would do so faster. Her memories moved back to childhood, when she'd been training as an adolescent. Vittonia was not so disorganized a place as Vorhazh, and nothing like Eregar. The soldiers in her land were trained to it early enough that each of them fought as a second nature. She'd felt bruises and lashes in the training yard before even entering her teens, and it was a grim reminder, nursing similar wounds now, how rapidly her young flesh had repaired them.

Then again, she hadn't been granted magical aid back then. Such things were too expensive by far for the mere grunts, however gifted. And Helena was under no delusions that youthful vigor would have let her body mend the sorts of ruin that had been inflicted upon it. When she'd been told how her new employers had left her healed, she'd immediately asked of the price. She'd panicked upon hearing a hundred gold had been spent, horrified at living under such a debt.

Solitaire, though, had just laughed. He'd said something she didn't under-stand, about one people called the British and another called the Yanks and how the former didn't pay for their healing while the latter were stupid. And that had been that.

It was stunning, but not as stunning as remembering him being by her side when she'd still thought her life was over. Holding her hand, whispering to her. Helena had gotten angry, somehow, after his description of her healing, demanded an explanation.

"Every life that's ever been lived is precious. You should be asking other people why they wouldn't save one for free."

He'd left her with that to consider it by herself, and Helena had decided that she would truly never understand the man, no matter how long she spent trying to gain his measure. She had gone about her business elsewhere in the mansion, motivated to find some form of distraction through sheer weight of confusion. The alternative was accepting the very real possibility that Solitaire was a good man after all, and such a fact as that might leave the skies themselves raining down upon the world in rebellion.

Fortunately, Velaharo Manor was a place of distraction, if nothing else.

There was a lot happening, and perhaps the least exciting among it all was the new arrival. Magnus, his name was. Helena had not seen his fight with Shango, but she'd heard it was one-sided enough that she could at least rely on the man not to embarrass her and Argar. If push came to shove. He was a typical Turskan, tough and hard, but not all together bright beneath his beady gaze.

Any other time she'd have relished teaching him his limits in a good spar, but such things were beyond Helena as she was now. She'd be weeks in the healing still, and not much good until it was finished. More distractions, then, were needed. Many more.

Argar was no more enthusiastic about the man than Helena herself, but to her surprise he was rather less apathetic about everything else around him. The giant seemed to have gotten into the habit of training, somehow. It almost felt surreal to see. He had that way of making anything he did seem ridiculous, as if it were some performance starring a ludicrously overscale puppet.

"You won your match pretty easily," Helena observed, finding yet another surprise in Argar's answering look. The man seemed actually offended by her observation.

"Course I did," he growled. "I'm just doing this to burn off some belly fat, that's all."

Helena looked at that belly and saw how it wobbled with every motion. She could certainly understand that of all sentiments. It had been strange, meeting with the Belahonts, largely because they'd been the first group Helena remembered who actually outdid the environment of her youth in bodily trim. All lean musculature and jagged abdominal ridges. Clearly there was some anatomical quirk left prominent in their family's blood, alongside the height.

Argar had none of that, but he was moving with a surprising speed as always. Enthusiasm, perhaps, giving a boost to his already unusual haste. Helena watched him for a good few minutes more until he finally tired of swinging the great weighted blades around, dropping them with so loud a clatter that she jumped. He made his way for the corner, and Helena thought he'd sit. Instead he just squatted there, eyes bulging and jaw tight.

"What are you doing?" She frowned.

"Exercise," he grunted. "Beam taught. It. Shut."

It was a few words less than would have been ideal, but Helena got his message all the same. Rolling her eyes, she left him to his exertions and turned her focus to his discarded training tools.

They really were rather big, she had to admit. Bending down, wincing as a few hastily healed muscles jumped in her back, she closed a shaky fist around one and tried to raise it up.

Obviously, she was able to lift it. And amazingly, she actually felt its weight resist her effort. Helena was wounded for sure, but she knew her own strength even diminished as it was, and the mass resisting her now was . . . insanity.

When she finally glanced over to Argar, he was properly seated. Apparently he'd finally earned himself an actual break.

"How much do these weigh?" she'd asked.

He'd grinned at that. Which was fair enough.

"Twenty pounds, for now." Argar had shrugged, with about as much modesty as Helena had learned to expect from Solitaire. "It's a start."

That had more or less been the end of their conversation. Helena was in no mood to continue watching him grin away while she couldn't at least give him a jab in response. She continued her study of the mansion and found no shortage of additional points of interest. Shango, of course, was at the center of her next bout.

"Ah, Helena." He grinned, sympathy burning in his eyes. She looked away from it, feeling sick just to catch a single glimpse.

"Sir."

"Sir," he echoed, smile slipping. "Right, well, anyway, keep an eye on this, would you?"

He handed her something, and Helena realized it was a bundle of . . . Yes, of cloth. Cheap, of course, and set out into a long, long strip. He moved away. "We're doing experiments. Alright, Elizabeth, go!"

The other new join, Elizabeth, started her sprint just as he gave the order. Something was tethered to her back, Helena realized, and that something was tugged and detached just as she took off. It was perhaps the finest sprint she'd ever seen.

It was fortunate they were in the largest hall of the entire mansion because anywhere else and it would surely have been dangerous to unleash such speeds. The woman seemed almost to disappear as she shot along the ground, crossing it in great loping strides and almost reaching the far wall before Shango's voice rang out.

"*Now!*"

Instantly, the woman threw something down, and she was decelerating after that. As Helena looked more carefully, she saw the something had been a bag, burst open and its contents spilled out on the floor. Shango was quickly moving to retrieve the object he'd handed her, gesturing her over to the spot Elizabeth had started her sprint from.

"Hold this down here," he ordered, handing Helena one end of the ribbon while he moved away with the other. There were lines on it, she saw, as the ribbon unfurled. Equidistant black etches. Shango seemed to count them as he continued unrolling it.

Finally, he stopped at the site of the dropped bag.

"As I thought," Shango noted, hurrying back. "Well, as Solitaire thought, but still it's good to have confirmation. You're just over two point seven times the average speed of an average man, as far as we can tell. About fifty percent faster than Beam, sixty percent faster than Solitaire, and seventy-five percent faster than me."

Elizabeth frowned.

"But I already knew you were all slow."

Shango glared at her, his good mood, apparently, barely broken.

"You can go now." He sighed, and she did, disappearing with barely less speed than before. When she was gone, Helena spoke.

"What was that?" she asked. Shango smiled, turning and gesturing to something. The object that had been linked to the rope originally tethered to Elizabeth. A tall thing, more wood than metal, and as alien as everything else the Belahonts ever made.

"This is a fairly basic measuring device. Rope hooks up to it. Once that's pulled a latch is released, water falls a measured distance, and one second passes before it hits the ground. Good for timing precisely. Solitaire designed it, and Beam built it during a break from work with Ardin. We've been using it to compare speed."

Helena watched it, thought, and tried to conjure up a question. She couldn't, and so her silence just remained for a few more moments.

"What is it?" Shango asked softly, seeing through her as always.

"None of you are acting any differently," she breathed. "I . . . I failed."

She'd failed. And a failed soldier was a dead one. Helena had learned that well enough. To try, to fight, was to resign yourself to the outcome. She hadn't, and yet her failure had yet to punish her.

Shango didn't put a hand on her arm. He merely sighed.

"Because you're our fucking friend, Helena." The man shook his head, as if bewildered at the very question. "Does that really need explaining? Now go and lie down. Corvan says you need some rest. Boss's orders."

He smiled, thin, weak, testing. Helena had planned to feign a smile of her own, but she never got the chance to do so. A real one erupted across her features entirely on its own, unprompted, irresistible and incomparably warm. It was the most wonderful thing she'd felt all day.

Almost enough to distract from that nagging still left in her gut, and that deep ache still plaguing every battered inch of her.

CHAPTER FORTY-FIVE

Shango's POV: Day 90
Current Wealth: 221 gold, 2 silver, 42 copper

We'd been busy, for the three days given to us before the tournament resumed. Very busy. Beam had been training like a motherfucker, of course, and Solitaire had started working on something new. I wasn't sure what, hadn't quite mustered the courage to ask. All I knew was it involved bulk buying a fuck ton of mercury.

No good could have come from that, I decided, so I just pretended it wasn't happening and hoped very hard not to wake up one morning finding out the building had been blown to bits by a Scouse maniac. The usual maneuver.

As for myself, well I had my own set of tasks to attend to. Largely compulsion based, to be fair, but we'd finally assembled a big enough range of people to do some *experimentation* and see exactly what each level of a stat actually meant. Elizabeth had helped me with the sprinting tests, and the Strength ones had been even more straightforward—just a matter of hoisting up increasingly heavy blocks of Solitaire's ice until they stopped yielding. The results were quite satisfying.

A 25 percent increase to Strength per level, which was about what we expected. Solitaire was pretty smug about that of course. What surprised us was the 8 percent increase to Speed. I'd been confused about the weird specificity of that number, until Solitaire had pointed out it was the exact cubic root of 1.25.

Smug asshole. One of these days he'd meet something as smart as he was. Actually, that was quite an eerie thought. I imagined there'd be quite a few bits and pieces involved.

"So what would this mean for us?" I asked. "You're sitting at twelve Strength now, right? And eleven Speed. Is that superhuman?"

He did some quick calculations.

"I'll be about six and a half times the average man's strength, and seventy percent faster give or take. I'm fairly sure that's world record breaking in both areas."

Well shit, that was encouraging. And we'd be getting two skillpoints per level, too.

My other tasks were less straightforward and dopamine releasing than just finding out how much we could lift; I had to somehow go about integrating our new joins. I'd expected Magnus to be the hardest one to organize, but he proved surprisingly malleable compared to Elizabeth.

It wasn't that she had *difficulty* following orders, of course. It was that she completely fucking refused to on a categorical level. It was like herding not just cats, but some bizarre cave creature that ate the fucking things, as well.

"Armor'd slow me down." She sniffed, as if that were the end of that. I actually short-circuited for a moment, pausing my futile efforts to put her in plate just to properly consider what I'd been told.

"It . . . will . . . It will also keep you alive . . . ?"

"Not if I get caught because I'm slower."

"Yes," I snapped. "Exactly then. And what if some idiot gets a lucky shot with an arrow while you're legging it in linen and wool?"

She hesitated, considering that, then shrugged.

"I'll make sure they don't."

It was like arguing with Solitaire almost. Just a complete refusal to even acknowledge the possibility of her actions having consequences, wrapped in the infuriating ability to *almost* make a half-solid argument justifying the sentiment. It was all I could do not to just start swearing blindly at her, and I took my leave.

Some victories, apparently, would require even the great Shango Belahont more time than that to achieve.

Our final matter of consideration was business, and that was by far the most notable. It was Phelia who called my attention to it, awaiting me in her—my—study with eyes as focused for work as ever.

It really was strange, speaking with her these days. Felt like I was in some fugue state given all our bedroom activity, and her complete and utter disregard for it the moment we were dressed and doing something else.

I followed suit.

"You had something to tell me?" I asked, taking a seat just opposite her. Funny how the distance we chose to remain apart hadn't shrunk at all since we'd started . . . Well, that was marriage I supposed. Or at least I assumed that was marriage. I'd not exactly had much experience with the concept just yet.

"Yes, I believe, given the hectic beginning to our arrangement has apparently been left in the past, we may now be best served looking for more . . . purely financial opportunities. Wealth, essentially, gotten through business. It is rather a more surefire way of bolstering one's coffers than simply killing people."

I widened my eyes, let my mouth gape open.

"You . . . What?" I gasped. "Not . . . Not killing people? How can that—"

"Enough, arsehole," she snapped, clearly not appreciating my hilarious wit. "You understand my point, though, yes? Particularly now, I think you'll agree your new company is far from suited for a large-scale conflict. And that's just the sort that you'd need to pay off my famil—our family's debt."

Was she just pretending to slip up so I'd be reminded that she didn't view us as a real family yet? I wouldn't put it past her. It was the sort of thing I might do, too, after all.

"Fine." I sighed. "Let's talk business, then. Which for the record I've actually got more experience with than I do mercenary work."

And most likely more experience than *her* for that matter, too. But we could cross that bridge when it came to it. Phelia was at least robust in her conversational skills, quickly bouncing back onto the main topic of discussion as if the distraction had never happened.

"Good. I doubt it will surprise you to know that I called you here having prepared several options for you ahead of time, each of which is . . . viable, at least, within its own area. But all of which will likely require some legwork to secure."

"Start with the most optimistic choice."

She did so, and I listened intently as Phelia moved through our options. Lord Wilskasai was the first among her chosen prospects, and I could see why quite quickly. He owned most of the city's mines. Elswick was a city ever under attack from . . . Well, pretty much everything really. When it wasn't orcs, it was undead. When it wasn't those, it was some enemy nation. One day I half expected a dragon would drop down and start burning everything. For now, though, it meant there was always a high demand for good steel.

I put that option on the solid-maybe pile, but made a note to ask Solitaire about the possibility of mass smelting later. It would be a lot less hopeful if our only option was diverting Ardin's efforts.

"Who are our other options?"

"The next up would be Lord Duriah, one of the more prominent heads of this city's martial families."

I'd heard that term before. Martial families, as the Elswickians called them, were those nobles who'd carved out niches for themselves by turning their families into a sort of elite fighting forces. One hundred men at arms was good, of course, when you were being attacked by orcs. But in a world where seemingly every human could muster *some* degree of superhuman physical power simply by training and practicing, there was a much greater difference made by elites. Sometimes you didn't have room for a hundred men to charge in at once.

Sometimes there were benefits to sending in a half dozen wrapped in steel plate and swinging swords hard enough to take limbs off with every hit.

I had a feeling that type would be rather difficult in a negotiation, though. Violent people tended to come with plenty of other traits packaged in. Few were pleasant.

"What does he want?" I frowned.

"Do you need to ask?" Phelia sighed. "Your staff, or others like it. Word has spread of it, you know."

"Ah," I noted. "No, definitely not. That's nonnegotiable. Long term we're best hoarding that secret to ourselves, believe me."

I didn't mind starting an industrial revolution, but I didn't want to kick-start one on Redacle's terms. Putting aside the exploitation that only increased as factories started emerging—and I wasn't sure looking at something as advanced as a gun would fail to inspire technological growth in other areas like that—our modern knowledge was our sole advantage, and I didn't want to see that reduced as the morons we'd been forced to share a world with started copying some of it.

Phelia, to her credit, seemed plenty understanding. I supposed even without out knowledge of the particulars it was fairly intuitive to realize how bad an idea it would be to give up the sorts of edges we had. Particularly when Solitaire was working on . . . something. Whatever it was he had his wits wrapped up in, I had a feeling it'd make people a bit volatile when he finally revealed it. Better volatile people without guns than with.

"So who's our last option?" I asked thoughtfully.

She hesitated, licked her lips, then sighed.

"Lord Byror. If we offer a truce, offer ourselves as subordinates, he may still wish to accept now that I have assets of more consequence to offer."

Solitaire's grin, pooling blood, a mangled friend, and a giant ticking time bomb just waiting to go off. I shook my head.

"Out of the question."

CHAPTER FORTY-SIX

Beam's POV: Day 90
Current Wealth: 221 gold, 2 silver, 42 copper

Apparently the tournament wouldn't just be doing alphabetic matchups from now on, but by sheer coincidence I was still the next one up in round two. I wasn't sure how I felt about that. Certainly not as opposed as Solitaire, at least, who looked to be on the verge of combusting as he spun one paranoid conspiracy theory after another to explain it. It was hard to dismiss him these days, though. People really did seem to be out to get us.

If nothing else, they'd be forced to do it in a tournament format now. A one-on-one fight. I'd be in my element when I came to meet their attacks.

Of course it helped that I'd been training, and preparing, and it helped that I was that little bit more dangerous now than in the last round. Helped more that I'd not seen too many in the last round who could've threatened me even then, and what helped most of all was the new trick I'd learned. I kept practicing it as I awaited my name to be called, focusing, conjuring the ethereal matter and letting it wash over me. It wouldn't do to show it off to the masses, that much still held. But there were ways around any problem.

My name was called, the moment upon me at last, and I hurried to answer it. I had no patience for dawdling, and I'd never been able to stand a wait even one second longer than was absolutely necessary. It was all I could do not to sprint out.

The arena looked more or less the same as it ever had, which was almost disappointing. My opponent strolled out shortly. He was a tall man, with features that were hidden to me by the heavy plate armor covering every inch of him. Well, I reckoned that was to be expected. Most of the first round's winners had been people wealthy enough to afford that sort of protection for themselves. It's not like I was in any position to complain. My own defense was even better.

Our match got started soon enough, and he was coming at me. A sword, this time, poor guy. I'd already gotten used to halberds well enough from my last bout, and I'd been training with a wide variety of weapons at every opportunity, tossing a few coins around to get decently skilled mercenaries to take some practice swings at me. Still, it was a relief to know I'd be in my field.

His first attack was a testing blow that I didn't even bother moving back from, just smacked aside. His strength surprised me, though, and it was that fractional warning that let me lunge away right before his follow-up could connect.

So, strength was against me. That was unfortunate, but not unexpected. I tried to remember this guy as he chased me and found the recollections drifting back. He'd been stronger than his last opponent, too, but my newly quickened eyes had no issue tracking his movements. I let him take a few more swings, learning his rhythm, then decided on my plan and stepped in. Instantly he sped up, revealing his true speed and bringing his blade down hard into the gap between two of my plates.

Just as I'd been waiting for him to. It hit the ethereal armor I'd conjured beneath my steel set, cracking through then stopping on the mail. I stumbled, wavered, let him think I was more injured than I was, and lunged the moment his guard drifted down. My rapier went clean between a pair of plates, too, but I made sure to watch out for blood before relaxing.

Admirably, the guy tried his best to stay upright, but there's only so much will and determination can do when the blood supplying it starts to run out. He collapsed to a knee, and the match was over soon enough. I watched him leave, then headed off myself.

Shango, I knew, would be circling around to meet with the guy. It was why I'd had to do without his input—he had to be primed and ready to strike up a conversation before anyone else. He hadn't tried to kill me, I knew that much, which meant that after Shango made his offer and headed back I could let him know, and we'd see if we got one more recruit. As far as schemes went it was probably a bit clumsy. Then again, what wasn't these days?

Argar was waiting for me as I took my leave from the arena, grinning as always.

"Poor bastard didn't have a chance, did he?" he noted. I tried not to be *too* smug as I replied, just shrugging.

"He got cocky. So you were watching then?"

"Aye, well, I plan on flattening you sometime soon. Figured I'd see what I could learn about how you move . . . Take advantage of the opportunity."

He didn't admit to being wrong, and I didn't prod him to. We just shared a look, a nod, and silently agreed to put everything behind us. It was the best outcome I could've hoped for.

Both of us were in the stands together soon after, where we found our seats waiting for us. Magnus was with Shango, continuing our new rule of never traveling alone, while Solitaire and the rest stayed at home to try to break as many terms of the Geneva conventions as was possible. It was almost nice, being outside of the increasingly cramped location we'd been steadily fortifying for the last few days, but that feeling didn't last long. The creeping fear of an attack only strengthened with every passing moment.

My hands tightened to fists as I watched the arena, not even noticing Shango's return until he was with us again.

"Nice fighting out there," he breathed, taking a seat, looking out at the arena just as I did. "We didn't get your opponent, sadly, but there'll be other shots. And you've guaranteed yourself a position in the next round either way."

I nodded, allowing myself to actually let that sink in. Another mountain of experience equal to the one we'd earned last time would mean another level for me, more power.

I'd be getting pretty strong pretty fast if I kept this up. I was almost desperate for my brother's other fights to hurry up and move past so I could find out what my new capabilities were sooner rather than later.

"How are your plans going?" I asked, suddenly finding myself considering the chances of Shango actually getting himself into the third round, and realizing that they were total shit. It wasn't that he couldn't fight, of course. It was just that he couldn't win fights.

Evidently, he was well aware of why I was asking because he suddenly let out an irritated huff.

"They're going fine. You just focus on kicking everybody's asses more, and we'll be doing well. I think another match is starting soon."

I glanced back down to the arena and saw that he was right. Both of us settled into our seats, eager as ever to see it.

We did see it, and we saw a good few others after that. The Challenger fought in the third match we watched, trouncing some poor sod as easily as ever, and Aja the Pit Hound was going against someone else shortly after. He didn't have any more trouble.

But neither of their opponents were *weak*. That was the unfortunate truth we were seeing, that as of now most, if not all our enemies seemed good enough to put up a solid fight against Magnus with equal equipment, and probably win with the plate armor that had now become most commonly worn among them.

More fights passed, and more notables caught our eyes. Almost before we knew it, things had moved along, and it was time for Argar's name to be called. I glanced over at the giant, half expecting to see fear in his eyes. I had, after all, been the one to tell him his limits, to shove against that unbreakable confidence and make it buckle.

It was a stupid expectation. I saw only the same certainty that always glowed behind his gaze. Argar stood in one swift motion and made his way down. I watched him go with a dry mouth,

"Good luck, man," I breathed abruptly. He looked back for a moment, grinning like always.

"Don't need luck" was all he said.

CHAPTER FORTY-SEVEN

Shango's POV: Day 90
Current Wealth: 221 gold, 2 silver, 42 copper

I had a lot to do, as always. That was life in Redacle. Do things, then find out you have more fucking things to do. My heading to the arena had been a break, a momentary recharge, an afternoon spent, if not resting, then diverting my focus to *differently strenuous* tasks and letting myself recover somewhat in all the areas of my brain reserved for the others.

Argar, as was his ever-prominent habit, had to ruin that by leaving my balls in my throat the entire damned time.

Oh, it all started out well enough. Things usually do, don't they?

Our bodyguard waltzed his way out into the arena as if he owned the place, and he didn't seem fazed an inch by all the hateful jeers thrown his way. I remembered then that he'd earned himself a reputation for brutality with how he'd dispatched the Soldier, which probably wasn't to our advantage. Solitaire, at least, had been subtle in exacting his revenge on the fucker sent to kill him— at least from what Beam had told me. Subtlety not only wasn't within Argar's vocabulary, but it wasn't within his physical capacity to even learn the word.

His opponent couldn't have been more different.

It was a small man, and that was my first hopeful observation. The second was that he was also an older one, probably as close to sixty as he was to fifty, and scowling that way only the properly tired and miserable were ever able to muster. As if the entire world were squatting without permission on his lawn. He peered up at Argar no more impressed than anyone else might have been looking at a regular-sized man.

Which was the beginning of my *less hopeful* observations. Following that singular pioneer of pessimism, I realized that his armor was quite well-made even by the standards of this tourney, that he held the fairly big and thick sword in one hand as if it weighed nothing at all. That even wearing twenty kilos of metal, he moved like he weighed nothing at all.

[Appraisal]
Statistics: Strength 11, Speed 13, Dexterity 10, Stamina 6, Toughness 10, Alertness 13, Charisma 6, Intelligence 5

Well, fuck. My breath caught in my throat as I drank in the statline. He had a fair advantage over Argar in more than one area. Speed and Alertness were both high enough that he'd be dancing around him, and that Dexterity . . . It was freakish. I was almost tempted to warn my friend, but the words wouldn't come out, held back by sense.

It'd just distract him, I knew. Just make him slow and stupid, and he'd need all the speed and wits he could get to come out on top here. Suddenly far less relaxed than I had been, I watched, tense and ready for whatever might happen.

The old man said something that I didn't hear, and it seemed to only irritate Argar. He lost his cool, came flying at him. It didn't work.

The axes were like blades in a blender, whipping around, coming one way and the other. I actually felt bad for the bastard stuck dodging them, almost. Argar hadn't gotten any stat increases from his three days of training—I'd been sure about that—but there was something different about how he moved now. A refinement, a practice. It wasn't much of a difference at all, but all those sluggish lulls between swings that an enemy of my or my brothers' speed were able to slip around seemed to have shrunk.

He was almost resembling an actual fighter, with an actual sense for his weapon's balance.

Still, he hit nothing but air. I watched the older man weave between axe swings, sometimes not moving more than an inch or two as he sent their edges flying wide of himself. It was almost hard to believe, a preternatural display of . . . No, not of speed, he wasn't just moving fast. I could track him just fine. This wasn't anything like the King.

He was just picking the exact right thing to do, every time, all the time, without fail. It was almost like watching Beam fight.

Argar's face twisted to a growl, and his body surged on now instead of his axes. Clearly he meant to smash his enemy down with a less avoidable attack.

It looked, for one moment, that he'd actually manage it. But the older man's sword just whipped up and smashed against Argar's helmet, stunning him with the instinctual flinch all men had to such an eye-approximate impact and interrupting his charge. While Argar still reeled and righted himself, the sword found a joint in his armor with surgical precision, passing between plates and drilling through chain mail. I winced at the sight as his leg buckled and he stumbled back.

"You are strong," the older man called out. "But undisciplined, poorly trained."

I barely heard him over the crowd, but I heard Argar clearly enough as he spat back his defiance.

"I've been training for three days, and that's all I need for you!"

He was charging in, an axe reared high, his body so painfully open to an attack that even I winced. The older man closed to punish him for the vulnerability, then stumbled back as Argar suddenly let go of his axes and whipped a fist out viciously fast. Faster than it could ever have come with two kilos of steel clutched tight. The older man moved at the last second, turning it into a glancing blow that sent sparks skidding and metal screeching as steel slid off of steel, but he was unbalanced, and Argar moved fast to punish him for the failing.

Argar wasn't deterred, not yet; he kept on coming. Leaning in, scrambling for the older man, and trying to lock his grip.

If he managed, I knew he'd have a chance. In a grappling match, covered with plate, the things that mattered were size and strength, not skill and side-stepping speed. I urged Argar on, did all I could not to stand up and start howling for his victory, watching with a dry mouth and tight fists.

But Argar's enemy was good at this, too. Very, very good. He slipped from Argar with a sliding grind of stiff plating, and backed off faster than I could follow. Argar barely snatched one of his axes up in time to ward the man off with another wide swing.

He was panting now, and all the hope drained out of me like helium from a punctured balloon. There'd never really been much of a chance at all, I saw now, not with such a weight of experience working against him. If we'd wanted Argar to win, we'd have been better pushing him to train a month ago. At least then there might've been some question at hand before he went down.

"You cannot win this, boy," the man called out, "But you are a resilient one. It will take time to defeat you. Surrender now and I will take you on as my apprentice. If what you say is true, and you really are only days into training, then you would be more than qualified to be my student."

Argar looked almost offended.

"I've not lost yet, you old bastard," he snarled, looking for a moment like he'd come on swinging again, but hesitating, holding back to regain his already wasted breath.

"Save me the bluster, boy. This is your final chance," the older man spat. "Give up. Save me the effort of beating you and you might go places under my tutelage."

Argar's fists, I saw, were tightening. Even from the hundreds of feet separating us I could make out the iron strength in his wrathful grip.

"Piss off."

Then it was the older man's turn to attack, and if anything he was deadlier on the offense than he was resilient in defense. Moving in like a snake, going low, melting back from a warding swing, and twisting around to strike from Argar's unprotected side. The giant was stumbling around to guard, just as the elder reversed his movement and hit the other. Metal screeched, Argar stumbled again, and then a new blow was coming.

Argar didn't avoid this one, either, but it bit a lot deeper than the staggering impact he'd taken seconds before. I winced, he winced, the fucking crowd winced as we all saw—almost *felt*—the edge of his enemy's steel neatly pass down.

Whatever his damned sword was made of, the old man had a nice edge on it. Even tool steel chain mail surrendered. But not without exhausting most of its attacker's impact.

Quick as lightning, Argar's punch caught the old man across his head and lifted him fully a half foot from the ground as he went sliding back. The bastard wasn't even close to up before five hundred pounds of screaming northerner came down hard atop him.

The match didn't last long after that.

CHAPTER FORTY-EIGHT

Solitaire's POV: Day 90
Current Wealth: 211 gold, 2 silver, 42 copper

Come to think of it, I was starting to see a few upsides to being stuck in Redacle. Here I could make all the explosives I wanted.

Which was nice, but boring. I had the mercury cooking elsewhere, a secret tool we'd use later, and that left nothing for me to do except focus on other matters of home defense. I'd already finished the welcome mat, which meant we needed something with a bit of *proactive* self-preservation power.

Killing people when they tried to stab you was nice and all, but it just couldn't beat killing them when they were still a mile away. So I tried to work on a more refined model of cannon.

That wasn't hard, at least. The last cannon I'd made had been a repurposed bell, and the one before that had been an antiair battery I'd set up during one paranoid afternoon when I kept expecting police helicopters to make themselves known above me. Neither one had been particularly fine work, and I had the luxury of time now. A bit of it at least.

One major factor was that I didn't need this to punch through any great weight of armor. We weren't dealing with modern people, or a giant creature, or even any of the actual powerful Redaclans. Kaiju-sized monsters or dark sorcerers were still a ways off from us, so I could just focus on spitting out iron for now.

Which was still annoying. I did have that old perfectionist urge I'd always had. The one that drove my mother to make sure her son could diffuse a DET charge in under fifteen seconds after rolling out of bed. I wouldn't settle for a cannon incapable of winning the Napoleonic Wars for a reason as petty as it being completely unnecessary, no sir!

God, maybe I really did need medicating.

Well, no helping that now. I got to work.

The fundamental principle of a cannon, really, was that it could squeeze an explosion. So I had to first decide what kind of blast I wanted. To do that, I'd need to know what I was going to be hurling.

I didn't need to kill a fortress, so I decided on a smaller projectile. Fourpounders, as they'd have called them in the age of actual black powder cannons, or in noncaveman terms an iron ball measuring about seventy-five millimeters from one side to the other. Then I realized I was being stupid. Why make a ball? Much better to use an elliptical slug. No need to re-create history just for the sake of it when there were more effective alternatives.

And there'd be no need for iron, either. Why not use lead?

It wasn't hard to get my hands on plenty. I just put an order in for our ever-growing horde of blacksmith minions and soon had plenty of the stuff. Lead melts at a hilariously low temperature, so I was looking at a nice big bucket of the stuff soon enough, pouring it out and doing my best not to breathe it in. After so long dealing with steel-liquefying heats it was almost laughable how overly protected I was, between my thick layers and superhuman flesh.

While I waited for my lead to arrive, I'd gotten to work on the actual barrel. This was a bit trickier.

Beam was at the arena. Ardin was busy. I'd heard from Shango that his bitch wife was able to dig up some stories of what had happened at Rinchester, too. If I was publicly seen ordering people to assemble a big metal cylinder, or if someone paid enough to learn from one of the smiths responsible that I'd done so quietly, a clever person would be able to figure out that I was re-creating the weapon responsible for turning so many Rotters into numerous smaller pieces of Rotter.

I considered the pros and cons, eventually deciding to call on Corvan and see what he could do.

"This is like your brother's staff," he said instantly. I considered lying, decided it wouldn't work, and pretended I'd never considered it in the first place with a nod.

"Exactly like that. Bigger, obviously. Imagine something ten times faster than an arrow and thirty times heavier, solid lead. That's the sort of weapon I'm describing here."

Most men wouldn't have had the slightest idea what I meant. It just wouldn't register to them. Such forces were beyond anything they had a common reference for. Corvan, though, was a magus. A strong one, and an experienced one. He hadn't told us most of his history yet, and I'd have bet there were a good few magical phenoms lying somewhere in it. He grasped the essentials nice and quick.

"Are you insane?" Corvan snapped. "Why would you want that? What do you think is coming for us?"

"Don't know, not sure, and I'm making sure to be overprepared for whatever it is. Now get to work."

Fortunately, he didn't argue for long. Also fortunately, I still didn't need a big gun, and we had plenty of iron stores already prepared. Now it would've taken a while to make steel, though I was working on a new method for that as part of Shango's—or rather his bitch wife's—business ideas. The good thing about black powder, though, was that its fundamental weakness meant durable metals weren't really necessary to gunify it.

Iron would do. I gave Corvan the dimensions and kept his measurements lined up while he heated and squeezed the hot metal, hammering and compressing the impurities away.

We'd formed the initial shape from molten iron, essentially casting it into a funnel of hardened air that left the final product stiff and hard. Brittle, probably, too. Which was why I had him put up a wall of air and hid behind a desk while we gave it a test fire.

The gun didn't explode at least, and our long practice hallway with its hundred-meter length—the longest one in the building—gave a few pointers on just where the shortcomings were.

After the first few shots, I did end up needing to replace the wall, but they were *very* educational. Notably in that for whatever reason the projectiles were spinning completely haywire. That was weird, and ahistorical, so I gave a bit of thinking as to why.

If I could punch myself in the stupid, I'd have stabbed it instead. Elliptical slugs weren't used with smoothbore barrels like the one I'd set up. I gave a few more practice shots with spherical balls, and sure enough they flew nice and straight. Ish. It would take a damned long time to affix the interior of the barrel with grooves for rifling, so it looked like I'd be stuck doing things like the redcoats had for now. Ideally with a less genocidal choice of targets.

"Not much good, is it?" Corvan noted. "Unless you're fighting a giant."

He had a point. The cannon wasn't that big, three hundred kilos in all, but that was still a fair amount to be doing much of anything with. Even on wheels, or an axle, it would take a lot of strength to turn.

So we got back to the drawing board because I quite liked the idea of a workable swivel gun, and already had a decent notion of how I might make my new toy light enough to work as one. It all came down to the metal.

Cast iron was all right. It worked, at least, but I could do better. Bearing in mind I had some steel on its way, I decided to try saving the few days that'd likely take by working around my issues instead. In the end I settled on a new design.

Once more, cast iron. This time, though, I had Corvan squeeze the cooling metal with rings of *wrought* iron instead. That was more flexible, less stiff, and gave easier. It provided a bit of flexibility to an otherwise rigid and brittle barrel, which allowed me to make the main structure that little bit thinner. I made all sorts of other ergonomic changes, too, mostly to stop the voices in my head that got pissy whenever something wasn't perfected to half a percentage point, and we tried a few more shots with round balls.

Their performance was far, far better. A very promising sign, made all the more promising by our newly slimmed-down gun. One hundred and forty kilos, not three hundred. It was still a heavy bastard, but light enough to work with.

All that was left was the actual swivel mechanism, and I got to that promptly. Then stopped, and started swearing.

Well, there were limits to raw knowledge and intuition. I'd need Ardin, or at least Beam, to do the fiddly smithing work needed to make all my new design's complex moving parts. Which meant we'd be waiting a while anyway. Hopefully nobody tried to murder us before they were freed up.

CHAPTER FORTY-NINE

Shango's POV: Day 90
Current Wealth: 211 gold, 2 silver, 42 copper

I wasn't much looking forward to my match, which, in my defense, was a fairly standard attitude to aim toward an imminent ass kicking. It was just so obvious what was coming. I wasn't Beam, not physically and *definitely* not technically. Magic aside, and it *would* be aside as per the rules, I had nothing on him in an actual fight. I couldn't even cheat with my gun.

Any round able to inconvenience him would very possibly bury me, so I entered the arena with no small amount of worry. That worry wasn't really reduced in the slightest when I saw a woman stroll out to face me.

She was tall, but not particularly well-built. After so long spent around giant, burly bastards able to one-hand a sledgehammer, I'd evidently developed quite a skewed sense for human muscularity because her impressively lean outline struck me as *skinny* rather than anything else. She moved well enough, though, hopping from one foot to the other and testing the weight of some short, broad metal blade held tight in one hand. A chain ran from its back, affixed to the base of her apparel.

I didn't want to be right, but guessed it was probably not a close-up sort of weapon. Just perfect.

"I don't suppose you'd be willing to talk this out?" I tried, nervously smiling and using the expression to hide my gaze as it flicked across her face. The woman's features were unmasked by any visor or helmet, and I hoped to read whatever emotions might flit across them. If she'd been hired to kill me, and decided to do so, there might be an explosion of uncertainty, or anger, or any number of other things.

But it was like looking at a statue. A very murderous statue, mind, that wasted no time in drawing its weapon and stepping forward. Her armor clinked and rattled with the movement, bringing my attention to it for the first time.

Interesting, not plate armor. But not cheap, either. It was solid steel made into smaller rectangular plates that dangled around her frame and shifted easily with each movement, or else lay crested around limbs and torso segments in solid walls. Easy to move in, I'd guess, but hard to break through. My hand tightened around the handle of my own weapon—a tool steel rapier that had been the thing best suited for Beam to train me in. It was heavily built as far as fencing steels went, to compensate for armor, but otherwise unchanged. A lot smaller than the weapons mostly favored in this world, and that lack of mass seemed particularly problematic all of a sudden.

[Appraisal]
Statistics: Strength 9, Speed 13, Dexterity 10, Stamina 7, Toughness 9, Alertness 13, Charisma 6, Intelligence 7

Well, there was a surprise. With an Intelligence stat that high I'd have to watch her. She'd be quicker than—

Slower than the bit of steel that suddenly came flying for me, that's for sure. I tried to duck and failed miserably, merely shifting millimeters and feeling it bite down in a gap between my metal plates. I feared, for one moment, that I'd been cut, but the chain mail beneath it held fast. Ardin had done a fine work— tool steel like the others. Lucky for me, he'd gotten faster at making it. Unlucky for me, my opponent was swinging again.

This time I was prepared, but her steel edge still twisted too jerkily and cleanly to follow, scraping along the armor around me and losing one of its own tips in the process. She withdrew it, scowling.

Well, that was medieval steel for you. Worse than the stuff we'd used back on Earth. If I could just get her to keep smashing my armor head-on, my enemy would be unarmed soon enough. She seemed to realize the fact, and moved to enact a new tactic.

It was like trying to keep track of an arrow that insisted on changing its own direction by the moment. Not a matter of focus, or anticipation, just raw speed. By the time I'd clocked it in one place, it'd already flitted by another eight feet to another. I sustained my futile effort of pinning down the fucking thing before it suddenly came down for me. I flinched, raising a guard, then swore as one last twist ran along the chain and whipped the end upward under my now-exposed armpit.

This time I *did* feel a cut, and staggered away. There was no blood outside my armor, and shifting inside it I could feel the chain mail was only down a few links, but that was a fucking close one. My enemy was more confident now, watching me from the seven or so paces separating us. Evidently, her weapon could do either a lot of damage or a little. A fickle thing based on momentum and centimeter-precise aim. Had I taken her best shot already?

I doubted it. And if they got much worse than that I'd be bleeding out sooner rather than later. The decision of what to do next practically made itself. I let out a roar and charged.

Now, I've never been the most intimidating of fellows. Well, if you ignore the fact that a black man is inherently scary to plenty of assholes, and that an African is inherently *savage* to plenty more, at least. What I have been, though, is six feet tall. And since being tortured by Beam's little exercise routine, I'd also had a fair bit of bulk to boast about, too. Adding the plate armor on top of that and I probably cut a very scary figure, sprinting and screaming and swinging.

Which was really something I'd been banking on having more of an effect than it did. But this woman didn't even flinch. She just watched me closing in like some idle fascination, calm and collected, biding her time until the perfect moment came. Her bladed weapon caught me right above the hip.

The biggest pain I'd felt since being beaten in that alley ran up my side, a burning, screaming lance stuck right in me and grinding itself deeper with every step. My body tried to seize up, muscles to tighten still, heart to pound right out of my chest. I ignored it all, turned it into more screaming as I closed at last to melee range, and swung.

Of course the bitch already had a shortsword up by then because God wouldn't have found it nearly as funny to give me an *easy* opponent. My opening slash was clumsy and unprofessional, like always, but I'd come a decent way since starting my lessons with Beam. It was straight at least, and forced her to take a sidestep in deflecting it. The impact ran right up my arm, back down to the elbow, and by the wince on her face I could see it did that and more for her.

Well, I had the strength advantage, and the armor advantage. And all the mass here was mine, too. Up close we were in my turf. It was a reassuring thing to know, and lent extra vigor to my next swings.

She didn't try to block these, just whipped back. The one advantage, I saw, to my rapier-like weapon was it meant I could get a lot more swings in a lot more easily than with a broader period-appropriate sword. On the other hand this also left me with a lot less momentum behind each one than a heavier piece. My enemy was beyond reach now, circling, eyes narrowed, cautious. I was just about to speak when she darted in.

Quick jabs, one, three, ten. I barely even parried a third, feeling the rest skid off my armor. She was moving to encircle me the next moment, and just as I twisted to keep her ahead, her next swing came down hard at a joint. It broke the mail, barely, and cut me like the first chained swing had. A tiny little nick dealing damage that was more psychological than physical.

I backed up. She closed faster. A leg found its way behind one of mine, my balance broke, and I felt myself lurch back, landing hard. Before I was up, the woman was on me, a knife drawn and pressed back down under my armpit. I froze.

It was the place she'd already cut into with her chained weapon, and she had a perfect opening to drive that steel in. This one wasn't so strong that no human on Earth could've matched her, but her physical power was still a good few times stronger than what most men would be generating. If she wanted to, if she'd been paid to, she could stick that knife in, drag it back, and cut all the tendons. Corvan was approaching the limits of his healing. He'd need to be taking breaks soon, long ones. Weeklong ones.

Was I about to lose the movement of my arm?

"Do you give up?!" she snarled.

I hesitated a literal instant before frantically nodding and losing myself the match.

CHAPTER FIFTY

Solitaire's POV: Day 90
Current Wealth: 211 gold, 2 silver, 42 copper

I showed up at the stadium soon after receiving word of my own match coming up. Turned out Shango had been handed an ass kicking. That was about typical. He'd always loved getting those back on Earth. It was different here, though, due to being a fairly massive inconvenience for all of us. I swallowed my frustration and tried to remind myself that it wasn't quite his fault he'd been born with a silver spoon lodged in his colon.

"So, a woman," I noted. Shango glared at me.

"It was a very strong woman," he growled. "And well trained. And she got lucky."

"Right." I nodded, grin blossoming. "A very powerful woman, of course. That explains it then."

"Fuck off." Shango seemed impervious to my attempts at cheering him up, and I could hardly blame him. He'd lost his shot to progress through the tournament and get another mainline of experience points. That hurt, a lot. More than any loss in prize money could have. And it made me all the more nervous for my own bout.

"It's not the end of the world," I noted, switching tactics quickly. "You have more time to focus on business rather than training now, and your combat power was never what made you an asset to begin with. It's not like Beam's dropping out, right?"

He did relax, slightly, at that. And I saw that there'd not be much more I could do. I headed off for my own match, feeling suddenly heavy at the thought.

My armor hadn't quite been finished yet, but Beam's fit me well enough. An inch too short, an inch too broad, but otherwise I slipped in ready for a fight. It was somehow a slight reassurance. Shango's loss had reminded us again that good steel didn't make us invincible.

Arthur Nightne strolled out, and I had to resist the urge to swear blind.

He was one of the tournament's favorites, a fairly tall, fairly lean man who, despite his not-particularly-bulky build, moved like a damned truck. He was wearing full plate armor like me, and a fairly large longsword that hopped from one hand to the other like it weighed as much as a pencil.

I knew this man was fast, strong, terrifyingly skilled. I knew all of this because he'd been one of our main characters back when Redacle was just a damned fantasy world.

The match began, and he closed fast, swinging faster. A feint—he always opened with those—and I bypassed it by throwing a quick lunge for his face.

There was no point in even worrying about guarding myself, knowing that his blow was faked, and I'd have definitely hit him had he not been so damned explosive in his speed. He swatted my sword aside, but I was already backing away before his counterstroke. My elbow ached from where the clash of our strength had sent an impact down my arm, and it was all I could do to hold the fucking sword he'd batted away so easily. This was not going to be a fun fight in the slightest.

Apparently, though, I'd shaken him. The idiot was probably trying to figure out whether I was a secret fighting genius or just ridiculously lucky, and I decided to take advantage of his uncertainty, closing in and pressing my sword to his, bringing my strength to bear. Whispering in the moment I had before being forced back.

"I know it's all an act."

He froze up instantly. And I smashed my forehead against his face with every inch of strength my entire body could muster, using the plate of my helmet as a bludgeon. It did its job well enough, hammering in the visor guarding Arthur's eyes and sending him back a step.

Only a step, mind. He was really quite strong.

Arthur seemed galvanized by the headbutt, but cautioned, too. He backed up, eyeing me, studying my moves. I knew because I was the one who'd written his habit of doing that into the character. It felt surreal to see it from the perspective of an enemy, and just a bit terrifying.

It wouldn't take long for him to get my measure, and once he figured out how much weaker I was, this fight would be as good as over. I'd have to do something clever before that could happen.

"What do you mean?" the knight asked. He was on me almost before I could react, but did just what I had. Swinging down, softening the impact right before it came, clashing our swords and making a show of pressing his bodyweight against mine. From this close, I could see one of his eyes had been near totally covered by the folded metal of his visor. His voice was all uncertainty and worry, almost fearful. That was a hopeful sign—a fearful enemy was half beaten.

"I know you're not a noble knight," I breathed, pushing back against him. "You've never voluntarily saved a maiden in your life, you spend most of your days desperately trying to *avoid* danger, and you've shoved more than one person in between you and it."

"Whoever told you this—"

"Nobody told me," I cut in, grunting as his strength became too much to bear and stumbling back. I realized my mistake an instant later when he swung for me with every scrap of strength he had.

Twenty-two Strength, on our system. Shango had checked. It was like being hit by a fucking car. My steel-clad boots screamed as they scraped against the ground, entire body sent sliding, then falling as my balance broke. I hit the stone, rolled, got to my feet just in time for a boot to catch my chest and send me flying all over again.

Very much like being hit by a car because this time, between the force and the lack of friction metal had on stone, my back actually hit the far wall of the arena . . .

. . . Ten meters away.

It was ridiculous. I almost burst out laughing then and there. Five, six kilojoules had just hit me? Accounting for waste energy at least. That wasn't the kind of impact a person took. It just didn't happen. That was comic book shit. And I was fighting it.

I got to my feet as fast as I could, and I was still barely up in time for Arthur to find me standing and swinging rather than lying back. My error was clear now—if I knew his secret, that his mythological heroism and quixotic valor was just a hoax—it meant I was a threat to the cushy hero's life he'd come to enjoy.

Arthur Nightne was a fucking bastard. A selfish, cowardly, conniving piece of shit who got by on misunderstandings, a great deal of genuine martial skill, and the fact that people were always willing to tell heroic tales about a goodlooking white man. I'd felt so clever writing him.

I didn't feel very clever now.

Because when you took a man like that and showed him a threat to the high life, his first instinct wasn't to ask any questions. It was to kill that threat before someone else could. My block was barely in time to stop his sword, and even as it did I was still forced down to one knee by the sheer, unbridled fucking strength on the other end. He was further advanced from me than I was from a normal human, and the screaming joints in my shoulders were evidence of the fact.

Only one thing caught my eye during the exchange over my own anatomical torture. It was the big dent left in Nightne's sword. Hope, that.

Being stronger than a polar bear didn't exactly make your weapons any harder, I supposed.

"I'm not going to expose you—" I managed, which, being honest, was an impressive feat alone given how quickly the fucker kicked me. His boot found all the heavy plates over my gut, which wasn't actually a weak spot in my armor at all. Somehow, he made it feel like one. My feet left the ground, and I flew a good foot or more upward before finally starting my gravitational drift back downward.

He beat me to it, of course, punching again. This time when I flew, it was without the slightest contact with the stone underfoot, and I practically bounced off the wall right behind me.

For the second time, I was in the dirt. It was only my mother's psychotic lessons that kept me from lying there helpless.

A stationary person is a dead person, she'd say. Right between *always remember to say please and thank you*, but just before *if somebody looks like they're planning something, best to gut them then and there*. My body was rolling before my brain even knew it had touched down, and even that was too late to keep Nightne's next kick from launching me again.

It really was getting quite tiresome, being thrown around. Not as tiresome as landing, though. This time I did a fine job breaking the fall, saving my precious neck and shoulders from being beaten by the hard stone by absorbing the impact with my face. I was up as fast as before, though, and bought myself a second by swinging out wide at Nightne's face.

"Do you really think I'd be telling you this if someone else didn't already know as insurance?!"

He hesitated. I'd bought myself seconds, at least. Nightne was many things, but stupid wasn't one of them. Now all I had to do was carve a handhold into him and see how I could work it. If not . . .

Fuck, the worst they'd do if he beheaded me after the match was called was disqualify him, and somehow he'd go down in history as a glorious savior for it to boot.

"My brothers know," I told him, speaking faster than I'd ever spoken in my life. "And I doubt even you could kill all of them together, not with my magic protecting them. But I have a way you don't need to."

He closed, and for one horrible moment I thought I was about to get one limb lighter. Instead, he just entered another feigned grapple. Squeezing a bit harder than was probably necessary.

"Speak fast," he spat. I spoke fast.

"We know how skilled you are, how strong you are, how fast you are. And we know how often you get thrown into deadly fights because some idiot thinks you want to be there. I'd like to offer you a job with some people who know better."

The pressure eased up a fraction.

CHAPTER FIFTY-ONE

Shango's POV: Day 91
Current Wealth: 197 gold, 27 silver, 14 copper

Solitaire lost his fight, obviously. It wasn't that he was a bad fighter, just that he'd been fighting Arthur fucking Nightne. Winning would've been basically impossible for all the same reasons losing would have been if his opponent had been a toddler. He did surprisingly well, though. Which obviously was evidence of some trickery on his part.

Well, there were benefits to creating the world you were stuck in. Having intimate knowledge of a few key players was one of them.

On the one hand, Corvan was more or less out of magic healing juice, so we had to fork over the cost of fixing ourselves up personally. That stung a bit, particularly when I heard how much lead and other materials Solitaire had gone out of his way to buy the day before. On the other hand, we had Arthur fucking Nightne on our team now. That was a big boon because he actually gave us a real shot at that prize money. I didn't think he moved as well as the King, or swung as strongly, but he surely had a chance, at least, of winning. I hoped so at least.

Oh well, there were other benefits to each round anyway. Even if seeing them this time around stung a bit.

[Appraisal]
Class: Revolutionary
Level: 14
Condition: Fine
Modifiers: +4 Speed, +6 Toughness, +3 Alertness, +5 Strength

Statistics: Strength 12, Speed 11, Dexterity 8, Stamina 6, Toughness 11, Alertness 11, Charisma 3, Intelligence 10
Inventory: Local wear, plate armor, shortsword, shortspear, knives (x3)
Class Abilities: Detect Element II
Current Experience Points: 448/480
Unspent Skillpoints: 0

[Appraisal]
Class: Dragonknight
Level: 16
Condition: Fine
Modifiers: +4 Strength, +5 Speed, +5 Toughness, +6 Alertness
Statistics: Strength 13, Speed 13, Dexterity 8, Stamina 9, Toughness 13, Alertness 14, Charisma 6, Intelligence 5
Inventory: Local wear, plate armor, rapier
Class Abilities: Beloved II
Current Experience Points: 246/520
Unspent Skillpoints: 0

Two levels, a thousand experience. Solitaire and I'd missed out on both opportunities by losing. There was a notable question of why Solitaire had seemingly gained three hundred points, but that didn't detract from my own lack of any. That lack stung more than any of the cuts I'd gotten had, so I did what I always did with the bitter taste of disappointment.

I washed it out of my mouth with something else.

Alora the Red Blade was her name, and it was a comfort to at least have gotten my ass kicked by a girl with a cool name. That cool name had a more practical effect, as well, because it made the act of tracking her down far quicker and easier. I found her at a tavern, strolling in with Magnus watching my back, and heading to her seat in the corner of the room. I'd not even finished sitting down before she spoke.

"Fuck off."

As openings went, not the most promising. I'd worked with worse, though.

"I just wanted to offer you my congratulations." I smiled. It bounced off her entirely.

"You want me to join you, like that idiot did, and like Arthur Nightne has," she replied, aiming her words like a dagger and sending them just as precisely through my verbal armor as her *actual* blade had been sent through my physical armor.

Well, I'd seen an Intelligence stat of seven on her. It was hardly unexpected that she'd see through the bullshit, given the obvious hints. Next time we'd have to try recruiting the clever ones first.

"Alright, fine, you've seen through me," I answered, deciding that my one remaining card was playing things straight. It was amazing how often that worked where all else failed. "I want to recruit you. You're fast, skilled, tough, and strong—"

"Not interested. You're trying to build an army, and that fight your Vit got into in round one was clearly some sort of demonstration against you. Whoever got Aja the Pit Hound under their thumb is fucking powerful, and I don't want to tangle with that."

I hesitated, before deciding to proceed.

". . . And you're smart, above all else," I finished. "I really do believe you'd be a great asset for my family, and I *know* we'd be a great one for you."

The woman looked at me in . . . Well, in very much the same way I'd always been taught to look at people. Fascinating.

"The question is whether I'd live long enough to benefit from that. And I really don't think I would."

It was a completely fair point, and it also served to frame exactly where I needed to target her uncertainties to move this conversation in my favor.

"You'll no doubt have heard that not a one of us has been targeted since then, and we've not done anything to draw the ire of the people responsible. We're stronger now, too, not least for *Arthur fucking Nightne's* presence. And if you signed on, you'd be looking at some new gear. Gear made by the same techniques and people responsible for the chain mail you felt your weapons bouncing off yesterday."

That one had her considering, a tiny little crack in the iron wall of her stoicism.

"Which, again, is useless if I can't use it. Who's to say you openly recruiting won't spur on another little attack?"

I smiled.

"I'm to say that, particularly because we'll be offering you shelter in my wife's mansion. A noble mansion. That mansion, as it happens, will be protected by the most powerful magics my brother and our magus can muster. You have heard of my brother, right? Solitaire?"

She swallowed.

"The one who . . . destroyed those Rotters."

"Yes." I smiled again. "And the one who made my staff. How about we step outside, and I can show you?"

I'd brought a sheet of iron for just such a demonstration. Maybe fifteen centimeters in either direction, and about one centimeter thick. Arrows would've bounced off it with barely even a dent left to show they'd impacted at all. My gun was more than enough though. My first shot took a corner right off; the second was centered better and gutted the plate. We had to prop it up again after both—the bullets sent it spinning through the air as they tore through.

Alora swallowed again, seeing the display. We were standing a good fifty paces back from it, and I let my smugness show as I hoisted the gun back over my shoulder.

"On a good day, I can fire this more than sixty times a minute," I told her. "And put a round—rather, a shot—through someone's chest from almost ten times the distance you just saw. It won't go through steel as well as iron, obviously, but if it hits a man in normal plate armor, it'll still smash through the breastplate, his torso, the backplate, and any naked people who happen to be standing behind him for good measure. We can make more, by the way."

"How many more?" she asked. "How quickly?"

"More." I shrugged. "You don't find out until you sign up, but I can tell you you'll get one if you want it. Armor, too."

"What good is armor anymore?" she scoffed. "With these things around."

I eyed her.

"Our armor will stop a glancing hit from one of these while remaining light enough for an untrained man, and even if the projectile penetrates it'll be slowed enough that a particularly tough person might still escape with just scratches and bruising. Our armor, at least, is very good. As you might have noticed, with how long you struggled fighting someone you could've beaten three of normally."

She was thinking now, and that was always the prelude to my victories. Get a person thinking and you were most of the way done with getting them to think what you wanted. I waited for the question, or questions, I knew was coming. I wasn't waiting long.

"What are your plans exactly?" she asked me. "What do you want?"

That was a big question. What *did* I want? Elswick? Not really, no. Peace? I was certainly going about it the wrong way for that. I was a few good deals away from living in luxury forever, and the deck was almost as stacked in my favor now as it had been the moment I shot out of my dad's dick.

Did I want justice, then? Yes. Basic decency and rights for the people of Redacle? Yes. Did I want to right the world's wrongs and straighten it all out like some damned hero? Yes I did. But how did I intend to do all that?

In the end, I could hardly have told her I wanted to conquer the entire world, so I just shrugged.

"What everyone wants, in the end. Power, influence, and to do the right thing. If you've heard of our exploits in Rinchester then you know how much my family's already grown in a few weeks so far. Why don't you stick around and see what we can do in a few more?"

She was thinking again, but she barely even needed to bother. I could tell by the deliberate pause and the intense furrowing of brows that I had her.

That was the thing with clever people—their default state was thinking. And their default thoughts, most of the time at least, were rational. It was hard *not* to get a rational person to fall on the side with guns.

CHAPTER FIFTY-TWO

Beam's POV: Day 91
Current Wealth: 197 gold, 27 silver, 14 copper

Solitaire had blown the house up, and Phelia was pissed.

Well, that was a mild exaggeration. As Solitaire was quick to point out—he hadn't blown the *entire* house up. Just a tiny, shitty corridor, and even that had only been blown up "a little bit." For some reason, though, this didn't seem to actually mollify Phelia much.

"You're insane!" she'd snapped. "A madman! You're a threat to us all!"

"If by 'us all' you mean the global capitalist hegemony responsible for the sustained oppression and exploitation of the working class," Solitaire had replied, "then yes, I am. You might say that my destroying that wall was merely symbolic of my intents to destroy the world order laid out by its parasitic oligarchs. That your brick and mortar was the stuff of oppression, and an indicator of what I intend for all of capital."

Phelia blinked, staring at him.

"What the fuck?! No, you're actually insane! You just blew my fucking wall up!"

"It was a shittily made wall." Solitaire sniffed. "If you don't want your things blown up, make them more explosion resistant. I could recommend we build it with rebar, you know. That's something your people are too stupid to have invented yet. Basically—"

It was not a very productive conversation. It was also one that begged a lot of questions, and I was quick in aiming some of the more notable ones at Solitaire.

"Why did you blow up the wall?" I asked, which got a sigh from him.

"I didn't do it *on purpose*," he grunted, as if it were somehow unreasonable to believe that the insane pyromaniac would ever even dream of such a thing. "It was an . . . accident. A project I'm working on got a bit out of control."

That surprised me. It didn't seem like him to make a mistake of that sort.

"You accidentally set off some black powder?"

Solitaire grinned.

"Oh, this wasn't black powder. I—"

Whatever he was about to say next was interrupted by Shango's return, our brother strolling in with Magnus in tow and a newcomer by his side. Alora the Red Blade. He'd gotten her, then.

I saw instantly where her nickname came from. The woman's hair was almost *crimson*, that's how red it was.

"What's going on?" Shango asked while the woman remained silent. She seemed hardly impressed by us all, even by Nightne, and her eyes were darting around the room silently, thoughtfully. Solitaire was first in answering.

"Phelia's throwing a tantrum because somebody chipped a bit of wallpaper."

"You blew a fucking hole in my wall!" Phelia snapped. Solitaire shrugged.

"There may have been a wall behind the wallpaper at the time, yes. But it wasn't in any of the parts of the mansion we actually use, so I don't see the issue."

He could have boiled Phelia alive and not left her skin as burning red.

What followed was not a long argument. Shango quickly came to side with his wife, Solitaire called him a "cunt-struck traitor," Phelia called him a barbarian, and I had to step in before anybody drew any paranoid conclusions from the events. Most likely somebody whose name rhymed with Politaire. Soon enough Solitaire and I were making our way out of the room and to another part of the occupied wing, giving everybody a bit of time to cool down.

"He's changed," Solitaire growled for the fifth time. "I swear, he has. That's what women do to a man, you know, change him. Make him all malleable and—"

"Solitaire, I'm really not in the mood for your misogyny at the moment," I cut in, deciding to just say it straight and hope it sank in. Fortunately, it did.

"Fine. Let's do the tests then. I need to wait for my ears to stop ringing anyway."

That, I had to admit, brought a smile across my face. I'd started to like the tests.

First up was the sprint, and that was satisfying as hell. As of now, apparently, with my Speed stat hitting thirteen, I was capable of managing a hundred-meter dash in seven seconds flat. World record breaking by a ludicrous degree, and I wasn't running it on anywhere near as controlled a ground as the Olympics used. After that came the lift.

We'd set up a sort of bench press for testing that, and Solitaire used his ability to provide the weights by freezing carefully measured cubes of ice. Thirteen Strength made me about equal to Argar, and Argar, it seemed, could use it to raise more than half a ton.

Five hundred and eighty kilos, that was about my limit. *Also* world record shattering. After this came the not-so-fun tests.

Solitaire heated up a bit of iron, and he stuck it on me. Barely. It was just a single strip, maybe half a square inch in area, held against the tip of my elbow. He'd done the same thing a while ago. I hissed, felt it burn as he held it there for exactly a second, then watched him pull it away. In a few hours we checked the mark, and kept checking it.

I'd still gotten burned, but not as badly as before. That pretty much confirmed his theory on Toughness scaling up at the same rate as Strength. It also served as a useful reminder for me not to get myself lit on fire. We weren't that durable. Yet.

"Tests complete." Solitaire smiled. "You're getting dangerous. I wonder how stab resistant you are . . ."

"Don't," I told him, cheerily enough regardless. Solitaire wouldn't *actually* knife me without asking permission. Probably. I was fast enough to avoid it either way.

He sniffed, put out at the denial, but clearly still pleased with our readings.

"Well I can do some calculations anyway. Your skin should be closing in on the tensile strength of copper as things are. Not stab proof, but certainly stab tedious."

Stab tedious was a lot less than I might have hoped for, but I'd just have to follow my usual tactics of trying not to get stabbed in the first place. They'd been working out well enough so far at least.

"What do you think this does for my chances in the tourney?"

His face fell.

"Not . . . as much as it might have, honestly. You're stronger than before but . . . Well, we're dealing with people around the twenties range at the upper end. And the odds of you running into one of them are doubling with each round. Sorry, man."

It was about what I'd feared, but still far from pleasant to hear it all put in such stark terms.

I wasn't that tough. Yet. But I had to be.

Argar wasn't hard to find. These days he was often outside—always a safe distance from the outer fence just in case anyone got ballsy with a bow—and doing his laps. I watched as he tore along the perimeter, face hidden behind his tool steel visor. I had to admit, it was impressive. And for several reasons.

Just a few days ago he never ran anywhere he could walk, and even now he was still carrying around at least a few dozen pounds of excess fat. He had to be cooking himself in that armor, to the point where I'd be worried about him dropping from heat stroke if it weren't for his impossible durability.

But he was persevering, and much more than I'd thought he had it in him to do.

"Alright, Argar, up for a bout?!" I called out. He gave the gesture, the small, quick one that showed he was nearing the end of his circuit—and his strength—and implored me to hold still. I wasn't holding for long. He finished quickly, always a fast bastard despite the size of his gut, and then he was standing poised and ready just a few short minutes later. For his ever-dwindling stamina, Argar sure as shit did recover fast.

I limbered up while he rested, and soon enough we were going at it. We'd sparred so much lately that there was a certain rhythm to it now. But I still felt something off. It wasn't that things had changed now that I'd gained my extra levels. It was the opposite—they'd stayed the same. Argar swung just as fast as ever, his strength proved just as big an issue as before, and I was tested just as much in keeping from losing my footing against his onslaught. All despite being superior in every way to my previous self.

Argar was stronger. He was faster, certainly tougher. And he was driving me back before I made the adjustment to stop restraining myself. Our sparring match didn't last much longer after that. His already diminished stamina finished emptying itself out, and while he panted and recovered I eyed him in thought.

"Let's . . . go and see Shango," I told him, suddenly suspicious. We reached my brother quickly, and he soon understood what was happening.

Shango looked at him the way I'd seen him look at a hundred others, eyes tightening and face twisting with concentration. Finally he spoke.

"Strength fourteen, Speed seven, Toughness fifteen . . . Alertness ten. Level twelve. He's improved."

Argar, clearly, wasn't following much better than usual, but I'd committed the levels and abilities of all our members to memory. He *had* improved.

Which made sense because there was no way four days of training was enough to cause the kinds of change I'd seen in him. It looked like we finally had our answer to how people in this world got stronger.

Push-ups, sit-ups, and plenty of juice.

CHAPTER FIFTY-THREE

Beam's POV: Day 94
Current Wealth: 197 gold, 1 silver, 17 copper

We were at the arena by the evening. None of us were fighting. We were into the next round anyway. We all had to show up, regardless, to watch the King. It was as easy a victory as ever, and my eyes apparently hadn't improved enough for me to see much more than I had before.

They hadn't improved, and this time there were only fifteen other people, not thirty, for him to be pitted against. Each round I had narrower chances of not being thrown against him.

"Don't suppose we've gotten any last-minute surges of experience?" Solitaire asked, aiming his question at Shango. Shango, for his part, actually did take a look. Then shook his head.

"Yeah." Solitaire sighed. "Things can never be that easy, can they? And you all call me crazy for wanting to build an anti-matériel rifle."

In fact, we all called him crazy for *actually* building one back on Earth, when nobody wanted to kill us, let alone anybody with superpowers. Bringing those sorts of details up, though, was never something he appreciated, so I just bit my tongue.

We were back at the house soon after, and busy. Solitaire disappeared into his now-off-limits section of the place, and we all steered well clear to avoid getting caught up in whatever explosions or other calamities he might unleash next. Deliberately or otherwise. Argar and I, on the other hand, had our training.

There were three days between each round, we'd learned. Shango was quick to tell us why—so that the wealthy could save a bit of money by letting themselves heal naturally after magical aid, while the poor were given too little a reprieve for their bodies' natural repairs to make any difference. Bastards.

Helena was still recovering, and she would be for a good long while, but she seemed to heal quickly regardless of what she said. I still felt a bit awkward looking at her, never sure what to say, and more awkward still when she started heading upstairs to spend time in Solitaire's laboratory. Still, if she had an issue with living in a constant state of near incineration, she expressed no such thing to anyone else. And it wasn't like her absence was felt in the training department, either. We had Magnus and Arthur now.

The former was good—as good as Helena maybe. The latter just ruined the fun for all of us.

I'll be the first to admit, I'd gotten used to being the best. Back home on Earth nobody in the entire world could actually match me, and barely a few could even challenge me. On my worst day, I'd lose to a few on their best, but for the most part I was uncontested as a winner. In Redacle, I was less of a big deal. And I'd known it. There were people in this world who could cut down trees with haymakers, and I definitely wasn't one of them just yet.

Arthur wasn't, either, but he was a damn sight closer to it than me. Than any of us. Even all fighting at once, Argar, Magnus, and I were disadvantaged in a match against him.

Twenty-two Strength, twenty-two Toughness, twenty-two, really, in everything physical. And he was a dueling champion to boot. Not as good as me, not quite, but . . . good. Good enough that whatever fractional edge in skill I had—and it really was smaller than the advantages I'd enjoyed on Earth—was offset easily by the sheer physicality he could wield.

At one point, Argar and I both shoved against him at once only to be forced back in a single move. Magnus swung from behind and missed even as Nightne *started* to move halfway through his swing's completion. We encircled, coordinated, and found ourselves confounded time and time again.

Really, that sort of sheer power just wasn't fair. And having Solitaire helpfully let me know that Nightne could probably have benched over four tons somehow only made things sourer.

Because as strong as Arthur was, as fast, as tough, he wasn't nearly equal to the King on a physical level. And that left me more terrified of round three with every damned sparring match we fought. It seemed only to spur Argar on, though.

And that was what gave me the drive to train even harder. Couldn't have the giant asshole getting better than me, could I?

Elizabeth wasn't a fighter, nor was she in recovery, but that was by no means cause for her to go without work. Solitaire and Shango put her right into the busy business of finding out more about our potential enemies in the next rounds. Specifically, more about the Challenger, and more about Aja the Pit Hound. We didn't bother with the King, for two fairly big reasons. The first, of course, was that virtually nobody knew anything about him, except that he was an outsider to the city who showed up only for the tourney. The second was that whatever we learned about him, he'd probably still eat us alive in an actual fight.

I was level sixteen, which was a good amount of progress from when the tourney began, but it wasn't nearly where I needed to be. And for the first time since learning of how we could grow stronger, I felt jealous of the native Redaclans. Argar, at least, could improve himself by just exercising. I was stuck killing.

After one particularly tough training exercise, in which Arthur had nothing short of bullied the rest of us with a training stick while we played defense, I found the knight taking a seat beside me and looking over. I'll admit, I actually didn't know a huge amount about him. The parts of Redacle I'd written had never featured characters like him—he'd always been more of a mid-tier, not a real powerhouse, and I liked my shonen-style fights.

Then again, knowing *little* about someone already meant I was starting with more knowledge than I did in most cases. Arthur Nightne was a legendary hero, a truly brave man, and a renowned example of chivalry and heroism. That was a start.

"You're getting better each time, I know it," he told me. It felt strange to be met with such unwavering friendliness, but strange in a good way. I let the smile grow across my features.

"I'd say the same, but we're really not giving you much pressure to," I noted. Arthur laughed, the sort of easy laugh of a man perfectly confident in himself, and still genuinely pleased to be recognized.

"Don't feel bad," he assured me. "I've always taken to the sword well, and I worked hard to get where I am. But don't treat me like some great measuring stick, either. There's far better warriors than me, somewhere out there."

In fact, they weren't nearly as rare as he was seeming to imply. The King of Blades, for one, but I knew for a fact that Arthur wasn't a top-ten fighter in our entire setting. Even if I hadn't, I could've inferred as much from fighting him.

A half-ton bench press wasn't bad on my part, and my shoulders still throbbed where they'd almost been wrenched from the sockets blocking his swings, but if I'd sparred with one of this world's best, bones would have broken. Instantly.

"Like the King of Blades?" I asked instead, deciding it would be kinder to direct things to a more local threat. Kinder, and more immediately relevant. I'd yet to actually get Arthur's opinion on the King, and his was an opinion I valued a lot. More, I realized, than anyone else's. My brothers were clever, but they weren't fighters, not trained ones. Arthur was. And he was a genius of a trained fighter at that.

His face scrunched up, suddenly tense. Without the helmet I could clearly make out tanned, handsome features sitting on top of a square jaw, and below a pronounced brow. Brown eyes rippled like pools of chocolate while he considered the question. God, he was such a damned hero, it was almost embarrassing to be sat so close to him. Who'd written this walking cliché again? Shango, obviously.

"The King of Blades is better than me," Arthur said at last. "Much better. I'll be honest, I don't like your chances of beating him as you are. I wouldn't like them, even if Magnus, Argar, and I were permitted to fight him at the same time as you."

It was a stark way of putting it, but not a wrong one. I happened to agree with his assessment.

"What have you noticed about his technique?" I pressed, hoping, at least, that Arthur's eyes would have caught more than mine. It seemed I was in luck. He paused for another think.

"Good," he replied. "Very, very good. Mechanical, practiced. But . . . Hmm, how do I put this? It's old. More experienced than talented."

I thought I understood, taking his meaning and running with it.

"You think he's getting on in his years, then?" I prompted. "Some grey-beard with decades of fighting under his belt?"

There were ways to exploit that. We'd not seen many Stamina stats raised that high in this world, perhaps for understandable reasons, and if he'd followed suit with that trend then a man past his middle years, or even well past them, might find that a critical weakness. Endurance diminished faster than raw speed or power as someone aged.

Arthur, though, still seemed far from confident. He just shrugged again.

"I think you're best looking for other fights to prepare for. That might actually yield some fruit."

Once again, he wasn't wrong. I headed for Elizabeth. With luck three days had been enough studying time for her.

If it wasn't, I had a nasty surprise waiting for me tomorrow.

CHAPTER FIFTY-FOUR

Shango's POV: Day 94
Current Wealth: 196 gold, 19 silver, 32 copper

'd been very, very busy over the last three days. I'd had to be. When one lost one's only chance in a while to snap bricks in half and do a quadruple back-flip, one found distractions to cope with the fact. Mine, as usual, was in work.

Phelia had been the one to bring the possible sources of wealth to me, of course, but it was Solitaire I'd gone to to find out our options. He'd asked for a few days while he worked on them, then, in true Solitaire fashion, delivered in seemingly the precise instant where my patience was about to run dry.

"Behold!" he declared, leading me to his workshop and proudly pointing at a weird, big vat. "My big elliptical pig iron blowy machine!"

The name could certainly have used some work, which told me it was an idea he'd coined independently. I took a long look at the thing, trying to figure out what it might do and how it might do it, then just gave up. However it worked, it wasn't intuitive enough for me to figure out. Solitaire evidently noticed how lost I was because he launched into the smug process of explaining.

"Alright, so basically we pour molten iron in, right? Standard shit. We do a lot of that anyway and already have the equipment to make it. The difference here is we also have a giant pump that I've set to be driven by either a superhuman, several humans, or a primitive steam engine. Pump pushes air, and thus oxygen, through which removes impurities in a fairly uniform way, keeps the heat up, and eventually turns the whole batch of iron into decent-quality steel. Decent being better than most of the stuff this world's idiots use, that is."

It was a lot to be told at once. I decided to start with the most crucial part.

"How much steel can we produce a day with this?"

Solitaire shrugged.

"Probably . . . I don't know, ten tons or something? It's not a really big blowy—"

"Don't call them blowies," I cut in. He spoke over me.

"But it'll still process quite a bit through sheer volume."

I stared at it, considering all the pitches I might make with something like this to back them up. For now, I decided, it'd be better not to let people know about it. This thing might have made as much steel as the entire city combined, or a sizable fraction at least. Being known as people capable of that didn't seem like it would be good for long-term survival.

"You did . . . very well." I grinned, mood lifting pointedly upward. Pointedly, and quickly. How had I not felt this way instantaneously? This was possibly the biggest thing Solitaire had made since black powder. And once again, it was ours.

Best to keep it under wraps, but we'd be fucking going places.

Phelia was where she always was, her study. My study, whatever. She was reading, as per usual, and didn't bother looking up at my entry until I actively spoke to her. Even then, I could see I didn't actually have her attention until what I was saying properly sank in.

"Solitaire can turn over a ton of iron into steel every day. If you can find someone to provide the iron then we can turn a pretty easy profit."

Her eyes couldn't have darted up faster, even if I'd lit myself on fire and shot her in the leg.

"Do you have any idea what this—"

"I do," I cut in, having gone out of my way to research and memorize as much of the local economy as was possible. Even if I hadn't, *shopping* for the stuff not too long ago would've made it abundantly clear anyway. I couldn't read still, but I'd made a step toward even that through learning with Helena. So was Solitaire, as I gathered it.

Geniuses that we were, both of us were almost as literate as the average five-year-old was back on Earth. Still, better than the average five-year-old on Redacle at least. Small victories and all that.

"Lord Wilskasai," Phelia said at once, and I nodded.

"Just who I was thinking. Mines, refineries, iron, right? What sort of deal do you think we might get from him?"

Phelia's brow furrowed at that, the book finally placed down as she dedicated the entirety of her not-inconsiderable intellect to the problem.

". . . The more we let him know we have, the more he'll want," she said at last. "Wilskasai is greedier than he is rich, and he is *very* rich. But also, fortunately, not an ally of Byror or his compatriots. And cautious of them."

I winced at the last part. Cautious didn't mean antagonistic, and often implied the opposite. Byror's animosity toward us was common knowledge by now. It meant we were fucking radioactive to any potential dealmakers who feared him.

"So how would you suggest we approach?" I asked her.

Phelia seemed surprised, and I wasn't sure why—because I'm an *idiot*—until she spoke next.

"You . . . want my opinion?"

God, medieval patriarchies. It was like something a cartoon world would have.

"Yes," I told her flatly. "Spare me the false modesty. You're cleverer by half than anyone in this city not named Belahont, and you know a thousand times more about it than I do. I want your opinion, and I will weigh it quite strongly once you've given it. So spare us both a bit of time and speak."

Say one thing for Phelia, say she was *fast*. I'd stunned her more, perhaps, than I'd ever seen a woman stunned—excluding those Solitaire had punched in the head—but she bounced back near instantly.

"I see." She swallowed, eyes burning with something too quickly vanished for identification. "Well, then, I think the best option here is to simply offer him returns from the profit of steel we make, asking for iron as payment. Make it a direct transaction with him. If you simply purchase large quantities of iron, and he finds out only later that you're turning it into wealth via this new steel-making method, then he may feel slighted. And—"

"Powerful men do terrible things when they feel slighted. Yes," I noted, nodding along. "Fair enough then. Good idea. When can you set up a meeting?"

"Now," Phelia replied. A nice surprise, and I sent her off to do just that.

Phelia really was quick. I had my meeting scheduled within the hour, and was waiting only a few more hours after that before it was ready for my presence. We used the time to prepare.

My clothing, fortunately, was made more *appropriate* by raiding one of the old wardrobes in Phelia's mansion. One of her relatives at least had been close to my height, and he had a nice outfit that both fit me adequately and smelled of such concentrated wealth as to congeal gold dust on the floor with every step I took. These were just the beginnings of our work, though.

Firstly, my accent was wrong. Yeah, no surprise there. When you were dealing with rich people back on Earth an African accent was *always* fucking wrong. It wasn't a case of specific bigotry here, though, more just generalized xenophobia. Redaclans weren't much trusting of outsiders after all.

I didn't take long to coach into a more appropriate pattern of speech, and from there I got down to working on the memorization of Wilskasai's preferences, history, views. More or less anything that might let me subtly influence him one way or the other. And it was work, too, because I didn't have an on-demand memory like Solitaire. Just a very good one. After that came the conversational practice.

"Wilskasai is one of the cleverest in the city, and all the more ruthless for it," Phelia had warned me. Suddenly I regretted deciding to make Redacle a land of skilled politicking and cerebral sparring. It would've been so much easier on all of us if its nobility had been violent, egomaniacal morons like in real life. At least Solitaire's view of rich people had colored most of their capabilities.

Eventually my hours slipped by, and the meeting loomed over us. I set out for it, Phelia in tow, Magnus following after to guard us. I'd come to suspect that an actual attack was unlikely to befall us at this point.

"Unlikely" and "suspect," though, were far from a certainty. Thus the fucking bodyguard.

Wilskasai's mansion was not bigger than Phelia's, which was a surprise. It was far better maintained, though. Its gardens had groundskeepers actively working, and as we were invited into the sprawling structure I found no shortage of servants and guards within. My wife had told me, at length, how wealthy the family was of course. It was different to be told than shown, though. I found myself tallying up the likely cost of keeping so many on payroll, then giving up once I counted past my two dozenth face.

If nothing else, there was certainly a lot of potential money here. I just had to wring it out.

Wilskasai himself received us in his office. This was not normal, nor was it proper. We were nobles, and Phelia herself was of old, pure blood. It was not the done thing to receive nobles in an office because offices were for receiving inferiors, as I myself had seen demonstrated quite well in my earlier visits within the city.

I knew Wilskasai wasn't the sort of man to make this mistake, either. It was deliberate on his part. I was of thin blood, my wife of empty coffers, and we were his inferiors in all but name.

Fine then, we'd just have to see how long that lasted.

"Lady Velaharo," Wilskasai smiled. "And Lord Velaharo, might I offer my congratulations on your wedding?"

He might have, and it would've been a fucking joke. One didn't address the woman first, either, in this land. I didn't care in the slightest of course, but Wilskasai would have. He was trying to get to me, another slight to remind me where we stood.

Which itself was an advantage. Because it told me the sorts of things he thought others would notice, and that implied that he himself would notice those very same sorts of slights. I was dealing with a thin-skinned man, then, who cared about how he was seen. A useful hint. Thanks, moron.

Wilskasai was a man in his middle years, average height and thin with cheekbones that seemed to be attempting an escape from his face and dull brown eyes. His hair was tousled, skin unusually pale, entire visage groomed to perfection. If I'd needed any confirmation about his vanity, I'd have found it in a single glance.

"Thank you, my lord." I smiled, showing all the deference a man like this would want and letting him see a shade of quivering ego. It would irk him to see his petty gibes go unnoticed, and thinking he actually got a reaction from me would hopefully improve his mood. It seemed to work.

"Oh, you can dispense with the formalities." He grinned, waving a hand as if he actually meant a word of what he said. "Please, I've been itching to meet you. Heard stories, you know?"

That I actually believed. There was no other reason he'd be slumming it with this meeting on such short notice.

"And I much appreciate being given the chance," I replied, showing just enough enthusiasm. "Hopefully I can make it well worth both our time."

Hopefully I could.

CHAPTER FIFTY-FIVE

Shango's POV: Day 94
Current Wealth: 196 gold, 19 silver, 32 copper

You're aware I do not usually deal with people like this," Wilskasai noted, sipping from a glass of wine. He didn't offer me one. Prick. "I am, you see, rather a busy man, and frankly I accept a scarce few of the numerous offers thrown my way."

I believed exactly half of that, but letting him know would only piss the old bastard off, so I stuck to my dull smile instead.

"Well, I believe you will find this one of particular note, my lord. My brothers and I have recently mastered the ability to convert barely processed iron into true steel in large quantities. Magic, of course, but a uniquely unstrenuous kind. I'm afraid our efforts to teach other magi have yielded little fruit, but . . . Well, we can still benefit others with just the ability known to us."

His eyes couldn't have lit up more brightly if someone had put a torch behind each one. Greed tended to do that to men, and particularly it tended to do that to the men who already had the most. Lucky then that they were the ones I usually ended up most incentivized to manipulate.

"And you are choosing to share this with me," he noted. "Why?"

Not the sort of question a man asked without reason, and I was perhaps the best person in the world to detect this one. Paranoia.

Solitaire talked sometimes about how he could smell people's emotions. I didn't think he was being literal. More likely it was just the best approximation for some empathic intuition he felt. More instinctive than deductive, more robust than precise. I couldn't do that. All my knowledge of others came from hard work and observation, which was why I paid particular attention to all the tiny ways in which Wilskasai's face twitched itself away from the norm I'd come to see in it.

"Because, frankly, you seemed the best option," I replied, carefully gauging his reaction. "Even putting aside your monopoly over the mines—which was no small factor—there's your relation with Lord Byror. He has no small amount of animosity toward me, and though he has yet to move against me overtly, or give me cause to suspect that he will in the future, I don't think my innovations would be well received by either him or any of his allies. You, though, stand apart from them all."

It wasn't flattery, but it was flattering. That was the best way to stroke a clever person's ego—so subtly that it seemed almost accidental.

Wilskasai had clearly been given a lot to chew on, and he did the smart thing of taking his time. I waited patiently, and without giving any indication that I was waiting at all. Finally, I got an answer.

"What sort of proposal would you be making?" he asked.

Really, it wasn't the sort of response he should've needed any time to consider in the first place. I didn't let that coax my guard down, though. Some clever people were slower than others. That didn't mean their judgments were less sound. Just more careful.

Intelligence 6

Wilskasai was smart, much smarter than most. I'd be an idiot if I wasn't extremely careful in how I handled him.

"You provide us with the iron for free," I suggested. "And, in exchange, you receive half of the profits we make by selling the steel it turns into. Assuming a twenty percent loss in material, that would be . . . what, five times your investment with each delivery of material? Seven?"

He eyed me at that, studious, thoughtful.

"Two thousand pounds' worth of iron," he began, "would be equivalent to around twenty silver pieces. You'd offer to turn that into more than two gold?"

"Two gold, just for you," I promised. "And we can process quite a bit more than just that. Give us ten thousand pounds if you want, and we'll be making you ten gold a day."

It was a very near thing, but I kept myself from adding how that would likely triple his current profits. Either he'd worked it out already, which meant it would impress, or he hadn't. If he hadn't, and was in the process, doing it quicker would only irritate him. This was the worst stage possible to do something as stupid as irritate him.

He already looked too torn on the offer for my liking.

"Did you know that Lord Byror had already requested a meeting with me before you?" he asked suddenly.

I hadn't, and I didn't like where this was going at all.

"No, my lord," I replied, hiding my apprehension. He didn't seem to be in the sort of mood for noticing it, either way, fingers suddenly drumming.

"Indeed, I was surprised myself. He told me about you, quite a bit about you. And, in particular, he stressed how . . . disadvantageous he would find your growing influence among the nobility."

My heart sank as Wilskasai continued.

"Double whatever you offer, that was what he promised. Lord Byror is an individually wealthy man, and the coalition he and his peers have formed . . . Collectively, they control most of this entire city's money. More than even the Anophes. I do not doubt for one moment that they can make good on their promise to purchase my iron for double the returns you are offering."

Well, there was capitalism for you. Once a ladder was scaled it wasn't hard at all to kick it down and keep others from following, it seemed that much remained true even when lords were the only ones allowed to scale. Byror had more money than me, probably by a factor of many hundreds of times. Perhaps thousands. If he felt his interests were best served by buying tons of iron at a loss, then he could just go ahead and do it.

That was a problem for me, but only if Wilskasai remained confident he stood to gain from Byror doing so. If his offer wasn't believed by the man receiving it, then its validity wasn't relevant in the slightest. Truth was no match for deception. This was why we lied.

I let him see surprise first, then just a slight whiff of confusion. Then, once I was sure he'd taken both in and started considering them, I finally spoke.

"I see. Forgive me, my lord, but do you believe they are so wealthy as to match our combined potential?"

Wilskasai clearly didn't get the implication all at once, and as I'd suspected he was the sort to get irritated when he thought someone else was holding more cards.

"Explain," he demanded sharply.

I explained. It was promising to see him hooked so quickly, but still not a guarantee, and so every word left my lips with the utmost care.

"Two gold a day is a handsome sum, to start with, but my brothers and I are still developing our powers. We will one day be managing double. We *might* one day be managing many times that. How long do you think Byror will be able to challenge that sort of profit with nothing but stored wealth and income? Perhaps weeks, maybe even months if he's willing to liquidate some of what he already owns, but eventually his wealth will dry out."

Wilskasai was thinking, I could see that much. Step one complete.

"You're selling me an alliance, at the cost of angering the most powerful people in Elswick, all on the promise of some unrealized potential?"

"Yes," I told him, figuring that flat honesty would go the furthest here. "It's a risk from your perspective, but I doubt you reached your current position without taking risks."

Clearly my guess had been correct, and that *was* the way to approach things. Wilskasai looked moved, but he still took his time in consideration. Every moment that passed left me closer to a fucking freak-out than the one before.

I hadn't banked on Byror poisoning the well for us, and that threw everything into question. It wasn't easy to make a promise capable of matching tangible offers of the sort he could throw around. I just had to hope my assessments had been right, and that Wilskasai really was as greedy as I'd guessed.

Eventually, I got my answer.

"I'll give you the first load to haul back to your mansion with you. If I don't get my two gold by tomorrow then we're never dealing with each other again, and I'll deny ever having so much as agreed to give you a chance. Is that clear?"

I relaxed, but only barely.

"It is, my lord. Thank you." It was a struggle to keep my expression or voice from twisting to match the awful tension still eating me alive from the inside out.

"Good. Now begone and let my servants lead you out through the back entrance. We never met, and this agreement was never formed, understood?"

"Understood." I nodded again hastily. I made a show of leaving in a hurry, as if intimidated by the old bastard, and it wasn't until we were already in a carriage with the pile of iron that I finally spoke to Phelia. It was reassuring, at least, that Byror could have it carted over to the estate so fast.

"That went . . . well," I began. It was hard to even say that much. Every word left me somehow convinced that the entire thing would crash down around me as I said it. Phelia, though, smiled.

"It went perfectly," she breathed. "Beyond perfectly. I've never seen anything like it."

I'd just like to say that having a gorgeous woman stare at me the way she did while saying that did not have the effect on me that it would have had on a lesser man.

That's a damn lie, obviously, but it feels good to at least keep up the pretenses.

"Thank you," I replied, about as intelligently as ever.

"This . . . This changes everything," she continued, barely even seeming to hear me. "Everything. This is serious income, sustainable, p . . . permanent, even."

I could see the gears turning, and watched as Phelia slowly ran through each one of the realizations I myself had already had. She really was clever.

"What can we use this income for?" I asked at last. She considered it.

"Well, you're recruiting, aren't you?"

We were, but that was something we'd already had the funds to do more of. The fundamental issue was that Byror could still outbid us, and that meant anyone we hired was suspect as a traitor. Unless . . . I grinned.

"Solitaire's new weaponry should make it a bit easier to instill loyalty," I observed. People were far less likely to betray people who owned the world's only cannons, I imagined. We'd done a lot today. A lot.

It was a whim, really, that had me pulling up my Appraisal once more. I hadn't expected to see anything.

[Appraisal]
Class: Emperor
Level: 15
Condition: Fine
Modifiers: +6 Toughness, +4 Strength, +4 Speed, +2 Alertness
Statistics: Strength 10, Speed 10, Dexterity 6, Stamina 5, Toughness 10, Alertness 10, Charisma 9, Intelligence 9
Inventory: Local wear, plate armor, repeater, shortspear
Class Abilities: Appraisal II
Current Experience Points: 173/500
Unspent Skillpoints: 2

Well shit.

CHAPTER FIFTY-SIX

Solitaire's POV: Day 94
Current Wealth: 196 gold, 19 silver, 32 copper

Everything nice I ever said about black powder had been taken back by the dawn of our ninety-fourth day. It was bullshit. I fucking hated the stuff; shitty, stubborn little powdered rat shit was what it was. I was glad we'd abandoned it in the nineteenth century because I'd be embarrassed to still use a piece of shit like that as late as the twenty-first, just as I was embarrassed to be stuck using it then.

Embarrassment changed very little, though, in the grand scheme of things. Actually it changed nothing, I was still dealing with the same shitting problems with the same shitting mechanisms.

But that was for another time. It's not that you need some vital context shown later to understand what I was doing, more so that it's just way more narratively satisfying if I record it as some big, epic reveal. Remember the exploding barrel when we attacked those gangsters in the ratpass? Or the makeshift cannon at Rinchester? Yeah, pretty cool shit. Way better than if it'd been spoiled beforehand. What can I say? I'm writing this journal to record my and my brothers' histories in Redacle, but that doesn't mean I'm not still a storyteller at heart.

As an aside, to this day, black powder can go and fuck itself. But I digress.

It really is hard to stress how bad of a mood I was in at the beginning of that day. It wasn't often, when you happened to be me, that a problem arose that didn't surrender to the blunt hammerblows of intellect near instantly. Some might expect that to mean that those few exceptions were fascinating, enticing novelties. To some extent, they were. For the first ten minutes. Then they became progressively more annoying, quickly graduating from blinking manually to lying in bed needing a piss, then moving on to crying baby on an airplane before finally settling at a level in excess of even Shango's bitch wife. Really, I'd been going through it.

But it was not all bad. When Shango got back from his meeting, he'd insisted on scanning me with his Appraisal. Sure enough, there'd been a change to my stats. Level sixteen, four skillpoints all to myself.

"What made you check?" I'd asked, and he'd just grinned.

"Do you know how many times I've struggled to make one of my deals since coming here?"

I thought about it.

"None," I guessed, and Shango grinned wider.

"None," he confirmed. "And I'm guessing that steel creator was the first time you've actually struggled to make something, intellectually, rather than simply remembering principles of science you already knew and implementing them."

Goddamn did I like how smart he was. Shango was absolutely right.

"So we can gain experience from tasks based around our own fields," I finished. "Maybe even others, but certainly by pushing ourselves."

That was the best news I'd heard in a while because it meant there was actually an advantage for us to find in my stepping out of my comfort zone.

"I do need a break so that I don't go insane and kill myself, though," I noted, and Shango sighed.

"Right, figured. We're heading off to watch the tourney soon. Want to come with?"

It seemed better than nothing, so I did. There was always something to gain by scouting out the competition with an extra set of eyes, after all.

Besides, our funds had dropped below two hundred gold, and betting had proved a decent source of revenue before. Shango had secured us a constant influx of wealth, as I'd learned when he'd returned earlier that afternoon, but we still stood to gain in the short term from a particularly lucrative wager. More money was, after all, better than less money.

For once, we were arriving at the arena earlier than any of our own side's fights. Some delay had befallen it, necessitating a later start in the day, but the main reason was that this round was where the competition became properly fierce.

Beam had watched by far the most matches previously, and according to him we'd gotten past the point where contestants weaker than Magnus could be expected to show up. Even disregarding the advantage of now-universal plate armor, people like Alora were looking a great deal less hopeful in their chances.

Which wasn't to say she was screwed because we'd made a few improvements to her gear, too. Her lamellar was all well and good of course, but the dash of tool steel we'd added just perfected things. Maybe she'd even make it to round four.

The Challenger strolled out as his name was called, and we all watched him receive his opponent. Shango was shoulder to shoulder with me, watching and appraising. His mood was fouled slightly, despite a general uptick from learning he'd gained experience through his politicking. That wasn't surprising. It never took him long to go from pleasantly surprised to bitterly disappointed not to have received his surprise sooner. Someone really ought to have a chat with him about that pessimistic streak.

Not me, of course. It would preferably be someone who didn't mine his own sleeping quarters as a cautionary defense.

"New guy is tough," Shango growled. "Physical stats all in the teens."

It was funny how much less intimidating that was than if we'd heard it a few days ago. I glanced at Beam, and Shango read the question on my face before I could ask it out loud.

"Thirteens, yeah. Essentially dead equal with him."

Beam for his part did not look particularly pleased to hear that. Maybe he'd gotten used to standing above everyone among our group. In any case the reminder of his own limits would probably do him some good.

And holy shit, it was one hell of a reminder.

The guy was quick, at least. His name was Kokatoa—a weird one that was foreign to Elswick and didn't ingratiate him to the crowds. His armor was of strange design, too, clearly not local work, and his technique was less local still. He came on like a damned cyclone, all unchecked aggression and precise aim.

But the Challenger wasn't all talk. Clearly he'd been trained by the best, and at no small expense to his own family. With an enemy this good we actually got to see some measure of skill from him rather than just brute strength. Things didn't last much longer than last time, though.

Strikes were met by parries, swords screeching on each other and shaking so violently with each impact that I thought they might shatter every time. Both were thicker than most historic examples in real life, needing to be built more robustly to survive their own wielders' strength for any length of time, but I saw the clear difference in their make as the Challenger's weapon continuously knocked flakes of steel from his opponent's.

The opponent in question was soon forced onto the defense, a position he was clearly far less comfortable in. I took it all in as best I could, but I wasn't Beam. Physically perceiving what was happening was about my limit.

Once it was all done, the Challenger took his leave, and his beaten enemy did the same shortly after. He wasn't hurt, surprisingly enough, having managed to stave off the majority of incoming damage right up until his own disarming. Not bad at all. I made a mental note of his name in case we were ever recruiting while he was in the area again.

Beam was the first of us to comment on the affair.

"So, the loser was as good as me," he breathed, clearly not liking the fact one bit. I didn't, either.

"You have better gear," I noted. "And certain other advantages outside raw statistics. But yeah, as good as you."

Not a promising sign in the slightest.

We watched a few more matches, and fortunately Kokatoa *was* still a cut above the norm. I was having a hard time seeing myself matching some of the fighters pulling up now, though, and a lump built in my throat as I thought of Beam.

I was done with this tournament, and none of what I now watched was my problem. But all of it was Beam's. He hadn't fought in this round yet, and with each person who fell, the odds of him going up against the King got higher.

The King, at last, was called through. He came out like some giant machine, freezing the blood in my veins as I watched him move. His opponent was some fucking guy who didn't even last a single swing.

He'd been as good as Beam, too, apparently.

CHAPTER FIFTY-SEVEN

Shango's POV: Day 94
Current Wealth: 196 gold, 19 silver, 32 copper

Alora eyed Aja the Pit Hound, glanced up at the organizers' box, tilting her head in thought. She then turned around and walked out of the arena without another damned word. The match was called as her loss, and Beam was left with the next match.

Luckily, our hidden enemies seemed to have run out of psychopaths and one-man armies by then.

We were tense, regardless, as Beam faced off against his enemy. A smaller man who nonetheless had physical stats almost on par with our brother's. Whether this was bad luck or another attempt at fucking us by the organizers, it was difficult to tell. Had it been the latter, though, they were in for a nasty shock.

This guy would've had decent odds at victory the day before. Not now.

Beam closed in and took him apart in a way that humans just didn't manage against other humans. It was like watching some machine at work, not a person. Wood in the chipper, meat in a blender. In under twenty seconds he was standing over a beaten-down, surrendering enemy surrounded by chips and flakes of shredded steel. His rapier was barely hurt and shone in a light that looked almost impossible for the day's intensity.

As a fact, it *was* impossible. Solitaire had had the idea to try conjuring some ethereal enamel for his weapon to add anti-armor capabilities, and three days had been enough time to practice it. This was the first time I'd seen it used in anger. It didn't disappoint.

Nightne came next, and I won't even bother describing his victory. It was quicker than Beam's, that's about what you need to know. Argar was the last. His was harder fought, but not by much. I hadn't paid much atten-tion to his training, but I was there when we were fitting him with his armor, and I swore he had actually dropped at least a few pounds around the belly. Certainly moved like it, too, because his enemy was probably the equal of Magnus, and had armor on top of that. It wasn't an advantage that afforded him much.

"I taught him that move," the man himself noted, watching Argar from the seat beside me. "Used in my home country. Good shield breaker."

The term *shield breaker* probably wouldn't have been used literally, most of the time, which only made it more impressive to watch Argar smash his ene-my's shield fully in half, then send the wreckage of wood and iron rimming flying to one side.

He still favored an axe, Argar, but he used it a lot better now. Seemed to have picked up more in six days than I had in weeks.

"So he's better than you?" I prodded Magnus, well aware of how easily his ego bruised.

The man sniffed, about as short-fused as ever. "Might be one day, but not today."

Elizabeth snorted beside him, eyeing the man as if he'd just drooled on himself.

"Didn't he throw you yesterday? Not like Beam, I mean. Actually throw you. As in he picked you up and . . . You know. Like a javelin."

Magnus glared. He tended to do that a lot, I'd found, and more specifically he tended to do it with Elizabeth. And Helena. The two of them seemed to have formed some sort of blockade. Of all our new recruits—save Arthur—none hated fighting as much as them, so it made sense to me in that regard.

Solitaire, being Solitaire, had suggested they were also sleeping with one another. I'd dismissed that as the ramblings of a pornography-obsessed creep, but he was undeterred as ever.

Down below, the fight finished in quite a spectacular degree. Argar smashed the blunt side of his axe down hard enough that, had his enemy not been super-human, I'd have been fearful for his life. As things were I saw a notable lack of any skulls being driven down into any spines and, thankfully, an even greater lack of consciousness. His enemy crumpled, and the match was called. Argar actually collected a fair number of cheers on his way out.

"He's become a bit of a favorite," Beam informed me, clapping along with so much of the audience. "This has always been a noble-dominated event, but there's enough commoners filling out the stadium that Argar's getting a follow-ing for his birth alone."

I smiled, happy for the big guy. Solitaire for his part smiled even more hap-pily as he collected a few silvers from betting. He'd come intending to wager quite a lot but had quickly decided against that as he'd realized the competition's quality. Fair enough. Better to keep less money than lose more.

One more match came, this one between two fighters that none of us considered particularly noteworthy. Their fight was barely more so, ending shortly and easily. With it ended the round.

We all sat there for a moment, processing our progress. Then I turned to Beam.

[Appraisal]
Class: Dragonknight
Level: 18
Condition: Fine
Modifiers: +4 Strength, +5 Speed, +5 Toughness, +6 Alertness
Statistics: Strength 13, Speed 13, Dexterity 8, Stamina 9, Toughness 13, Alertness 14, Charisma 6, Intelligence 5
Inventory: Local wear, plate armor, rapier
Class Abilities: Beloved II
Current Experience Points: 386/560
Unspent Skillpoints: 4

God, could he actually win this thing?

CHAPTER FIFTY-EIGHT

Shango's POV: Day 95
Current Wealth: 200 gold, 18 silver, 49 copper

Beam put all his skillpoints into the physical stats he usually picked, making his new average fourteen. I might've guessed. The particulars of what this meant numerically were lost on me, but what I did understand was that it made him a *very fucking scary* individual. More so than before. More so by far.

And it still left him more than just a few points behind the majority of the tournament's strongest enemies. There'd been hope, for a while, but seeing the creeping pace of his empowerment now had dashed that completely. Three rounds left. Aja, the Challenger, and the King were all still in the running. And so were Beam, Argar, and Arthur. The odds of one of our boys going up against the tournament's heavy hitters were almost one hundred percent. The odds of it being someone other than Arthur, who could actually come out on top . . . Not a lot lower.

I was in a fouler mood leaving the arena than when I'd entered it. As usual, Solitaire was the one to notice.

"Worried about Beam," he noted.

"Worried about Beam and Argar," I replied, tension still solid and pointy in the center of my chest like I'd swallowed a bag of nails. Solitaire thought for a moment.

"I won't lie about his chances of avoiding a tough fight altogether." He sighed. "But I think his odds of victory are better than you might think. Has he ever let us down before?"

Strange, being asked that question, because I honestly couldn't say he had. Even against the vampire, once he'd gotten his powers back, Beam had come out on top. But that enemy had been far closer to the version of him fighting it than our sources of concern were now. It did something for my nerves, but not a lot. We kept moving.

Velaharo Manor felt cooler than usual when we entered it. I took a moment to realize it was because the most deranged man ever to crawl out of Liverpool had taken most of a day's break on repeatedly firing cannons indoors. It smelled nicer, too. Black powder, I had learned since setting foot in Redacle, had a faint rotten-egg odor that was far from pleasant.

I even took the time to make my way through the greenhouse. Apparently the Velaharos grew a bunch of cacao plants recreationally.

Phelia's eyes were tight with concern as we returned, and Helena's seemed scarcely less so. Both let out sighs of relief upon finding out we were into the final round.

Only Helena's caught in her throat. Only Helena, I supposed, had seen firsthand what we'd be facing there.

"You should drop out," she suggested, eyeing all the soon-to-be contenders at once, but giving Argar and Beam a particularly large shard of her focus. The former snorted, the latter kindly smiled, and Nightne remained stony faced and square jawed as ever while he replied.

"I appreciate your concern, my lady, but I am afraid I simply cannot. I promised to aid my new lord in this tourney, and by God I shall."

Lying bastard. It was almost surreal to watch how good his performance was—how successful in drawing approving, awestruck eyes from across the room. He really was one of Solitaire's more amusing characters.

"We have a few days in any case," Beam noted. "Might as well use them, eh?"

He just wanted to have another go against Arthur, now that he'd strengthened himself even more. Which was fair enough, I reckoned. I watched him and the others head off, then turned my focus to Phelia.

"Any news from Wilskasai?" I asked quickly. Her face was drained of its apprehension incredibly quickly. I supposed a fucking huge shit ton of money tended to do that to a person.

"He sent word back. Just a sentence. Our delivery was acceptable, and he will continue our correspondence."

I let out a deep breath. The deal had been agreed upon, of course, and I'd felt confident that Wilskasai would hold to it—in no small part due to my receiving an experience reward . . .

. . . Could I use that to tell the future? No, I bottled that possibility away for later. One thing at a time, Shango.

"Excellent," I told Phelia. "Then we have a bit of income secured."

A bit was underselling it, though it would still take us literal decades to fully pay off her family's debt at this rate. Still, progress at least.

Phelia seemed to be having the very same thoughts, or else something different was gnawing at her because her own excitement was quite muted, too. It didn't stop her from smiling away, in any case.

"Husband . . . Shango," she began, seeming suddenly uncertain. "I . . . I'd just like to say thank you. For everything. I know it was politically advantageous for you, but . . . still, you've changed everything for me. Given my family a future. I won't forget that. Thank you."

It was somehow uncomfortable, seeing the look in her eyes, but I swallowed and nodded anyway. Eager to just move on from the conversational topic and into less awkward territory.

"Obviously we'll need to reinvest this," I noted. "It's not bad, of course, but a few gold a day won't pay your debt off anytime soon. What sort of things could we get into that would make the most of our . . . assets?"

Phelia was thinking before I'd even finished speaking, like usual, and I got my answer spectacularly fast.

"Mercenary work is never scarce in these lands," she replied instantly. "And with . . . your brother's assets, I'd wager we could become rather successful in the business."

I noticed that she'd said "we" instead of "you," but I didn't think about it. Phelia had given me something far more concerning to take note of.

"Did something happen between you and Solitaire?"

She'd practically flinched at the mention of him, and not in any trivial emotion like disgust or contempt. I'd seen fear in her face, heard it in the quiver of her voice, felt it as she spoke. That didn't come from nowhere.

Phelia didn't meet my eye, but she didn't avoid it, either. Replying quickly, confusedly, as if my question were somehow unprompted.

"You heard about the wall incident, no? In fact you even walked in midway through our argument about it. This estate is the only thing I've managed to halfway preserve of my family's legacy and . . . Well, he keeps destroying it. He keeps destroying it and mocking me for wanting him to stop. Do you—" She caught herself, inhaled, continued. "Suffice is to say, you know I have no love for Solitaire."

I felt like I'd just been gutted. The arguing, the bickering, it'd struck me as petty somehow. It hadn't occurred to me what this place actually meant to Phelia. Crumbling mortar and cobwebs aside . . . this was where she'd grown up.

But I was being distracted. God, she was such a good liar she almost had me of all people fooled. Almost.

"What did he do?" I snapped, angry now, mind racing. There were any number of possible answers. That was one thing I'd learned since coming here. That however dangerous and twisted this world was, one of the scariest fucking things in it had always been the bastard I called a friend.

Phelia backed off, deceptive calm turning to a shaky fear. I realized after a moment that it was me she was scared of. Of course it was. A Redaclan might fucking hit his wife for lying to him.

"I'm sorry," I continued, forcing myself calm. "Really, I am, but . . . Please, what did Solitaire do? I need to know."

She told me after a moment's pause. I listened, and listened carefully. I kept myself calm, considered what she was saying, and when Phelia was done I nodded.

I felt numb, but that was nothing new, either. I felt like that every time Solitaire did something I'd assumed would be beyond the pale. Every time he found some new limit to the ever-moving line of tolerance for his behavior. I took my leave from the room, heading off to see him.

Solitaire was where I'd come to expect him, in his laboratory. This time he seemed to be frowning over a sort of pump mechanism, but I hadn't the time to ask about that, or try to imagine what it might be for.

"Alright, Shango," he said without looking up. I didn't answer, just stepped over his greeting and closed in.

"Phelia told me what happened."

Solitaire paused. He looked up, gauged my expression, then shrugged.

"I needed to know we weren't being endangered more by her secrets. If she didn't want me to do something like that, she shouldn't have gotten Helena almost crippled by lying."

There wasn't the slightest shred of regret on his face, and I just sort of exploded when I realized the fact.

"What the fuck is wrong with you?" I snarled. "Mentally, what exactly has gone wrong in your brain that you can behave like this?"

Solitaire met my outburst without even blinking, seeming more bored than anything.

"Shango, you're wasting both of our time," he sighed. "Just drop it. This is getting tedious."

I stared.

"What is?"

"This," he snapped, gesturing at seemingly everything at once. "This little dancing around. Your game where you pretend to be outraged and disgusted every time I do something important for our survival, while continuously failing to actually stop it. We both know you don't really care, not enough to do any-thing about it."

It was all I could do not to shake with rage. I stared at Solitaire, tried to find something to say. Couldn't. There were no words for him.

"I give up," I said at last. "You win. Congratulations, Solitaire, you've finally managed to convince me that my best fucking friend is beyond help."

There were tears in my eyes, and that only deepened my fury.

"I'll work with you for now because I need to, but . . . I don't want to speak with you anymore outside of that. What we're doing is . . . helping people. That's more important than you or me, but outside of that . . . go fuck yourself. We're done."

I turned from him before he could say anything that might threaten to change my mind and took my leave.

CHAPTER FIFTY-NINE

Solitaire's POV: Day 98
Current Wealth: 211 gold, 39 silver, 22 copper

My mother had been right, the fucking bitch. She'd been a violent, paranoid, crazy cunt, responsible for ruining my life and, I was almost convinced, a fairly prolific serial killer. But she'd been fucking right, too. Friends were just enemies who hadn't taken swings at you yet.

Humans. They were all the fucking same. Animals. Pigs. Dull, grunting cows. They didn't know anything because they didn't *want* to know anything. And they called the people that did crazy, unstable. They diagnosed them as schizophrenics or paranoids. They shoveled pills down their throats until they stopped noticing inconvenient truths and were content to stuff them away in the loony bin. Unless they lived outside the West, of course. Then they just got vaporized by some fucking drone pilot.

Well not me, never me. The fucking cunts could come for me a million at a time and I'd get rid of them all. Stupid rats, I'd like to see their diagnostic abilities when I'd finished turning this entire steaming shit pile of a planet into a radioactive wasteland. I could do it, too. Nukes? Fucking easy. Any idiot could figure it out. Maybe I'd even try to give myself a challenge and see if I could do something with antimatter.

For the time being, though, I was still stuck with the shitting, dull idiot technology this world had left me, and that was taking long enough to improve on already. Still, I'd been making progress. Ish. Not nearly enough for comfort, though, and not nearly as much as I'd have hoped to make before the day of the tourney's next round. It was with a heavy heart that I watched Beam and the others head off for it.

From the mansion, that was. *I* wasn't leaving the damned place, not with all the time I'd spent setting up my perimeter. I'd noticed a "jogger" outside the mansion lately, bastard. He was a spy, readying to send out the word to his bosses if enough of us left it at once and send in a bunch of bastards to steal all our stuff. Well, he had another thing coming with me, that was for sure. I could practically imagine the thugs he sent in finding the . . .

Anyway, that was for another time.

It was just me, Magnus, Alora, Elizabeth, and Helena in the mansion. Not including Shango's bitch wife, of course, who was fortunately still giving me a wide berth. Very fortunately because if she started whining about some new minor infraction like it was the end of the world I was going to hurl either her or myself through a fucking window. Things were rather calm around the mansion, which was why I was surprised to find myself with company while I worked.

Elizabeth and Helena, both at once. Apparently they were taking a break from scissoring each other into a coma, and that made me suspicious. Not to sound paranoid, but if someone modified their usual behavior even slightly, the safe thing to do was always assume they were about to try and kill you.

"You're still working," Elizabeth began, looking at the fruits of my labor with a considering eye. Then a confused one. She was clever—most of our group were—but there were some things that pure cleverness didn't help much with. I was processing mercury, compressing air, carefully locking mechanisms into one another with millimeter-scale precision. It wasn't the sort of work one unfamiliar with modern technology would grasp.

"I'm still working," I replied, deciding to hurry and save her the embarrassment of having her ignorance displayed fully. "I reckon there's decent odds our enemies make a move once the tourney is over, or possibly before. Our being almost half the current participants is probably half the reason they haven't done it yet."

Both women looked rather perturbed at that. Good, it was a bloody perturbing thought.

"They had Aja the Pit Hound maim me," Helena muttered, eyes hitting the floor. "If they can bring him on for another assault . . ."

"Then I'll shred him to bits," I told her, finding my voice louder than I expected. Sharper. Oh God, was I getting *protective*? That was revolting. I was acting like a damned human. "Relax," I added. "You saw what I did at Rinchester. What's coming next is going to be a lot more powerful."

"How much more?" she challenged. "Because he was wielding draconian bronze, wearing plate that might even have stopped Shango's staff. He moved like a damned cyclone. Do you have anything capable of measuring up against that?"

It was an interesting question. I'd specifically designed Shango's gun with our own growing strength in mind and allowed its power to hit heights that would've produced far too much recoil for a normal person as a result. And Helena probably wasn't wrong that Aja's plate could've put up a fight against it all the same.

He wasn't invincible, not in the slightest, but there was a fair-to-good chance he could've taken a big notch out from a squad of modern-day marines before going down.

But I'd designed my new projects with *that* in mind, too. And I gave my subordinates the rundown. By the time I was finished even Helena's brown skin seemed noticeably paler, her eyes widened to dinner plate dimensions with shock.

"How is that even possible?" Elizabeth gasped.

I'd admit, it was satisfying as hell to get that sort of reaction from her. I just humbly shrugged.

"My people are very good with moving parts, and I'm smarter than all of them by a mile. I've never actually made one of these, mind, but give me a while and I'll have all the kinks hammered out."

And, if I was lucky, a big snack of experience points, too. I was fairly sure I'd gotten a few for my last creations at least, and these were taking me much more work than those had.

"You could fight a dragon with that," Helena muttered.

In fact, I couldn't, but better to avoid letting her know. We needed morale with the sorts of threats we were staring down.

"We'll be fighting a lot less than a dragon, in any case," I noted. "So, as I said, relax. We have this. Particularly with Arthur bloody Nightne on our team, eh?"

Helena smiled with slightly less of a fragile twist to it than I'd seen before. That was progress at least. I knew what sort of effect a beating like hers could leave psychologically. If I could so much as chip away at that I'd consider it a personal victory.

The two women did not leave me alone, which isn't a sentence I'd *normally* consider a bad thing. They were, however, blessedly silent—which *is* a sentence I'd normally consider a *good* thing.

I got quite a bit done, too. My reloading mechanism was going smoothly, pneumatic system slowly but surely coming around to levels of reliability I'd almost let myself think were impossible within this world, all while I took the measure of exactly what point my springs would and did recoil down to the millimeter. Everything was coming together—almost enough for me to unveil this to you, the readers.

As an aside, if you are reading this, sorry about the booby trap. It probably took most of your fingers off, maybe a hand. Not actually sure why I'm setting it up as I bury this journal. Just habit I suppose.

It was later on, hours later, that I was finally interrupted in my glorious work. The others returned home. Shango was with them, and I didn't glance his way even a second on account of him grabbing hold of our friendship and violently fucking it to death right in front of me. Beam, though, deserved my attention, and when I gave it to him . . .

Well, his face stunned even me into silence.

CHAPTER SIXTY

Solitaire had been hunkered down in the house for a while when, the day before the tournament's next round, he'd headed out. No warning, no reason given. He just fucked off. Scurrying away down the streets and returning so sneakily and suddenly that we'd barely even had a chance to realize he was gone and start panicking.

I wasn't that shaken. He just tended to do stuff like that. It was his coping mechanism—one of many—for when something got to him. Granted, it was a bit disturbing to think he might be feeling nervous. Both for what it implied of my chances in the tourney . . . and because he currently had access to ridiculous volumes of explosive material.

He'd come back, though, and he'd come back grinning. That was how I'd gotten my new weapon, all verified and cleared with the organizers before its use of course. And viciously effective. Why was it always the most unstable, disturbing moods that saw him at his most productive? Perhaps some things were better left unanswered.

Aja the Pit Hound was up first when we arrived at the stadium, and thank fuck he wasn't fighting me. Or Argar, which would've been worse actually. Because I could actually take him. We all watched him demolish the poor bastard thrown out before him, a fairly remarkable warrior in his own right who'd have beaten all but a few of us as we were. He might have even taken down Solitaire.

Definitely didn't take down Aja, though, and the fight was over near instantly. The Challenger was up next, against the only other man in the quarterfinals that I can't recall the name of to this day. I'll let you guess for yourself which of them won. After that came a horrible realization, followed by confirmation of my growing suspicion.

My name was called, and Argar's came after it. We were to fight each other.

I glanced over at the giant and found him grinning. It was such a typical response on his part that all I could do was laugh.

At the very least, I knew I was guaranteed a place in the next round. Argar was frankly quite lucky to have gotten as far as he did, even with Solitaire's armor and his growing physical strength.

We both came into the arena at once, weapons out and eyes hard. Argar's were a sight more *amused* than mine, I had to say, but he seemed to be taking everything seriously all the same. That was concerning. Give me a relaxed, cocky asshole to surprise and beat any day over whatever I was facing now.

It wasn't that Argar might have won, just that he'd still have been able to make a fight of it. He'd improved almost as much as me over the last few days, hitting the early learning curve for his standard training and, apparently, possessing some ridiculous innate talent that saw him improving from it several times faster than usual. We were a lot closer than I'd have liked.

And that was all the considering I was given time for because he went for me after that.

He swung. I parried and fell for his feint hook, line, and sinker. Argar's axe was coming back around faster than I would've thought possible, and I just barely dipped beneath it. His boot was next, but he'd tried that trick before, and I dodged it easily. I gave him a little smack across his head, just a reminder of who he was dealing with. His reeling stumble only lasted a moment before he was back again.

Fighting Argar was like fighting a seizing man, all unpredictable flailing and raw physicality. But there was something new to him that hadn't been there a week ago. Degrees of technique, scraps of order mixed in with the chaos. It made him more dangerous, not less, and forced me to keep my guard up as I dodged.

But I just had to keep my guard up. Argar was faster, not fast. Strong, not unmatchable. The gap between us had shrunk from when we first met after all, and it would shrink ever more. His strength had already slowed in its growth. Mine was showing no signs of stopping.

The axe hurtled from his hand, and my sword came down to gently rest on the crook where pauldron met helmet. Argar froze, stared, then sighed.

"Bugger it, you win."

I withdrew my weapon with a smile.

Back in the stands, I actually found it hard to even watch the damned fighting that followed. I was too eager to see what benefits I'd gained to my experience.

That didn't last long, of course, when I realized that it was the last match of the day. And there were only two fighters left.

Arthur walked out into the arena, test swings cutting the air as he limbered himself up. He didn't seem the slightest bit perturbed despite everything, and somehow his confidence gave me a boost to my own. I was still sore where he'd thrashed me in training bouts, despite my own improvements. Perhaps, just maybe, if anyone could do it . . .

The King of Blades entered to a volcanic detonation of cheering, which fully reversed my growing confidence and left my mouth dry as sandpaper.

It was almost hard to believe the height difference. Arthur was very tall for this world, at least my height, but there was still close to a foot separating the top of his helmet from the King's. One was close to seven feet tall, height bolstered by the centimeters of steel encasing him, and the other was well over.

But height didn't mean much. The King had overcome a bigger gap already. What mattered was how they fought, how they moved, how they struck. And that was what I watched out for as the two enemies closed in as one.

Over the course of the tourney, I really had improved. I actually caught the King's movement this time. Barely.

It was a heavy swing, and Arthur caught it at the edge of his blade. He slid backward, actually slid backward. Two hundred pounds of man, and probably five hundred more of armor too thick and heavy for a normal human to wear. I saw scrapes left in the stone under his heels where they dragged, and it was clear by the exertion of his body just how far behind the King's strength he fell.

Arthur didn't hesitate long to reply, stepping in and throwing quick, short jabs at his enemy. He was moving still, despite the block. Strength enough that he could stave off injury, if not effort, in the process. The King met his attacks, turning them away, backing off and controlling the space between them expertly. Even so, I could see there was no advantage for him in technique. Arthur took that category by a hair, and I was more advanced than that from him. Which meant the King wasn't perfect. He could be surpassed. He could be beaten.

But it was hard to imagine Arthur managing that because the King soon moved past his testing jabs and came on again, forgoing the careful feeling out of an enemy, simply spurring the fight on into explosive violence at the peak of their strengths. And his peak was far higher than Arthur's.

Arthur was stumbling back, then dodging one way and the other as great guillotine swings hurtled for him. One missed so widely as to hit the ground, smashing a torso-sized chunk of stone to pieces and sending flecks of it to rain down upon the crowd. My ally did his best and fought no worse than he ever had against us. Better, really. But there was just a limit to what could be managed against an enemy like this. He was slower, and the gap in power was bigger by that than far. Blows started to connect. Grazing, scraping blows at first, but they deepened and accelerated in their ruination of his armor.

Tool steel, modern steel. Good steel. But for all its effectiveness, and all Ardin's genius at working it, it wouldn't have stopped an anti-matériel round, and it didn't stop the ten pounds of mystery metal now slamming into it hard enough to cut a SWAT helmet completely in half.

Red flashed in the air, a fleck of blood drawn where one blow had gone deeper in the rest, and I knew from that moment on there'd be no winning this. Arthur continued retreating, stepping back even as he fended off the endless army of attacks raining down on him. The ground at his feet became littered with scraps of mangled metal, and sparks were spat into the air so thickly it was like watching a cascade of burning matches.

Then I saw it. Arthur's back was about to hit the wall, his retreat about to end. The King was moments from accomplishing the very same snare Solitaire had been subjected to by Arthur himself, and there was no greater chance of it failing than there'd been last time. It was over.

But Arthur surprised me, then. And he surprised the King, too. One single unexpected swing sent his sword's tip screeching along the helmet of his enemy, leaving a discolored rent where tool steel hit magic steel and knocking the King's head to one side.

Then the King of Blades' own sword came down, making a quick end of the business.

We all watched as Arthur was carried from the arena—gently, of course; he was a fairly popular minor noble after all—and the crowd reached a new level of murmuring. I turned to see Shango's face was tight, hands balled into fists that were tighter still. He was on the verge of shitting himself.

But I smiled. Because I'd seen for myself that the King could be hit now. Could be parried, dodged, tricked. And if all of that were possible, then he could be damned well beaten.

"What are my experience rewards looking like, Shango?" I asked.

CHAPTER SIXTY-ONE

Shango's POV: Day 98
Current Wealth: 211 gold, 39 silver, 22 copper

I was not on the verge of shitting myself, for one thing. Let's get that out of the way before anything else. Beam seemed to have an exaggerated impression of how worried I was at the time of Arthur's defeat.

And to be clear, I was absolutely worried. This was a man I'd seen cut a cow carcass fully in half in training with one swing. A man who could hoist the four-hundred-pound Argar off the ground and throw him like a beanbag, all while fighting off two others of our best. And he'd been beaten. Beaten soundly.

But Beam was grinning away, as if he'd just been told the secret to living forever. When his question came I realized why, obviously, but it was still a shaking thing to see. He was so damned sure of himself it actually made me jealous.

"Alright then," I replied, feeling my irritation grow to levels that were perhaps unfair to him. It wasn't his fault that . . . Well, any of what was happening had happened. And I wouldn't take it out on him.

[Appraisal]
Class: Dragonknight
Level: 19
Condition: Fine
Modifiers: +2 Strength, +6 Speed, +6 Toughness, +7 Alertness
Statistics: Strength 14, Speed 14, Dexterity 8, Stamina 9, Toughness 14, Alertness 15, Charisma 6, Intelligence 5
Inventory: Local wear, plate armor, rapier

Class Abilities: Beloved II
Current Experience Points: 306/580
Unspent Skillpoints: 2

I winced.

"One level up," I told Beam, sighing. "Two skillpoints."

It wasn't that much of a surprise, with his newly grown strength and a decent chance of going up against either Argar or Arthur—a guaranteed win for us one way or the other—this had possibly been the least risky round for us so far. His power, of course, had suffered in its rewards as a result. Beam's smile did seem to have a notch taken out of it as he realized that.

Beam spent his skillpoints soon, in any case, and I took in his new statline. It probably said a lot about how well we'd been eating regarding such things that I found the two-point improvement a trifling difference.

[Appraisal]
Class: Dragonknight
Level: 19
Condition: Fine
Modifiers: +2 Strength, +7 Speed, +7 Toughness, +7 Alertness
Statistics: Strength 14, Speed 15, Dexterity 8, Stamina 9, Toughness 15, Alertness 15, Charisma 6, Intelligence 5
Inventory: Local wear, plate armor, rapier
Class Abilities: Beloved II
Current Experience Points: 306/580
Unspent Skillpoints: 0

It was an improvement, I told myself. It was a big one. We'd just needed a lot bigger. The knowledge was heavy in my gut as I got to my feet, and all of us headed our way back to the mansion.

Solitaire convulsed when we saw him, but didn't attack outright. Somehow I'd convinced myself he might, that with our friendship dashed he might just pull off the mask entirely.

But no, that was stupid. He wasn't a monster; he was a person. Just a bad one.

"Arthur lost," he echoed, licking his lips, twitching in all the ways I knew betrayed a growing urge to blow something up. "Well, that's hardly unexpected. The King was always tougher. We knew that going in."

We had, at that, but it was another thing to see such a wide gap demonstrated clear as day. Not to mention to our own not-inconsiderable detriment.

"Cheer up," Solitaire cut in, slapping Beam on the shoulder. "We still have your new weapon, and none of the other contestants have seen it now, right? At least I'm guessing not. You don't seem to have used it on Argar given he's stand-ing there and not . . . You know. Congealing."

Beam smiled, mouth twisting, despite everything, inexorably upward as he nodded.

"Right," he breathed. "Yeah, that's true. Not a small advantage to be kept from the King, either."

"Not a small one at all." Solitaire grinned. "And it gives you very good odds of getting past the next round as long as you don't fight him."

I did notice that even he wasn't trying to convince Beam of his odds against the King of Blades himself. Which was fair enough because Beam was too smart for that to possibly work.

"Are we . . . done with the tournament?" I asked suddenly. It was a weird way to phrase my half-formed sentiment, so I gave the matter of cohering it into verbal form another go. "I mean . . . We've gotten plenty from it now, right? Beam's one of the deadliest people in the city already, whatever comes next, right? A few weeks ago we were talking about the entire thing being out of our league and not worth the fee of entering. Now . . ."

Now we were speaking, straight-faced, about the odds of reaching the finals. Everything had been such a frantic, desperate blur that I'd barely even noticed it happening, but somewhere along the way of our participation . . . we'd become powerful.

Properly fucking powerful, not just capable of bullying alleyway thugs. A laugh started building at the back of my throat for a moment.

Then it died, shriveled up, and started to excrete foul-smelling liquids as Solitaire spoke up, thus reminding me of our decapitated friendship.

"We should start planning our next move. We've narrowed the possibilities enough that we can make educated guesses about what our situation is likely to be soon based on essentially just four scenarios."

He so obviously wanted us to ask, to give him the prompt needed to "natu-rally" demonstrate how great and clever he was. I couldn't be fucked dealing with his infantile narcissism anymore.

"There are two scenarios just purely based off of whether Beam comes out of the tournament significantly stronger than he is now or not," I noted. "So I'd guess that the other two are also coming from a single coin-flip variable. And it's you, too. Are you suspecting we might be attacked by Byror and the Dead Edge?"

Solitaire's face fell, which didn't satisfy me in the slightest. Just made me feel more . . . nothing.

"Yes, I am," he said at last, bitter in an instant. I wasn't naive enough to think he was that irritated to have been robbed of his bragging. No doubt, he could sense exactly what and how I was feeling. It was one of a million brilliant things about him. And it was wasted, like all the fucking rest.

"So you think we have few enough realistic possibilities for our new situation that we can plan for all of the likely ones from here."

Solitaire nodded. "Already started planning." He shrugged. "And I reckon, if the worst comes to pass, we should expect some kind of attack. We've been kept safe until now by the optics of one noble attacking another, even indirectly, but your deal with Wilskasai, our growing effectiveness in the tournament, and the big display we've given everybody of our tool steel among other things . . . I reckon there's a chance we've made ourselves too big of a problem to ignore."

I wanted to blame him, but that would've been unfair. Even if Solitaire had been the only one attracting attention, and he certainly hadn't, there was every chance of Byror and his cronies eventually moving against us anyway. We'd had no choice but to strengthen ourselves.

"When do you think your projects will be finished?" I asked. Solitaire scowled, that way he always did when a problem had the audacity to confound him.

"Depends. I need more mercury, and I think the alchemists in this town have slowed their sales to us specifically because of Byror."

"Leave that to me then," I replied, finding another stab of anger at the revelation. That bastard had his tendrils everywhere, and he seemed not to ever tire of using them to fuck us over. "I've made one impossible deal lately. Reckon I can manage at least a few more."

Besides, we were talking about probably more than a few dozen people. There were always a handful of cowards in any group of that size, and we'd suddenly found ourselves with no small amount of weight to throw around.

"So we all have our nice little jobs then." Solitaire smiled, practically dripping with sarcasm. "Let's get to them. There's still a few things I can work on while I wait on the mercury, at least, and the rest of us could use some R and R in any case. Big day coming up soon, right?"

His eyes flickered to Beam, who seemed suddenly to have graduated from mild disquiet and into full-blown fear over the duration of our conversation. I couldn't blame him. As intimidated as *I'd* been watching the King of Blades beat someone capable of going sword to sword with a space marine, I didn't have to fight the bloody bastard.

"Big day coming up," Beam croaked, nodding and taking his leave. Arthur headed out after him, moving with a bit of a limp. The King hadn't hurt him that much, but nobody could take hits like that and not come out with a few bruises. A quick Appraisal told me he'd lost a point or two from most physical stats, which wasn't a surprise at all.

Perhaps one day I'd start being unbalanced, when people around us got hurt. But I reckoned we'd still not become powerful enough for that sort of complacency just yet. And I realized, then, that we maybe never would.

Not if things went wrong over the next week or two.

CHAPTER SIXTY-TWO

Beam's POV: Day 101
Current Wealth: 216 gold, 16 silver, 45 copper

Arthur was easier to fight, at first. Oh, part of that was me becoming more powerful of course—but I'm not egotistical enough to have believed for an instant that I was meaningfully closer to him. His soreness was what did most of the heavy lifting, lowering his physical abilities to a level more akin to the Challenger or Aja the Pit Hound, and that combined with my progression of power to just barely let me fight him in such a way that was *almost* not embarrassing.

Well, we all had to take whatever victories we could, I supposed. Particularly when they were against a man capable of putting his fist through a solid brick wall with arm strength alone.

It was made worse, too, by the fact that I was only *sometimes* fighting with my weapon of choice. Helena's healing had gotten along quite some length over the course of the tourney, and though it would still be a while before she was actually fighting, the woman could properly exercise again. When she wasn't doing laps, or practice thrusts to resharpen the corded musculature of her body after weeks of watching it soften, she was tutoring me on spear work in preparation for the next bout.

"You're doing it too shallowly," she'd snap. When I wasn't gripping it too hard and thus throwing off my accuracy, or holding the shaft at the wrong points for ideal control, or any number of other imperfections that the King of Blades would surely punish me for. I came to think I was an idiot, eventually, until she let it slip one day that I was apparently the fastest learner she'd ever seen. Apparently her standards were just ridiculously high.

Helena wasn't the sort of teacher to be gentle as she broke hard facts to a student in any case. I appreciated that because it meant that when she told me I'd improved by a lot I actually had cause to believe her. I wasn't nearly as good with a spear as a sword still, of course, and I probably wouldn't ever be, but in any case it was progress. A small victory, and I'd be taking every victory I could get.

My training was more of a coping mechanism than anything else as the days trickled by and my worries grew, but it wasn't the only thing restoring my confidence. Shango returned one day with a broad grin on his face and a new light in his eyes, which I only understood the context for after having it explained.

"I've leveled up."

It was the sort of news that takes a moment to sink in, which in retrospect is disturbing. It was very, very good news, sure, but also fairly simple and certainly not unprecedented. That I had such a hard time letting it actually solidify in my mind probably says more about the sort of week we'd been having than anything else.

"How much?" I asked instantly.

"One level." He shrugged. "But it's better than no levels. Some of those alchemists were tough, and very scared. I'd not gone in expecting to sway them. Then I did." He was grinning more openly than I'd seen in days, and damn if it wasn't a refreshing sight.

"Equally balanced stats now," he continued. "I'm sitting at elevens for everything. Huh. Remember when that was impressive?"

God, I did remember. When we used comparisons to real-world athletes as measuring sticks and milestones. As of this moment, Shango was the only one of us that even really worked to do justice, not counting our subordinates. And I had a feeling he'd be growing soon enough as well.

Even if I might not be getting much further than where I already was. That thought stung, lowering my just barely raised mood all over again.

"Good for you." I smiled weakly, and Shango was nice enough not to embarrass me by pointing it out.

Soon enough, the time had come for me to march out into the tournament. My every step toward it felt heavier than the last. It was strange. I'd fought in more matches than I could count over the years, and within the last few months I'd tested myself in more than one fight to the death. None of them struck me as fearfully as my approach did now.

I suppose I'd never been waiting to fight an enemy so clearly beyond me before. No matter who I fought today, I'd be the underdog, and I didn't have any friends to help even the playing field, either. It was a horrible novelty.

"You'll do fine," Solitaire told me, unprompted. I turned to stare at him and found that *he* was already staring far more intensely. I nodded, somewhat disconcerted, and forced a smile. If he was speaking like this, worrying like this . . . Well, I'd never *seen* him do so before. He must have been unnerved.

How terrified did I look to inspire that sort of response?

Soon, he was at my back, and I was waiting in the stands for my name to be called. I wasn't kept waiting for long.

And neither was Aja the Pit Hound.

Armored, armed, and trembling with a mix of terror and adrenal strength, I entered the arena ready for blood and any other fluids that might find themselves painting the place. He did much the same, writ stiller.

I realized, then, that I'd never actually been that close to the Pit Hound. My first time experiencing it was a shaking one. He was big, very big. Taller than Solitaire, broader than Argar. The plate armor strapped about him made it difficult to gauge anything concrete about his physical proportions. The outer shell of steel had to be an inch thick at least, but there was clearly no lack of musculature beneath. Staring into his visor, I felt like I was locking eyes with a black hole.

The match's start was declared, and Aja drew his khopesh. I drew my own weapon.

A spear. The new one, made by Solitaire, measuring easily ten feet in total length and made of dense tool steels and light woods across its entire body. With luck, even my current opponent wouldn't be able to hack it in half with that draconian-bronze edge of his weapon.

But when had we ever been lucky?

The Pit Hound was charging, and I backed away, jabbing low and high, testing his guard. Well, there wasn't much to be desired in it. His sword was everywhere my spear tip was, mostly through skill but partially from the great weight at the end of my weapon. The Pit Hound was barely forced to halt his rush, which was all that saved me. If he got past my weapon's length, he might be on me before I could swap to my sword.

He circled, cautious now, and I realized why. He wasn't seeing any reason to charge in after me.

So I had to sweeten the deal. I thrust again, stepping forward now and throwing my whole weight behind it, an overcommitted stab that would leave me too open to possibly answer any counter attacks he might manage after the fact. The khopesh knocked my spear aside, but not entirely off-kilter, and its tip crunched into the edge of Aja's breastplate.

Had Solitaire been a *normal* person, that might have been all she wrote. He'd have shrugged off the impact, come flying at me, and hacked me to pieces in moments. Fortunately, my friend was nuttier than squirrel shit.

The tip of my spear, which I'd been told was crammed absolutely full of something called mercury fulminate, detonated the moment its metal blade met strong enough resistance to be pushed back into the section of shaft behind it. I looked away just in time to spare my retinas, but even from over two yards away I felt the concussive force of the blast and was sent stumbling by it. My heels scraped the ground, head shaking, vision blurry.

But I was just peachy compared to poor Aja, who seemed to be simultaneously attempting a new world record for both clumsiest and longest backflip. Looked like he succeeded, too, as he only came down face-first onto the stone after flying a good ten or so feet.

There was a big blackened section to his plate armor that was still spitting out thick smoke as he tried to sit up, and I could just barely make out dents and cracks along the sheet. He moved slowly, dazed and with no excess of vigor after his little impromptu gymnastics, as well. He'd been hurt; he'd been worn down.

I'd been given an opportunity, and I closed in to make full use of it. The vampire's rapier leapt into my hand and whistled hungrily through the air.

By the time I was on the Pit Hound, he seemed mostly recovered but still favored one side as he moved to parry my swing. His return stroke almost caught me, but I just barely ducked back from it.

He was taking the offensive, then, trying to force me back and keep me running. I had no intention of allowing that of course, twisting into one of his swings and letting it slide over my sword as I braced it against myself.

God, I still almost got disarmed. It was like trying to block a cavalryman's lance, sheer, inhuman force placed behind a single mass. I stumbled away, forced myself to regain my balance, and shot in. Jab, jab, jab. Quick, light feints at his face followed by a bigger swing down at the damaged section of his armor.

Predictably, he moved to block the blow. That was fine because I'd been ready to twist it down into his thigh at the last second. The plate there quivered and cracked under my enhanced weapon.

I backed off again, eyeing the damage, looking for any flecks of blood. Little, and none. That was fine. I'd just have to keep chipping away at him.

Clearly, Aja knew, too. He was attacking again. God, did he attack.

Left, right. His swings were like scything swipes, threatening to behead me as easily as a blade of grass. Down, up. His sword was a falling guillotine, a roaring volcanic jet, all mass and speed and deadly, mutilating precision. My arm was numbing with every blow I guarded, strength too little by far to contest the sheer pneumatic might driving his every swing.

Scared, champion?

It was a familiar voice, one I'd not heard for a long time. The one who apparently gave me my magic and lived in my head.

Piss off, I thought, and I heard laughter echo through my thoughts.

That's the spirit. Now aim it at him.

I did, though there was a big difference between the right spirit and the strength to back it up. I made an opening I knew Aja would go for and twisted from the path of his blow before letting one of my own catch his arm mid-swing.

Blood. Finally, blood. Crimson and sticky, hot and dribbling down the crook of his elbow where my sword had bitten down. Aja stepped back, clearly surprised, and I closed in to capitalize. I managed two more swings before he regathered his wits. One was parried entirely. The second, though.

The second came down on another section of his breastplate, further torturing the metal.

Whatever the vampire's rapier was made of, it was at least as good as the tool steel Ardin was working. That, and my enhanced cutting edge courtesy of my own ethereal conjurations, meant that it was just armor-piercing enough to threaten Aja.

He knew it, too, but he didn't get panicky and overly cautious like most men did once they started losing. Just focused more. A new assault struck me, and this time I found my fatigue had grown too much to continue blocking for long.

His khopesh came down on a pauldron, cutting through and nicking the flesh beneath. Another slice took the plating over my stomach. I was bleeding more than him now, which meant time had just taken my enemy's side, and things were only worsening from there. I couldn't beat him.

So I changed styles entirely, abandoning defense. I waited for the moment of his swing, then stabbed for him. His sword came down first, hitting my backplate and leaving the deepest cut I'd felt so far on my body below.

My strike, though, was the deadlier one. I felt the tip of my rapier go through Aja's plate armor, the chain mail beneath, and bypass the padded underclothes like they weighed nothing. It buried itself in his chest like a shovel in dirt.

Both of us fell at once, blood leaking everywhere. The stadium's noise became distant and incoherent, like buzzing insects in my ears. I groaned, shifted, thrashed slightly as I felt my body protest at the slightest motions, fell still.

They are about to declare you a beaten man.

It was all I got from my friendly little voice, and it was all I needed. Aja and I had fallen at once. Would they decide the victor based on which of us was most damaged?

No. This tournament would use any excuse they could to hand me the loss. So I needed to get the fuck up and take it from them.

My newly acquired injuries screamed as I moved, reminding me with every inch that my body was falling apart at the seams. I ignored them, just as I ignored the growing weakness in my core left by absent blood now pooling around me. Moment by moment, I got up.

Standing upright, I could see that Aja was still twitching, but barely. I held myself aloft just long enough to have it all declared my win, smiling as I did. Then, the moment it was all over, I collapsed.

Funnily enough, I thought I remembered being like this once before, as well. It had . . . Yes, it had been right after arrival, I thought. Right after we first got attacked by that bear. I did hope we didn't get dropped into crippling medical debt again this time.

Then again, that would just be bloody typical of this world. When had we ever been lucky here? When had we ever had the easier time of things?

Strong hands came to grasp me, carefully hauling me from the arena, and I let myself drift off.

CHAPTER SIXTY-THREE

I was getting so tired of watching my friends get hurt. I didn't even really feel fear anymore. How fucked is that? Beam was lying there looking like tenderized beef, and I couldn't even muster *fear*. Just . . . emptiness.

He lived, of course. And it wasn't even a particularly near thing. I tried to tell myself that was why my reaction had been so blunted, but . . . Well, I'd never been as good at lying to myself as I'd been at lying to others. Fortunately, Beam was awake soon enough, and before then I had ample company.

"He fought like a demon," Magnus breathed, staring at him with a newfound respect. I had to admit, even through the terrible cold centering me, it was hard not to feel a similar sensation in my own thoughts.

Beam had surprised us all, and not unpleasantly. My heart had almost stopped when Aja's name was called, and I'd watched every move of the fight certain I'd watch a repeat of his torment of Helena. Instead, my friend had won.

Granted, he'd won by opening the fight with a fucking anti-matériel spear thrust, sure. But we won most of our fights with a good old-fashioned cheat these days, and I reckoned we owed the bastard a bit of payback in any case. I'm not a sadistic man, and I consider myself a true believer in restorative justice, but damn if it wasn't satisfying seeing the sword slip past Aja's armor that first time.

"Good on you, mate," Elizabeth whispered, kneeling down beside Beam, eyes fiery and hateful. None of it was directed at him. "Good on you. Did good by Helena, boss, and I won't forget that."

It was a stark reminder just how much I was indulging myself, and I turned to Argar.

"Can you take him back to the mansion?"

"Aye." He nodded, bending down to hoist Beam up over his shoulder with surprising care. It might've been amazing, any other time, to see a combined two hundred and fifty pounds of man and metal plucked up off the ground so weightlessly. But this was not any other time.

"Magnus, you go with him. Rule of pairs, remember."

The man looked irritated to have been forced away from the stadium right before the King's fight, but he obeyed all the same. Soon enough it was just me, Elizabeth, and Alora staring out into the arena. My spirits, though, were lifting slightly. Because I'd glimpsed something of Beam as he was being carried away.

[Appraisal]
Class: Dragonlord
Level: 20
Condition: Unconscious
Modifiers: +2 Strength, +7 Speed, +7 Toughness, +7 Alertness
Statistics: Strength 14 (9), Speed 15 (10), Dexterity 8 (4), Stamina 9 (3), Toughness 15, Alertness 15 (13), Charisma 6, Intelligence 5 (3)
Inventory: Local wear, plate armor, rapier
Class Abilities: Beloved III
Current Experience Points: 526/600
Unspent Skillpoints: 3

Another level, irritatingly close to *two* actually, but we'd take whatever we could get right now. Beam would certainly be needing whatever small boosts came his way for the next bout.

Oh, who was I kidding? He'd be needing a fucking howitzer.

Solitaire made himself known just before the match. It surprised me, but perhaps not as much as it should have. Sitting down, he stared out into the arena, fidgeting, analyzing. Looking for whatever information he could scrounge up on the enemy our friend was going to face. I'd have done the same thing.

The King made his entrance to as enthusiastic a reception as ever, and, bizarrely, the Challenger's own response seemed muted and small by comparison. He wasn't a short man, didn't wear light armor, and wielded a fairly sized sword. Somehow everything about him seemed diminished through comparison with the King. They met in the center of the arena, already within a few paces, both apparently eager to test themselves against the other.

The signal was given, and they both moved in to fight.

It was the Challenger who swung first, but the King stopped it without the slightest effort. At least I think he did. It was really more of a deduction. I didn't manage to physically *see* the movement at all.

A metal clang ran out through the stadium, but the King was already swinging before it had crossed the dozens of meters separating me from the source. Remarkably, the Challenger managed to sidestep, countering with another swing that, of course, came nowhere near his enemy's body.

Watching it all was an exercise in . . . hopelessness. The Challenger was faster, stronger, and tougher than Beam was, even now, and he could barely even lay a finger on his enemy. We should've expected as much after seeing Arthur's performance—in fact we sort of had—but actually seeing it happen . . .

Fuck. Was that even a human in there under the helmet?

It didn't take long for the Challenger to be beaten, not long at all. A few seconds at most, and the crowd loved every moment of it. I was starting to wonder what enjoyment they even got from watching the King fight. Surely from their perspective he was just blurs of motion, then falling enemies.

Power, I supposed, had an appeal inherent to itself. Solitaire looked as grim as I felt once it was all over.

"Beam doesn't have a chance." I sighed. "Forget winning. He'd be lucky to last five seconds."

Solitaire hesitated, looking thoughtful, then nodded.

"Yeah," he agreed. "Let's go and see how he's doing. Corvan must've started his healing by now."

Well, it wasn't like we had anything better to do. We both headed back to the mansion.

Fortunately, Corvan wasn't anywhere near as slow in his healing as he'd been the last time Beam had gotten this hurt. He'd already exhausted most of his magic on the efforts by the time we found him, and Beam himself was awake and conscious.

Certainly not having a good day, of course. There were limits to Corvan's magic, as ever. Beam might've healed himself just as much by simply waiting a few weeks, which wasn't to say he'd gained nothing. Just that we'd really be banking on the three days before our next round to add a bit of supporting magic to his recovery.

"You really do need to stop getting almost killed," Corvan was grumbling. "It's getting tiresome for me."

Beam ignored the joke, grinning up at me.

"What sort of benefit did I get?" he asked eagerly. "Felt like more than one level this time."

"It was just one." I sighed. "But you got three skillpoints. Looks like our theory about getting one more every ten levels was correct."

That seemed comfort enough for him, and I watched the familiar sight of his concentration as Beam spent the skillpoints on more power.

[Appraisal]
Class: Dragonlord
Level: 20
Condition: Worn
Modifiers: +3 Strength, +8 Speed, +7 Toughness, +8 Alertness
Statistics: Strength 15 (14), Speed 16 (15), Dexterity 8 (4), Stamina 9 (8),
Toughness 15, Alertness 16 (15), Charisma 6, Intelligence 5 (3)
Inventory: Local wear, plate armor, rapier
Class Abilities: Beloved III
Current Experience Points: 526/600
Unspent Skillpoints: 0

Whatever minor comfort I might've extracted from the sight of his progress, it withered and died underneath the King's shadow. But not enough that I didn't notice one thing of interest.

"Oh, shit, your class name. It's changed."

Beam blinked. "Changed how?"

"Dragonlord, not Dragonknight. Any idea what that means?"

I wasn't really putting much hope in that magic voice in his head explaining anything, but figured it was worth asking. No luck, in any case.

"Hopefully this'll give him something new." Solitaire shrugged. "I'm guessing his Beloved has leveled up?"

It had, actually. I confirmed it with a nod.

"Then spend a few days trying to see what else it can do now. With luck you'll have something that turns the tables. Like a magic anti-tank cannon you can conjure."

Fat chance, but we'd need to check every possibility we had anyway. I watched as Beam waltzed off to do his work and let my eyes fall down back onto Solitaire.

"We have a few days before the tourney's over and the enemy can attack without causing a disruption," I noted. "How close are your projects to finishing?"

"Close," he assured me. "And I think we can expect to catch them unawares if we're not too obvious in Beam's power-up this time around. If they knew we were growing exponentially between rounds, rather than just revealing hidden strength, there's a good chance they'd have attacked already even despite the disruptions it'd cause."

I had to admit, he wasn't wrong. Leave it to Solitaire to needle out all the ways a person might attack him. Leave it to him because God knew he couldn't be trusted with much fucking else.

CHAPTER SIXTY-FOUR

Shango's POV: Day 104
Current Wealth: 222 gold, 0 silver, 37 copper

The day was on us, and it felt bloody awful waking up during its morning. Everything was stiff, slow, like my own body was delaying my arrival in the arena for knowledge of what was awaiting me there. Beam, I knew, would be feeling all that times a thousand. I tried to comfort him as we headed out to the stadium; it didn't work. I didn't blame him. I reckoned, if I ever made my way to fight someone capable of cutting cars in half, I'd be owed a bit of grumpiness, too. More than a bit.

Conversely, the crowd seemed more excited than ever. Assholes.

We didn't bother getting comfortable because none of us expected to be here for long. There'd be no fights today except Beam's after all. Beam's and the King's. He was called down for it before we'd even settled in.

Solitaire, having come with us, placed the bet we'd all agreed on, and we watched our friend march out with a single long hope.

Please, man, just manage to last one single minute. It's all you need—one minute.

The King stormed out into the arena, all glinting metal and reptilian grace. Beam stood where he was and prepared to meet him, sword clutched tight, body trembling with either fear or whatever insane emotion struck uniquely him in such times. He didn't have another bomb-spear, we figured that'd been a one-hit-wonder and he'd need to fight with his weapon of choice from beginning to end just to last.

We all held our breaths, the audience excreted theirs as a single roar of excitement, and the match began.

Beam charged in, then wavered and stopped. He circled the King, looking for an opening or guarding for an attack, and he soon found the latter as his enemy took one step forward and lashed out a sweeping blow to cut the space before him. Beam's sword was up to guard it, but his body went flying. We all heard the screech of metal on stone as he slid all the way back to the far wall, shoulders impacting it hard.

The King was already closing the distance by the time he stopped.

It was a near thing, but Beam was barely up in time to keep the sword from catching his armor directly. I winced, hearing the sound of metal hitting metal. It was like a damned car crash, sheer weight and speed—sheer force. Beam's knees bent, body curling down to disperse the impact and reduce his body's strain.

Unfortunately, the King wasn't content to leave things at that. He kicked Beam while his guard was still busy with the sword, and this time he completely left the ground before flying away, soaring through the air and coming down hard.

. . . On the other side of the stadium, a dozen meters away.

For one moment I worried Beam wouldn't be getting up, but he did. Barely. He was wispy, shaky, unsteady on his feet. The King bought him less than a second by launching him—he crossed the space separating them faster than should have been possible.

Beam was barely turned and ready for his follow-up.

It wasn't a fight, not at all. It was . . . I don't even know what. *Bullying.* Beam was utterly helpless. Even fighting defensively was hurting him just through the sheer difference in physical prowess.

". . . Fourteen seconds," Solitaire whispered, voice tight and terrified. He was scared. We all were. Give us a fight, we'd fight it. Give us a big one, even, full of thrashing mouths and innumerable enemies, and we'd figure something out.

What did you do with this? How did you fight something like *this*?

Beam, it seemed, planned on figuring it out.

He discharged attacks as the King came back for him, quick ones, light, fast, testing. He only got three jabs off before the King turned to a new swing, and it was over before I even saw it.

This time, though, Beam actually withstood it. Sort of. He jumped before it hit, let the impact send him flying into the far wall, and bounced off, landing on his feet, balance kept, force dispersed, body intact. For now.

But the King had already shown how meaningless distances like that were to him. He closed back in, entire stadium seemingly within the reach of his arm. Beam tried to avoid him entirely now, skirting away, even almost running at one point, but it was never enough. The King just closed, stalking toward him with that ludicrous speed, shrinking the gap one meter after another.

"Twenty-two seconds." Solitaire groaned as the brutality continued.

He wasn't even fucking halfway there, and the King seemed as tireless as a machine. Down, down came the sword. Right into Beam's guard. This time they were right in front of the wall, and every hit was forcing Beam back into it. I saw his armor deteriorating by the moment, tool steel crushed, bent, and mangled as it impacted the stone.

I saw the *stone* taking damage, even, big chunks of it cracking and crumbling away where a hundred kilos of human and metal thudded into it. We'd kept Beam's armor short of the multicentimeter thickness common to this world's superhumans, hoping he could use the lack of weight to equalize his enemy's speed advantage. That had been a damned failure, and now it seemed he was feeling the lack of protection.

A particularly hard swing sort of squeezed Beam against the wall, then sent him exploding out from between it and the King. He flew head over heels, stumbled, and bounced, rolled away to stop in a heap. Once more, he'd crossed the arena. Once more the King was standing over him in an instant.

"Twenty-six seconds," Solitaire breathed.

"Do you yield?"

The King's voice rolled out, low and grating through his helmet. We all paused—the audience paused. Shit, the rats in the sewers probably paused. But Beam didn't. He took a few moments, of course, *seemingly* to steady himself, but really to buy a few more precious seconds. Then, finally, he answered as he stood.

"Sorry, but no. My friends have too much riding on this tournament. I need to keep fighting you."

The King studied him for a brief moment, then nodded.

"Then good luck, warrior."

He moved like the embrace of death, and I didn't see the hit before Beam was already flying away.

This time, there'd been no block. The sword had caught him right at his—thankfully yet undamaged—breastplate and hacked through. A glancing, light blow, but one that had still cut clean through the steel, mail, and gambeson beneath, and through the ethereal plate Beam was covered in for good measure. Blood drizzled out of his gashed-open chest in thick rivulets that hung in the air as his body soared past them. He only stopped when he thudded once more into the far wall.

Once more, and perhaps no more than that. I felt sick watching him lie where he did, slowly gushing out more of his blood, and Solitaire's hands tightened about the railing so hard that the wooden structure shivered at his grip.

"How long?" I asked him.

His voice was low as he answered, hopeless.

"Forty-one seconds."

Beam was groaning, writhing around. I couldn't tell how mobile he still was. The bleeding, at least, seemed to have slowed, but it was still a big gash he'd have taken. I couldn't imagine things going on much longer now.

The King reached him, and then Beam took a page out of Solitaire's book.

He took away one hand from where it had been held tight against his chest wound, then flicked it out. A splash of blood struck the King clean in his visor, sending his head back a step as he was briefly—ever so briefly—stunned. Beam turned the move into a roll just as his enemy's sword came down, sliding between his legs and taking off at a run.

The King turned impossibly fast at the sound of him, nearly taking his head off with a blind swing, but after that he remained where he was, pausing a few more seconds to clean the blood from his visor and face, to restore his own vision.

Beam didn't bother attacking, which was just as well. He'd not have achieved anything in the process save to exhaust himself. Instead he stood and rested, panting in more strength while his enemy prepared another attack.

"Fifty-four seconds." Solitaire gasped, sounding painfully tense as he realized what I did.

Six seconds away, and a dozen meters between them. Beam had a fucking chance.

The King took one last moment to ready himself, then charged. He was on Beam, swinging, feinting. His real attack came through but still found Beam's sword anyway and sent him flying back. The King was faster and more diligent in his pursuit now, closing in to skewer Beam while he was still sprawled out. He barely managed to block the sword, letting its force compress him down into the ground and sending cracks reaching out across the stone as his armor screamed.

"Sixty—"

Beam paused, and something in the air changed.

CHAPTER SIXTY-FIVE

Beam's POV: Day 104
Current Wealth: 222 gold, 0 silver, 37 copper

What is happening?

It was the voice, the one that always spoke up in those moments that most mattered to me. This time, I heard more than just its usual collected confidence. I heard doubt.

And I understood why because we hadn't told it about the scheme.

The King was so strong, even lasting a minute against him would have been a challenge for me. So we made it one. A big one, with Solitaire dropping a hundred gold coins onto the attempt—knowing that Byror's interference kept us from spending much of them anyway—and wagering them against my lasting until that sixtieth second. We'd taken a risk, threatened ourselves with a setback, and given me a challenge. Because there was a lot to gain from five-to-one odds—five hundred gold in this case.

And our experience had always been derived from potential gain.

This task you set yourself, it was a fierce one, the voice echoed, probably reading my thoughts rather than catching on, but no less smug for it. *And I acknowledge your tribute of glory. Bask in my power, champion, and make it yours.*

Before I could even formulate a thought—let alone a response—I knew exactly what it meant by power. It was my Beloved, my armor, a weapon of ethereal magic against my skin. It was all of this, and a thousand, million times more. I gasped, the King stiffened, and the change began.

It started with my skin.

Hot, itchy. It was like boiling water hissing down atop it in tiny droplets. Could that even still hurt me? I wasn't even sure, but I became more certain as the pain worsened, then changed. It was tight the next moment, and growing tighter. Fingers and hooks digging into the epidermis, pulling it taut, tearing it at the seams. Then stillness. I felt its weight now—it had weight?—and I felt a calm certainty from it. I wasn't given the chance to consider the sensation before a new change was coming.

A deeper one, this. It went down into the viscera beneath.

My muscles were spasming, screaming. It was like the lactic burn of a difficult exercise, felt for days and days, compressed into moments. The bones permeating them shifted, too. Grinding and popping as their joints fractionally turned, elongating, thickening. Hardening.

My vision turned red, mouth suddenly full of salty blood, ears ringing so loud I couldn't hear the screaming crowd. Then it was over.

I was on my knees, blinking. My body was fine.

No, it was more than fine. I felt exhilaration that hadn't hit me since my first gold medal, and I felt it with every ounce of myself.

Then I remembered where I was, what I was doing. A fighter, fighting. A champion winning.

In one motion I leaped to my feet and snatched my fallen rapier from the ground, wrapping it in its ethereal cutting edge mid-swing. It was complete just in time to catch the King's pauldron. A solid connection, good, and made with more strength than I could ever have mustered before.

Somewhere in my convulsive episode, I'd spent my experience. That wasn't what was happening now, though.

Because I hadn't had nearly enough to smash so long and deep a crack across the mystery metal protecting my opponent's body.

He slid back, almost like I had. Only a yard or two, mind. With all that steel he probably weighed close to five times what I did. But it was a start. I closed in while he was still reeling with surprise, swinging again. The King raised his sword to guard, but I twisted, letting mine slide along its edge just right and sending it low for his arm.

Like the genius he was, he foresaw the attack just in time to whip his limb aside—even throwing in a counter as he did. I smacked that away, noting with satisfaction that my arm was only *throbbing* rather than *tantruming* at the disparity of our strength. My riposte was like a bolt of lightning.

The King saw through my feint, then saw through the next. There was no third—until I saw a weird tension to him one moment before swinging low for his thigh, and instead flicked my blade upward to scrape along the visor of his helm. It served well to make the King flinch, opening him for a thrust to the chest that left another split in the metal's face. He swung fast enough to almost catch me as I darted back, and suddenly we were four paces separate. The whole exchange had lasted only a second or two.

As one, we started pacing.

This wasn't cat and mouse, not anymore. I was stronger now, a predator staring down a predator. The creature I'd been, scrambling away and cowering in the corners, that *thing* wouldn't last a minute against me now.

But it had lasted that long against the King. Which made me the deadlier monster. Time to prove it to everyone.

I closed in, apparently surprising the giant with my aggression. He adjusted quickly—genius, as I thought—and feinted in a way so painfully obvious that I was almost insulted. His following body check was more nicely done, but still sidestepped simply enough.

What surprised me was his sudden pivot, sending his sword twisting around to slice a notch out of my plate armor, ethereal undersuit and . . . Yes. And a bit of the shoulder beneath.

No wince caught me, and I didn't anticipate the pain that failed to show. I knew, instinctively, that I was beyond such things now. My blood sizzled and hissed for a moment before I reformed my plate, carefully dropping a layer down to compress the wound. I hadn't been capable of that before, and so I did it again to my earlier cut to stem more of the leakage.

The King was on me by then, demanding that I do other things with my focus.

I'd fought someone faster than me once, and it had been quite the interesting novelty. The difference was bigger now, even with my lighter armor, but . . . it was manageable. The King was skilled, but I'd fought more skilled. He was strong, but I saw now that there were limits to the physical force he could throw at me. His sword chased me everywhere, thirsty and darting in to drink its fill. I barely kept it at bay, but managed all the same, watching the man wielding it and waiting for my moment.

The moment came. An instant of pause, a slight delay, a habit so tiny and unfelt that even I needed an entire three glimpses to realize it was there. My rapier found the mark I'd already left in the King's breastplate, and I felt something softer giving beneath the stab this time.

He didn't let me enjoy it for long before taking a hand from his weapon and punching me. That one, I will admit, fucking hurt.

For the dozenth time that day, I flew like a shot put. My body crashed into the wall, bounced off it, hit the ground hard. I realized, then, that the King hadn't really put his back into the other swings. Not holding back, just fighting like a man who knew he'd win. Sparing the excess strength.

I got to my feet, head perfectly clear, body perfectly fine. Impact of stone and metal barely even a dull throb at my shoulder blades. I glanced where the wall was cracked and crumbling, glanced back where the King was closing and staring. Grinned.

He wasn't fighting anymore like a man who knew he'd win.

We crashed into each other like waves on the ocean, twin storms. Our bodies were the convulsing hurricanes, always twisting and jerking, never where we seemed, always on the move. The swords between us were flashing bolts of lightning, forking between our forms and spitting sparks into the air as they kissed and bit. The ground cried out where our booted heels crunched down, cracking, shivering. The crowds screamed, but not as loud as me.

This was combat; this was a *fight*. This was a man whose head was worth the taking, who'd leave all the halls in all the world echoing with the sound of my name.

This was something to give a purpose to my little brother's death and prove that his genius hadn't been wasted after all.

I ducked a swing, parried another. My boot found the center of the King's chest, hurting him about as much as harsh language but breaking his balance for that precious moment I needed to scrape another chunk from his armor. This time I leaned back from the punch he tried to retaliate with, right into the foot he'd slipped behind my heel.

For one moment, I was stumbling. Not long, less than the blink of an eye. But long enough for him to swing one last time and catch me directly along the chest.

CHAPTER SIXTY-SIX

Shango's POV: Day 104
Current Wealth: 722 gold, 0 silver, 37 copper

So, Beam lost. No surprise there. We'd all been waiting for it to happen. It had been where the day's generally grim tone had come from. Each of us had headed out of the house to see our friend fight an unwinnable fight, and then inevitably lose. The only reason we'd even sent him out had been the King's general reputation for decency and honor. Had we thought he might cut him in half after or during his victory, we'd not have even humored a course of action besides forfeiture.

That said, Beam had done a *lot* better than any of us even imagined. And I'd caught his entire performance with the best vision around.

[Appraisal]
Class: Dragonlord
Level: 22
Condition: The Dragon
Modifiers: +10 Strength, +14 Speed, +14 Toughness, +14 Alertness
Statistics: Strength 22, Speed 22, Dexterity 8, Stamina 9, Toughness 22, Alertness 22, Charisma 6, Intelligence 5
Inventory: Local wear, plate armor, rapier
Class Abilities: Beloved III
Current Experience Points: 306/640
Unspent Skillpoints: 0

He'd been a monster. Every bit Arthur's equal physically. And with his natural advantages of ethereal armor and weaponry to boot.

That, and the way he'd fought. Not just dexterous, not just skilled—and he was, of course, both. It was the *unrelentingness* of him. Like some wild animal, or a homed-in attack dog. We had plenty of chances to examine Beam as we carried him out of the arena, and I could see firsthand he'd taken some serious wounds even outside the one that knocked him out.

His visor was absolutely mangled, steel caved in almost into his skull. The King's glancing slice had cut his shoulder down to the bone, and everywhere we stripped the plate away from his flesh revealed more bruises and scrapes underneath. Even standing with injuries like that would have been impressive. Fighting?

Fighting through them, that was something inhuman.

But Beam wasn't in that state now. I checked as much myself.

[Appraisal]
Class: Dragonlord
Level: 22
Condition: Unconscious
Modifiers: +5 Strength, +9 Speed, +9 Toughness, +9 Alertness
Statistics: Strength 17 (14), Speed 17 (13), Dexterity 8 (4), Stamina 9 (4), Toughness 17, Alertness 17 (15), Charisma 6, Intelligence 5 (3)
Inventory: Local wear, plate armor, rapier
Class Abilities: Beloved III
Current Experience Points: 306/640
Unspent Skillpoints: 0

There'd been a time when I would have soyjaked at seventeens across the board, but it was just that sort of day. Besides, the poor guy didn't have seventeens *now*.

We had Corvan ready with his magic-healing stuff, but there was really only so much to do. He was still slightly weary from the day before, and Beam really had taken a lot of damage. He woke up, at least, but Corvan wasn't skittish about the results.

"He won't be fighting anytime soon." He grunted. "He'll be healing for at least another few weeks."

Well, that was better than *decomposing* for a few weeks, so I decided I'd take it.

Beam was thankfully up without any great delay, which was particularly good given we actually didn't have much diagnostic ability when it came to human brains. His return to consciousness was abrupt, blunt, and awkward. Lots of quick convulsions as his limbs took a moment to realize they weren't still fighting. We all stood around him, watching to ensure nothing was wrong, which probably didn't do anything for his nerves, but at least left us conveniently placed for a few questions on his part.

"Did I win?"

It was just such a Beam thing to ask. We couldn't help ourselves. Every single one of us burst out laughing.

"You drew a bit of blood," I said at last, seeing that Beam was now scowling after apparently working out he'd not had such a great performance. "A damn sight better than anyone else, but . . . You don't remember it?"

With the manic relief of seeing him alive and cognizant running out, that was the next big concern. Beam hadn't fought like a man disconnected from what he was doing. A blackout like this . . . That was concerning.

He certainly seemed concerned, too, because I saw his face tighten with thought.

"I . . . No, I do. Bits and pieces. And everything up to the minute mark, or thereabouts. But not . . . not everything."

This smelled like a later problem to me.

While Beam was getting updated on the handful of things we'd done since his defeat, namely arguing loudly about what to try to spend our new money on, I headed off to see Phelia. I still felt that knot in my stomach as I did.

It had been my fault, what happened to her with Solitaire. And while she'd put us all at risk by withholding information . . . I couldn't overlook what my friend had done. Done again. The unilateral decision on his part, all the trauma.

She'd be without it if I'd just been a bit less easygoing. And that made me think of how many other people might still be *alive* or killed in less messily cruel ways.

Phelia was in the bedroom, and thankfully she had her clothes on. Reading, like always, looking up as I entered, tense.

"I didn't want to interrupt, in case . . . something had gone wrong," she said quickly. "Your brother, is he . . . ?"

"Alive." I smiled, actually having worried for a moment at the concern on her face. "Beam's fine. He actually drew a bit of blood from the King before going down."

Phelia's stare was almost like a child's: pure, undiluted awe.

"That's . . . unprecedented?" I guessed.

"Not quite," she conceded. "But almost. Only one other has managed it, and he's been competing here for over a decade. Your brother must be very strong indeed . . ." Her voice grew edged slightly. Fuck. Woman-deciphering mode.

Phelia was pissed, but not about anything she felt confident in confronting me on. Clearly this was important enough to be hinted at so soon after the more serious topic, but not immediately vital given that she was skirting around it.

I didn't take long to narrow things down.

"You've noticed how our power improves with time," I guessed.

"I have," Phelia replied. "Care to explain that?"

It was a good question. *Did* I? I wasn't sure. Phelia was family, technically, kind of. But that didn't mean she enjoyed our full trust. I'd protect her the same way I would anyone else—because people being hurt was bad—and I had to admit I'd come to enjoy her company somewhat. The fact that she was drop-dead gorgeous and regularly had sex with me had nothing to do with that at all, I assure you.

Still, did I want to explain?

She'd already lied once, by omission, albeit for fairly understandable reasons of needing to secure a place in our family. Might she betray us again?

Perhaps, but it would be a lot more likely to be betrayed if I evaded, or lied and got seen through. Phelia's last deception had come when she thought she *had* to for self-preservation. Keeping her informed and feeling like she had my confidence seemed like the best way to prevent another.

"My brothers and I are unique," I said at last. "Completely. In how we gain power particularly. We don't do it by just training and working hard like others do."

Nodding, Phelia frowned at that, rearranging information in her head to see if it fit with what I was saying. The smart thing to do, of course.

"What do you do, then?" she asked. "Defeat enemies?"

"Good guess, but not quite. Mostly we seem to . . . accomplish goals. The harder, the riskier, the more power. We seem to be able to get a bit by beating magical enemies, too, but for the most part it comes from accomplishments."

Phelia took barely a heartbeat to process everything.

"So, when we set up the deal with Wilskasai . . . ?"

"Yes," I confirmed. "I became a bit more powerful from that."

Phelia shivered, drawing the *next* smart conclusion, her lip curling as she voiced it.

"And Solitaire is making progress on bypassing that technological gap he's been struggling with . . ."

Which meant another truckload for him. Fair enough for her to be worried, though I still wasn't. I knew he wouldn't turn against me, at least. That was perhaps all I could say for the bastard, but I could say it, nonetheless.

"We need him," I assured her. "And besides, I don't see him reaching Beam's level now, do you?"

We hadn't even tested Beam's level, but I was fairly sure we'd be looking at close to a ton for the bench press at least. His stats weren't *that* far from Aja the Pit Hound's anymore.

And that was to say nothing of his new ability. That berserker state made him a physical equal of Arthur. It was hard to imagine much withstanding us

now. Not with someone like that on our side. The two of them could've slaugh-
tered the rest of us all at once.

Phelia only nodded stiffly.

"I understand." She sighed. "Just . . . control him, please?"

A request, not an order. She was too smart to think she had any real duty
binding me, even if our names were tied together now.

"I will," I promised. Binding myself anyway. It was hardly the first time.

Ian B. Urns is the coauthor of the Author's Nightmare series, originally released on Royal Road. He writes dark fantasy stories with all the action, humor, and horror he can cram in. Having penned six novels thus far and developing his skills with each new book, he hopes to continue expanding into other genres. Urns lives in the United Kingdom, where he avoids natural light and eye contact with other living things.

A. C. Erinle is the coauthor of the Author's Nightmare series, originally released on Royal Road. A Nigerian novelist who favors character-driven fantasy and world-building, he has penned several books now, sharpening his writing skills with each one. He spends his free time frolicking in nature and otherwise enjoying life, before marching back into his Writing Hole. His stories are dark, but they never fail to be optimistic. Erinle currently resides in Lagos.

RESPAWN YOUR CURIOSITY

follow us on our socials

 podiumentertainment.com

 @podiumentertainment

 /podiumentertainment

 @podium_ent

 @podiumentertainment